THE MIDDLE GENERATION

A Novel of John Quincy Adams
and the Monroe Doctrine

M. B. ZUCKER

HISTORIUM
BOOKS

First Edition published by Historium Press

Images by Imagine & Public Domain
Cover designed by White Rabbit Arts

Visit M. B. Zucker's website at
www.mbzucker.com

Library of Congress Cataloging-in-Publication Data on file

Hardcover ISBN: 978-1-962465-05-2
Paperback ISBN: 978-1-962465-06-9
E-Book ISBN: 978-1-962465-07-6

Historium Press, a subsidiary of
The Historical Fiction Company
New York, NY, U.S.A.
2023

Other Novels by M. B. Zucker

The Eisenhower Chronicles

A Great Soldier in the Last Great War

Theodore Roosevelt and the Hunt for the Liopleurodon

To Hyman and Cynthia Cohen

Table of Contents

A Map of the United States of America, 1817

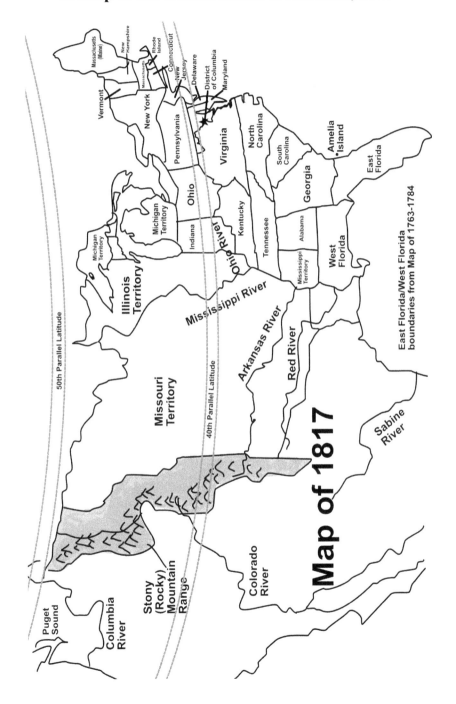

ADVANCED PRAISE

"This captivating read offers an insightful portrait of one of the most important figures in American history: John Quincy Adams. The author's ability to portray the distant, flinty Adams, as a flesh and blood human being represents a remarkable achievement. This is historical fiction at its best, for the characters who animate Michael Zucker's novel ring true from the first page to the last.

Zucker's novel is full of vibrant portrayals of all the key figures from the so-called Era of Good Feelings, including James Monroe, Andrew Jackson, John C. Calhoun, and Henry Clay. *The Middle Generation: A Novel of John Quincy Adams and the Monroe Doctrine* is an entertaining and enlightening read that all students of historical fiction and of American history will enjoy."

-Stephen F. Knott, former Professor of National Security at the Naval War College and the author of *Coming to Terms with John F. Kennedy*

"M. B. Zucker goes well beyond a story of simple political intrigue. He offers one of the most moving literary portraits of a President I have ever encountered."

-Dr. Jeffery Tyler Syck, Author of *The Revolution of 1828: John Quincy Adams, Andrew Jackson, and the Origins of American Democracy*

"John Quincy Adams is one of a small group of presidents whose major achievements to his country preceded and followed his time in the White House. In this splendid account of Adams's years as Secretary of State, Michael Zucker, a rising star in the area of historical fiction, recaptures JQA's extraordinary vision and true greatness."

-Alvin S. Felzenberg, Presidential Historian and Author of *The Leaders We Deserved...Rethinking the Presidential Rating Game*

Foreword by Dr. Jeffery Tyler Syck,

Assistant Professor of Politics at the University of Pikeville and author of *The Revolution of 1828: John Quincy Adams, Andrew Jackson, and the Origins of American Democracy*

There has quite possibly never been a more experienced and prolific American diplomat than John Quincy Adams. Over the course of his career, he served as Ambassador to four different major European nations and negotiated the end of the War of 1812. In 1817, his diplomatic work culminated in his appointment as Secretary of State. It is at this point in his career that M. B. Zucker picks up his narrative. The following pages tell the exciting story of Adams' attempts to stave off war with Europe, negotiate the acquisition of Florida, and draft the famous Monroe Doctrine. All while running for President of the United States.

However, it is not this aspect of Adams that makes him such an interesting figure. While attending Harvard, a young John Quincy Adams came to a startling realization—he was not a very good person. His whole life was built around a fanatical quest for glory and he was far too inclined to do whatever it took to acquire it. A lesser man, faced with this realization, would have attempted to rationalize his own depravity. But such intellectual dishonesty was not for an Adams. That very day he vowed to work ceaselessly toward his own moral perfection. A gripping and Sisyphean quest that litters the pages of his diary.

It is this endeavor that makes the life and thought of John Quincy Adams so moving. It is true that he met more of the nineteenth century's leading figures than almost any other American statesmen, that he dominated the diplomatic life of the early republic, and that in his final years, he served as the chief opponent of slavery in the House of Representatives. But all of this pales in comparison to Adams' deeply human search for goodness.

To fully capture this aspect of Adams is no easy task. Biographies have struggled for centuries, yet that is exactly what M. B. Zucker does in this thrilling tale of political intrigue and human nature. Somehow, he manages to expose the heart of Adams to the reader without papering over the inherent contradictions in his life. In this way, he performs a service of unparalleled importance.

Even if John Quincy Adams' noble quest for virtue does not appeal to you there is a great deal we could all stand to learn from him. For John Quincy Adams' many lessons are as relevant for the twenty-first century as they were for the nineteenth century: his dedication to the American republic, his disdain for simple-minded political factionalism, and above all his vision of a nation in which each and every human soul can be elevated. In a time dominated by a strange mixture of turbulence and tedium, what teachings could be more important for all people to embrace? Of course, we would do best to learn these things from the great man himself but since, for obvious reasons, that is not possible, we must turn to the second best thing: M. B. Zucker's touchingly beautiful portrait of words.

Jeffery Tyler Syck
Pikeville, Kentucky 2023

Serit arbores, quae alteri saeclo prosint.

He plants trees for the benefit of another age.

—Cicero

PART ONE

MISTER ADAMS
LATE 1817

I

"A MOMENT PLEASE," the President said. "The nation's security must endure my tardiness."

The senior Cabinet officers, formed of Mr. Calhoun, Mr. Crawford, and myself, competed for the straightest posture to fill the interlude. To this day, I wonder if we were cognizant of the practice.

The lesser officers—I mean *secondary*—abstained, for they knew their place. They were cautious men. Attorney General Wirt rarely spoke before knowing the President's opinion and Mr. Crowninshield was a volume of doggerel in a bookcase bearing Homer and Shakespeare. The Secretary of the Navy, he looked to Calhoun for mentorship.

Calhoun sat straight as a spear and won the contest. I blamed my failure on distraction from my swelling eyes, an ailment that had worsened since my return from Europe. The truth was my defeat lay in the inferiority of my physical proportions. Atop Calhoun's square face was dark hair both full and groomed. His only unattractive features were his lankiness and the seriousness that shone through his eyes, and though uninviting they mesmerized me.

The President was ready but first studied his Cabinet. A year since his election and we were finally together. He radiated pride. Satisfaction with his choices? Or a validation of his decades-long journey to hold the office? Likely both.

"I wish to continue framing our meetings with written questions," he said. He raised a set of cards. "I've found it a constructive mechanism for guiding our discussions. But before I distribute these, let us welcome Mr. Calhoun to his first appearance as Secretary of War."

We showed our approval by converting our table into a tambourine. It shook more violently than we anticipated, though we should have given its miniature size. Calhoun bowed his head but his attention remained fixated on the room's details. I knew because he held the exact look I did two months prior. Neither of us anticipated its humble furnishing.

Allow me to relate our seating arrangement. The President was at the table's head, his back to an empty fireplace whose shelf held two lit candles. I sat to his right while Calhoun and Crawford were on his left. Wirt and Crowninshield squeezed together at the other end.

I remind myself that this small jaundiced yellow room served as a mere surrogate for the President's Office while the nation rebuilt the Executive Mansion following the late war. The December sun, situated in the west, provided poor illumination. Four more candles flickered, dispersed. They made visible a globe standing in the corner and a map of our Union hanging from an adjacent wall. By the door stood a coat rack holding our winter garments. It was a quaint room, stuffy, and insufficient for what was to be the world's greatest nation. It lacked the quirks and wonders of Jefferson's office a decade prior, with its inventions and books scattered about and birds flying overhead.

The President was taciturn until we fell silent. Then he placed the five cards at the table's center and we all took one. "Both questions concern South America," he said. I glanced at him before reading the card. His outfit was a conscious reminder of his service during the War for Independence. For example, he wore knee breeches instead of trousers. It was a generation out of style, though I ought not critique another's fashion for I knew little of the topic as my wife was apt to remind me. The first question read:

Has the executive the power to acknowledge the independence of new states whose independence is not recognized by the parent country and between which parties war exists?

The throbbing in my eyes worsened. South America's wars of independence against Spain were the Department of State's business. The President ought to have consulted me before taking the question to the Cabinet. Perhaps Calhoun also deserved input. But why should Crawford, the Secretary of the Treasury, get an equal voice? Such consensus building was cowardly.

The Cabinet officers joined eyes. We turned to the President and signaled in the affirmative. A moment longer than necessary and he understood. He looked pleasantly surprised.

"The power exists," he whispered. Then louder, "But is it prudent?"

Our eyes joined again, communicating positions through facial gestures. Crawford, that pig-looking man, settled his stare on me. He sought to lure me into his trap.

"We again agree on the wisdom of such an action."

"Hardly," I said.

"Do you mind clarifying your position, Mr. Adams?" the President asked me.

"Granting recognition to the South American republics gives us moral credibility but is a stupid decision."

"Will it cause a Spanish declaration of war?"

"At a minimum. What prompted this discussion to change our policy?"

"The United Provinces of La Plata have sent an emissary and ask to be recognized."

"I know, Mr. President. Mr. Clay invited them so he could attack the administration in Congress. The Speaker will do anything to stand centerstage and wreck you, sir. We don't know if the United Provinces will survive—"

"On the contrary," Crawford said, "they've built a stable government in Buenos Aires." Calhoun's left elbow touched the table, pushed to the side by Crawford's mass. His tobacco-colored eyes studied us both. "General San Martín's victories in Chile will remove remaining royal encampments in that region."

"For now," I said. "The Spanish will regain momentum since Prince Metternich has restored King Ferdinand on the throne in Madrid."

"You're making my point for me," Crawford said. Did he care about the rebels or did he only exist to antagonize me? "We have no reason to fear a war with Spain. Her army is occupied in South America and Lord Nelson destroyed her navy at Trafalgar 12 years ago." He said to the President, "Intervening for the rebels will lead to a hemisphere of republics. We should relish—"

"The rebels are hardly moral exemplars," I said. "They've just as much blood to wring from their sleeves."

"How many thousands did Spain kill when reconquering Venezuela?" Crawford asked. "How many civilians?"

"General Bolivar's Decree of War to the Death states the rebels will execute anyone of European descent unless they actively support him."

"Who will remember it once he wins the war? Ferdinand's return changes nothing because Spain is a dying empire."

"Then why not allow such inevitability to come to us? Why wage an unnecessary war?"

"Because *risking* war—which isn't guaranteed, considering Spain's weakness—endears us to the rebels." He said to the President, "It can forge lasting alliances."

"You think I should lead the country into war less than a year after my inauguration?" the President asked. "The last war ended two years ago."

"A war we won," Crawford said. "I am not advocating for—"

"You believe recognizing the United Provinces, and the other rebels, leads to war with Spain. Or endangers it."

Crawford's head retracted to his shell. "I'm saying we shouldn't fear—" His words petered away. He wasn't a serious thinker or advisor. Calling him opportunistic was an understatement. Professional opportunists traded stories about him within their nests. "A potential war would be short and in our interest."

"How?"

"The Florida Territory is ripe for picking. Spain can't control it or Texas."

The President turned to me. *Lead the counterargument.*

"Presidents Jefferson and Madison each attempted to wrestle Florida from Spain. Each failed and suffered the political consequences."

"Madison secured a foothold in West Florida," Crawford said. "Today's situation is different than theirs. Spain has moved its Floridian troops to South America. That's why so many slaves flee there and why the Seminoles can invade my native Georgia and scalp my neighbors."

Calhoun's eyes narrowed. The President noticed. "You've been quiet, Mr. Calhoun. Do you have something to add?"

The Secretary of War inhaled. His shoulders, scrawny as they were, expanded as he donned a stoic mask. "We must remember the Seminoles claim the land in Georgia and the Louisiana Territory that we bought from the Creeks following General Jackson's wartime victory." His posture relaxed.

An excellent point. Indian affairs were the Department of War's prerogative and Calhoun did his research. A competent colleague, at last. He came from South Carolina, the most opinionated Southern state. I was surprised he could operate so methodically.

"It makes little difference," Crawford said. His hand waved dismissively, causing a draft. "The Seminoles are attacking our citizens and they can do so only because Spain can't govern the region."

"I remind the Secretary of the Treasury that American military forces under General Gaines and the Northern Division are already conducting an operation to disrupt the Seminoles clustered near the Georgia-Florida border," Calhoun said.

"This is irrelevant to the original question," the President said.

"I have made an adequate argument for why we shouldn't fear provoking war," Crawford said. *Adequate*. Crawford aimed for mediocrity and failed to reach it. This defined his existence and was why I left our meetings with headaches. One could not help but escape his presence worse than before.

"You're ignoring the most important factor," I said. "Europe will not sit calmly as we destroy Spain's empire. Particularly the Holy Alliance."

"Can the Alliance cross the Atlantic?" Crawford asked.

I asked the President, "Are these the questions you wish to weigh, sir? Over recognizing a band of rebels?"

"Answer the question," Crawford said. "The Holy Alliance is made up of Prussia, Austria, and Russia. Of those, only Russia is a naval power but they don't even have a warm-water port to access the eastern Mediterranean."

"And if Britain joins them?"

"Britain opposes the Alliance, which exists to promote absolute monarchy. Not even George III believes in that."

"Must I give you a history lesson? Must the Secretary of State look upon the Secretary of the Treasury as his pupil?" I asked. Crawford chuckled. "Britain partnered with the states forming the Alliance to thwart Napoleon's attempt to rule the world. It was at that time that

Napoleon kidnapped Ferdinand from Madrid, triggering the uprisings across Mexico and South—"

"This is disgraceful," Crawford said to the President.

"Mr. Crawford is correct, Mr. Adams," the President said. "Speak with a tone becoming of a Cabinet officer."

Still more pain within my eyes as my muscles contracted with anger. I reformulated my thoughts. Crawford wouldn't let himself be persuaded. I spoke to the President and Calhoun and maybe the others.

"The United States of America exist between two extremes. We state that our citizens must surrender a portion of their sovereignty to a representative government that will act on their behalf. The Holy Alliance rejects this vision. They believe that God placed monarchs on Earth to rule the rest of us. They conflate us with French revolutionaries —" Turned to the President, who supported that revolution two decades prior "—and with Napoleon, who they hold responsible for plunging Europe into a war that lasted a generation. But the French Revolution is the other extreme. The people's sovereignty could never be granted to institutions in even a limited—"

"This lecture is unnecessary, Mr. President," Crawford said.

"It *is* necessary," I said. "We must appreciate that the Alliance wants to keep the peace in Europe and prevent a duplication of the French Revolution and Napoleon. That they see the South American rebels and *us* as part of the same movement. A movement which we call freedom and they call anarchy."

"Britain is more liberal than the Alliance. She—"

"They joined together against Napoleon and they'll do it again if they see us, a rising nation, waging a war of conquest against the Spanish Empire." I said to the President, "Britain has the world's most powerful navy. Your house is being built for a second time in 20 years because Britain burned it down. And France, where the Alliance reinstated the Bourbon monarchy—"

"You mean to scare us," Crawford said. "Europe hasn't recovered from Napoleon's wars. Six million people died."

"The Europeans' taste for war mirrors our own people's taste for whiskey. I was in St. Petersburg when Napoleon invaded Russia and I witnessed the barbarism that ensued. Europe's peace does not protect us. They can concentrate their power against—"

"Britain sympathizes with the rebels. She won't allow Metternich to invade this hemisphere."

Bang!

The President struck the table. His jaws pushed against his cheeks as his slow mind processed our debate. He was not a bad looking man for his age but his head was too small for his stature.

"Mr. Adams," he said, "how do you think Lord Castlereagh will react to the collapse of Spanish power in Florida?" He referred to Britain's Foreign Secretary.

A liquid had built in my right eye for the past minutes. I dabbed it with a handkerchief.

"Castlereagh offered to broker negotiations between us and Spain last year, when I was minister to the Court of St. James. I declined. Britain wants Florida for herself and I suspect her hand in the Seminole raids."

"So you *do* support our annexing Florida," Crawford said.

"Of course," I said. "But we must do it while avoiding war with Europe. We barely survived the last one."

"We're better prepared," the President said. "My administration has set the Army at 20,000 men, larger than it was before the war under Jefferson or Madison."

"Britain has 35,000 soldiers in Canada alone, sir. In Europe, fear and respect are the same. We must strengthen our manufacturers and our Navy—" Glanced at Crowninshield "—prove we can stand alone before they see us as an equal."

The President shifted backward, hands clasped. He mulled over my point. It took him several moments to think through an issue and reach the same conclusion that I would have found in an instant.

"You alluded to my domestic policy." His eyes aimed downward, his words meant for all. "The press called the present moment *the Era of Good Feelings*. But our Union almost broke during the war. New England's open talk of secession was unacceptable."

"I agree, sir."

"Let me speak, Mr. Adams."

"Sorry, sir."

"That's all right. The Federalist Party—which was nothing but an extension of Alexander Hamilton and his patrons—is dying. It is a mere

New England regional party and I don't expect it to survive another five to ten years. That gives us an opportunity unknown since early in President Washington's tenure. I want America to be a republic free of partisanship. No divisions between North and South, between New England merchants and cotton plantation owners. This is one country. A country of free individuals. None of our citizens are oppressed or are deprived of the property they earn. Discord doesn't belong in our system. My visit to New England this summer convinced them of my intent." He shifted forward with his arms extended to balance his weight. His eyes focused on Wirt. "We must take the best ideas from all the Union's corners. I changed my mind on the Bank of the United States to lead by example. A moderate government will attract the nation's brightest minds and we can sort through their proposals. There will still be some extremists. The Mr. Randolphs of the world. But a new national consensus shall be our legacy. A happy, peaceful, and prosperous Union."

Silence. No one wanted to challenge the President's optimism. He did it himself. To Calhoun, "What do you advise regarding the United Provinces?"

Like the President, Calhoun collected his thoughts before speaking. I wondered what his eyes studied behind me and assumed it was the overlapping shades of gray on the coat rack.

"I agree with Mr. Adams," he said. Wirt and Crowninshield sighed. I was not surprised they'd joined with Crawford. He likely promised them jobs in his administration should he win the 1820 election after destroying the President and me. Or, less cynically, they favored him as a fellow Southerner and could not think beyond regional prejudice. "But I don't know if I predict a similar doomsday if we recognize the rebels."

The President nodded. "We'll defer recognition for now." Calhoun and I glanced at each other. My first victory as Secretary of State. Validation rang through my bones. Had the President any intention of changing his policy or did he only wish to watch us debate? Either way, I won. "Let us turn to the second question."

I paused and took a breath and lifted the card. It read:

What should be done about Amelia Island?

Wirt turned to the globe. I *tsked* with my tongue, a habit I developed as a rhetoric professor at Harvard. He turned back, his brow a misshapen ridge. If he did not enjoy my response he should not have earned it.

"Unprepared, aren't we, Mr. Wirt?"

"I am merely reminding myself of the island's—"

"It is near the Georgia-Florida border, right off the Atlantic coast."

"Pirates have captured the island," the President said. "It has become the center of their smuggling operation. Should we respond?"

"Is *pirate* the appropriate label?" Crawford asked.

"What would you call them?"

"*Patriots* or *revolutionaries*," Crawford said. I scoffed. "I'm sincere. A rebel faction called *The Supreme Council of the Floridas* captured the island and are using it to harass Spanish shipping."

"They're pirates," I said. "They threaten our shipping too." To the President, "Pirates are pirates, sir. They cannot be tolerated off our flank."

"What do you recommend we do about them, Mr. Adams?" the President asked.

"We must seize Amelia Island." Crawford shook his head and I raised my voice. "We must deny the pirates its use."

"You're a monarchist, like your father," Crawford said. My left hand squeezed my right under the table. "Why else would you support Spain over the rebels?"

"You're mischaracterizing my views."

"It's the only logical conclusion from what you've said today."

"Maybe if you could grasp—"

"I am not interested in your continued bickering, gentlemen," the President said. He retrieved a handkerchief and dabbed his forehead. To Crawford, "I consider those occupying the island to be pirates. Is there a reason I shouldn't remove them?"

"Yes. They're allied with the rebels. Removing them will be seen as entering the war on Spain's behalf and siding with monarchy against the new republics in Venezuela, Columbia, and elsewhere. We would betray our values and poison our relationships with those countries."

Wirt and Crowninshield nodded. The President returned to his contemplative expression.

"I disagree with Mr. Crawford," Calhoun said. Words I hoped to hear hundreds of times. "Sympathizing with the rebels does not mean we must tolerate criminals."

"And if it damages our relationships with the republics?" Crawford asked.

"This is a small incident, sir. It will not cause much confusion about where our heart lies."

The President's eyes shifted between Crawford and Calhoun. They landed on Crawford. *Have you another point? No?* They returned to Calhoun. "What would be the fastest unit to deploy?"

"General Graves and the Northern Division," Calhoun said. "Graves is engaged near the Georgia-Florida border. We could disengage the division and redirect them—"

"That would leave Georgia vulnerable to a Seminole offensive," Crawford said.

"Allow me to speak." Calhoun turned to the President.

"Please continue."

"The Southern Division is stationed in Tennessee. It could take Graves' place."

"Is such a reorganization necessary?" Crawford asked.

"I want to capture Amelia Island as soon as possible," the President said.

"Isn't the Southern Division commanded by General Jackson?" Wirt asked.

"Yes."

"I know his victory at New Orleans made him a hero, but he's undisciplined. Can we trust him?"

"The Attorney General is right," Crowninshield said. "Jackson imposed martial law on New Orleans for months after the victory and imprisoned a judge who ruled against him."

"I don't see how we can avoid utilizing him if we wish to capture Amelia Island and repel the Seminoles simultaneously," Calhoun said.

"I agree," the President said. He asked Wirt, "Does an offensive against the pirates require congressional approval?"

"They menace our shipping. We can say the operation is defensive in nature."

"As I thought." To Crowninshield: "Do you have any concerns about establishing naval superiority around the island?"

"No, sir. I don't expect meaningful resistance."

"I concur," Calhoun said. "Casualties will be negligible. Fort San Carlos will be ours by New Years Day 1818."

"Excellent," the President said. Crawford frowned, meaning events had taken a proper course. "I've one more point to discuss. It regards your department, Mr. Calhoun."

"Sir?"

"Before you assumed your post, General Graves informed me that the Northern Division was short an engineer and that this might affect the Seminoles operation. I transferred one from the Southern Division to his command. I thought it routine but General Jackson protested that I'd sent the order directly instead of to him. He's declared that he won't allow the transfer to proceed without his permission and has instructed his officers not to obey me without his blessing. I reminded him that I am the Commander in Chief and he has to accept my decisions. He disagrees. I fear he will not cooperate with this operation until the situation is resolved. What do you advise?"

All eyes were on Calhoun. The President was testing him. His place in our hierarchy depended on the answer he crafted on the spot. He had it in seconds.

"What if the Department of War enacted a new policy whereby division commanders are sent instructions for them to convey to their subordinates? The Department can hold in reserve the option to send orders directly in case of public emergency." One of the best minds I had the pleasure to witness. I had to make him my partner. He continued, "This compromise will convince General Jackson that he won his dispute with you while the presidency and the Department of War maintain their dominance over the military."

The President smiled. I led the Cabinet in battering the table again, closing the meeting.

II

I EXITED THE Executive Mansion and heard hammer strike metal and concrete. A cacophony of sound from a city in repair. I inhaled until my lungs strained and my heartbeat slowed. A cold breeze carried away my agitation. I felt like myself again. Afternoon marched toward evening and I wanted to visit the Department of State before the day's end.

A *swishing* caught my attention. I saw a young Negro at one of the Mansion's columns applying white paint over the scorch marks left by British torches in 1814. I judged him to be in his late 20s or early 30s. He wore a green shirt under a yellow vest and a wide straw hat sat by his feet. An expression of content, if not joy. Perhaps mundane.

I approached, holding files behind my back. "Greetings, young man."

He paused and lowered his brush. "Yessir?"

"What is your name?"

"Peter. What's yours?"

"My name is John Quincy Adams. I am the Secretary of State." No reaction. "Do you know what that means?" He didn't. "Have you heard of the Department of State?" No. "The Department of State manages United States foreign policy and diplomacy. I direct the Department and advise the President on those subjects." He nodded, trying to understand. "Are you a painter?"

He looked at the brush. "Sometime*sss*."

"How would you describe yourself?"

A moment passed. "Master Monroe is my owner," he said. My nose wrinkled, slipping through my constraints. "He took me and six more from Highland to repair this buildin'."

"Do you know what this building is?"

"Of cours', sir. Master Monroe lives here. He's the President."

I nodded. "And where do you live?"

"Here." He pointed at the Mansion. "The other Negroes and I live in the bottom of the buildin'."

"In the basement?"

"Yessir."

I gestured to the column. "You're doing well. Very professional work."

"Thank you. Sir."

"Where did you learn?"

"Master Monroe had another Negro teach me. So I could work at Highland."

"I see. Do you feel—your *master*—treats you well?"

"Well enouff'."

"Are you satisfied? With your life?"

Light dissolved from his eyes. His defenses fell. "I guess." A pause. "Others got it worse."

"Others of Master Monroe's Negroes?" A moment and then he nodded. I decided against prying further. "Thank you for the conversation and for your service to our country," I said.

"Yessir. You too."

I left the Executive Mansion and turned back to see Peter once more. Anger rose in my heart at seeing a slave toil at the foremost republic's most important building. Slavery was among man's greatest evils and incompatible with America's promise of liberty. I'd never questioned this and I wasn't alone. The prior generation's giants, including Father and—regardless of what he did in his private life—General Washington, understood the contradiction and hated it but accepted the compromise as necessary to maintain the Union under a republican government. They predicted slavery would disintegrate in the following decades. Yet 30 years passed since the Constitution's drafting and slavery flourished. I had no reason to doubt their genius. To the contrary, my peers and I feared that living in their shadow doomed us to mediocrity. So I held my breath for slavery's end and the Union fulfilling the creed Jefferson wrote over two score years ago.

My office stood at the intersection of 17th and G Street, a short walk from the Executive Mansion. Washington City's winter was worse than when I'd served as senator a decade ago. A volcano erupted in the East Indies in April 1815. Ten thousand died and temperatures dropped in the Northern Hemisphere. I was in London but heard of snow in New England that summer. The poor farmers and their disrupted harvests. The climate only partially recovered and so I donned my winter gear from my time as minister in St. Petersburg. This drew mockery from Washington's citizens. Mrs. Adams found their response mortifying but I thought it endearing.

Pennsylvania Avenue was Washington's most important street, if any of the unfinished roads deserved the name *streets*. Having served in St. Petersburg, London, Berlin, Amsterdam, and Paris—during the 100 Days—Washington hardly appeared a city, let alone a capital, with its wide distances between buildings. I was still adjusting after a decade in Europe, which was both more developed and wicked.

The war proved that Washington was too close to the water to defend. British flames found the public buildings with little toil. Many feared traitors had helped. The city was amidst reconstruction and slaves did most of the work. Once the architects' plan was realized our population of 10,000 would surpass a million and until then I and others navigated these bird bones. Its best feature was the lush scenery past the city boundary, reminiscent of *A Midsummer Night's Dream*. This was surely the unanimous opinion of our visitors during those years.

Crack!

I'd stepped on a bottle and leapt to avoid glass piercing my boot. I growled at the brown spikes rising from the snow. Whiskey. One report told me most Americans annually drank over seven gallons each. Western farmers were more than happy to fulfill this growing appetite. It was cheaper than water. I was not one to abstain from a drink but moderation was vital to a productive life. *Woe to those who rise early in the morning to run after their drinks, who stay up late at night till they are inflamed with wine. They have harps and lyres at their banquets, tambourines and flutes and wine, but they have no regard for the deeds of the Lord, no respect for the work of his hands.* Isaiah 5:11.

I continued and saw a candle already lit to illuminate the road. Strange, as the sun hadn't retired. It was likely a drunkard on duty. I retrieved a cigar from my pocket and lit it with the fire. Ah, warmth. Cigars brought me daily happiness. A stress relief.

I approached my office and saw a strange figure through the snow. She held a Bible in her right hand and extended a pamphlet with her left. I wasn't interested.

"Sir?"

"Why are you in the cold?" I asked.

"Are you drunk?"

"No—what?"

"Are you—"

"Do you need shelter, ma'am?"

"No."

"How is your home? Does your husband abuse you?"

"I am quite well. Would you care to discuss temperance?"

"No, thank you."

"How about slavery?"

"No, ma'am. I must visit my office before dark."

"I understand." Her posture sank. "Care for a pamphlet?"

I sighed. "Would it offend you if I decline?"

"Maybe."

"I already have too many papers waiting in my office."

A pause. "May I ask what you do?"

"Does it matter?"

"I'd like to know."

"I'm the Secretary of State."

Her posture restored itself. "Mr. Adams." I bowed. Snow hit my neck, which might feel nice if I weren't already chilled. "Your father is a great man." I chuckled. She attempted repair. "You might be too one day." A pause. "I'm sorry, sir."

"That's all right."

"May I ask your opinion on slavery?"

"Must you?"

"You might stand for President one day."

I hesitated. "Slavery is ancient and simple. Freedom is modern and complex. I've no doubt which will survive."

She smiled. "Thank you, Mr. Adams. It's an honor to speak with you."

"Likewise, ma'am. Don't stand out here too long. Find warmth."

I entered the department building. It housed all federal agencies until the individual complexes were replaced. A boring design, its classical roof and tan brick resembled a school, which it was, given the torrent of information that washed over all of those within its halls. I climbed the wooden stairs to the second floor where the Department of State had five rooms. The spectacled woman who owned a fruit cart by

31

the Department of War's entrance stared at me. Her face was a cracked timepiece judging me for arriving late to class. I examined her with repressed disgust and yearned for my department to be solitary again.

Our main room was empty aside from Mr. Brent, my right hand who was three years my junior, and a youngster I didn't recognize. Half a dozen desks sitting in two rows of three controlled the space's center while file cabinets literally and metaphorically blocked the sun along the rim. Any open space on those pasty walls wielded maps of every continent.

"Where are our clerks?" I asked. "Slade, King, and Ironside. Where are they?" I referred to the men who directed the Bureau of Archives and Laws, the Department library, and the dispersing agent of pardons and passports.

"We received—" Brent paused. His face projected thoughtfulness while disguising cunning. "I sent them out on individual assignments. I didn't expect you to stop by today. Slade is mailing instructions to our ministers. Ironside's at the patent office and King's at the Capitol."

"All right," I muttered. I moved toward my private office by the opposite wall and paused. It was ridiculous that each minister required two sets of instructions, one for procedures and one with assignments. I gestured to the youngster. "Who's this?"

The youngster turned to Brent. Brent said, "This is Matthew Maury. I've hired him as a translator."

"Don't we already have a Maury?"

"His father is the consul in Liverpool."

"I see." I nodded at Maury. "A pleasure."

"Likewise, sir."

Brent said, "We received—"

"The clerks ought not leave the office until we've restored the Department from its wartime disruption," I said.

"We have."

"Your standards are lower than mine, Daniel." I faced my office but turned back to him. "We need everyone working here. Congress drops more and more chores on us, as though no other federal organ exists. We need to think about the 1820 census. Index the federal and state laws. And so on." I finally entered my office, leaving the door open if they wished to follow.

My office was bare. I didn't bother decorating since it was temporary. A bookcase, a file cabinet, and maps of North America and the world on the wall opposite my desk, which sat under the sole window. Lord Castlereagh and other European ministers would weep, not laugh, if they saw it. But a renovation was coming and the plans I formed there would allow my successors' importance to dwarf theirs a thousandfold.

The daily stack of three dozen newspapers was on my desk. Every day I read them and cut out important articles for my files. The *National Intelligencer* sat on top. The administration's mouthpiece. I saw the main story was that New York's government passed legislation to build a canal in Lake Erie.

"Any developments in the Cabinet?" Brent asked. He stood in the room near the door while Maury occupied its frame.

"Oh, yes," I said. "It was the most productive yet. The President recommitted to not recognizing the United Provinces." Maury appeared as though struck in his chest. "Yes?"

He hesitated. Then, "Shouldn't we recognize them, sir? They carry on our revolution."

"It's not that simple. Such an action risks war with Europe."

"Oh."

I said to Brent, "The President also decided to capture Amelia Island."

"Excellent," Brent said. "What do you think of Mr. Calhoun?"

"I detect great potential in him. He's clearly ambitious."

"Could he join our side?"

I smiled. "Perhaps." I sat behind my desk, lifted the *Intelligencer*, and read about the canal. It would revolutionize New York State. Governor Clinton pursued it because President Madison had vetoed a large internal improvements bill the day before leaving office in March. Madison claimed the Constitution did not grant the federal government such authority. I didn't take such a narrow view of government power and agreed with Clinton that internal improvements were critical for our growth.

The *Intelligencer* contained an interesting wrinkle. Martin Van Buren, Clinton's foremost opponent in the New York senate, fought the bill by claiming the canal's construction would raise taxes. Once Clinton acquired the votes for its passage Van Buren switched sides and voted for it. The article called him the *Little Magician*.

I snickered. A public life must be anchored by virtue. Otherwise it was a wicked grasp for power. Denial was a virtue. Pleasure was a vice. Characters like Van Buren were why most Americans were cynical about politics.

I turned the page. An article about Washington's reconstruction. One sentence about the new public buildings stood out: *a beacon to remind us how much may be lost by false security, or by want of union and energy of action.*

Exactly. It was peculiar that Americans declared victory in the late war when the Union almost perished. Our capital fell to ash and Jackson's triumph at New Orleans didn't change that.

Brent hovered over me. "Yes?" I asked.

"We received a communication from Mr. Gallatin." He referred to our minister in France. "King Louis rejects our restitution claims for the six million dollars their navy stole from our vessels during Napoleon's reign."

"On what grounds?"

"He claims the monarchy isn't responsible or liable since the theft occurred under a different regime."

I snorted. "Mr. Gallatin desires an argument?"

"He does."

"Tell him to look in *Mare Liberum*. It—" Turned to Maury. "Write to Mr. Gallatin. Instruct him to look in *Mare Liberum*. It's Hugo Grotius' book about the freedom of the seas. A book of law. He'll find the answer there." Maury raced for a pencil and paper. I said to Brent, "A new government doesn't erase a state's debt. It can't. Otherwise every country would borrow money and artificially reestablish its government to avoid repayment."

"You know it doesn't matter what we say to Louis. He won't listen."

"I know. It doesn't mean I won't torture him over it," I said. Brent chuckled. "Have you read the *Intelligencer* yet?"

"No."

"It has an article on our false belief of security. It's right. But we have an opportunity to ensure that no foreign empire can ever threaten us again."

Maury returned as my sentence ended. "How's that, sir?"

"Our population has doubled since ratifying the Constitution and will do so again in the coming generation. That means greater wealth and power. We need geographic security to fulfill our potential."

"How?"

Brent smiled. "The first of many lectures." To me: "Enjoy him while he's ripe."

"We take advantage of the Spanish Empire's collapse. Their decline mirrors our rise. Once we have Amelia Island we'll use it to open negotiations for purchasing the Florida Territory. We'll also improve our relationship with Britain."

"I thought you didn't trust her," Brent said.

"I don't. But we can't resist her and the Holy Alliance simultaneously. Her navy rules the waves so she controls our access to markets abroad. With Napoleon vanquished, she can dedicate her full attention to squashing us." My cigar was now a stub and I fiddled with it. "No one in Europe blesses our growth. We'll do it anyway, but it's impossible without pacifying London."

I retrieved a knife from a desk drawer and cut out the *Intelligencer* article. I handed it to Brent. "Archive this for me." Brent left to do so. Maury followed.

The United States were to dominate North America, meaning Europe's presence in this hemisphere had to be eradicated. North America was to be one nation, speaking one language and professing one political system. That we would absorb Texas and eventually Canada was as much a law of nature as that the Mississippi should flow to the sea.

Internal improvements would strengthen our economy and trade would bind the world together. Perhaps the New Englander in me necessitated that thought. Free trade and a single, global system of measurement would foster world peace.

A great vision. It was achievable with the right decisions. I had to win over the President. Crawford and Clay would undermine me for their own gain. Calhoun was the key. We'd woo the President together and the three of us would produce victories that earned the public's support. Then Congress would support us or suffer electoral defeat.

That was my goal as Secretary of State. If I succeeded, the people would see my wisdom and allow me to continue my work as President.

III

MY EYES, STILL irritated, were now heavy as I arrived home and I prayed Mrs. Adams had had one of her good days. We'd rented a house at C and 4 ½ Street. A modest home but our family fit well enough. The neighborhood was uninspired, even by Washington standards, the indiscernible buildings standing in file rows like minutemen awaiting approaching redcoats. Its worst feature was a jail-turned-slave pen a mere block away.

I entered the home and saw that the dining room fireplace embers were abating. George, my eldest, slept nearby. John and Charles, my younger sons, attended Boston Public Latin School and lived with the Welshes, our friends. Two chambers—the dining room and kitchen—were at the front while a cluster of minute bedrooms inhabited the rear. The dining room had a table with six chairs, a cluttered bookcase, and portraits of Cicero and George and Martha Washington.

I approached my son and saw a French study book opened so I couldn't read the title and painted metal toy soldiers organized for battle. I kneeled and shook his shoulder until his eyes opened.

"Were you studying or playing?"

He groaned. "I was studying and took a break."

"You don't have time for games if you're to enter Harvard as a sophomore."

"I know, Father," he said meekly.

"I will make our name proud," I said in French. In English: "Translate for me." He failed, barely trying, and I paced about. "Don't you want to make something of yourself? To get somewhere—anywhere—in the world? To earn my admiration rather than be a burden?" He wept. I stood over him so my words carried greater force. "Control yourself. Be distinguishable from the placenta once attached to you."

He begged between gasps: "Stop, Father."

I froze, stressed from my day. I chose to be kinder. "What battle were you reenacting?"

A moment. "General Washington's victory at Saratoga."

"Washington wasn't at Saratoga. It was Gates. You can't even waste time properly."

He hugged his legs.

"Work for another hour before retiring for the day. Read scripture before bed. It's medicine for the soul. We are all, son, unwilling to confess our own faults, even to ourselves. Our consciences either disguise them under false and delusive colors or seek out excuses and apologies to reconcile them to our minds."

He nodded and I entered the kitchen. A claustrophobic space made worse by protruding counters, stuffed shelves, and a round three-legged table at one end. A pot of stew waited for me. I was too drowsy for hunger.

Ellen and Antoine released their grip on one another. Ellen was our cook and Antoine was a young Belgian man I'd hired as my servant. They were the best-looking pair in the family, though that said little.

"I take it Mary's asleep?" I asked, referring to my wife's nine-year-old niece living with us.

"Yes, Mr. Adams," Ellen said.

"And Lucy?" My wife's servant.

Ellen hesitated. "She's in bed."

"Did Mrs. Adams yell at her again?" More hesitation. "Be honest."

"Yes, Mr. Adams. Mrs. Adams had another episode." My head drooped. "She fainted and we put her in your bedroom. She might be awake now."

I lacked room to express my frustration and so squeezed my fists. "I needed her to have a good day."

"I'm sorry, sir."

I turned to leave and paused. "You may restore your embrace."

Our bedroom was pitch black. Curtains resembling a sorcerer's cape altered it into a lightless mausoleum. Misaligned portraits of our sons and a pamphlet about repairing buggy wheels cluttered a night table while the closet door remained ajar from when I left that morning. Mrs. Adams opened her eyes. *Paradise Lost*, her favorite book, sat beside her face. Her hair grayer and her body plumper than when we wed. Self-induced stress was a greater culprit than age.

"You fainted?" I asked. She nodded. "Do you need laudanum?"

"No," she whispered.

"Do you know the source?"

Louder now: "I again instructed Lucy—"

"Do you want her to quit?"

A sigh. "I don't care."

"What *do* you care about?"

"You know the answer. I can't stop thinking about Baby Louisa."

My spine used to stiffen at such remarks. No longer. "It was five years ago."

"As if that matters." Her posture rose. "She—she was everything. And you, in your heartlessness, you don't even—"

"Of course I do. I loved our daughter more than anything. But we cannot live *within* mourning. We still have children to attend to. Lives which must go on. We cannot afford, nor should we want, to be consumed by a single tragedy. We must accept it as a dark chapter and —"

"Do not lecture me. You haven't the right."

"A right derived from what?"

"Look at how you treat those dearest to me. Like Baby Louisa. Like Father."

I shook my head. "Your father was in the wrong. He brought it upon himself."

"You merely had to pay off—"

"I was not about to allow his creditors to blackmail me, Louisa. To blackmail our family."

Screaming now. "Instead you allowed for his humiliation. He had to flee London for America, a country whose revolution he supported—"

Joined her screaming. "Do you know the insult to my virtue—"

She scoffed. "*Your* virtue?"

"Yes, my virtue. It's my most valuable possession. My life's foundation. As if I had the money to pay off his creditors when I'm supporting our family on a government salary."

"He died a broken man. A man who'd been—"

"He lied to us, Louisa. To you."

A lower octave. "He was the only one who cared. Who ever cared."

"People care for you."

"Who?"

"Me."

"Really?"

"Of course. And our family."

"They don't respect me."

"That doesn't mean they don't care."

"It's a prerequisite." She turned to the curtain. "I ask so little from life and I get even less."

"Self-indulgence is pathetic."

"I just want a happy family. That's all."

"Life isn't meant to be happy."

"Yes it is. At least, that's what I believe."

"A foolish belief. Everyone feels stress but adults put it aside and keep going."

A pause. "I should join our daughter beyond the grave."

"Or don't listen to me. Whichever's better."

I undressed in the mirror and became blue. My handsome days were behind me. Balder and rounder. I mentioned my eye troubles and will inform you of my hands later. I wished to hide from the world and never appear in public again. No one should have to see this.

Some quiet minutes. Then, "Let's leave for Braintree the day after tomorrow."

"Why?" she asked.

"Getting away from the city will clear your head. We'll spend time with my family instead of the vultures circling Washington."

"Can you afford to leave?"

"No, but your health is more important. I'll return before the upcoming congressional session."

"You're underestimating the time required to visit New England during winter."

"Not if we travel by steamship. I'll tell Brent tomorrow that he must run the Department for a few days. He'll understand."

"Daniel is a considerate man." A pause. "Can we visit John and Charles?"

"You can. I won't have time."

"They need their father."

"They'll have to do without. For now."

IV

BRENT WAS NOT pleased when I informed him of my plan to leave Washington and take Mrs. Adams to Braintree. He asked about Amelia Island and I told him to not expect news for two weeks and that I would return before Congress formed an opinion. Then he asked what to do if the President changed his mind on recognizing the United Provinces and I said he would not do so this soon after making his decision. Brent raised concerns around half a dozen other issues—Britain's claim to the Northwest, a change in the Seminole crisis, and the weight and measurement report among them. I combated each argument and we settled on two conclusions—I trusted him to run the Department in my absence and a respite would help Mrs. Adams tame her depressed spirits. He was fond of her and she of him.

Off we went. Mrs. Adams and I rode a steamship—I believe it was the *Savannah*—to Massachusetts. A stop in Trenton. I first encountered this new form of travel in September, when I returned from Europe and visited my parents before going to Washington to be sworn in. I considered myself a man of science and read all I could. Life was changing for the better. Man was no longer shackled to the ground. He could outpace a horse. Cross the country in days. People of different states would meet, the Union would consolidate, and ideas would spread. The next rung of the ladder this side of Gutenberg.

We'd spent the September trip socializing with passengers from both sides of the Atlantic. This time we conserved our energy and avoided the cold. At least I did. She sat under an awning to breathe fresh air while I stayed in my cabin writing a poem. Poetry was my passion and if I could choose a talent I'd make myself a great poet. Alas, it remained no more than an outlet. I'm normally private with my work, but I'll show you my creation:

> *O that the race of men would raise*
> *Their voices to their heavenly King,*
> *And with the sacrifice of praise*

The glories of Jehovah sing!
Ye navigators of the sea,
Your course on ocean's tides who keep,
And there Jehovah's wonders see,
His wonders in the briny deep!
He speaks, conflicting whirlwinds fly,
The waves in swelling torrents flow,
They mount, aspire to Heaven on high,
They sink, as if to Hell below:
Their souls with terror melt away,
They stagger as if drunk with wine
Their skill is vain,-to thee they pray,
o, save them, Energy divine!
He stays the storm, the waves subside,
Their hearts with rapture are inspired
Soft breezes waft them o'er the tide,
in gladness, to their port desired.

I joined Mrs. Adams for the next wing of our journey—Trenton to Massachusetts—and though not allowed in the female quarters I didn't fear reprimand.

"Care to sit?" She was still under her awning, holding a half-empty glass.

"I'll stand." I had my hands behind my back. "Do you feel better?"

She nodded. I hoped she was truthful. "Where are your thoughts?"

"In London," I answered.

"Anticipating what Castlereagh will do in the Northwest?"

"No. With Mr. Bentham."

"Ah. An interesting man."

"I miss our walks."

"You miss your debates. It took Europe's foremost philosopher to match wits with you."

"Please." Only a false humility in part.

"Truly. You won't speak to me about your work but I've no doubt you're too intelligent for your enemies," she said. I smiled. "What topic occupies you?"

"You're interested?" She sighed, which confused me. "Monarchy is on my mind, given the Alliance's threat. I'm dissecting our discussion of whether removing George III is worth a British civil war."

"And you, ironically, opposed the proposition."

"Correct."

"That wasn't a question."

Another smile.

◆ ◆ ◆ ◆ ◆ ◆

We arrived at Peacefield, the family farm, by carriage the following night. Braintree was 12 miles from Boston and two miles from the sea and was the epicenter of the Adams lineage. Our arrival startled my parents. Mrs. Adams hoped to excite and so we sent no advanced warning. Mother was disappointed I was to only stay a short while but Father knew I had business in Washington and questioned why I came at all.

"George could not join?" Mother asked.

"Not until he improves his studies," I said. My parents exchanged a look. I paid it no mind. They offered us a bath but I informed them we'd already bathed that week.

The house was saturated because Tom, my brother, lived with my parents along with Nancy, his wife, and their five children. My parents, lacking time for preparation, placed us with two toddlers—Frances and Isaac—in a cramped upstairs room for the night. The house had Father's office and four bedrooms on the second floor, the largest two containing the adult couples. The ground level had a sitting area, the dining room, and the kitchen. The fireplace in the sitting area warmed the house during the winter months but I recalled my family sleeping in its vicinity. They would do so again as the weather worsened. My parents had a farm that they used to produce animals and wood. They kept their surplus for themselves and considered independence a virtue.

I'm reluctant to call the home my parents' because the deed was in my name. My savings were the only reason Father's failed investment in a London bank did not cause foreclosure. It was the least I could do to repay what they'd done for me. Mrs. Adams wished to sell the property once my parents passed but I had no such intent. Our family's presence in Braintree was a monument to the century-and-a-half we'd been in this hemisphere.

I awoke shortly before five—late by my standards—and strolled around the farm. The sea breeze did its worst but it could not halt my thinking. Luis de Onís y González-Vara, the Spanish minister to the United States, would call upon us to return Amelia Island to Spain once we expelled the pirates. I had to convince the President to show Onís that Spain couldn't defend Florida and Texas against American power and to surrender them without a fight in exchange for compensation. But what if Crawford convinced the President that my ploy was too risky? What if it was? What if Madrid instructed Onís to persevere? Would the President act or would Florida slip through our fingers? He'd lose the next election if Britain controlled Florida and Cuba beforehand. Who would replace him? Crawford? He'd sell the Union to Britain or even Metternich and reign as puppet-governor.

I sought contingencies. Would Calhoun stand with me? How long until Onís contacted my office? What if the pirates resisted our men better than expected and corpses required burial?

Mrs. Adams' sadness demanded my focus so concentrating on work proved impossible. Our daughter died five years ago, when we were in Russia. My wife's heart broke in ways even I couldn't contemplate. Baby Louisa was as lovely an infant as ever breathed the air of Heaven. She was at the age when the first dawn of intelligence began to reward the parents' pains and benefits. Every gesture was a charm, every look a delight, every imperfect but improving accent at once rapture and promise. To all this we bid adieu. Mrs. Adams was inhuman for a year after her passing. She wanted to follow our daughter and leave our sons and me. Especially me.

Sunlight emerged and delicately caressed the landscape. It illuminated Tom's approach. A whiskey in his hand. He was skinnier and had a fuller scalp than me but this failed to hide his misery. I remembered his green coat with gold buttons from his 18th birthday.

"Mornin'. You must be frigid."

"Already?"

He shrugged. "It helps."

"It masks."

"Then a mask is what I need." He took a defiant swig.

"Remember Charles."

Anger melted his shallow exterior. "I'm not him." A pause. "Our brother was a warning."

"Of what?"

He hesitated but I pressed through my gaze. "Of the cost of being an Adams."

"What do you mean? Our name bears a virtuous—"

"Of course *you'd* say that. You're successful."

"You mustn't blame—"

"We both hated law, brother, but Father won you a fancy job in Europe. For me, he offered space in exchange for shame."

"I did not come here to argue, Thomas."

"I don't want to argue either." He drank. "But don't judge me."

I forcefully shifted my attention. Pigs in the distance. After some quiet, "I miss the farm."

"Why?" he asked.

"People in cities care only about money and status." I waited for a remark that did not come. "How's Nancy?"

He shrugged and his face jittered as he thought of an answer. Instead he took a sip, to my disappointment. I wanted to move our interaction in a constructive direction. Something he'd enjoy.

"What do the people of this state think of me?"

A moment. "Your leadership in ending the war and your new job have overshadowed memory of the Senate recall."

I nodded and said, "Good," softly, because he expected it. "Voting for the embargo was correct, the best of the available options, regardless of what unemployed merchants in Boston might—"

A gust of wind pummeled us. We were uncomfortable but we each refused to retreat inside. A contest of stubborness. Farm animals were a poor distraction now and I moved my thoughts to my work.

"John! Tom!" We turned and saw Mrs. Adams. "Breakfast is ready!" I looked at Tom and we silently acknowledged our foolishness. "Come!" my wife shouted. "Your mother lacks patience!"

♦ ♦ ♦ ♦ ♦ ♦

The ladies raised the fire and prepared cornbread and boiled eggs. Mrs. Adams knew not how to operate a farm when we wed but Mother mentored her, albeit not joyfully. We gathered in the sitting room. Tom's rascals were close to the fire and the adults formed a disjointed ring around them. I sat next to Mrs. Adams and Tom and Nancy were across from us. Father was behind the children so he could enjoy the fire while Mother was furthest away. I watched Father bite into cornbread, his eyes the loaded muskets of his years. The man who pushed independence through the Continental Congress and prevented war with France at the cost of reelection. He sported a lion's mane but it was gray and backward, going down his neck.

"So, Louisa," Mother said between mouthfuls, "how are you liking marriage to a high official?"

Mrs. Adams was already in better spirits. She smiled and finished chewing. Her natural light, the feminine complexion that drew me to her those years ago, was on display.

"I'm sure you recall the pressures of being a hostess in Washington," she said. Mother and Tom both turned to Nancy but Mother then returned to my wife.

"John never served in the Cabinet," Mother said, "but I know the wives of Cabinet officers must host regularly. Probably more than in our time. As wife of the Secretary of State, you'll be considered the capital's leading hostess other than Mrs. Monroe."

"I wish…" Mrs. Adams' words petered off. She asked me, "Do you mind if I explain what's happened?" I signaled I didn't but focused on my food. "We were informed upon our arrival in Washington that we were to pay our respect to the city's leading families. Members of Congress and the Senate and those sorts. We discussed this and decided it was more effort than we cared for and we've been shunned ever since." Mother shook her head. "Mrs. Monroe told me we'd breached protocol and we've spent the last weeks repairing our relationships."

"How is Mrs. Monroe as hostess?"

"She's reclusive. The opposite of Mrs. Madison. That's another reason why she asked me to alter my approach."

"She wants you to act as the administration's hostess?"

"Yes."

"A dereliction of duty," Mother said. "Don't you agree, John?"

Father waited a moment. "I suppose. Don't care for mindless chatting myself."

"I think it's noble of you to bear responsibility that's not your obligation," Mother said. Mrs. Adams smiled. "Have you started?" I snickered. "Yes, Johnny?"

"Tell them," I instructed Mrs. Adams.

"Are you sure?"

I nodded. "It will amuse them."

Mrs. Adams returned to Mother. "John had several friends over for dinner and cards. After they settled in, I departed to find the men some candles when I saw my copy of *Rob Roy*. The new Walter Scott novel. Have you read it?" Mother shook her head. "It's wonderful. I began reading and forgot to return. Later I heard the men, including this one—" she looked at me "—tripping over furniture in the dark."

Nancy laughed. Mrs. Adams turned to each of us to judge our reactions. She had expected her story to land with greater effect. Perhaps I was wrong to encourage her.

"Were you drunk?" Mother asked me.

"Yes. It was a special occasion. I don—"

"You must avoid serving too much alcohol," Father told Mrs. Adams. "It's a national problem. Dependency on drink is something Johnny doesn't need."

Tom's fury was magnitudes greater than earlier. Nancy stared at Mrs. Adams and me, not hiding her sadness and wanting us to know it.

"You will grow in your role," Mother said to Mrs. Adams. "I have nothing but confidence in you."

"That's very kind."

"It's the truth. I misjudged you when we first met. I thought you were a spoiled London girl and I'm sorry for getting you so wrong."

"This isn't nec—"

"We should be partners." Mother smiled. "We can guide Johnny together. We'll build a great man."

"My mother and wife, conspiring?" I asked.

"You can try to stop us if you'd like," Mrs. Adams said. This earned the laughter she craved.

"Ha ha," I said sarcastically before sipping coffee.

Mrs. Adams looked at Mother. "You remain the guiding planet around which we all revolve."

Nancy pushed her way into the conversation. "Tell me, Louisa. How are parties in Washington? The ones you don't host?"

Mrs. Adams chuckled. "Still exhausting. Count your blessings that you didn't marry a politician."

Nancy withdrew into her seat. Mrs. Adams turned to me for direction but I was preoccupied. She turned to Mother, who shook her head. Back to me, staring until I met her eyes.

"Done eating?" Father asked me.

There was still food on my plate. "I can be."

"Good. Let's take a walk."

"Let Johnny eat," Mother ordered. Father grabbed his cane. "It's freezing."

"Let's walk," Father said.

We exited the house. The wind had calmed but the air was colder, besting the sun's efforts. I tracked Father as we walked the trail we'd used many times before. A flickering of memories. Some pleasant, others buried. The worst moment of my youth happened there—Father, with Mother's blessing, pressured me into breaking my engagement with Mary Frazer, a young girl to whom I'd pinned all hopes of happiness.

Father was silent and I decided to prompt him. "I don't seek counsel on policy."

A moment. My words went unheard. Then, "Good. I don't seek to give it. I am too old and have been out of action too long to be useful."

"Unlikely."

"I'd rather discuss issues closer to home."

"Go on."

He sighed. "Your mother was my closest advisor. And my wisest. When I look at you and Louisa…" A moment. "Do you talk to her about your work?"

"No."

"You should."

"Louisa has a limited understanding of politics and world events."

"Teach her. Bring her up to speed. Though you're wrong. She was a minister's wife in Europe. Befriended Emperor Alexander in St. Petersburg. Witnessed Napoleon's conquests. My image of her was forever changed when she told me of how she crossed the continent with young Charles alone for six weeks and French soldiers intercepted them in a Russian carriage. Her improvisation saved your family."

"That does not mean she knows how to manage France and Russia."

"You're making a mistake, Johnny." He made eye contact. "I'm fond of Louisa. Marrying her was the most important event of your life." Turning away. "No matter what office you may obtain."

I turned backward, not wanting us to go out too far in case the wind resumed.

"How are the boys?" he asked.

"What?"

"I asked *how are the boys*."

"Oh. They're fine."

"How old are they now?"

"George is sixteen, John is fourteen, and Charles is ten."

"How is George's education progressing?"

I groaned. "I don't know what to do with him. He's stupid and weak."

"What does Louisa think?"

"She's soft with him. With all of them. Charles' French is improving but the others are behind. A shame children are not clay to be made according to the fancy of every potter."

"Remember that an education should include a knowledge of history in general and of England, France, Holland, and America in particular. Have them read whatever legal text you can, no matter the age. And the memoirs of great men."

"I know, Father. I remember how you raised me. I model my approach to fatherhood on you."

"Just don't pressure them too much."

"Is such a thing possible?"

"Yes. Look at your brothers."

"But look at me."

"What about you?"

"I didn't turn out like Tom and Charles."

"I suppose not." He growled within each breath. I wanted to return home soon. "I wish you'd had more success as a lawyer. You could have been great but you are too disposed to despondency."

"It didn't interest me."

"You didn't give it a chance. Spent your law school years playing cards and chasing girls. The profession requires time to earn appreciation."

"It was a bad fit. My mind doesn't work that way."

"You determine how your mind works." He looked back and then said to me, "Realize where you started in life, Johnny. History won't give me my due. I won't be credited for my role in the Revolution. The parts performed by General Washington, Mr. Jefferson, and Dr. Franklin will be exaggerated instead. But we are still one of America's leading families. You came into life with advantages that will disgrace you if your success is mediocre."

"I am the Secretary of State."

"You must become President."

He started toward home. I followed. "My position makes me heir apparent. The last three Presidents all held my office before ascending to the Executive Mansion."

"That's not a guarantee."

"A guarantee is impossible."

"It was for General Washington. You are not he, but it can still be done."

"How?"

"Find a way, Johnny. And you must win two terms, to make up for my loss to Jefferson. Restore the family legacy."

I swelled with anxiety. This was the period where I'd succeed or fail to fulfill my destiny. I was again the eight-year-old Father took across the Atlantic during the War for Independence.

"You once told me that you studied politics and war so I may study mathematics and philosophy, and I had to study mathematics and philosophy so my children could study painting and music."

Father chuckled. "There will always be a need for politics, son. If men were angels no government would be necessary. I am not advising you. I'm telling you. You must achieve the presidency. For your own worth and for mine. For our family's. You *must* succeed."

"Yes, Father." My mind raced faster than I could follow. Crawford. Onís. Metternich. Only a few of the obstacles I faced. It was now an issue of life and death. Failure would destroy me and my family. A disgrace for generations. Through history. My name synonymous with shame.

Mother waited for us as we approached home. "Louisa is chatting with Tom and Nancy."

"I was reminding Johnny of our expectations of him," Father said.

"Yes! We shall have a two-term President in this family."

Father chuckled, embracing the joke at his expense. My anxiety doubled.

"Remember to not look back or shrink from your duty, however arduous or dangerous the task assigned you," Mother said. "And never forget virtue. It's equally important. Purge any Old World values you absorbed from your soul. Your great intellect counts for little if virtue, honor, and integrity aren't added to it. I'd much rather you found your grave in the ocean while returning from Europe than see you an immoral profligate or a graceless man."

The highest goals that parents could have for their child. The heights of ambition and virtue. They wanted the impossible, yet I had no choice but to obey.

"The first and deepest of all my wishes," I said, "is to give satisfaction to my parents."

PART TWO

FLORIDA MAN
1818

V

I AWOKE SOON after three O'Clock, which was too early for rising. I returned to bed but was up at half past four. The difficulty I found in stirring earlier each morning than the preceding one was that I lost necessary sleep and had the most painful drowsiness the ensuing day.

Pain forced me up. I'd taken an afternoon nap and eaten too much before bed and now paid interest on my indulgences. I lit a candle with our home's fireplace and used its illumination to brush my teeth. A blend of burned bread and soap. My teeth were poor quality and I suspected my parents giving me mercury to combat smallpox as a boy was why.

Next I wrote a diary entry for the prior day's events. I had a diary since I was 12. Father gave me my first volume while in France and I titled it *Diary by Me*. The entry read:

5 January 1818

My wife who for some days has been troubled with a bad cold and cough was bled this morning by Dr. Hunt. Cardelli was here and told me of the arrival of Mr. Bulfinch, the Architect of the Capitol. At 11 O'Clock I called at the President's, where I found Mr. Crowninshield and nine or ten of the Members of the House of Representatives from the Districts of Massachusetts interested in the fisheries, consulting upon the subject of the proposal to be made to the British government. After examining the map and some conversation, several of the Members asked for time to write to their districts for information and I undertook to reconcile Mr. Bagot to wait until the February Packet for the proposal. Crowninshield had received dispatches with information about Amelia Island on the 23rd of last month. Mr. Calhoun afterward came in with the same dispatches and the President appointed a Cabinet Meeting for 11 O'Clock tomorrow morning to determine what should be done with Amelia Island. At the office I had visits from Mr. Gaillard, the

*President pro Tempore of the Senate, and his colleague Judge Smith, and
had a conversation with them on various topics.*

     I put my diary aside and picked up the Bible. The Bible was
humanity's interpretation of God's word and was the most perfect
document produced by our hands. It taught of benevolence and humility.
The source of civilization's virtue. A call to never be tame or abject, to
never show oneself yielding or complying to prejudice or intractability
which would lead astray from the dictates of one's conscience. The first
chapters contain our earliest history, of Eden and immortality revoked for
our transgressions. Thus showed the consequence of selfish and slothful
behavior and for wanting what was God's.

     I couldn't push my parents' message from my thoughts. I had to
meet their expectations of both future achievement and virtue. The
outcome was beyond my control yet failure wasn't an option for I
wouldn't live as a disappointment. I turned to scripture for help, starting
with John 1:12.

     *Blessed is the man that endureth temptation: for when he is tried,
he shall receive the crown of life, which the Lord hath promised to them
that love him.*

     Virtuosity was more important than outcomes. Right? That's how
Mother raised me. Yet she and Father were clear that they expected me to
reach the pinnacle of my profession and society. An outcome that
mattered. I read Jeremiah 10:23.

     *O Lord, I know that the way of man is not in himself: it is not in
man that walketh to direct his steps.*

     Reading the Bible was itself a laudable occupation and scarcely
failed to be a useful employment of effort, but reflecting upon it was
equally essential to give it the efficacy of which it is susceptible. That's
why I set apart a small portion of every day to read and observe it.

     I turned to Cicero, the greatest statesman and philosopher of all
time. His name personified eloquence in Latin thought. The master of the
language, as was Shakespeare for English, Cervantes for Spanish, and
Dante for Italian. Cicero taught us that having a brave and great spirit
meant disdaining things external and prioritizing our duty to society over
prestige or else battles for hierarchy would transform a government for
the people into one for the few or the one. He reminded me that my life

was less valuable than serving my country. He demonstrated this when he died defending the Roman Republic from Caesar, Mark Antony, and Octavian. His writings were humanity's defining achievement besides scripture.

These works renewed me and I labored on the measurement report before walking to the Potomac with Antoine. January's snow covered Washington. Swimming and walking were my favorite forms of exercise and this achieved both. It surprised me that more citizens did not take advantage of the river. I swam one or two hours every morning and Antoine rowed behind me to ensure my safety. I competed with myself to see how long I could swim without touching the river bottom. I lasted ninety minutes that morning before joining Antoine in the boat. I only wore a cap and green goggles so Antoine directed us back to the river bank to gather my clothes.

This was my morning routine. Routine shaped my life and granted me sanity. It led to improvement and improvement was a better goal than specific outcomes. It allowed me to become my best possible self.

Nations, like individuals, required improvement to survive. America needed internal improvements to fulfill her destiny as the wealthiest and most powerful nation in history. Roads and canals would stimulate her expansion across the continent I intended to conquer. They'd foster our citizenry's financial and cerebral growth. Government's sacred duty was guiding the improvement of the governed. That's why the slavery powers and the Holy Alliance were the enemies of progress.

Improvement meant working toward virtue. Perfection was possible for only the divine and the insane but our duty was to aim for it anyway and slow progress over time bettered our nature.

The luminous bodies in the sky faded as the sun appeared. Time for work.

VI

"PLEASE BEGIN, MR. Calhoun," the President said.

Calhoun's image was softer than I'd yet seen. Childish pleasure seeping through his mask's crevices. "Amelia Island is ours." I led the applause and the other three officers reluctantly followed. His solemnity told us he wasn't done. "We suffered no casualties." More applause. Weight lifted from my bones.

"I'll send Congress a message," the President said. He gestured to a form beside him. "It will notify them of the operation and our date for withdrawal."

"Why should we withdraw?" I asked.

A touching of eyebrows. "That was my intent."

"I wasn't under the impression that that was our next step."

"Spain will want us to return the island to them. It's why we ordered our soldiers not to remove Spanish property."

Calhoun glanced at his notes. "The property consists of four cannons that neither the Spanish nor the pirates put to effective use, shown by neither proving able to defend their position."

I asked the President, "What if we refuse to withdraw?"

"We risk violating the Law of Nations," Wirt said.

"Spain couldn't defend the island and lost control of it."

"Weren't you terrified of provoking war with Spain?" Crawford asked. "That's why you opposed recognizing the United Provinces."

Of course Crawford changed his mind in order to disagree with me. He was a man who learned by watching the mistakes of those who took his advice.

"It's very simple," I said, turning to Crawford and then the President. "Mr. Onís will contact me regarding developments on Amelia Island within days. Keeping it shows Spain they can't control it or the Florida Territory." I said to Crawford, using his arguments against him, "It will be the basis for why they should sell Florida to us. Returning the island loses that advantage."

"You're deliberately provoking a diplomatic incident?" Crawford asked.

The President asked Calhoun, "What do you think?"

"Mr. Adams is correct. We'll never have a better opportunity to negotiate for Florida's sale."

"And if this provokes the Holy Alliance?" Crawford asked.

"Over Amelia Island?"

"You both thought they'd wage war over recognizing South American republics."

I said, "If you think capturing a pebble in the ocean is the same —"

"It's territorial aggression—"

"—as intervening in the South American war, you are not fit to advise the President on matters of foreign policy."

Crawford protruded his bottom lip, crossed his arms, and turned to his protégés. "The Secretary of State is in over his head," Crowninshield said, "and risks provoking the war with Europe he preached about in our last meeting."

"Both steps were correct," Calhoun said. "We had to dislodge the core of piracy and now we possess a vital tool for negotiations." Calhoun wielded an independent mind, sound judgment, keen observation, and I respected his eloquence.

Crawford said to the President, "I told you invading Amelia Island was unnecessary and I was right."

"Were you?" Calhoun asked.

"Yes. It was a ploy hatched within Mr. Adams' mind and it appears Mr. Calhoun was in on it."

"Is that so, Mr. Adams?" the President asked. "Is this a ploy?" My mind structured a response. "Because if it is, it's a good one. Controlling Florida will remove the largest threat to our southeast."

"These actions risk American lives," Crowninshield said.

"Not really," Calhoun said.

"The pirates could have killed our men," Crawford said.

I was about to say the ploy would make America invulnerable to foreign attack when the President said to me, "Are you confident you can use this to negotiate Florida's purchase?"

"With enough time, yes."

"How much time?"

"I'd rather not commit to a schedule, sir. I wish to maintain flexibility."

"Very well. I'll modify my message to Congress. Don't embarrass *our* administration, Mr. Adams."

"I won't."

The President asked Calhoun, "Any news on General Jackson?"

"Yes, Mr. President. The Southern Division is in position. On your order, it will move into the Florida Territory and strike the Seminoles." A pause. "Jackson itches for a fight."

"Do his letters make for an entertaining read?"

"I'll share some with you. I've never seen anything like them."

The President said to us, "We're still agreed on deploying General Jackson?" A joining of affirmative eyes. The President to Calhoun: "Instruct him to begin his operation as soon as possible." Calhoun penned his instructions. "But inform him not to attack Spanish fortifications. The Seminoles are our opponent. Not Spain."

"Yes, sir."

The meeting ended. Another victory. Time for my move.

VII

"MR. CALHOUN!" THE Secretary of War had longer legs than I did so I raced to catch up once we'd left the Executive Mansion. "Mr. Calhoun!"

He paused until I reached him. "Yes, Mr. Adams?"

"Are you going to the department building?"

"I am."

"So am I. We can walk together, unless you object."

"Of course not. I appreciate the company." We walked toward 17th and G Street.

"How is your family?" I asked.

"They're well."

I didn't expect this answer. That the Calhouns' baby daughter recently passed had gone through Washington circles. I had hoped to establish a connection between our common losses but he was so logical he wouldn't allow it. His eyes revealed no emotional clouds blocking his judgment's rays. He was possibly the most formidable man in Washington.

"How is the Department of War treating you?"

He snorted. "Perhaps only you can fathom the catastrophe I inherited upon assuming my post. Though my department is the larger and more complex of the two."

"Still, it's admirable the President served in both our jobs simultaneously during wartime."

"Yes, he worked himself to the bone."

"How many clerks do you have?"

"34," he said. "Plus 18 Indian agents outside of Washington."

"Really? I have six."

"Again, my department is larger. We're modernizing the Army and I spend 15 hours a day on paperwork."

"Hmm." A pause. "We seem to agree on most issues that arise during Cabinet Meetings."

"I've noticed that," he said. "I appreciate not standing alone against Crawford and his lackeys."

"The first four Presidents were preoccupied with Europe's wars. The Atlantic world is now peaceful and we have an opportunity for growth."

"The nation is a young Hercules. We must follow his example." He'd started walking faster than me and slowed his stride. "Doing so requires innovative policies, both foreign and domestic."

"Such as?"

"Think back to President Washington's policies. He raised tariffs to fund internal improvements and increased the Army. Those are sound policies for today. I'd also like to establish a military academy for the brightest minds of all parts of society."

"You don't align yourself with Mr. Randolph?"

"You *were* an ocean away during the war. Clay and I battled the ultra-state rights congressmen for years. They're ambitious men without the talent for national politics so they'd rather leave the central government impotent."

"I'm surprised, Mr. Calhoun."

"Why?"

"You're the leading man of South Carolina, the state most afraid of the federal government."

"Not all of us, Mr. Adams. Not all of us." He navigated around frozen mud. "I consider myself between extremists like Randolph on the one side and Pickering or Hamilton on the other."

"As do I. As does the President." His nose wrinkled and I restrained a smile. "Do you disagree?"

"The President agrees with National Republicanism but, like Madison, holds that an amendment is needed for the central government to fund internal improvements." A pause. "The General Welfare Clause is adequate." Another pause. "Their stance is asinine. Madison's veto of the Bonus Bill the day before he left office and the President's similar attitude leaves the nation as vulnerable as it was before the war. A war we barely survived. The President knows we must expand to defend our vital interests from Europe and the Indians but won't fund the improvements to mature our economy."

His words surpassed the opening bars of *Voi che sapete* in their beauty.

"I agree with everything you're saying. How would you feel about forming a partnership?"

His tongue betrayed nothing but his eyes signaled his pleasure. "I'd like that." Perfect. "The President listens to us when we speak in unison. A partnership will mutually benefit us and the country."

"My thoughts exactly."

"Besides, we face a rival pair."

"Who?"

"Crawford and Clay. They're devious and will destroy the President—and us—to achieve power."

"You think so?"

"You don't? Clay was my ally but I weep at what he's become. He uses his position as Speaker of the House to reduce the President to one term. Crawford is even worse. There's never been a man in our history who's risen so high of so corrupt a character."

"Do you consider him a disloyal Cabinet officer?"

"Please tell me you're not naive."

"I like hearing the words."

"Oh. Crawford doesn't have opinions about South America or Amelia Island. He opposes whatever we say because we're his rivals for the presidency. His report on the nation's finances was outrageous. He claimed we have to cut the military because of the national debt, yet the nation prospers and needs larger arms, not smaller. He'll say anything to undermine my department. His allies accused me of giving contracts to friends and he nearly murdered my advisor, Mr. McDuffie, in a duel. All for political games. I loathe that man. Wish the President would fire him."

"We can't call for that. The President dislikes infighting within the Cabinet."

"I know." He paused. "There shall not be another President from the Revolutionary generation. The torch is passing. If we stick together, Mr. Adams, we shall triumph over our adversaries and define the coming era of American politics."

VIII

I SPENT THE afternoon reading a myriad of dispatches from Europe. The first one was from J. A. Smith. It was a notification from Earl Bathurst that Princess Charlotte expired during childbirth. I wrote a letter to George III expressing sympathy on our government's behalf for his granddaughter's passing and for the stillborn male child.

Congressman Rhea of Tennessee visited me and he brought some forms. I told him to return tomorrow. I next sent Senator Talbot of Kentucky a note and on the way home I stopped at the Branch Bank. My book was balanced.

I found Mrs. Adams standing in the doorway. She startled me and I didn't like her expression. Why was she up after her bleeding yesterday morning? She looked mortified. Her eyes didn't express depression or lifelessness. Something else was the problem.

"What's wrong?"

She silently moved back and turned, leading me into the dining room. Three Indians waited. I felt panicked but remained stoic, which was difficult because I wondered if they were Seminoles here to murder me and my family as part of the war. I was powerless to stop them.

"Do any of you speak English?" I asked.

The one furthest left said, "I do."

"What's your name?"

"I am Kusick. These are Longboard and Miko. Menawa sent us."

"What tribe are you?"

"We are Muscogee. Creek."

I breathed and relaxed and then turned to Mrs. Adams. "Get the Madeira." She returned with a bottle. Longboard, the Indian in the middle, spoke to Kusick. "Is something wrong?"

"My friend does not drink rum."

"This is wine."

Kusick relayed the message. Longboard nodded. "He will drink it."

"Excellent." Mrs. Adams distributed the glasses. I whispered to her as she delivered mine, "Everyone is all right?"

64

"Yes."

"Good. Wait in the bedroom." She exited and I turned to the Indians and gestured at their light outfits. "You must be freezing."

"No," Kusick said. "We coat our skin in bear and goose grease. Traps the heat. And our fur coats are made for such weather."

"Very well. Were you Red Sticks?" The Red Sticks were the Creek faction who opposed America in the late war. I hoped they weren't. Lower Creeks were our allies.

"Yes."

"But you're not Seminoles," I said. "You should be grateful we're combatting your enemy." He offered a small nod. More of an acknowledgement than appreciation. "The Department of War manages Indian affairs. You would be better speaking with Mr. Calhoun."

"Calhoun is an unreasonable man."

"Why?"

"He's forced dozens of tribes to sign treaties that renounce their land. He bribes and threatens us."

"He believes that Indians will be annihilated if they live near white populations. That they must move west to survive."

"Yet he takes our children into schools so they will learn your religion."

"Hoping they'll one day assimilate."

"And if we don't want to?"

"You may not have a better option."

Kusick spoke with his colleagues for several minutes. Then: "Calhoun is an unreasonable man."

"Am I reasonable?"

"We hope so, Adams."

I knew what the white man did to the Indians. In 1600, over ten million lived in North America. Mr. Morse's recent survey for the administration estimated there were now less than half a million. Sad that Russian tyranny had a better record of tolerance than us. But I was a representative of the United States government.

"I consider Indians to be a disunified people. A savage people. Look at how the Seminoles murder American children."

"The white man murders Muscogee children."

"That's true."

"Why are whites not a savage people?"

"We make use of the land."

"We ask the United States for land grants. We wish to use the land too."

"I lack the authority to negotiate such a deal. I'm sorry." I sipped my Madeira. Longboard and Miko had finished their glasses because Kusick did the talking. They spoke until I interrupted. "Why did you not request an appointment at my office? Coming to my home is inappropriate."

Kusick translated and this amused them. "We tried," he said. "Brent declined us because we lack the title of *minister*."

"Are you allied with Spain?"

"No."

"Britain?"

"No longer."

"What do you think of our efforts in Florida?"

"We will never sympathize with Jackson. He is the Devil."

"You allied with Britain and we defeated you."

"20 million acres. Half our ancestors' land. And you allow pirates to flee Amelia Island with their booty. How is that fair?"

"We had no jurisdiction to try whether it was theirs."

"The United States operate through guns."

"Do you have any other requests? Otherwise, it's time you left."

Kusick translated for Longboard and Miko. Longboard asked a question and Kusick wanted clarification which Longboard gave.

"What will the United States do after defeating the Seminoles? What happens to us?"

I sighed and said, "I can't answer you tonight." Kusick was disappointed. "I'll ask the President and have my office give you his answer."

They accepted this and departed.

IX

I WENT TO the Capitol Building later in the week. It had only begun its restoration from the British inferno. The Hall of the House of Representatives was further from completion than I expected. The marble pillars surrounding it occupied two-thirds of the space. I thought them in poor taste, for the marble of the shafts was so dark that they cast gloom over the whole. I prayed for the men working there that this incarnation of the building earned a better nickname than its predecessor. We called it *the oven* when I was a senator.

I entered the Speaker's office. The door was open and Mr. Clay worked at his desk. He waved me in. Clutter piled in the area's rim and every available nook. The only spots spared were his chair, the center of his desk, and a small space for guests. An ostentatious portrait of Jefferson occupied the space where a shelf could have hung to hold more rubbish. His walking stick balanced off his desk's back left corner and it held his top hat, waistcoat, and winter coat.

"Good morning, Mr. Adams. It is still morning, yes? Not afternoon?"

"You asked to see me?"

"I did." He released his pencil and handed me a large document. "I wanted to give you this in person." I restrained myself from ripping it in two and then lowered it and saw the sadistic, idiotic smile comfortably situated on his lips.

"You're subpoenaing me?"

"My investigative committee is subpoenaing the Department of State. Detail is paramount, Mr. Adams. I know that you know this. Don't worry, we're subpoenaing the Department of War too." A chuckle. "I want every scrap of paper the administration has on the invasion of Amelia Island and its withholding recognition from the United Provinces." He gestured to a chair that held a pile of books across his desk. I saw the open space on his shelf where those books stood hours before. "Please, sit."

"I'll stand. On what grounds—"

"Do not fake outrage with another politician. A tremendous storm will soon burst upon you about Amelia Island. My sources tell me a letter exists where Mr. Crowninshield says the Navy left two vessels behind on the island, and—"

"The United States government now controls the island and you will not get away with bullying the administration into serving you."

"I must reign the administration in. It acts as a rogue branch of government."

"I've kept Mr. Forsyth and the Committee on Foreign Relations informed on every step of our actions."

"That is inadequate. Mr. Forsyth is less of an administration ally than an administration tool."

"He's a mild man of good talents. It's unprofessional of you to —"

"I shall end the administration's support for Spain in the war."

I needed a moment to process that claim and I gestured to the door. "Can we close this?"

"By all means."

I shut it and faced him. His eyes were lighter than Caribbean waters and would have soothed those under their gaze had they not contained a leviathan of mockery. His greatest joys were mint juleps and torturing me. "That's an absurd claim."

"On the contrary, Mr. Adams, how else ought I interpret the administration crushing a rebel base meant to harass Florida and the Spanish blockade of Venezuela? The withholding of recognition is hardly a neutral action when the rebels fight for freedom against history's most brutal empire."

"What do you hope to gain by subpoenaing the administration?" I paced what little I could and was annoyed I couldn't hold my arms behind my back.

"For the public to know the immorality of its actions." Excitement drained from his tone. "Then I'll have the House vote on recognizing the United Provinces. And Chile, while I'm at it."

"Congress cannot overthrow the executive."

"Congress is an equal branch of government. What I'm doing is legal."

"But you're setting a dangerous precedent. Your ploy will fail. Our allies will block your effort because your victory will bring us into the war."

"We ought to take a limited action, at a minimum." His clasped hands now sat on his desk, pressing down some papers. "Spain's blockade of Venezuela targets civilians as well as the military. We should disrupt it."

"If the Holy Alliance supports Spain?"

"Britain will aid us."

"You wish to start a global war?"

"Spain killed 40 million people when building her empire. Did Genghis Khan butcher that many? For three centuries, that monstrosity has sat atop the thrones of Montezuma and the Inca. Spain erected the most stupendous system of colonial despotism the world has ever seen. The most vigorous, the most exclusive. She locked—"

"This is ancient—"

"This history is crucial for understanding why we stand able to dismantle such a regime. She imprisoned Spanish America from the world. Foreigners couldn't enter it and the natives were kept ignorant of each other. Mexicans could not enter New Granada, for example. She's regulated how agriculture may be used to rule the most basic elements of her subjects' lives. Thus the olive and the vine, to which Spanish America is so adapted, are prohibited wherever her culture can interfere."

"American boys shouldn't die for olives and vines."

"How about defending republicanism? You're comfortable with a monarch who answers to Metternich crushing a republican uprising in this hemisphere?"

"You think Spain will win without our involvement?"

"I can't say. Neither can you. What do you believe is worth fighting for if not free government?"

"Our national interests. At least until we've accumulated greater strength."

"Building a league of hemispheric republics is in our interest. We'd stand with friends in a world that hasn't escaped Augustus' shadow."

"I'll gladly extend my hand to them, after they've won their war alone."

"If they'll accept our friendship after we didn't lift a finger—"

"Their friendship isn't worth American corpses."

"How does Louisa stand your interruptions?" He smiled and saw I wasn't amused so his smile grew. "It's the doctrine of thrones which says man is too ignorant to govern himself. You arraign the dispositions of Providence Himself to suppose that He created beings that must be trampled on by kings. Self-rule is the natural government of man. Just look at the Indians."

"They slay each other at rates—"

"All their warfare spilled a fraction of the blood Spain has. Or Napoleon, for that matter. Population density decides freedom or tyranny. Liberty is overthrown when people are crowded together in compact masses. This would be true even if they were philosophers. The people of Spanish America are spread out over a vast space, and so their physical and moral conditions both favor liberty."

"Their moral conditions?"

"Nothing within Catholicism is unfavorable to freedom. They merely must separate religion from government, as we have."

"Even so, remember General Washington's warning about waging war for fellow freedom fighters. He proclaimed neutrality during the French Revolution."

"One reason among many why I favor Jefferson."

"Even he questions Spanish Americans' ability to govern themselves."

"Please. They're as intelligent as any other people. They have nine universities and have advanced science as far as we have. Read the writings of Supreme Director Puyerredon of La Plata. His pen rivals that of Jefferson or Madison."

"If you say so." I looked at the subpoena. "The island and recognition," I muttered and compiled a list of relevant documents in my mind.

"Should I have demanded more?" A pause. "Does the administration plan to annex the Florida Territory? My sources tell me —"

"Your source is Crawford. Don't pretend you're special."

"Fine. Crawford told me you're communicating with Mr. Onís. Should I have subpoenaed your letters?"

"Of an active negotiation?"

"Yes, if the administration is acting contrary to American interests."

"Contrary how?"

"Does the President plan to annex Florida?"

"You know he does."

"I do. It's the only reason why he would hold onto Amelia Island. You're using it as leverage."

"The President shall succeed where Jefferson and Madison failed. What's your objection?"

"That seizing Florida appears ambitious. We're already accused of interest in expansion."

"Spain can't control it. That's how the Seminoles attack our citizens."

"You believe Lord Castlereagh objects to our recognizing the United Provinces but not to territorial expansion?"

"Not if we do it diplomatically."

"Is a mediocrity, such as yourself, up to the task?"

"Your reputation for charm remains a mystery."

"The President chose you for Secretary of State because the rest of his Cabinet is Southern and you're from New England. He needed geographic diversity."

"Jealousy motivates your every thought and action, sir."

"Comfort yourself however you'd like. General Bolivar reads my speeches to his army. What have you done to deserve your position?"

"I spent 17 years in Europe. More than any other American official. How are my qualifications questioned by the man who I saw go to bed as I awoke every morning in Ghent?"

"Yet I was still more effective than you."

"Ha!" I turned to the door for a moment. "You flatter yourself."

"You were prepared to grant Britain fishing rights in the Mississippi River."

"I was trying to end the war." Shouting now.

"And I knew to hold out for better terms." On his feet.

"Why discuss finished business? Good day to you, Mr. Clay."

"Wait."

"Yes?"

"Is it true the President has deployed General Jackson to Florida?"

I hesitated. "Why didn't you include it in your subpoena—"

"I'm not going to subpoena an active military operation, Mr. Adams. That could kill our boys."

I hesitated again. "Yes."

His head dropped. "I feared as much. We must repel the Seminoles but they still have rights we ought to respect. General Jackson isn't the man for that. He has—a history with the Indians."

I nodded. "What he did to the Creeks—"

"He's a monster. The most dangerous man in the Union."

"He's our generation's biggest hero."

"Which makes me weep. The victory at New Orleans owed more to modern cannons built in factories than to Jackson."

"An interesting argument. Still, he's an asset to our security."

"You say that because he's your tool. Do you foresee him as your running mate in 1820?" he asked. I didn't answer. "Be wary of Jackson. Don't believe you can control him. He's chaos personified."

I didn't know what to make of his advice. He appeared sincere. "Have a good day, Mr. Clay."

"And you, Mr. Adams."

X

I SAT CRAMPED at the end of the main table in our dining room. I tried to focus on my soup and not look at the 20 souls situated on either flank. Tightly packed in the narrow space. Mrs. Adams was on the other end. She'd come into her own as Washington's leading hostess, though her powers had yet to reach their zenith. Part of me delighted in once again seeing her as the urban socialite I'd fallen for back when our guts were trimmer and our faces less wrinkled. It was her greatest talent. She'd charmed the Prussian king and Russian emperor during my ministerial years.

Yet if I lived another two centuries I still would not grasp humanity's interest in socializing for its own sake. It wasted time that could be spent reading or improving oneself. Instead, I was forced to speak on topics that did not concern or interest me and pretend to care about others' thoughts. How dull. Something within men and women sought to curry favor with others, especially those above them within the hierarchy so as to raise their placement within it. They desired power over others to more easily get what they wanted from them.

I preferred doing that by producing results, like leading the peace negotiations in Ghent. People cared about each other to the extent they proved useful. Results meant more than making socialites feel good about themselves. It was upsetting when parties were in my own home so I couldn't leave my wife to socialize on our behalf. These people filled every room as Mrs. Adams had removed our furniture to make space for them. Poor me.

Mrs. Adams arranged for a performance of *Twelfth Night* after supper. My favorite comedy but I had to bide my time until then, listening to those who loved their own voices drone on and on. I heard a conversation between my wife and a woman named Mrs. Cowell.

"How are the children, Louisa?"

"They're well. George shall soon interview with Harvard. John and Charles are rapidly completing grammar school."

"Charles too?"

"Yes. He has the fastest mind of the three."

73

"Wonderful."

"You may have heard that Mary, my niece, moved in with us."

"Oh, I hadn't." Mrs. Cowell turned to the other guests for guidance. "Is she visiting the capital?"

"No. Adelaide, my sister, is ill."

"I'm so sorry. What of your brother-in-law?"

"He's deceased. Various relatives were assigned the different nieces and nephews and we got Mary."

"Well, it's quite compassionate of you." Mrs. Cowell looked at me but I didn't bother meeting her gaze. To my wife: "How old is she?"

"Nine. We're happy to have her. Mary's a pleasure and she provides free entertainment as she wraps my boys around her fingers."

"Really? How so?"

"They compete for her affection. She flirts with George since he's here but she receives a daily stream of letters from John and Charles. Nothing for me, of course."

"You look surprised," Miss Vail said to me. Dozens of eyes turned my way.

"I've not heard of this," I said.

"Of course you haven't, John," Mrs. Adams said. Our guests chuckled. "It didn't appear in your measurement report." The chuckles increased to laughter, which quickly faded. They were wary of mocking the Secretary of State. I grumbled and they left me alone. Not interested in banter. Mother told me to be seen and not heard.

"So, Mrs. Adams." I recognized that voice. Mr. Webster. I was wary of his presence all evening. He'd been a leader of the Federalist minority in the House but left office to practice law when I returned from Europe. He could often be found arguing before the Supreme Court. I didn't trust him.

"Yes?" my wife asked.

"Do you hope to live in the Executive Mansion in 1821?"

I did my best to ignore the situation and blow on my soup. I had no desire of validating Webster's scheme and resisted urges to watch Mrs. Adams' reaction. My eyes flickered and I saw why he was called *Black Dan*. His dark hair and height made him an imposing figure.

"I've no interest in politics," Mrs. Adams said. I felt her eyes on me, seeking approval. I wouldn't give it in front of these serpents.

"I hoped for a stronger answer," Webster said. "Mr. Adams understands that the Constitution is a compact between the people, not the states."

All eyes turned to me. I couldn't remain coy without it being obviously intentional. I looked at my wife.

"My attention is entirely focused on my present duties. I've no ability to think of future elections. Besides, nothing would serve the country better than the President acquiring another term in office."

My platitudes disappointed our guests and they returned their attention to Webster and then to other topics. I didn't care for Webster's compliments. He was a residuary legatee of the old Federalists who placed his ambition over his values and possessed no principle less elastic than Indian rubber. He proved this by calling for New England's secession during the late war.

The next hour vexed me. Lucy and Ellen served a roast with an assortment of vegetables and I listened to the uninteresting and at times unintelligent conversations surrounding me. Such evenings dulled my focus and made my work more difficult. Forced socializing endangered American security. Yes. I ought to tell that to Mrs. Adams. And the President. Finally a shadow fell over me and the night's most exciting event commenced.

"Alex!" I said. "How are you, sir?"

"I'm well, Mr. Adams." It was Mr. Everett, my secretary from when I was minister to Russia.

"What brings you from Boston?" I could sense the guests were put off by my sudden energy. Good. They should know how they bored me.

"Legal work wears at my mind. I hope for a policy job."

"Is that why you're here?"

"Of course not."

"Good. It would be inap—"

"Though I'd consider myself in your debt if you know of any sources of employment."

"I'll keep you in mind." A pause. "The guest lists for these parties are so long that I—"

"There's something we must discuss."

"Oh?"

"Can we speak elsewhere?"

I saw that Mrs. Adams glared at me for breaking decorum. "No."

He was annoyed and bent closer to whisper, "My political contacts warn me that Mr. Clay and Mr. Crawford conspire to destroy you."

"Trust me, I'm aware." I leaned closer to him. "What have you heard?"

"Clay is behind the efforts to recruit American privateers on the rebels' behalf." He paused. "He's breaking the law. You must strike back."

"How would I, besides referring the matter to Attorney General Wirt?"

"You must stand for President in 1820."

"I'll do no such thing."

"Clay and Crawford won't be so noble. Clay is looking for ways to undermine the President and is building support in the West. You must place yourself on equal footing if you and the President are to survive."

"My enemies' moral failings are their problem, not mine."

"But—"

"We should cease this discussion for now." Many guests stared at us and Mrs. Adams was furious. I said to Everett, "Let's set up a time to continue this."

He agreed and left me to return to my irritation.

XI

"THAT DOES NOT answer whether the Empire claims the mouth of the Columbia River."

"Do you not know that we have a claim?"

"I do not know what you claim. Nor what you don't claim. You claim India. You claim Africa. You claim—"

"Perhaps a piece of the moon."

"No, I've not heard that you claim any part of the moon, but there's not a spot on this habitable globe that I know of which you do not claim."

I sat behind my office desk. Across from me was Mr. Stratford Canning, British minister to the United States. His older cousin, George, was a high ranking official in their Foreign Office. Canning was my junior but had proven himself as a capable diplomat during Napoleon's era. I'd asked him to visit me to resolve issues between our nations left over from Ghent. I had to secure America's interests without transforming the world's mightiest power into our foe. Friction with London must be negligible so we could confront Spain and the Holy Alliance. Britain joining our enemies would be catastrophic, the end of my mission and possibly of the Union.

He was unremarkable in his looks but his immaculate dress outshined any of our congressmen or clerks. He looked down his nose but I believed this to be a tactic and that in truth he admired me even as he diligently pursued Britannia's interests with a shark's vigor.

"My government was hurt that yours sent a warship," he read his notes, "the *Ontario*, around South America to the Columbia River without notifying me first."

"The United States have claimed that region since Lewis and Clark."

"Don't confuse the issue. I won't discuss a resolution to the Pacific Northwest. Only to the *Ontario*."

"The issues are intertwined. Addressing the regional dispute makes resolving the *Ontario* easier."

"No, it allows America to violate British territory."

"It's not British territory. Which is why we should—"

"The *Ontario*'s presence precludes broader negotiations."

"Will the Lords of the Admiralty resist the *Ontario*'s presence?"

"No. Which is quite the olive branch to a minor country behaving aggressively."

"In response to Canadian aggression. They seized Mr. Astor's base of operations for the Pacific Fur Trade Company during the war and gave it to the Canadian North West Company."

"He abandoned the area."

"Because he knew they'd take it by force," I said.

"The British Empire has already pledged to return the area to Mr. Astor."

"It does so at a glacial pace and Astor is a businessman who loses money in the meantime."

"So America and Britain are in crisis because the American government does a businessman's bidding?"

"Don't pretend that the East India Tea Company isn't pulling Parliament's strings. If it didn't, the separation between our nations wouldn't have been necessary."

"This is irrelevant."

"I'm referencing the arrogant attitude with which the British Empire treats the United States. You blacken us every way possible and retard our development."

"Don't take it personally."

"This isn't a joke. The Empire encroaches south of the 49th parallel out of jealousy. You aim to check our future settlement of the Northwest."

"I told you we planned to return the area to Mr. Astor," he said. "But the *Ontario*'s presence makes it impossible."

"Why not agree to a trade? We'll withdraw the *Ontario* in exchange for your returning the area to Astor."

"That would be a concession to a minor power. We need something in return."

"What if we claimed we didn't know the Canadians were present there?"

"How—"

"We'll claim that we thought the North West Company withdrew once the Empire acquired the area. That the *Ontario* was deployed to restore American possession and, because the Northwest is so remote, we didn't see it as aggression. Build the entire problem as one of confusion."

He thought this over. "I'm satisfied with that framework." He wrote it down. "I'll send it to Lord Castlereagh."

"We don't seek war over the Northwest fur trade. I'll even instruct the *Ontario* not to commit any hostile acts until it's withdrawn, unless it faces opposition. You've said the Royal Navy has been ordered not to resist it, so this should go smoothly."

"Excellent. Lord Castlereagh will be pleased."

"How is he?"

Canning shrugged. "He faces much criticism at home. He believes, correctly, in my view, that Britain must be engaged in the Concert of Europe to keep the peace on the continent. But the public and the press see it as betraying Britain's approach toward Europe since Henry VIII."

"A public servant is a modern Job. He must weather such—"

"I see him more as Jonah. He wants to run away. It's unclear who shall portray the whale. Perhaps a new conqueror bringing another war."

"We had a most productive relationship when I served as minister to the Court of St. James. He's a cold man but not a repulsive one."

"I'm pleased you like him so much." A pause. "As we've addressed the *Ontario*, would you care to discuss the rest of the Pacific Northwest?"

"Yes. Our old claim—"

"You told me. The Lewis and Clark expedition."

"No, before that. America purchased a large tract of the area from Indians in 1787."

"I've not heard of this. You do realize that Spain also claims the entire region? And Russia eyes it?"

"Let's worry about our two nations for now."

"Very well. What would satisfy America?"

"If we set the boundary at the 49th parallel of north latitude."

"Out of the question. That would give you the entire Columbia River basin and Puget Sound." He pointed to my map of North America on the wall behind him. "You'd monopolize that route to East Asian markets."

"Anything less surrenders part of the Louisiana Territory that we purchased from France."

"Which Britain doesn't recognize because it violated the Treaty of San Ildefonso's clause that France could not sell the territory to a third party."

"Perhaps we can coax your recognition."

"Proceed."

"The arbitrary line set in 1783 is a nullity," I said. "The region wasn't explored and so it was built on ignorance. Our position is that a straight line boundary will be easier to survey than boundaries built around watersheds."

"What eastern boundary do you have in mind?"

"From the Stony Mountains to the Pacific Ocean."

"I'm still uncomfortable committing to a firm border in the Northwest. It might prevent a repeat of the *Ontario* incident but it reduces future flexibility when the region is only now being settled. What if I agreed to your border, and in exchange, we established freedom of navigation for civilians?"

"I'd want an expiration date for such a policy."

"Twenty years?"

"Make it ten."

"Done."

"Excellent. The President will approve."

"As will Lord Castlereagh. He wants to avoid conflict over such a marginal issue."

"He won't have it when Britain learns to respect our territorial integrity."

"Must I remind you what happened in 1776 and 1812?" he asked.

"No. The American-Canadian border is now stable. We won't invade again."

"Tens of thousands of Canadians shall sleep soundly."

"Good. Keep what is yours and leave the rest of the continent to us."

"You treat me like a schoolboy."

"In that case, my young pupil…" I looked at our prearranged list of topics for the day. "Would you rather discuss slavery or fishing next?"

"Slavery." He read a document. "Lord Castlereagh authorized the following proposal. He wants to suppress the slave trade."

"We already withdrew from it under President Jefferson."

"That's why Lord Castlereagh believes your government will cooperate. His idea is for the vessels of nations who've already withdrawn from the trade to stop the vessels of other nations who've also withdrawn with the goal of intercepting slaves being illegally trafficked."

"You can't be serious," I said. "That's a barefaced attempt by the Empire to obtain the right to seize other nations' ships during peacetime. I remind you, sir, that such action was the proximate cause of the late war."

"America claims to be the nation of freedom. A claim that results in her having the weakest government on Earth, a government so weak that the Union will dissolve within a few years. Yet she still placates the Southern slave powers."

"Americans won't join an arrangement that lets the Royal Navy search our ships."

"Is there an evil greater than slavery?"

"Yes. Impressment during peacetime. We'd be making slaves of ourselves."

"Perhaps I'll go to Virginia and ask the Negroes if they agree with your assessment."

"You may do as you like, Mr. Canning. No ship involved in the trade may fly our flag, so any ship the Royal Navy stops could not ask our government for help. This double standard is made worse by the reality that only British vessels pursue smuggled slaves and so only they would be allowed to stop other nations' ships."

"America could join our endeavor."

"You know the South's prejudice makes that impossible."

"How foolish of me to expect the nation of freedom to cooperate."

"I've had quite enough of your tone, sir."

"My tone?" he asked.

"Yes. I thought you wished to discuss the Empire's restitution for the property stolen from our citizens during the war."

"We can."

"The Treaty of Ghent authorized our nations to select a friendly sovereign or state to arbitrate. Let the search begin."

"I'll notify Lord Castlereagh. He'll send options and we can compare lists." He wrote a note. "Should we take a break?"

"Let's keep going."

"Very well. Should we discuss the Nova-Scotia fishing boundary or the West Indies trade war?"

"Neither." I decided it was time to raise the most important issue. I had to be graceful. "What is Britain's intent in Florida?"

Canning folded his arms. I wondered why he still wore his winter collar and decided his upbringing overrode his youthful attitude. "Britain recognizes the Florida Territory as part of the Spanish Empire."

"Really?"

"Of course."

"Yet it slips from Spain's fingers. Ferdinand has moved all his military forces to South America and cannot prevent the Seminoles from harassing Georgia."

"Does America covet Florida?"

"Does Britain?"

"Don't toy with me, Mr. Adams. We both know you're corresponding with Mr. Onís."

"That regards Amelia Island."

"Which you're using to prove Spain's weakness. Your course is easy to decipher. Why raise this subject? Are you asking if Britain will interfere with your effort?"

"Yes."

"The only way we'd accept an annexation is if we acted as mediator."

A preplanned trap. I'd no choice but to spring it. "What terms would Britain seek?"

"Spain wishes to keep her grip on Florida and Texas, so an arrangement where America gets Florida but does not expand past the Mississippi River is fair."

"Exactly what I should expect from British mediation," I said. "In all her mediation, or offers of mediation, her justice and policy merely serves herself."

"We want Madrid as an ally. Siding with America drives her toward France and the Holy Alliance."

"That is Britain's goal?"

"Yes."

"Then why did the President's fact-finding mission in South America report an influx of fighting men and weapons to support the rebels?"

"Lord Castlereagh has said those are isolated incidents. Britain hasn't granted the rebels recognition."

"Oh he's said that, has he? The report detailed how Britain is organizing legions within General Bolivar's army." I struck the desk.

"Since Napoleon's defeat, many of the men who comprised His Majesty's military are unemployed and the weapons manufactured to fight the emperor are collecting dust. It should be expected that some of those assets would make their way to a new conflict and make themselves useful."

"It's clearly an organized effort. One that British control of the sea and of Jamaica and Trinidad allow for with ease."

"Why would Britain back Bolivar?"

"The removal of Spain's monopoly on the Spanish-American market. Both to open that market and to establish a new, British monopoly."

"You think we claim all of Spanish America?"

"Not as formal colonies, but as importers who have no other options. I expect our next group of fact-finders will note British merchants moving into the southern half of this hemisphere. Your course is as easy to decipher as it is duplicitous."

"No more than yours."

"You oppose our efforts so as to pretend to be Spain's friend and keep her from Metternich but really you're why she's suffered a string of recent defeats at Bolivar's hands."

"You deduced our strategy." He pretended to applaud. "My congratulations to you. Now what will you do with this information?"

"I could inform Mr. Onís."

"To what end?"

"To make clear to Spain that Britain isn't her friend."

"You think he'll sell Florida to you once you've opened his eyes?"

"Yes, if it saves him Texas and a larger confrontation with us."

"I see," he said. "Well, you'll be disappointed to know that Ferdinand is aware of our support for Bolivar."

"I don't believe you. Why would he tolerate a backbiting ally?"

"Because he wouldn't dare oppose us and, like the rest of Europe, he's against American expansion. You underestimate, Mr. Adams, how greatly the British establishment despises the idea of America growing into a middle power on the world stage after having spent over a century resisting French efforts to unify Europe under her control."

"In that case, everything we've agreed to today, from the Columbia River to the arbitration over stolen slaves, can be undone like that," snapped my fingers, "should Britain oppose our purchasing Florida. We can become another big problem for you."

"That would push *us* toward the Holy Alliance. Remember that the nations comprising the Alliance were joined with us against Napoleon. I recall that America stood with the emperor when he threatened our existence."

"King George and Lord Castlereagh will have to choose whether they'll allow Metternich to destroy liberalism across Europe and the world merely to oppose America."

"We can do business with Prince Metternich. You can't."

"Have you met him?"

"I saw him several times when I worked under Lord Castlereagh at the Congress of Vienna. He's a vain man but a brilliant intellect. He sees liberalism as a dissolving, decomposing principle that separates men and loosens society. He thinks your country allows individuals to achieve greatness but that it doesn't form an efficient mass and so isn't truly progressive. He knows your hypocritical calls for freedom caused the French Revolution which slaughtered a generation of Europeans." Canning leaned forward. "You don't appreciate how close Lord Castlereagh and Prince Metternich are. They collaborated in Vienna to restore Europe and have a kinship. No one wants to see America and their chaotic ideology spread more than they already have. You think highly of yourself, Mr. Adams, but remember that Metternich outfoxed Napoleon. The Royal Navy is all that stands between the United States and his reactionary claws. Proceed wisely."

He'd bested me. Debate could clarify my hope for the future but it couldn't ensure it. More than my ambition was at stake.

"Should we adjourn?" I asked.

XII

I RECEIVED ANOTHER visitor in my office a few days later. Mr. Manuel Aguirre was the United Provinces' Commissary General of War. Brent led him to me and closed the door so we could speak privately. I returned to my desk and gestured to the opposite chair but Aguirre pretended not to notice, standing for now to feign politeness later. He held a sealed packet.

He carried himself awkwardly even by my standards. The timidity and constrained, high pitched voice of a mouse. Balding but compensated by a handsome mustache.

"Would you rather converse in English or Spanish?" he asked in English.

"You're my guest. You choose."

"Let us use English. You are generous to host me and so we should use your mother tongue."

"Very well. Is that for me?" I pointed to the packet.

"Yes." He placed it on my desk. "May I sit?"

"Please." I gestured to the intended chair but avoided eye contact so he knew I knew of his fakery. I opened the packet with a knife I pulled from a drawer. It contained two forms. First was a letter from Supreme Director Puyerredon to the President of the United States. The second was the United Provinces' Declaration of Independence. It read:

> *We, the representatives of the United Provinces of South America, in general congress assembled, invoking the Supreme Being who presides over the universe, in the name and by virtue of the authority of the people we represent, and protesting to Heaven, and to the nations and inhabitants of the whole globe, the justice by which our wishes are guided, do solemnly declare in the face of the Earth, that it is the unanimous and indubitable will of these provinces to break the repugnant ties which bound them to the kings of Spain, to recover the rights of which they were despoiled, and invest themselves with the high*

*character of a nation, free and independent of King
Ferdinand VII, his successors, and the mother country.*

I put the papers aside. "I'll give these to the President."

"Thank you, Mr. Adams." He stooped in his seat.

"You said in your note that you have a proposal for our government."

"That's correct."

"What is it?"

"Everyone knows that you are writing back-and-forth with Mr. Onís to purchase the Florida Territory. The Provinces believe, in light of our recent victories against the Spanish tyrants, that we can capture the territory if your government lets us use Amelia Island as a temporary base. We would deliver Florida to you and ask for your government's recognition in return."

I'd anticipated this visit's intent was a request for recognition but I'd not expected such an odd wrapping. "Are you a proxy for Mr. Clay?"

"Of course not."

"I know how disappointed Clay must be that he went through the effort to subpoena my department, denounce me and the administration on the House floor, and still lose the vote to recognize the Provinces 45 to 115."

"Sir, I assure you—"

"It doesn't matter, Mr. Aguirre. The United States won't grant recognition at this time and are uninterested in a British-armed military seizing Florida. Your proposal is no different from when the pirates controlled Amelia Island in December."

"We're not pirates, Mr. Adams. The Provinces did not authorize those adventurers."

"That may be, and the United States did not intend to appear unfriendly to the Provinces when we dislodged the pirates. We are as friendly as we can be while remaining neutral."

"But why do the United States insist on neutrality?"

"You are an adept observer of global politics. You know that recognizing the Provinces could cause war with Spain and the Holy Alliance. No, we'll remain neutral until the rebellion has won and recognition is no longer contentious."

"The Provinces are disappointed. I will have to explain this to the Supreme Director and the Council."

"Avoiding a showdown with Prince Metternich and Emperor Alexander is worth a slower start to our bilateral relations."

He paused. "What if our offer was more interesting?"

"How so?"

"The United Provinces will open its ports to your vessels and merchants. But this offer comes with a limited time constraint. You and your President must decide quickly."

I snorted. "Did your government instruct you to give me an ultimatum?"

"No. This is my idea."

"It's a highly unusual statement."

His cheeks retracted until his jaw bones jutted out. "I apologize."

"Don't worry, just learn for the future if you're to continue on as a diplomat. Making threats about port access can kill sailors. As a colonial possession, your ports were accessible only to the Mother Country. But you are independent now, or will be soon. It's customary under the Law of Nations that independent states don't shut their ports to other states without cause. We've already opened our ports to you, despite withholding recognition, for example. I want any future communications on this subject to be in writing."

"Access to your ports does us little good. We are not a maritime nation. We have neither ships nor seamen."

"You have privateers."

"Only to harass the Spanish."

"We won't close our ports to you without cause. I suggest your country train its diplomats in basic awareness of global conventions before sending more agents abroad. Consider this free advice."

"We do have agents abroad. Three of them."

"Oh?" I asked. "Where are they?"

"We have one in London, one in Vienna, and one in Madrid."

"You have one in Madrid?" I asked. He nodded. "King Ferdinand received him?"

"No, he stayed with the British minister. I believe he's hiding in Paris now."

"I see. But Prince Metternich received an agent?"

"Yes."

"Interesting. He's probably extracting information from him to give to King Ferdinand. Metternich is hostile to your country's existence as an independent state."

"We are aware." He paused. "We'd made Ferdinand an offer but he rejected it."

"What offer?"

"To end the war. We proposed he send Don Carlos, that infant brother of his, to become ruler of an independent South America. He said *no* and that's when the Provinces issued the Declaration of Independence."

"Hmm. A mistake on his part. Now he's going to lose the war after piles of carcasses. I wonder what Metternich advised at that juncture."

"I do not know."

XIII

I MET WITH the President alone in his office two days later. I felt groggy from the spring afternoon sun. We sat in our normal positions at the Cabinet table. I explained the tentative agreements I'd made with Canning regarding the *Ontario* and the Northwest before moving on to the Florida Territory.

"He said Britain will stand by Madrid."

"Did he give a reason?" the President asked.

"The predictable one. She wants Spain as an ally within European politics and this is something to offer, even as she sends troops and weapons to Bolivar."

"Do we think King Ferdinand and Mr. Onís know about British involvement?"

"Canning says they do."

"Do you believe him?"

"Yes. It's too large a presence for even the Spanish to miss."

"And Ferdinand is so desperate to hold Florida that he'll accept British help," he said. I nodded. "You still believe we can convince him to sell it to us?" I nodded again. "Hmm." A pause as he looked down, his eyes on some notes but not reading them. "Will Britain align with the Holy Alliance if we annex Florida?"

"Canning said as much. That the entire European establishment will stop the annexation by any possible means."

"Is he sincere?"

"No."

"How do you know?"

"A powerful America does not threaten Britain's interests to a fraction of the extent that absolute monarchy's expansion does. Canning and Lord Castlereagh know that."

He shifted posture so he leaned back in his chair. He stared at the ceiling while he analyzed the various factors the way a horse navigates a rocky and untrodden trail. He'd earned the nation's respect for his service in both our wars with Britain but he'd failed as a diplomat and betrayed President Washington during the French Revolution. Had he grown or had I reason to worry about his judgment?

He lowered his eyes so they were just above making contact with mine. "There was another meeting that you wish to discuss?"

"Yes, Mr. President. I met with Mr. Aguirre the day before yesterday. He's—" looked at my notes "—the Commissary General of War for the United Provinces."

"Did he request recognition?"

"Yes. He made a couple of odd offers to strengthen our interest."

"Such as?"

"The first was that the Provinces will conquer Florida and trade it to us. She'd need Amelia Island as a base," I said. He looked contemplative. "You're not considering it?"

"Would it not resolve our problem?"

"It would place a British-funded army on our border and break our neutrality."

He sighed. "You're *confident* your negotiations with Mr. Onís are the better option?"

"Unquestionably."

He thought it over. "Very well. Write a report detailing the substance from these meetings and send it to the other Cabinet officers and the House Foreign Relations Committee."

"Is that necessary?"

"Yes, Mr. Adams. I want consensus within this administration and with Congress."

"Very well, sir." I wrote a note and noticed the President staring at me. "Sir?"

"I'm having second thoughts about our present course."

"I can tell."

"Can you?" Sarcasm in his voice. "Mr. Crawford warned me of a rumor that Spain is prepared to seize our ships in Havana Harbor in response to our holding Amelia Island." I didn't answer so he would finish his thought. "We should evacuate the island."

The coward. If he weren't the President I'd have slapped him. "No, Mr. Pres—"

"This is serious, Mr. Adams. Should it happen, we'd have to retaliate by invading Cuba. That would cause a larger conflict with Europe."

Damn Crawford. My plan was unraveling. I had to escape failure's tentacles. "We must remain vigilant, Mr. President. Spain is bluffing."

"We're talking about the end of my presidency, even if events don't spiral out of control. We need a new strategy."

"What do you have in mind?"

"I want to write our ministers in Europe to inform the local governments of a conference to discuss Spanish America's future," he said. My mouth opened but he raised his hand. "We'd ask for control of Florida in exchange for organizing the conference."

"That would invite Europe to decide this hemisphere's destiny."

"I think we overestimated our strength. We can't remove them. Not yet."

"We *are* strong enough. The world must know that the United States are no longer Britain's former colonies. We're independent with our own foreign policy."

"I fear you're too hasty and are leading us into disaster."

"I'm not. I promise you I'm not. This will work."

He turned away. His frantic eyes darted about the room like a cornered cat. I wished we trusted each other.

"Have your negotiations with Mr. Onís been in person or only through letters?" he asked.

"Only the written word. I've held off meeting him until we were further along."

"There's no time. Meet with him and make a deal. You have two weeks or I'm changing our approach."

"I cannot possibly—"

"The framework for a deal, then. Get it done."

"Yes, sir." I gathered my papers and paused. "Sir?"

"What?"

"A Creek delegation visited my home and asked what our government intends to do with them and the other Indian tribes after General Jackson's campaign against the Seminoles is over. I told them I'd speak with you and send them a reply."

A moment. "I've thought about this issue a great deal since assuming office. Our growth is vital, yet I desire benevolence. I'm going to propose to Congress that we give the Indians land west of the Stony Mountains. They'd be safe and can preserve their separate tribes."

"I see." I wrote a note. "Thank you, sir." I turned to leave.

"Wait, Mr. Adams."

"Yes, Mr. President?"

"Since you've raised the topic, I'd like to discuss how the Seminoles campaign should end. Whether we should force their surrender or withdraw General Jackson before that."

"Have we received any reports from him?"

"No. But the communication route is long and difficult." He looked nervous again. I didn't know why, unless his thoughts had returned to Spain.

"Jackson's campaign proves to Spain that they can no longer govern Florida. I'd advise you to leave him there until after my negotiations with Mr. Onís are concluded."

He nodded. "Very well. I won't withdraw him." He looked increasingly unsettled. I wished I knew why. "Goodbye, Mr. Adams."

"Goodbye, Mr. President."

XIV

MR. ONIS AND his guests arrived at the Department of State's main room. "Thank you, Mr. King," I said to the clerk who escorted them. He nodded. Onís and the other Spainiards stood near the door. "Come in." Onís advanced slowly, the other three following as one unit. He was a handsome man for his years, his late 50s. Dressed not only in three layers but wearing medals awarded by his master. His eyes revealed a cold pride in his Spanish heritage, a ruthlessness trapped by his nation's weakness. A medieval man in a revolutionary age.

"Mr. Adams," he said in English.

"Welcome, sir." A pause. "Are these your daughters?"

"They are." He stepped to the side. "Meet Madame de Heredia and Miss de Onís." They bowed their heads upon his speaking their names. Neither expressed warmth or personality and I gathered that Onís used them as props to portray his humanity.

"A pleasure," I said. "How are you enjoying Washington City?"

Their eyes shifted to Onís for guidance. "They like that it is more relaxed than my previous postings," he said. He turned to his secretary and said in Spanish, "Take mis hijas outside and wait for me."

"That is not necessary," I said. "You can wait with Señor King. It is humid outside."

"No," Onís said. To his secretary, "Do as I commanded, Señor Noëli." Noëli nodded and he left with the girls. Onís breathed deeper after winning our first skirmish. I was unbothered. Such symbolism was childish. What troubled me was the President's cutoff coming closer every hour. I fought to hold my anxiety at bay. I needed every ounce of my diplomatic experience to prevail.

Onís and I were alone, as King had followed Onís' lackeys. "Would you care to enter my office?" I asked.

"Yes, gracias."

Two cigars waited on my desk. "Would you like one?"

"Yes."

I gestured to the candle and he thanked me. "Shall we begin?"

"Yes. Let us return to English." We took our seats, the desk between us. "My master, his Catholic Majesty, wants the United States to know that the truth is of all time."

"The observation that truth is of all time, and that reason and justice are founded upon immutable principles, has never been contested by the United States. But neither truth, reason, nor justice consists in stubbornness or assertion or in the multiplied repetitions of error."

"My master agrees. He wants to know why the United States have not withdrawn their military from Amelia Island and returned the island to him."

"Spain's weakness let pirates capture it. The President believes that the United States must control the island to prevent a recurrence."

"The occupation infringes upon Spanish sovereignty."

"Spain lost the right to control Amelia Island when she failed to defend it."

"You give a gross insult to my master and the Spanish monarchy, importing that they are of no more consequence than a dead old hen. But if Spain is weak, it is ungenerous to insult her weakness, which is owed to the unparalleled effort she made to deliver Europe from tyranny."

"The President has no intention to return the island. We did not act aggressively toward Spain. We acted defensively, and how could we surrender the island unless we're sure it won't be reoccupied by adventurers?"

"Your military's withdrawal is a prerequisite for any further negotiations."

"I have stated the President's position."

"Then we have nothing left to discuss. My daughters shall be spared from humidity after all." Onís stood.

"I wouldn't leave so hastily." I cocked my cigar at an angle and drew deeply as I surveyed him. "That Spain will lose the Florida Territory is inevitable. I'm offering you the chance to receive the best possible terms."

Spain's pride battled its weakness in every twitch near his eyes and mouth. His posture followed his standards' plummet into a cavernous trench. We waited several minutes in silence. Then, "If we continue, we must clarify the borders between his Catholic Majesty's empire and the United States. Your people repeatedly violate our territory, especially in Texas."

"Our infractions are minor compared to what your failures in Florida have cost our citizens. They have lost millions between the Seminole raids and the slaves who've escaped to Florida as a safe haven."

"You mentioned this in one of your notes." He sat. "My master cannot afford to compensate your people. The wars against Napoleon and the South American insurgents have drained his treasury."

"Let us approach the principal issue. We want Spain to cede East Florida and to renounce all claims to West Florida. In exchange, my government can recognize Spain's claim to Texas and absorb part of the debt your majesty owes our citizens."

He processed my overture. His right hand clutched his cigar as the nails on his left dug into his knee. I assumed that hurt but he didn't appear to mind. I presented a confident posture, leaning over my desk and puffing my cigar.

"There are several issues to weed through," he said.

"Of course."

"Should I list them?"

"Please do."

"I see three that prevent your idea. One: my master does not recognize the legality of your purchasing the Louisiana Territory from France. Two: Britain will never approve of our relinquishing Florida to the United States. And three: any deal must include your government's pledge to never recognize the South American insurgents or states they say they've established."

"Where should we begin?"

"Let us discuss Britain."

"I spoke with Mr. Canning within the past month. He said Britain will not approve of this transaction unless she acts as mediator. But he stated the terms Britain desired and the President said they are unacceptable."

"What terms?"

"Are you aware that Britain is aiding General Bolivar?"

"Yes. General Morilla's victory in Caracas would have ended the rebellion had Bolivar not received four new British regiments." He placed his cigar in his mouth, not realizing that it needed to be relit. "Castlereagh also presses my master to remove Spain from the slave trade."

"Then why feign friendship with Britain?" I gestured to the candle on my desk.

"Britain will rule the world for the rest of this century. Waterloo ensures that. We must take what she'll give us."

"The United States will not place themselves at Britain's mercy."

"That is for Britain to decide. She burned this city three years ago."

"Then General Jackson won at New Orleans."

"Oh, yes. More land you stole from his Catholic Majesty. But there's no question that the Duke of Wellington could put Jackson's head on a pike if Castlereagh told him to."

"Our population grows at a faster pace than any other in the Atlantic world. Britain will never rule us again."

He was unconvinced. "Should my master ally with you against Britain?"

"It would be foolish for us to ally with a weak empire against a strong one."

"Then my master will never choose to antagonize Britain by transferring Florida."

Ash fell from my cigar onto my desk. "I repeat: nothing can stop the United States from acquiring Florida. I only hope to expedite the process through reasonable terms. Britain won't interfere because Castlereagh knows he is less threatened by a powerful America than by the Holy Alliance."

"You are an arrogant man."

"Perhaps. But deal with me or lose Florida in exchange for nothing."

"The United States would show the world their true colors and destroy their relationship with his Catholic Majesty and his successors for a generation."

"While advancing our peoples' security in the process. Florida's fate is not something King Ferdinand or Lord Castlereagh can decide."

He finally understood I was sincere that we would tempt Britain and bear the consequences, that fear of retaliation would not save his master. He wrestled with whether such a clash was in Spain's interest, regardless of the outcome. More silence.

"The United States must never recognize the insurgents."

"Never?"

"No."

"What about in 1900?"

"No."

"What about in 2000?"

"Don't joke with me, Adams," he shouted in Spanish. "This is vital for his Catholic Majesty's reign."

I said in English, "The United States will not recognize the rebels while the war is ongoing. But it is absurd to make that request indefinite."

He growled. "This is the compromise—any United States agent going to Buenos Aires or any other rebel city must pay a fifteen per cent ransom for two ships that belong to the Spanish Philippine Company that —"

"I'm not going to the President with that proposal."

"What will the United States cede?"

"I've stated our position. We won't recognize the rebels until after the war." I maintained my stoic face and he wouldn't look at me. "We'll also assume up to five million dollars that Spain owes our citizens."

He nodded, smoke flowing through his nostrils despite his cigar now bending 30 degrees. "I assume the United States want my master to recognize their control of the Louisiana Territory?"

"It allows us to determine the borders between our countries on this continent."

"My master believes that Jefferson and Napoleon violated the Law of Nations through that sale. The Treaty of San Ildefonso prohibited it."

"It is in his interest to recognize the transaction."

"Is it?"

"Yes. Like losing Florida, our control of the Louisiana Territory is a fact and there's nothing your master can do to change it. But he does have the power to clarify your empire's borders."

"This is an unkind world. Where do you believe Louisiana ends?"

"The Pacific Ocean."

Finally he showed me his eyes. "What?"

"Napoleon told us that the Territory included the Mississippi River and all lands whose waters flow to it. That includes all land east and north of the Sabine and the Rio Grande."

"That cuts deep into Texas."

"It's what we purchased."

"We need Texas as a buffer between the United States and New Spain." He referred to Mexico.

"We'll adjust our claim if Spain recognizes our control of the Louisiana Territory. And since this bears repeating, I remind you that your master can't prevent our controlling the Territory and I'm granting him the chance to determine where it ends."

He marched to the door and threw his crushed cigar on the ground. He froze. I pitied him, knowing his desperation to save his country from global humiliation. But I couldn't relieve pressure and still win. He returned, standing, a dog struck by his owner.

"May I clarify where Spain wishes to place the border?" he asked.

"I'd hoped you would." We approached the map of North America. He studied it and placed his finger on the paper.

"Here." He moved so I could see. The Sabine River. His finger traced the Arkansas River and the Red River. "This leaves Santa Fe within our control."

"We could accept that arrangement, if Spain withdraws her claim to anywhere on the continent north of the 42nd latitude." I pointed to the Pacific Northwest on the map.

"You Devil!" He leapt to my desk and struck it. Then he laid his weight on it and I feared he'd vomit. He took some minutes to regain control of himself. "There will be war before his Catholic Majesty grants that concession."

"There will be war if he doesn't. Before you say the Alliance will save you, know that Mr. Canning and I negotiated a decade-long joint claim to the region between our countries. Britain wants Spain to withdraw."

I waited and watched a broken man. It had taken every argument I could muster, some of them real, most of them bluffs, but I'd won. Then he returned to me, a sweaty disaster, but smiling and breathing through his mouth.

"I cannot even tentatively make these concessions until I write to his Catholic Majesty."

"That would take months. The President demands an answer. At least the framework for—"

"It is impossible. I will come to you the day I hear from him."

"What if we reduced the scope of our negotiations? Center it around Florida and the Texas border? We can delay our discussion about the rest of the Louisiana Territory."

"I ask that we end for the day. I am exhausted. I shall have dinner with my girls and write to my master before bed."

"I insist that we make at least some provisional decisions. Something that I can give the President."

He snorted. "Have a good evening, Mr. Adams."

Onís left. I waited until I was sure of his absence and then entered the main room. No clerks were present for me to vent to. I returned to my desk to process what had happened.

My entire scheme. Ruined. The President's insecurity did not give me the time to force Ferdinand's hand. Perhaps even then my goal was unrealistic. Spain wasn't collapsing fast enough and Britain would never tolerate our taking advantage. If the President didn't remove me from my post I'd still be a shadow of what I'd hoped.

I didn't sleep that night, instead imagining a conversation where I explained my failure to my parents. Heartbreaking. The end of an entire life plan. I dreaded the coming weeks.

XV

I DROPPED MY pencil on my desk at dusk. I had to get home—Mrs. Adams and I had plans to dine with Mr. and Mrs. Cruft. I spent the days since the Onís meeting reliving recent events and became obsessed with determining my mistake and concluded my goals were unobtainable. America was unready to become a middle power and I was stupid to think my hand would guide her to such. The country would suffer for my arrogance. Europe would spot our hunger and unify to deprive us. The President had no hope of winning in 1820 and my enemies would take his place. My arrow aimed for prestige and struck plunder.

Speaking of my enemies—the President told me to appoint Westerners to the next openings within the Department of State. He said the West was angry he'd chosen me instead of Clay and he hoped this would appease them. This thwarted my plan to appoint Everett, from Boston, to the next vacancy. It was obvious that Crawford had the President's ear and that Crawford did Clay's bidding. How was I to run a department filled with Clay's henchmen? Everett was right, they wouldn't stop until they'd destroyed me.

I had to control my thoughts and tug them from such dark corners. I gathered my things, exited my office, and found Judge Hay, the President's son-in-law, speaking with Brent in the main room. Maury and Ironside listened. Hay was twenty years older than Eliza, the President's daughter, and was an advisor in the President's inner circle.

Their conversation fell to its grave in my presence. "Mr. Adams." Hay bowed his head.

"Good evening, George. Do you bring a message from the President?"

"I do."

"Is it his list of names for future clerks?" I asked. Maury and Ironside looked at each other and leaned toward me.

"No," Hay said. "The President spoke of an emergency that requires your presence at the Mansion. He asks that you go there immediately."

Was this it? Had the President learned of my failure and decided to fire me? "Do you know the subject?"

"No, I'm sorry."

I kept calm before Hay and my subordinates. I had to accept my fate with dignity. I turned to Maury. "Send my wife a message." He grabbed a pencil and paper. "Tell her that the President needs me and I'm going to be late."

I raced from the department building to the Executive Mansion. Most people had already gone home for the day and all but two who saw me knew I was in no mood to speak. My most charitable interpretation for that pair was that they were blind. One I think was a temperance advocate. The other I hadn't a clue. I tugged my collar to prevent it from sticking to my neck. It was humid out but at least it wasn't summer.

I entered the Mansion and made my way to the President's office on the second floor. The President and Calhoun were waiting. The President stood while Calhoun was at his normal seat at the Cabinet table. Papers scattered before him, his hair a mess. I'd never seen him so pathetic.

"Shut the door," the President said. I did so and suppressed my panting.

"Your son-in-law spoke of an emergency," I said.

"Yes," the President said. To Calhoun, "Tell him."

Calhoun raised the paper closest to him. "I received a letter from General Jackson."

"Really?" I asked.

"Yes," he said. I'd never imagined him looking so anxious. "He conquered the Florida Territory." A pause. "All of it."

I was stunned. The United States controlled Florida? My instincts raced to calculate contingencies but I restrained them to focus. "Did he explain why?"

"He said the Seminoles retreated instead of engaging him. So he pursued them. He burned their lands and villages and even lured the leaders, Himomathle Mico and Hills Hadjo, onto a boat by waving the Union Jack. They're now dead."

"My God. What of the Spanish?"

"Defeated. He took the fort of St. Marks to resupply his forces and seized Pensacola because he thought the Seminoles were hiding there. The Spanish governor surrendered." He looked at the name. "José Mascot." He turned the page of Jackson's letter. "He asks for permission to invade Cuba."

The President was silent. I tried to read his eyes. Anger? Fear? Would his voice carry animalistic grunts or cries for help? Had his slow mind processed this development?

"Clearly we won't approve of—"

"There's no need to state the obvious, Mr. Adams," Calhoun said. "We couldn't approve of this even if we wanted to. The administration is dead." To the President, "Clay will impeach you for this."

The President turned from us.

"We're not dead yet," I said. "What are the biggest risks?"

"The diplomatic consequences," Calhoun said. "Committing an act of war without consulting Congress. Defying civilian control of the military. Those are the big three."

"Right," I said. My mind raced. There had to be a way to frame this positively. There always was in politics and diplomacy. "Let's start with the third issue." I looked Calhoun in the eye. "Whether or not Jackson disobeyed his orders depends on what his orders were."

"We should never have involved Jackson," Calhoun said. I heard emotions bubbling in his voice. "That was our mistake. He doesn't listen to anyone, including his superiors and civilian masters."

"What were his instructions?" I asked. He didn't answer. "Didn't the President say to tell Jackson not to attack Spanish positions?" Calhoun stared at me, warning me to stop. I kept going. "Did you include that in your note?"

"No." He spoke softly and with anger. I glanced at the President, who still faced a window. "I forgot."

"You forgot?" I asked.

"Yes. Yes, Mr. Adams. I forgot." His voice rose. "I work each day until I can no longer think. As do you. As does the President. I made an error."

"If you did not place that restriction on him, how could he violate it?" I asked.

"Instead I was complicit in this international crime," he said. "Or negligent, at best."

"I have something to say," the President muttered. Still at the window, where moonlight outlined his silhouette. "I sent General Jackson follow up instructions. He'd written to me about whether to take East Florida, since Spain can't control it." A pause. "I told him that great interests are at issue and it was up to him to carry our course to triumph. It made sense at the time."

I analyzed the President. Did he face away from us because he was scared? Or was this something else? An epiphany blossomed. I'd misread him. He was devious, not slow. He knew I'd never convince Onís to relinquish Florida and so he achieved his aim while setting up Jackson and Calhoun to take the blame and suffer the fall. His anxiety was not of my failure but of Jackson's victory reaching this city's ears. A master of political chess. Maybe. Or his negligence risked destroying us in scandal. That felt less likely and it didn't matter. Our survival depended on his. I'd treat him as he wished to be seen, a benign man. Time to forge the triumvirate.

"What I'm hearing," I said, "is that General Jackson made a broad reading of vague instructions. He's an aggressive man who took his order to pursue the Seminoles to an extreme, given that he was never told not to."

"The press won't care about such nuances," Calhoun said.

"This is Washington City. Nuances are how we function."

"So you want us to say we intentionally conquered Florida?"

"Yes."

"That creates larger problems. We'd be responsible for an act of war without consulting Congress and against a country with whom you're negotiating."

"Don't you see? This turns the negotiations on their head."

"By breaking them."

"It doesn't matter. Florida is ours. Onís will have to take the deal I offered him."

For a moment, a brief but crucial moment, I watched the President's ears rise. Ever so slightly. He smiled. They lowered and he turned to us, his expression serious, his focus on me.

"Surely we must return Florida to Spain," Calhoun said.

"Must we?" the President asked.

"What would justify our aggression?"

The President knew I was his tongue. "One moment," I said. I paced in circles as they watched me. Hands behind my back. My mind was my best and only weapon. Then: "We claim self-defense."

"You're mad," Calhoun said.

"Remember why we deployed Jackson. Spain lost control of Florida and the Seminoles were attacking our citizens in Georgia. That means Jackson was acting defensively. He's ended the Seminole threat." To the President, "The defensive use of force doesn't require congressional approval and is legitimate under the Law of Nations."

"Clay won't accept that argument," Calhoun said.

"He doesn't have to. We just need a majority of our citizens and the press. The people will love us. We acted boldly in their interest."

"What if Spain severs relations?"

"She won't. She'll accept whatever we give her. And if she doesn't, we'll keep Florida and ignore her tears."

"What about Britain and the Alliance?"

"The Europeans will protest but they won't go to war over this." To the President, "This wasn't a land grab. We wanted a stable border and Spain couldn't provide it. Why should we suffer our women and children being butchered? Spain forfeited her right to the Florida Territory. That's our argument."

"But why did Jackson take Pensacola?" the President asked, getting me to think.

"Because the Spanish governor would have counterattacked."

"That's a weak argument," Calhoun said.

I shrugged. "If the question is dubious, it's better to err on the side of vigor than of weakness. To side with our officer than with our bitterest enemies."

Calhoun knew the President sided with me. My perceptions of them had flipped. "I still fear that Clay will argue we're defending the indefensible," Calhoun said.

"He will," I said. "But he'll fail."

"Especially if our argument is made preemptively," the President said.

"Sir?"

"The press doesn't yet have this story. But they will within weeks. I'll wait in Highland through the aftermath. Mr. Adams, write an open letter giving the argument you made here tonight. Frame it as though Jackson made reasonable decisions based on what knowledge he had as his theater's commander. Be as detailed as possible. Address every counterargument you can think of. Because Clay will use whatever he can against us. Break his momentum before he has any."

"Where should I publish it?"

"The *Intelligencer*. Address it to Mr. Rush." He referred to our minister in Britain. "Lord Castlereagh is our most important audience."

"Yes, well, he's likely pulling the Seminoles' strings."

"Perhaps don't say that. Not yet." The President smiled. "We mustn't antagonize Jackson. He has a larger following than any of us." A pause. "Our fate is in your hands, Mr. Adams."

PART THREE

AMERICA'S NAPOLEON
LATE 1818 - 1819

XVI

I RELEASED THE *Intelligencer* and enjoyed breathing at my chosen pace for the first time in months. My open letter, 10,000 words long, had set the narrative about Jackson's invasion. The overwhelming bulk of Americans supported him and the President was happy to let the brash soldier have his moment in the sun as he secured his policy victory while avoiding responsibility for it. Our critics scrambled what arguments they could but were denied their chance to strike. I focused on diplomacy instead. Onís left Washington in protest and said he'd sever our negotiations unless Jackson was punished. I expected the fool to return within a month and was more concerned about Canning as an emerging wrinkle threatened our relationship with the British Empire. All of that waited as failure's agony withdrew and my confidence retook its throne, stronger than ever.

Mrs. Adams entered the social room, where I sat beside the fireplace. Her face won Plato's contest for the ideal image of dread. She held a letter.

"What is it, Louisa?"

"John," she said softly, "Your father wrote us. Your mother has passed."

I slowed my thinking to control my emotions. "I see." I looked at the ash in our fireplace which Lucy hadn't cleaned since winter. This was unsurprising news, as Harriet Welsh, our friend in Braintree, wrote us several times recently about Mother's declining health but the impact was hardly softened.

"Your father says he'll bear this with fortitude."

I nodded but Father's mention proved too much. My thoughts spiraled. I endeavored to prepare my mind for submission to divine will. Oh, God, pass from me. I had no mother on Earth. Gracious God had to support Father in his deep affliction and support and comfort her children and prepare us to rejoin her society in the abodes of the blest.

Mother was an angel, a minister of blessing to all human beings within her sphere. Her heart was an abode of heavenly purity. She had no feelings but of kindness and beneficence yet her mind was as firm as her temper was mild and gentle. She'd known sorrow but she kept it silent. The personification of female virtue—of piety, of charity, of active and never intermittent benevolence. She was more to me than a mother, she was a spirit from above watching over me for good and contributing to my conscience by her mere existence. What must it have been to Father and how would he support life without her, for she was his charm? Not my will, heavenly father, but thine be done.

I was not good enough for Mother. Unfit to be her son. Why, oh why, was she burdened with a defective son? I should not have fought with her. She knew best and she only wanted me to have a life worthy of our name. Both career and—both career and other things.

I glanced at Mrs. Adams and suppressed memories I'd no wish to relive. I had to succeed, to triumph in my post and become President. It's what Mother wanted. What she and Father wanted were all that mattered and that's what they chose, that, and for me to live a virtuous life.

If there is existence beyond the grave, Mother is happy. But if virtue alone is happiness below, no existence on Earth was more blessed than hers. She married in 1764 at age 20 and had five children. Only two sons survived her. She had seen the world, its glories without being dazzled, its vices and follies without being inflicted. She'd suffered often and severely. She rose with the dawn and superintended the household with all-foreseeing care. An ardent patriot during our Revolution who taught her children unbound devotion to their country.

But oh, Father, my aged and ever-venerated Father. What solace was left that could attach him to life? Merciful God, be thou his stay and his staff, and in thy sovereign goodness prove for him consultations, as this world cannot give.

"John?" Mrs. Adams paused. "Your father wrote a postscript." Another pause. "Our sons arrived from Boston. They're well."

"Good," I whispered. Wiped tears from their ducts and noticed their predecessors on my chin and lap and wiped them too.

"She and I became allies so recently. I wish we'd managed to discover the goodness in each other sooner. She wielded the art of softening the asperities of nature and molding them to her will. There was so much I could have learned."

I watched my wife and appreciated that she let me feel my emotions peacefully but I worried this would cause her another health crisis.

"Are we off to Braintree?" she asked. I shook my head. "Why? We must console your father and we can see our sons."

"I'm needed here, Louisa. I'm going to Highland tomorrow to speak with the President. Jackson's invasion is the most important event of my tenure thus far."

"Why do you defend that man? He's a barbarian."

"His pursuit into East Florida was justifiable. Clay will attempt to destroy the administration and we must plot our next move."

"It feels wrong to not join your father."

"You can take the trip alone if you wish."

A moment. Then, "No. We'll wait until it's timely for you."

XVII

THE PRESIDENT'S ESTATE at Highland was adjacent to Jefferson's at Monticello. His two-story, 40-by-30 foot wooden dwelling presided over 3,500 acres. A fireplace, wooden floors, basic furnishings, its simplicity evident when compared to Mount Vernon, yet alone its neighbor. It would have been quaint had there not been 40 slaves working the plantation when I arrived. The domestic quarters stood near the home while field slaves lived farther out.

I met the President in a modest den with access to the outside. I was surprised to find Calhoun already there. A nervous shell of how I'd once pictured him. Our chance to utilize the triumvirate was ruined when the President said he didn't wish to start until Crawford arrived. I turned to Calhoun for support but he was silent. I expressed concern that Crawford would send our discussion's details to Clay but the President dismissed this and stressed the importance of the Cabinet's unity during this challenge. We waited almost two hours for Crawford to join us, during which time I mentioned Mother's passing. Calhoun said depression after a loved one's death was rejecting divine will and that providence intended it in kindness and Mother was happier in Heaven than she was with us.

Crawford glacially crawled into his spot and the President said, "Let's begin with the British civilians that General Jackson captured." He read his notes. "Alexander Arbuthnot, a merchant. Robert Ambrister, a former Royal marine. Jackson accused them of leading the Seminoles and said Arbuthnot gave them material support and Ambrister trained their forces. He held a two day long court-martial that found them guilty. Neither were allowed representation or witnesses. Arbuthnot said he sold goods to escaped slaves and Ambrister said his goal was toppling *Spanish* rule. Jackson executed them the next day."

Calhoun and Crawford were taciturn. The President said, "Their deaths have caused more noise than any event since Jackson's route at New Orleans." To me, "How do we expect Britain will react?"

I cleared my throat. "I don't think they'll declare war, but the agreements reached on the Northwest are dead. I'll set up a meeting with

Canning as soon as I return to Washington." A pause. "This is proof that Britain is behind the Seminole attacks in Georgia."

Crawford said, "What about the gentlemens' ple—"

"Do not be blind, sir. Britain has targeted us since independence. Every Indian war waged upon us is traceable to the instigation of British agents. They've disavowed it each time but we've felt their misdeeds each time. Don't mistake me. I'm sorry that Englishmen were found among the Seminoles, but the British government has allied with that tribe since the late war. These executions will deter foreign attacks on our citizens and our borders. Hopefully, for years to come. That may grant value to their deaths."

"Reduce your tone," the President said. "You'll offend the British government more than we already have."

"This action may convince Spain to settle with us," I said.

"That's a good point," Crawford said. "Perhaps we should instruct Jackson to shoot any white man found helping the Seminoles on sight."

"Is that a sincere recommendation?" the President asked.

"Yes."

Crawford agreed with me? I needed to reconsider my position. He probably thought his idea would hurt the administration.

"What is the most recent news from Congress' investigation?" the President asked.

"The Military Affairs Committee condemned Jackson for executing the British civilians but ruled his other actions acceptable," Calhoun said.

"Is Clay satisfied with that outcome?"

"He instructed the committee to continue investigating Jackson."

"Jackson's his starting point," I said. "Clay sees him as his main rival for political leadership in the West."

"He sees the General as a menace," Crawford said.

"You should know I've taken additional steps since Mr. Adams' open letter," the President said.

"What steps?" I asked.

"I sent Jackson correspondence to ensure we survive Congress' investigation. I ordered him to return the forts of St. Marks and Pensacola to Spain. That should placate Mr. Onís into reopening negotiations. I also told him that the restrictions given to General Gaines during the prior incursion were meant for him too and that he acted on his own responsibility by transcending that limit." To Calhoun, "I said someone at the Department of War will modify the official records as needed. I don't expect him to cooperate even though it's in his interest to claim he followed but misunderstood his orders." A pause. "My understanding is he's spending his time finding escaped slaves and sending them back to the South."

"I fail to see why we shouldn't court-martial him," Calhoun said.

"We shouldn't do anything that requires us to return Florida," I said. "We can still secure its transfer."

"I'm not saying to return it. I'll point out, though I shouldn't have to, that I'm the one with the most to lose if Clay destroys Jackson." His dark eyes on me. "The argument that I wrote him confusing orders makes me look inept. I'd rather say he disobeyed us, which is true, since it minimizes harm to our public images."

"Jackson's too popular," the President said. "Court-martialing him would alienate our supporters. It's better to let Jackson and Clay collide. Only one will be left standing, if we're lucky. Or neither, if we're luckier. While they waste time, Mr. Adams shall complete his negotiations with Mr. Onís."

"I fear you're underestimating what Jackson's victory would mean, Mr. President," Calhoun said. "He'll feel emboldened. He already hopes to provoke a war with Spain and conquer Mexico. He wants to become a modern Hernán Cortés."

"That's right," Crawford said. "We should court-martial him now, while we still can." Had he reversed himself again? Thoughts moved through his brain as grains through an hourglass.

"I understand my plan is risky," the President said, "but it's the only one that allows us considerable reward and avoids losing the public's support. The decision is made. Let's proceed carefully."

XVIII

"I FEEL AS though I'm squashed among cargo that's crossing the Atlantic," Brent said. "Did you expect it to be this packed?"

"Yes," I said. "It's the biggest rhetorical event of the season and people will take any excuse to not work."

"We're here."

"This is work. For me."

We sat in the upper gallery in the Hall of the House of Representatives. Clay was to speak about Jackson's invasion of Florida to the Military Affairs Committee. His largest effort to sway public opinion. He refused to accept the Committee's ruling that Jackson's conduct was mostly acceptable and sought to place four new resolutions meant to censure the General. Censuring Jackson would remove Clay's rival and open a broader investigation into the administration.

I inspected who from Washington's elite were among us. Most had sent Mrs. Adams condolences for Mother's passing. I spotted Crawford and Crowninshield two rows ahead. I felt anxiety and contempt whenever I saw Crawford. How could a man serve a President while conspiring against that President? Did he wish to enter history as a traitor—a Judas or an Arnold? Or did he not care about such notions as justice? I did not understand why the President ignored the pleas Calhoun and I made to recognize the Secretary of the Treasury as Clay's ally. Crawford would only require three pieces of silver to betray the Lord.

The ministers of all the countries with whom America had established relations sat together. Onís was the exception as he'd not yet returned to Washington. Canning led the group. I wished to speak with him but such a conversation was impossible at that moment. We would see each other soon enough. Beside him was the Baron de Tuyll, Russia's minister. He'd been a major in the Imperial Army during the war and could always be found clad in black and red. His was an earned arrogance for he methodically pursued his goals so that those opposed couldn't stop him even with advanced warning.

A less threatening fellow sat on Canning's other flank. Mr. Hyde was France's minister and was among the least popular men in Washington society. He supported the Bourbon monarchy through the entire revolutionary era. Napoleon had exiled him to this country. He settled in New Jersey and condescended to Americans. The President hated him and viewed Hyde as disagreeable, ill tempered, and obscene. In one famous episode, Hyde invited Senator Barbour of Virginia to dinner and arrived drunk several hours late.

I noticed the entire Senate had adjourned for the day and sat together in the gallery. That body contained 44 members. Three out of four were Republicans, the rest Federalist remnants. The Senate embodied the even split between free and slave states within the Union. The free states were New Hampshire, Vermont, New York, Pennsylvania, Ohio, Indiana, Illinois, Massachusetts, Rhode Island, Connecticut, and New Jersey. The slave states were Delaware, Maryland, Virginia, Kentucky, Tennessee, the Carolinas, Georgia, Alabama, Mississippi, and Louisiana.

Ironically, the senators seated closest to me were the Massachusetts delegation. Mr. Pickering was my colleague and antagonist from my old Senate days. But Mr. Rufus King had my respect. He was the Senate's leading opponent of slavery and had worked with Washington, Hamilton, and Father, supporting policies like the Bank and the Jay Treaty that were critical to the Union surviving its infancy. I wished for us to be allies but he disapproved of my serving in the President's southern-dominated administration. He likewise sought to admit his youngest son to Harvard.

Mr. Gaillard, President pro Tempore of the Senate, was with Judge Smith and looked in my direction. Gaillard and I had an amusing conversation early on in my tenure. He'd asked if there was a new system of etiquette established regarding visits to Cabinet officers. I'd hoped there wasn't because I found such rules a waste of time. He said the Senate adopted a rule long ago—Mr. Burr was its author—saying senators should only visit the President. King, my clerk, referred him to the book where this was documented. I'd been in the Senate for five years and had visited every Cabinet officer at the dawn of each season. I told Gaillard I would conform to whatever arrangement was found proper.

An interesting trio—Senator Talbot from Kentucky, Senator Fromentin from Louisiana, and Senator Sanford from New York. Fromentin recently returned from France. Sanford, less glamorously, visited my home last week. He told me he wished for employment abroad and spoke of a young protégé who desired to become an agent in South America. I told him our postings were prioritized for Westerners and I could only grant the young man Consul in Buenos Aires but the position lacked a salary. This wouldn't satisfy his protégé. He gave me the man's name and desired office.

Justice Story was the only Supreme Court magistrate I could find. He was placed on the Court when I declined—I was minister to Russia at that time. He was Chief Justice Marshall's closest ally. The Court was the last bastion of Federalist power in an otherwise Republican-ruled government. I hoped it remained as such. Their rulings strengthened the Union as the ultra-states rights Republicans pushed us toward faction.

Leading ladies were in attendance. The House allowed them but the Senate didn't. Mrs. Crawford and Mrs. Crowninshield were among them. The most interesting was Lucy Brewer, a female marine who'd served on the *USS Constitution* during the late war. I didn't see my wife. Probably at home writing to friends in Braintree and Boston. We'd received many remorseful letters about Mother.

Mr. Cobb, congressman from Georgia and chairman of the Military Affairs Committee, opened the debate. The Speaker rose and the room hushed. He placed his notes aside and the women in the gallery leaned toward him. Clay watched his congressional colleagues and then looked at the gallery. I suspected he saw me because he smiled.

"Mr. Chairman, in rising to address you, sir, on this very interesting subject which now engages the attention of all of Congress, I must be allowed to say that all inferences drawn from my painful duty of unfriendliness either to the chief magistrate or to the military chieftain will be wholly unfounded."

My stomach churned at his two-faced niceties.

"I approve of the conduct of this government. Spain has no cause for complaint. Having violated the treaty of 1795, that power subjected herself to all consequences which ensued and it belongs not to her to complain of those measures."

He turned to the women.

"She is the sovereign of Florida and we accordingly treat her as such for its purchase. In strictness, we ought to have demanded of her to restrain the Indians. Failing that, we should have demanded a right of passage for our army. But, if the President had the power to march an army into Florida without consulting Spain or Congress, he had no authority to authorize hostility against her. If the gentleman succeeded in showing authority was granted to General Jackson to take Spain's ports, he would only have established that unconstitutional orders were given. But no such orders were given."

He reviewed the history of our war with the Creeks, which he claimed as the true cause of the Seminole conflict. He introduced his four resolutions. The first criticized the executions of Arbuthnot and Ambrister. The second was a law prohibiting the military from executing any prisoner without the President's authority. The third denounced Jackson's capture of Spain's forts. The final one clarified the illegality of the military from entering any foreign territory without Congress' permission besides pursuing a defeated enemy. I found the speech predictable and unmoving until he reached his climax.

"Recall the free nations which have gone before us. Where are they now? How have they lost their liberty? If we could transport back to when Greece and Rome flourished and ask a Grecian if he did not fear that covering their chieftains with glory—some Philip or Alexander—would one day overthrow his liberty?"

To the senators: "The confident Grecian would exclaim, *No! No! We've nothing to fear from our heroes, our liberty is eternal*. If a Roman was asked if he feared the conqueror of Gaul might establish a throne on liberty's ruins he'd have instantly repelled the insinuation. Yet Greece fell, Caesar crossed the Rubicon, and not even the patriotic arm of Brutus could save his country.

"I hope not to be misunderstood. I am far from intimating that General Jackson cherishes any designs inimical to the liberties of this country. I believe his intentions to be pure and patriotic. I thank God that he would not, but I thank Him still more that he could not, if he would, overrun the liberties of this republic. But precedents, if bad, are fraught with the most dangerous consequences."

To me: "Beware how you give a fatal sanction in this infant republic, scarcely two score years old, to military insubordination. Remember that Greece had her Alexander, Rome her Caesar, England her Cromwell, France her Bonaparte, and that, if we would escape the rock on which they split we must avoid their errors.

"I hope gentlemen will deliberately survey the awful isthmus on which we stand. They may bear down all opposition, they may even vote the General the public's thanks, they may carry him triumphantly through this House. But if they do, in my humble judgment, it will be a triumph of insubordination—a triumph of the military over civil authority—a triumph over the powers of this House—a triumph over the constitution of this land. And I pray most devoutly to Heaven that it may not prove, in its ultimate effects and consequences, a triumph over the liberties of the people."

Clay stepped away from the floor and grabbed a glass of water. Adulation discharged from every crevice and women's hats rained onto the House floor. His colleagues shook his hands in between his sips. Then they lifted him onto their shoulders and carried him out. The gallery emptied as many followed.

Brent and I stayed, along with some others. I'd not appreciated how Clay saw Jackson as an existential threat to the republic. Jackson was Alexander, Caesar, Cromwell, and Napoleon. I'd assumed Clay shared Crawford's opportunism and his assault on Jackson was meant to pierce the administration's flank so he could encircle us. But what if he was sincere? And worse still—what if he was right?

Clay's speech would spread through the Union over the next weeks, challenging my open letter. Whichever prevailed would decide if the President would enter his death throes.

XIX

THE PAIN IN my eyes returned. Within days they'd swell and become unusable. I had to work through my discomfort until then. This happened periodically but I resented it. To be undermined by something *so* trivial. How was one *so* defective to achieve greatness? I suppose Cicero and General Washington had their ailments but they bore them with grace while I was rendered immobile. It didn't help my already declining physical appearance and fueled the image that I was a porcupine to avoid unless an argument needed winning. I fought to look presentable as I stood on Pennsylvania Avenue at the trail leading to the Executive Mansion, along with Mrs. Adams, Calhoun, and his wife. Thousands lined the street hoping to glimpse the Union's biggest hero.

Congress voted down all of Clay's resolutions, proving that in Washington men praise you to your face but abandon you when it counts. The end of Clay's investigation, the administration was victorious. But the General remained controversial. That's why the President, refusing to dismount this deadly horse, arranged for Jackson's procession to reach the Mansion while refusing to meet him.

I failed to restrain my sadness at seeing the reception Clay and Jackson received. They were loved, touching people's hearts as I did not, could not. Something was wrong with me, more than my eyes. Ingrained in my nature. I told myself I didn't need affection, that a virtuous leader was unpopular, but the jealousy still stung.

Mrs. Calhoun was her husband's first cousin, once removed, and eleven years his junior. Her eyes were black, even darker than his, and too large for her face. I suppose I'd learn to enjoy having small spots of the lightless universe watching me. Calhoun disliked speaking in groups and wanted me to take the lead once Jackson arrived. We hoped to bring the General into our partnership. He'd be a valuable ally. I feared he and Calhoun were mutually angry about the invasion. Their tension could push Jackson toward Crawford, who I suspected would abandon Clay, in his defeat, for the rising star, despite the Secretary of the Treasury spending the crisis linking everyone in the administration but himself to Jackson.

Hyde recently met with Crawford and he warned me Crawford had drafted a letter to Onís proposing the Mississippi River as the boundary between the United States and the Spanish Empire. An apology for Jackson's invasion. He'd sabotage the General, the President, and the country, but I'd expect nothing less from a viper who preyed on other serpents. I sent my own letter to Onís to resume our correspondence. It had to reach him before Crawford's did.

There was a crescendo of noise from the crowd as Jackson's carriage arrived. I noticed there were no Negroes among them, strange as they usually enjoyed seeing our leading men. The crowd was thick and I couldn't glimpse the carriage until just before it reached the trail. A slave helped the General and his wife exit the platform. They approached us. I thought I heard the bullets lodged in his chest clatter. It was my first time seeing him. Tall, but not giant. He wore a blue uniform coat with gold buttons and cuffs and trim. An air of command rooted in his ability to outfight and outshoot any other American. Eyes were pulled to him as the planets to the sun.

"Mr. Adams."

"General Jackson."

Our parties greeted each other. I gestured to the Mansion but he didn't budge.

"Will the President meet me?" he asked.

"Not today. He wants to avoid controversy."

"I understand." He was visibly disappointed but I didn't know if he was insulted.

"You and your wife must dine with us on Monday," Mrs. Adams said.

"I shall decline all such invitations for the coming weeks," Jackson said. "The President is right, I'll avoid engagements until passions have cooled."

"You may not have long," Calhoun said. "The President appointed you as governor of Florida." A pause. "Congratulations."

"Is this exile?" Jackson asked.

"No," Calhoun said. "You're the obvious man for the job." I was glad he avoided feuding with the General. I trusted his character even though he'd lost my respect in this crisis.

"Hmm."

"It is a blessing," Mrs. Jackson said to her husband. "We'll establish the Protestant Sabbath in the territory."

"Most of Florida is Catholic, ma'am," I said.

"It will be good for them."

I glanced at my wife and she took Mrs. Jackson and Mrs. Calhoun aside so I could speak with their husbands.

"Where is Mr. Clay?" Jackson asked.

"I imagine he's in his office in the Capitol," I said.

"I shall duel him for what he's done."

"Gen—"

"He called me *Caesar.*"

"I know. But he's been beaten."

"Not yet. He breathes."

"Please reconsider."

"Then I'll have his ears," he said. I turned to Calhoun and then back to Jackson. He grunted and said, "I thank God that there is such a place of torment as Hell."

"For now let's settle for the embarrassment he feels for being Speaker and lacking the votes to punish his enemies." I paused. "I suspect my open letter contributed to his defeat."

Jackson didn't respond, as though I'd not spoken. Then, "Yes, I heard about a letter." Said with casualness that implied minimal thought. I was disappointed. I'd hoped my letter would win his gratitude but this man only felt resentment.

"Have you talked to the press about the Seminole war?"

"Not yet."

"It's inevitable. You mustn't contradict the administration's story that your instructions were unclear and that you acted defensively."

"That's true enough. I attacked Spain's forts because my scouts told me they were arming the Seminoles. The Spanish are a wicked race. Florida under their rule was the Babylon of the South. I destroyed it and brought us peace. Will the government return it as they have the forts?"

"No, and restoring the forts is temporary. That's why it's important you maintain the administration's story. I'm negotiating to put on paper what you made fact. You should also say that acquiring Florida is more important than Texas."

"I disagree with that statement."

"It's the only way to reach a deal with Spain."

"Why does that matter? Spain is weak."

"But Europe is strong. A deal with Spain will secure our interests without war."

"I see."

"You must help me sway public opinion, General."

"Where will you place the Texas border?"

"The Sabine River."

"That is too far north. Southerners will take offense."

"Florida is more important. Our enemies must not use the Florida rivers again, as Britain did in the war. There lies the South's greatest threat."

"I suppose that's right." Jackson turned to Calhoun, who stood awkwardly off our flank. Back to me. "Will saying this help the President?"

"Yes," I said.

"Then I shall do it. Though it is he who is in my debt. The President is an amiable character. It is acceptable that he should win the next election. We must keep Mr. Crawford from power."

Could it be? "You dislike Crawford?"

"I have trouble accepting that human nature is capable of the baseness which that man has shown."

I tested him. "He has not spoken against you in Cabinet Meetings."

"My sources tell me he instructed Georgia's delegation in Congress to vote against me in the recent inquiries, despite my action's necessity. He has no principles."

I met Calhoun's eyes. We'd succeeded. General Jackson had joined our partnership and, because he would serve in Florida, he could not threaten us in Washington.

XX

"WHERE IS GENERAL Jackson's record of the court-martial?" I had trouble focusing on Canning. Two weeks had passed since Mother died and I could no longer stop sadness from interfering with my productivity. My decision to separate those feelings from working hours had departed from recent memory and was no longer instinctive. It was time to visit Braintree and receive closure but for now I was trapped in Washington, prioritizing the nation over my emotions.

"What?" I asked.

"The court-martial, Mr. Adams. General Jackson's record of the court-martial. Of Arbuthnot and Ambrister. I want a copy."

"That is under the General's control. Congress voted not to subpoena his papers."

"Yes, which shocked me after Mr. Clay's address. Legislatures are odd bodies." His eyes dropped momentarily. "Surely the administration has it."

"General Jackson refused to grant the Department of War access." This was untrue, as the President had altered Jackson's papers, but I could not say this to Canning.

"The President tolerates defiance from a military officer?"

"General Jackson is both popular and stubborn."

"I see."

"Does Lord Castlereagh understand our government didn't authorize this invasion?"

"He does, but he also believes no circumstances existed that warranted the executions. Jackson's record will reveal any such circumstances."

"We should change topics. The President will not endure the political cost of challenging him."

"Parliament desires blood. Londerners burn Jackson in effigy. Lord Castlereagh could have war if he held up a finger."

"Will he hold it?" I asked. Canning studied me, testing for the insecurity that great powers exploited in weak ones. I didn't grant it.

"No. He won't."

"Is our cotton too good?"

He snorted. "He was impressed by your letter in the *Intelligencer*."

My eyes swelled and I winced in pain. "So, he will not break relations over Florida?"

"No. He will not waste our military's time in North America when Metternich and Alexander are our primary threat."

It was over. Neutralizing Britain denied Onís his last hope. British acquiescence was the largest obstacle to fulfilling my destiny. I'd gambled, based on my analysis, that London would tolerate an annexation, despite the warnings I'd heard everyday for two years. I was right.

"I am pleased to hear that, sir. Quite pleased."

"I can imagine."

"This means Castlereagh has abandoned his plans for Florida?"

"Plans? What plans?"

"Don't pretend to deceive me. Britain was transforming Florida into a gun aimed at our chest. She was behind the Seminoles' aggression and plotted slave revolts in the South. All that has been undone."

"You are a strange man, Mr. Adams. Are you unsatisfied with Lord Castlereagh's decision?"

"No."

"Then let us move on. Didn't your mother tell you to let sleeping dogs lie?"

Mother's mention broke what remained of my feeble separation between sadness and work. Canning realized he misspoke and apologized. I recuperated and he asked to discuss South America and British complaints about our trade laws. We discussed these subjects for another hour and I went home early. Mother's death weakened my spirit.

XXI

NEWS CAME THAT Harvard accepted George as a sophomore. An ideal reason to visit Massachusetts. The President acknowledged this but was hesitant for me to go before reaching an agreement with Onís. I knew Britain tolerating the annexation would prompt Onís to crawl back to me. He wrote of returning to Washington and the President allowed me to schedule our meeting for after my trip. He had a heart—often too much of one—but it benefited me in this case.

George complained about leaving Washington. His effort to win Mary before his brothers was more important than his desire to escape my guidance. I told him to overcome his feelings because they impeded his improvement and education. He'd given no signs he could bear the burden of being my oldest son or a member of society or of our species. He needed a break from Mary. He'd groveled to her for months to no benefit. Time apart would clear his head and allow his lips a respite from their time with her bottom.

Antoine helped bathe me in the Potomac the morning before our departure. I spent the first steamship ride telling Mrs. Adams I planned to rent Mr. Hancock's old house for George to live in Boston. It was close to campus and provided room for us during visits. She asked about other options but I assured her my plan was sound. Then we discussed Mother and I inquired as to whether she was satisfied with her life. Mrs. Adams suspected she wasn't because Mother had an inner strength that was insufficiently challenged. I asked for clarification given her experience in the Revolution and as First Lady and Mrs. Adams said Father held the posts and Mother, instead of becoming President, settled for raising one. I told her I was unsure of what she meant and advised her not to speak on topics of which she didn't know.

♦ ♦ ♦ ♦ ♦ ♦

No one greeted us in Peacefield. I briefly worried but the house was undamaged. I instructed the carriage driver to unload our bags and I entered. Father and Nancy were despondent, him with a near-empty bottle of cider on the table beside his chair and her on the ground grasping her left leg. There were markings of dried tears on her face and arms. I suspected they were processing Mother's death but even so they sat amongst a shameful disarray. Gobs of grief surrounded them and left our trio toiling to stand. We were Corsica, Malta, and Elba amidst a Mediterranean of rubbish.

"*Johnny.*" Father's voice blended whimper and growl. Bloodshot eyes. He'd never looked so broken. 84 and lost without his partner in life. How long before he followed her?

"I sent a letter alerting you of our arrival over a week ago," I said. Father didn't answer and instead gestured to Mrs. Adams and George, acknowledging them. "You did not write back." Silence. "This is over Mother?"

"No." Father asked Nancy, "Should you tell them or should I?" Nancy shook her head. So she was conscious. I noticed old pliers Mother used to build musketballs during the war by her head. Father said to us, "Tom's missing."

"Heavens," Mrs. Adams said, moving toward Nancy.

"When did he leave?" I asked.

"Four days ago," Father said.

"Five," Nancy muttered. Her eyes still closed. I turned to George but he appeared clueless, as always.

"Did he say where he was going?" I asked.

"If we knew where he was he wouldn't be missing," Father said.

"He's fallen in with evil companions," Nancy said. "It's the only explanation."

"What's your plan to find him?" I asked.

"Your letter," Father said. "We knew you were coming. You and Louisa can find him."

"And had we not come?" I asked. Father turned to Mrs. Adams and Nancy. I didn't know why, as though my question was unreasonable. I took Mrs. Adams to Father's office. "I must go to Boston. Josiah Quincy will know how to find him." I referred to a lawyer and the co-executor of my parents' estate, along with me.

"I remember where he lives," she said. "Near Harvard. Let me find him. George will accompany me."

"No, Louisa—"

127

"You must stay here and comfort Nancy."

"What? You're bound to be more attuned to her—feminine feelings."

"Nancy doesn't trust me, but she's fond of you. It has to be you."

I turned from her. She was right, or probably was. It felt odd not being the one taking action. Within an hour she and George were on a carriage to Boston. I tried speaking with Nancy but she retired early. Father fell asleep in his chair and I guided him to bed. I settled into the room occupied by Frances and Isaac, Tom's children, on the second floor. Memories of my brother thwarted my rest. He'd shown so much potential and was my secretary when I was minister in the Hague and Prussia. More importantly, he *liked* people in a way I couldn't. A human touch. I could never repay him for transitioning Mrs. Adams into the family. A role she mentioned for years.

My standout memory was also the first of my diplomatic career. President Washington and Hamilton sent me to London to convey secret information to Mr. Jay, who was negotiating to avoid war. Upon our arrival I thought I'd lost the document and it was Tom who found it. Failure could have wrecked Washington's diplomacy and his administration and Father's hope of succeeding him. I was never happier with Tom and we were suspicious of British rifling through our correspondence.

I said a prayer for my brother and made one last attempt at sleep. I pictured a meadow and distorted the image to trick my mind into thinking it was losing consciousness. It worked and I slept for three hours.

◆ ◆ ◆ ◆ ◆ ◆

I awoke to find Nancy on the porch drinking coffee and applying pencil to paper. "Good morning."

"Morning." Her eyes held their focus.

"What's that?"

"'Adventures of a Ruffle.'"

"Pardon?"

"A story I'm writing."

"I didn't know you wrote."

She nodded. "I give them as presents. This one is about how vanity is always sure to defeat its own plans."

"Is it poetry or prose?"

"Prose."

"Ah. I prefer poetry myself." I gestured to a chair at the table's end. "Do you mind?" She shook her head. I sat and retrieved a cigar from my pocket and lit it with the candle Nancy had placed at the table's center and then I leaned back, took a puff, and wiped gunk from my eye. I admired the landscape, a nice break from Washington. Back to Nancy. Time to commence the comforting. "Why did Tom leave?" I asked. Nancy released her pencil. "I'd hoped he could reconcile his failed ambition with virtue for—"

"He left because he heard you were visiting."

"What? Tom and I have a good relationship."

"He doesn't hate you, but you remind him of his shame. Of being an unemployed lawyer as an Adams. Living with his father and subsidized by his brother."

"He resents that I help him?"

"His heart does. His mind does not."

"Unbelievable." I clenched my cigar within my jaw.

"And now *you're* filling with pity, despite being the least deserving of it in the family."

"I'm not asking for pity."

"Not verbally."

"Do you resent me too?"

"What I resent is your parents destroying my husband the way they did Charles."

"Don't speak of them that way."

"I'm right. You contorted yourself for them and Tom couldn't but he broke himself trying. He should have chosen his own destiny instead of entering law."

"Would you have married him if he wasn't a lawyer?"

Her face was scarlet. "No. I wanted to marry an Adams but I married the wrong one."

"What, you wish you'd married me?" I folded my arms.

"Yes, but don't flatter yourself. It's not *you*, per se."

"Charming."

129

"I wanted a life in Washington. That may not sound glamorous to you, but you don't know what else to compare it to." A pause. "Did you know your father reads aloud every letter Louisa sends him? Every drop of elite gossip? I wanted that life. Instead I have to hear about it."

"Louisa doesn't love Washington. Quite the opposite."

"Then we can switch. I'll move to the center of power and she can marry a failure."

"Do not speak of my brother with such—"

"Do you realize the children and I go to bed hungry some nights?"

This caught me off guard. "Repeat that."

"Yes." Her smile contained light sadism. "Your in-laws can't afford food. You don't send enough money and Tom earns nothing."

"This is unacceptable."

"I agree."

I turned from her. I needed time to think through their financial problems. "So you wish to live among the powerful but resent my parents for pushing us toward power?"

She snorted. "When you word it like that…" She returned to her story.

The sun peeked over the horizon. The farm's eastern fields undulated in the morning breeze and the sun cast a litany of colors as its palette rotated counterclockwise on Newton's disk. "Remember that with pride comes disgrace, whereas humility brings wisdom."

She released her pencil to avoid breaking it. "You will not speak to me about pride. You're the second most powerful man in America and plan to become the first."

"Ambition is good so long as it is rooted in virtue."

"Is that what separates us? You have virtue and I don't?"

"No, just—do not allow a desire for popularity to overcome the dictates of your conscience."

"I'll remember that," she said with venom.

I left her shortly thereafter. Fear of the future and a failure to reach expectations had corrupted my sister-in-law. I spent the day's remaining hours wandering the home and farm, speaking to no one, contemplating Tom and Nancy's concerns.

♦ ♦ ♦ ♦ ♦ ♦

The next day, I walked to the United First Parish Church in Quincy. It was three miles from Braintree. The Puritans established it but it had become Unitarian. An old building. Locals had discussed replacing it for years. I opted not to invite Father or Nancy. He was too slow and she was too angry. Mother rested there and I placed white roses on her tomb.

She left us in her 74th year. Had she lived in the age of the Patriarchs her every day would have been filled with deeds of goodness and love. The delight of Father's heart for 54 years, the sweetener of his toils, the comforter of his sorrows, the sharer and heightener of his joys. He'd told me with an abundance of gratitude that in all the vicissitudes of his fortunes the cheering encouragement of his wife had been his never-failing support and without which he should never have lived through them. I begged to die a righteous death so my end could be like hers.

"Mother," I whispered, "are you there?" No reply. "The family needs me and I need you. I don't know what to do. Father's lost without you. Tom's gone. Don't know if Louisa will find him. And Nancy—you always liked her more than Louisa. But she's angry. With Tom. With me. With life. With you. A person shouldn't live like that. Unfulfilled, and worse, hungry. What should I do? Take her and the children to Washington? How would I afford that? George is leaving, but Louisa's nieces and nephews come and go every month. I can't..."

I sighed.

"There are times when I wonder if it's worth it. If entering the ground is better than struggling with the living. I try to do good, to fulfill what you wanted of me. But villainy exists and it would be easier to die than to fight. Especially when I can't win. But what would happen to my soul..."

I tried to predict what Mother would say. She'd think my problems were minor compared to hers. The Revolution, the new government, the separations from Father and her children. I missed her wisdom, of deeper penetration than Washington or Dr. Franklin. She guided me away from errors of passion.

Expel the mist, Johnny.

Now I was hearing things. A phrase she wrote in her letters. It sounded so clear. Her voice. As though she were with me.

Subdue your passion and generosity will accompany your effort.

Classic Mother. Her lesson hadn't changed since my birth. I thanked her and returned home. I spoke to no one and the subsequent day was similar. I thought about Tom and Nancy and my coming joust with Onís.

♦ ♦ ♦ ♦ ♦ ♦

Night came. A carriage approached and I rushed outside. It was Mrs. Adams and George. They had Tom. George, the carriage driver, and I carried him into the house. "Place him face down," I said. "He'll choke on his vomit."

Nancy cried and slapped her husband and cocked her hand again. I jumped between them. "Let me! Let—"

She fell and a storm rained down her cheeks. Mrs. Adams embraced her and Nancy mumbled something.

"What's that?" my wife asked.

"I'm never taking my eyes off him again. Never again. I'll follow him everywhere he goes."

Mrs. Adams strengthened her grip. Nancy relaxed. Father approached Tom and grabbed his shoulder. I wondered if he'd strike him too. He didn't.

"My son," he said softly. "My boy." He hugged him. "I knew you'd come back." To Mrs. Adams, "Thank you, Louisa. Thank you for bringing him home."

Mrs. Adams nodded. Once Nancy was settled I led my wife to Father's office.

"Thank you," I said.

"You're welcome."

"Where did you find him?"

"Behind a pub. Drunk."

I checked on Tom and returned to Mrs. Adams. "Do you know what happened?"

"Mr. Quincy spoke of tension between Tom and your father."

"Father?"

"Yes. He said your father's criticisms have become more frequent since your mother passed."

"Hmm." A pause. "So this wasn't about me?"

"It sounds like your father compares you both to insult him."

"I must speak with him."

"With your father?"

"With Tom. Father's too old."

"Wait until tomorrow. He'll be sober."

"Right. Take George back to Boston tomorrow. I'll give you the money to secure the Mr. Hancock house and a ticket home."

"You won't come?"

"I have to return to Washington. This business with Tom used up my time."

"The nation comes first," she said glumly.

"Such are our lives." I turned to exit but paused. "Thank you. Again."

She smiled. "You're welcome, John."

I slept better that night. Mrs. Adams and George left before the dawn. Father told my wife to write him more and that her humorous tales of the capital were delightful. Nancy wore a dreadful expression. I woke Tom at nine and put him on the porch with some coffee. I paced around the table, searching for words.

"What is it, John?" He held the cup with both hands and elbows on his knees.

"I'm sorry you never found your place in the world, Tom."

"What does that mean?"

"A man—a person—must have an identity. The autonomy to make his own decisions. To have a skill and put it to use."

"Do you have that?"

"Of course."

"And you chose it?" He shook his head and muttered, "This family."

"Tom, I spoke with Nancy. She told me she and the children are underfed."

"She said that?" A hint of anger.

"Yes. Why didn't you tell me?"

"How could I? It's humiliating."

"I'll make you a deal, Tom. I'll send you an annual stipend. In exchange, you and Father must reconcile."

"*He's* the one angry with *me*. He shouts at me that I'm a failure and a parasite."

"You misunderstand. I'll send you a thousand dollars a year and I want you to tell Nancy and Father you're earning an income. I don't care what you say you're doing. Law, bartering, whatever. But the family will appreciate you."

"You have that money lying around?"

"No. I'll take out another mortgage on this house."

"Can you afford that?"

"No. It might ruin me, but I'll figure it out."

"Louisa agreed to this?"

"She doesn't know. She can't or she'll kill me," I said. He laughed. "This stays between us. No one else."

Tom shook his head and laughed. "Thank you, John. You have no idea—"

"You're welcome." He cried and I placed my hand on his shoulder. "You're going to be all right, Tom. You're all right."

XXII

KNOCK KNOCK.

"Come in," I said. I looked up from my measurement report and placed my pencil on my desk. The door opened and Brent entered.

"Mr. Onís has arrived."

"Send him in."

"Let me clarify: his carriage waits outside the building. He asks for you to join him."

I growled. "This is a breach of diplomatic custom."

"I know."

"He cannot dictate where I sit."

"Should I tell him to leave?"

I thought it over. "No, I'll go. Some norms are foolish. And childish." I got up, grabbed a file containing my notes, and exited the building.

The day's heat, though near as great, was more endurable than yesterday. The difference being that yesterday the wind, being southerly, was like a gust from an oven. This day it was northeast in the morning and now east so it was cooler on the skin. Yet the hottest part of the day was coming and it crept upon me with a languor and lassitude and relaxation so I could hardly move. Great heat stuck in my throat and made speaking an effort. All this to say that I wanted to solidify the terms with Onís before the day's zenith arrived.

I approached the carriage at the street's edge. The drape was partially open, a compromise between blocking out the sun and inviting me in. I tapped the window to signal my arrival. The curtain parted and revealed the tragic scene of Onís' defeated face.

"Care to join me, Mr. Adams?"

"I would be honored." I climbed aboard.

He turned and spoke Spanish to his driver through a small curtain. "Go around the ciudad. Do not stop. I do not care about the destination. Just keep moving." To me, in English, "I was sorry to hear about your mother."

135

"Thank you." I had no intention of getting sentimental with him. The horses *clip-clopped* and the carriage vibrated and started moving. Onís rode backward and I forward. "Shall we begin?"

"Yes. My master wants a deal between Spain and the United States."

"So does the President."

"I must know: were you aware of General Jackson's invasion during our last encounter?"

"Does that matter?"

"Yes. It will tell me whether you were devious or clueless about what transpires in your government."

"As my letter in the *Intelligencer* stated, Jackson took a broad reading of what were admittedly vague instructions from the President and the Secretary of War and pursued the Seminoles as a defensive action based on the information he had at the time."

"Clueless then."

"Believe what you wish."

"Why hasn't your government punished Jackson? His Catholic Majesty views such an action as a precondition for a deal."

"Then he will get no deal. The controversy over Jackson is settled as far as our government is concerned. He now serves as the Florida governor. We gave your master an olive branch by returning the captured forts to him." I leaned forward. "You must understand, this is your last chance to make a deal to protect your master's interests."

"Do not threaten me, Mr. Adams."

"I'm stating a fact. Make a deal with me in this carriage or your master will lose Texas and my government will recognize the South American rebels within a week. Florida falls to the United States as the apple did to Newton. You've nothing left to offer us."

His chin jutted out but I saw it quiver. "What is your offer?"

"The same one I made months ago. Cede the Floridas. Recognize our control of the Louisiana Territory with borders at the Sabine River and the 42nd latitude. In exchange, the United States will not recognize the rebels until after the war and will absorb up to five million dollars that Spain owes our citizens." He didn't respond. "You've been beaten. Take the deal. I remind you that Britain now supports our efforts."

He looked at his notes. "May I make a counteroffer?"

"Must you? This isn't a negotiation anymore. You had your chance and missed it."

"His Catholic Majesty requires greater concessions. More than Texas. He cares about the honor of Spain and the glory of the monarchy. He talks as though he is Charles the Fifth."

"Three centuries have passed. Three centuries that have not been kind to Spanish power."

"Spain will accept the Sabine as the Texas border, if the border is the river's midpoint."

"That's unacceptable."

"At least grant Spain access to the river."

"I will not. The United States must have full control for navigational and commercial purposes."

"Then what if we moved the northern boundary for the Pacific Northwest? Something to protect my master's honor."

"His honor is not my concern."

"Place it at the 43rd parallel."

"No."

"Yes."

"I feel that we are not reaching a deal, Mr. Onís. Instruct your driver to return me to my office. Do not write to me again. I cannot express the disgust I feel about having to carry on correspondence with you on subjects we evidently cannot adjust."

"Surely the President would be satisfied with a boundary at the 43rd parallel."

"He may be. I am not. The United States can do better."

"Do you realize that if I cannot secure a concession that a rebellion will occur in Spain? You ask my master to commit suicide."

I opened the file and handed him a single sheet of paper. "This is a letter I wrote to Mr. Hyde. It explains that the United States shall recognize the United Provinces since Spain is not negotiating in good faith."

"I negotiate in good faith!"

"No, you don't. You intentionally delayed an agreement at our last meeting and left Washington City."

"Did you already send this to Mr. Hyde?"

"Yes." A bluff.

"*Why?* I thought you said you would not grant recognition before the war ends."

"I can send another letter retracting this statement. But there is no point in delaying recognition and forming new alliances if Spain won't accept our offer. I can also send a letter saying the President will ask Congress to annex Florida without a treaty."

"That would cause war."

"A war Spain cannot fight. Your master can't even stop Bolivar from crossing the Andes to liberate New Granada."

"What about the Holy Alliance?"

"We'll accept the diplomatic consequences. I don't fear them since Britain endorsed us."

"Yes, because Britain allows her citizens to be murdered as long as her wealthiest men earn a profit."

"I'll be as clear as possible: if the next word out of your mouth isn't an acceptance of my offer, I will *personally* arrange for your return to Madrid so you can tell your king in *person* why he's losing Texas on top of everything else."

He leaned back, a vanquished man. His eyes watered and he resisted crying but couldn't control himself. "You lack a heart. You— you're a reptile, not a man." A pause. "I accept the deal. Let's return to your office and write out the terms."

"Very well."

Onís gave his driver new directions. I allowed myself a moment of happiness. The most important day of my life and my biggest accomplishment, at least since ending the war at Ghent. Acquiring Florida and a definite line of boundary to the Pacific would precipitate a great epoch in our history.

◆ ◆ ◆ ◆ ◆ ◆

"I congratulate the Secretary of State on his triumph," the President said. "The Adams-Onís Treaty is heading to the Senate and soon the United States will touch the Pacific Ocean."

I studied my fellow Cabinet officers. Calhoun restrained his jubilation. He knew he'd chosen his partner well. We had the momentum to vanquish our rivals. My confidence in him hadn't recovered but he could serve as my lieutenant.

Wirt and Crowninshield looked smaller than usual, like the pawns Crawford used to disrupt the board's left flank as his right side crumbled. That was too harsh. They cared about our national interests but knew Crawford's defeat stunted their advancement. I wondered if Crawford's partnership with Clay would survive now that they'd failed. He turned to the President.

"Let us not forget General Jackson's contributions."

"Yes, the General played a vital role," the President said, "but Mr. Adams displayed greater diplomatic judgment than any American since Dr. Franklin. I include my role in the Louisiana Purchase." He smiled at me. It wasn't large, because his expressions never were, but I appreciated the effort. "Do you have any ideas for the rest of your term? Five years is a lot of time."

An invitation to explain my grand vision. Securing Florida made such openness safe.

"My aim for the duration is to dismantle Europe's grip on this hemisphere. They cannot be allowed to oppose our ambitions."

"What ambitions?" Crawford asked.

"The world must familiarize itself with the idea that our dominion is the entire North American continent."

"Is that our goal?"

"Yes."

"How will it happen without war?"

"Think of how the sun keeps the planets in its gravitational field. It *pulls* them toward it. The United States are the sun of North America. Foreign territories cannot resist our pull. We shall absorb European claims. Spain has possessions to our southern border and Britain upon our northern border. It is impossible that centuries will elapse without finding these annexed by the United States. No spirit of encroachment or emption on our part renders it necessary, but because it is a physical, moral, and political absurdity that such fragments of territory, worthless and burdensome to their owners, should exist permanently contiguous to a great, powerful, enterprising, and rapidly growing nation. We will expand where we can and otherwise wait for our enemies to fade. For now."

Silence. Then the President banged on the table. Calhoun followed. Wirt and Crowninshield capitulated. Finally Crawford knew it was too awkward to resist and joined the others. They unified behind my vision and I'd never felt so secure in the Cabinet.

PART FOUR

LIBERTY AND JUSTICE FOR SOME
1819

XXIII

YOU BOAST OF studying hard, pray, for whose benefit do you study? Is it for mine, or for your uncle's? Or are you so much of a baby that you must be taxed to spell your letters by sugar plums? Or are you such an independent gentleman that you can brook no control, and must have everything you ask for? If so, I desire you not to write anything for me.

Tap tap.

I saw Mrs. Adams standing in our bedroom doorway. "Who are you writing?" she asked.

"George. He complained that Tom checked on him in Boston and told him he isn't studying enough. I'm offering some fatherly advice."

For some reason, she looked as though a tiger was carrying off her niece. "The *Intelligencer* was delivered." She raised the paper.

"Wonderful," I said. She gave it to me.

The headline was that William Jones, president of the Bank of the United States, had resigned. I was not surprised. The bank's western land speculation and credit extensions for investors created a bubble which now burst, causing nationwide bank failures. Many envisioned the worst economic crisis since Jefferson's embargo or even the catastrophe after the Revolution. The President's reelection wasn't assured after all, should he receive blame.

I prayed this toppled Crawford as Secretary of the Treasury but worried Congress would cut the military. This made my mission more difficult and I thanked God the Onís treaty was completed before this news. I'd barely succeeded and this would have thwarted me.

"Ahem."

I lowered the paper and saw that Mrs. Adams hadn't moved. "Yes?" I asked.

"What does it say?"

"It's about the hard times, dear. Europe's recovery since Napoleon's downfall means they don't require as many imports from us. The South produces more cotton than British mills require and so London banks are reducing our access to—"

"I already know this."

"Oh?"

"I overheard it at the Capitol."

"When were you at the Capitol?"

"This morning."

"*Why* were you at the Capitol?"

"The Missouri debates are fascinating. I was gathering information to write your father a letter. *He* respects my opinions."

"Politics is no place for a woman, Louisa."

"Don't be a hog. I went with a group of ladies to watch Mr. Pickering's speech."

"*Pickering.*" I hated that man. "Wait, Pickering's a senator."

"Correct."

"Women aren't allowed in the Senate."

"Vice President Tompkins was our host. He didn't seem to mind us surrounding him."

"He's a drunkard. How was the speech?"

She snickered. "'Twas a tax upon those who've passed the age where imagination blazes at each electric spark and produced an epic poem which delights upon first reading but fatigues upon revisitation."

"Did you rehearse that?"

"Possibly. His rhetoric is unnatural."

"So I hear." I leaned back on the bed. "Missouri." A pause. "Missouri. I know its application to join the Union is controversial. I first heard of it after Jackson's exemption but I can't say I've followed the developments. So focused on Florida."

"They're applying to be a slave state. They'd be the northernmost one and would give the slave powers a majority in the Senate."

"One reason I wanted the Northwest was to offset annexing Florida. Slavery spreading northward undoes that. This is troubling. Very troubling."

"Are you close to Mr. Tallmadge?"

"I believe he's in the House and represents—New Jersey?"

"New York. He's the main protagonist of this drama."

"I see." A pause. "I like him. He backed Jackson's invasion despite criticism from his Federalist supporters. A true leader." Another pause. "I should sit in on the debates."

"You'll attract attention."

"How do you know?"

"Because the ladies had more eyes on me than on Pickering."

"Hmm. They must be trying to discern my views."

She scoffed. "That's an awfully self-serving interpretation."

I shrugged. "I'm being honest."

XXIV

MRS. ADAMS AND I sat on the House balcony, which was full but not as packed as during Clay's recent speech. I looked at the congressmen and was reminded how many were freshmen. Members of Congress voted themselves a pay raise near the end of Madison's presidency and this proved unpopular so the voters sent many talented men home.

I watched Mr. Tallmadge make his way to the podium. I hadn't known he was sick, the end of his life and career was near and so he took a stand for righteousness. Mrs. Adams told me on our walk to the Capitol that Tallmadge lost his son a few months ago. Our wound from losing Baby Louisa was still bloody and I felt the anchor weighing upon Tallmadge's mind. I admired him.

"I know my proposed amendment has proven controversial," Tallmadge said, "especially with my Southern friends. But I remind them that it is a moderate proposal, and—"

"No!" shouted half a dozen voices from the Southern delegation.

"It *is*," Tallmadge said. "It frees those yet to be born in Missouri and only after they turn 25."

Mr. Cobb from Georgia pointed at Tallmadge. "You kindle a fire that only seas of blood will extinguish!" Tallmadge shook his head and many Northerners shouted at Cobb to sit. I recalled that Cobb opposed Jackson's invasion. He was not to be trusted.

"If a blood sacrifice is required to redeem this nation's disgrace, I will contribute my mite," Tallmadge said. Southerners shouted at him again. "I ask my Southern friends, do you not speak of slavery as our original sin?"

"*No!*" most Southerners shouted in unison. I heard a few dissenting voices but they were overwhelmed. The Southern position surprised me. I'd thought all Americans, even those who slavery profited, understood its evil and awaited its demise. My view of my country suffered its first crack.

Only a third of Americans lived in Southern states yet they held nearly half of all House seats because of a wicked clause in the Constitution which counted slaves as three-fifths of a person when determining each state's number of representatives. Slaves couldn't vote and they shouldn't have counted until they were free and enfranchised. It was cruel to count them so their masters could oppose their interests and unfair to Northerners held hostage by the over-represented South.

Clay looked smaller than normal in the Speaker's chair. He'd hardly said a word and his stare gave an impression of blindness. What was he doing? He hadn't recovered from his failed investigation into Jackson and I questioned if he held the sway to navigate a constitutional crisis. More importantly—what did he think about this issue? He owned 50 slaves at Ashland, his Kentucky plantation. Did he view the institution as a necessary evil or something else?

"I am unaffected by this language," Tallmadge said. "My purpose is fixed and interwoven with my existence. Its durability is limited with my life. It is a great and glorious cause, it is the freedom of man, it is the cause—"

"Why do you care if other men own slaves?" Cobb asked. "It doesn't affect you."

Tallmadge said to Clay, "I have the floor, Mr. Speaker. The gentleman from Georgia—"

Clay signaled Tallmadge to silence. "Is your aim to destroy slavery in this country or contain it to where it already exists?"

"Contain it. My proposal is moderate."

"Would spreading slavery not dilute it?"

"On the contrary, spreading it would cause disunion," Tallmadge said. The Southerners shouted. "I speak the truth. It would turn our accumulated strength into a positive weakness. It is a poison in the bosom, a vulture on the heart. Nay, it—"

"We all know you are Governor Clinton's pawn," Mr. Randolph said, standing. "This amendment is Clinton's scheme to seize power from the President, even if he must break the Union to do it." His index finger rose above him.

Randolph was a Virginian. A Quid leader, meaning he rejected the President's effort to govern by absorbing some Federalist ideas, like the Bank. An extremist and owner of over 300 slaves. I disliked his screeching voice and childish looks. That was judgmental, but in fairness, I spared no one from my opinions.

"That claim is insane," Tallmadge said. The Southerners booed him. He turned to the Northerners and gestured for help. Mr. Taylor of New York stood.

Randolph spoke first. "Admitting new states shouldn't be controversial and slavery is what the people of Missouri desire. The opinions of utopians and businessmen are irrelevant."

"The Constitution gives Congress the power to make needful regulations," Taylor said.

"Who determines what is needful?"

"This body, according to the Constitution. So if a regulation prohibiting slavery within any territory is deemed needful, Congress has the power to make the same."

"Northern demonization of slavery will incite rebellions," Randolph said. "As will free Negroes. They set a bad example. The South will have a French Revolution on its hands." The Southerners booed the prospect. "Now, if we were to send the freed Negroes elsewhere—" The Southerners booed again, attacking Randolph. He sat down and Mr. Smith from South Carolina, a Calhoun enemy, took his place.

"No more federal intervention into the South! That includes their damn bank!" Southern applause and Northern boos.

These sounds formed a cohesive unit representing legislative denseness. Another noise, one of metal scrapping metal, rose under it and formed a jingle. The Capitol Building still lacked windows and so this racket proved exigent. The congressmen quieted. Both they and those of us on the balcony waddled to the nearest windows and openings, peering out in groups.

Below was a carriage pulled by 15 Negroes. Half a dozen men were at the front and behind them were women and children. They were naked or half-naked. The master cracked his whip, striking a woman with cobra-like ferocity. An American flag hung off the rear like a cloak.

I swelled with anger at this display. An obvious protest against Tallmadge's amendment. Several men and women looked at me and I had to control myself.

Clay told the congressmen to ignore the protester and resume the debate. They returned to their seats but the discussion was ungainly. Cobb called the amendment a Federalist plot to divide Republicans between regions. This was an inept comment but it held an interesting point. A new alignment emerged before me. The House was divided by region and not party. Madison's *Federalist 10* said regional blocks would find balance but the West's rise undid such balance.

I watched for several more hours as the debate regained its momentum. The dawn of a tragedy. The prior generation imposed a philosophy of freedom on a slavery-obsessed society and hoped freedom would prevail. The following generation said *no*. Now these forces would wreck the Union. This was *Hamlet*, whose waffling introspection mirrored Congress' endless dispute.

It was a contemplation worthy of the most exalted soul whether the total abolition of the great and foul stain upon the North American Union was practicable. The Tallmadge amendment didn't give an answer. The House narrowly passed it but the Senate voted it down.

XXV

I SAT ALONE—not physically, but in my heart—at a table in the Calhouns' rented house. Compared to our house, which was a speck beyond Uranus, theirs sat comfortably among the terrestrial planets absorbing the sun's warmth. I drank Madeira and ignored surrounding conversations for my mind's sake, but only in part because I hoped to hear something interesting, or better yet, something useful.

The Tallmadge amendment's defeat did not end the controversy surrounding Missouri's statehood application. On the contrary, there'd been no debate more passionate since Hamilton and Jefferson. I was unsure of a way forward. My job was foreign policy, yet I kept weighing options. None worked. I stumbled over the same problem again and again—the slave powers ruling the South wouldn't surrender the institution making them rich and those of us who believed in the Bible and the Revolution viewed them with righteous horror. I had yet to absorb the passion with which Southerners defended the practice and couldn't escape the sound of the Negroes chained together and circling the Capitol.

The piano stopped, breaking my concentration. I looked at Mrs. Calhoun on the piano bench. She was with child, probably six months. The woman was perpetually pregnant in those years. The Calhouns appeared a happy couple. I was glad for them but envious. Mrs. Calhoun came from wealth and funded her husband's career and life in Washington, including parties like this one.

Mrs. Adams hovered over her, watching intensely, eyes wide and unblinking. She usually lacked excitement about anything, which depressed me, but music stimulated her deepest passions. Her father encouraged her interest in art and that interest attracted me to her. I was sad and perplexed when it faded and I relished its return, even while knowing it was temporary.

My wife's words cut through the surrounding chatter: "Can you play the *Moonlight Sonata*?" Mrs. Calhoun nodded and began the first movement. The ghost's cry set an interesting atmosphere to the festivities, fitting the national mood. My gut tightened as I feared Mrs.

150

Adams might sing—I hated the female voice set to music—but instead she closed her eyes and took several contemplative breaths.

My focus broke again when one of the Calhouns' slaves replaced my Madeira. I noticed Mrs. Margaret Smith engaging Mr. Calhoun in conversation across the round table. Smith was an interesting woman and a prominent novelist. Her husband owned the *Intelligencer*.

"Any news on Hector?" Smith asked.

Calhoun sighed. "No, unfortunately. The catcher I hired believes he's in Philadelphia." He leaned back in his chair, surmounting its frame. "They're fast, you know, and strong. That's why they're so valuable. I question if he'd have gotten so far if I'd stayed in South Carolina."

"But your service to the country is invaluable."

"You're too kind."

"Do you know why he left? Any word from your domestics?"

"I suspect free Negroes seduced him. He was a sleepy fellow and he wouldn't have left on his own accord."

Surrounding noise increased and I leaned closer, desperate to hear every word without being noticed.

"What do you think about Missouri?" Smith asked.

"Northerners—" words cut out "—doing. Negroes will rebel and people will die."

What?

Calhoun continued, "Evangelicals pervert the Lord's words to attack slavery. They'll let Negroes think their actions are justified."

"—image of God?"

"You tr—Devil's Advocate—curse that Noah put on Ham for seeing him naked—Israelites enslaved Canaanites—"

"—risk—uprising—"

"Britain knows—destroy the South," Calhoun said. "Northern merchants are in the pockets of London bankers and—politicians do their bidding."

"But what if—"

I noticed Calhoun turning in my direction. I looked down at my plate and then my lap. I felt mortified, hoping he didn't catch me eavesdropping. I raised my face and saw he focused on Smith. He hadn't noticed me.

I was stunned. Though I knew Calhoun was from a South Carolina plantation I thought he was enlightened about slavery, like General Washington. I had to clarify his stance, but not tonight.

"Rubbish," said the woman sitting to my left. She wielded the London accent I'd frequently heard at the Court of St. James.

I turned to her. "Pardon?"

"Oh, nothing," she said. "Just listening to a private conversation." She smiled and gestured to Smith and Calhoun. "It's a bad habit."

"What's your name?"

"Fanny."

I nodded. "Call me 'John.'"

"I know who you are, Mr. Adams."

"That's fair. What do *you* do?"

"I'm an actress. My troupe is touring the States."

"Ah. I love theater. It got me through my time in The Hague during the French occupation. What's the play?"

"*Othello*." My face must have scrunched, given her reaction. "Not a Shakespeare fan?"

"Oh, I am. *Hamlet* is the greatest work of literature since the revelation. But *Othello* is inferior."

"I'm sorry you feel that way. I consider it one of the great tragedies."

"Desdemona's fondling of Othello is disgusting. A viewer's terror and pity subsides immediately when he smothers her in bed because she's had her desserts. Her misfortunes are just for her having married a Negro."

"I'd thought you wise enough to oppose slavery, sir."

"I do. This is a separate issue."

"Really? If you're the best the Americans have, perhaps the soliloquy ought to change from *I hate the Moors* to *I hate the ni*—"

"I said no such thing. But who can sympathize with Desdemona? The lesson of *Othello* is that black and white blood cannot marry without —" I felt Mrs. Adams grab my shoulder. I looked at her. "What?"

"John…"

I noticed many eyes staring at me, including Calhoun's. Then I saw Fanny was furious. I apologized and didn't speak another word that evening. Why did I bother talking to people when I couldn't connect with them? I was too peculiar and didn't belong anywhere.

Should have stayed home with my books.

XXVI

"YOU'RE EARLY," CLAY said. He was in the midst of writing a note. I saw the stress running from his eyes down to his jowls, a mask he couldn't remove no matter how hard he pulled lest he tear his face.

"I give myself extra time to avoid tardiness," I said. "It's not always necessary but the policy is validated when it is."

He nodded, not listening to my poor attempt at small talk. He finished his task and dropped his pencil and then looked at me and I saw repressed nerves in how he held his eyes and lips.

"Take a seat." He gestured to the chair opposite his, this time lacking the book pile. I complied to show gratitude for his fitting me into his schedule. "What can I do for you, Mr. Adams? I assume you're here to tell me that Spain's government ratified your treaty with Mr. Onís?"

"Not yet. Ferdinand is taking his time. I'm here to ask about your plans for handling Missouri." I gestured to a candle on his desk. "May I?" He nodded and I lit a cigar.

"Is this an administration inquiry?"

"No. I ask as a citizen."

He studied my sincerity and tapped his finger on the desk. "I won't speak of Missouri, but we can discuss slavery more broadly, if you'd like." I appreciated the respect he showed me. Perhaps he contained hidden depths.

"That will do."

"Let's analyze the problem. Slavery declined after independence in part because the French Revolution and Napoleon's wars limited global trade for three decades. Peacetime spawned a resurgence and cotton's value has doubled. The credit squeeze has made no impact. Last I checked, a pound is worth 27 cents."

"How much has production expanded?"

"At least ten times since the dawn of this century."

"Really?"

"Oh, yes. Maybe more. There are individual acres in the South annually producing hundreds of pounds of cotton. The Southeast will be exhausted soon but Jackson opened the Alabama and Mississippi

Territories by removing the local Indians. Plantation owners are moving hundreds of thousands of slaves there, meaning thousands of Negro families are torn apart, since we renounced the Atlantic trade."

A shiver down my spine, both at the evil he described and the non-subtle implication that I'd contributed to it by annexing Florida and supporting Jackson. Did this mean his opposition to me was genuine, not jealousy? Was he right and I wrong? I felt chills, goosebumps, and sweat. I needed to fill time to avoid awkwardness and I noticed my cigar's foot had landed on the floor.

"So, our fathers' belief that slavery would die—"

"They were wrong," he said. "The opposite is happening. Clearly."

"Is it too late to stop it?"

"That's the question." He kept tapping his desk. "I've spent many days pondering this. A great many days. Especially recently." A pause. "The conclusion I've reached is that restraining slavery's growth before it overwhelms the republic can only happen gradually and that slaveholders must be compensated."

"That validates Negroes as their property."

"Which matters more to you, Mr. Adams? Winning the argument or producing change? *My* concern is that emancipation opens another problem: white people will never share the country. No one likes competition, especially with those they deem beneath them. Imagine being a farmer or manufacturer and losing to a former slave. That's humiliating and whites won't let it happen."

"So—"

"They also fear Negroes will want revenge, which should dispel any Southern claim that slavery is benign. Negroes are the most corrupt and abandoned of all Americans but it's not their fault. It's their condition. Anyone put in that predicament would have similar results. They won't be slaves once—if—emancipation comes, but they won't be free either."

"What can be done?"

He studied me again, then: "If I explain my vision, I want your word that you won't tell anyone. Especially the press." I nodded. "Everyone knows the obstacle is white hatred for Negroes. That's why they don't want millions of free Negroes living beside them. But I suspect they'd accept emancipation if the freed slaves were sent outside the country."

"Are you a member of the American Colonization Society?"

"No, but I know they have a similar plan."

"What's the timeline?"

"We'd emancipate and export 52,000 Negroes a year. That's the number of slaves born annually and removing that number would keep their population consistent as the white population grows, reducing white anxiety. Eventually they'll be comfortable enough for total emancipation."

"Where would they go?"

"Has the President not discussed with you the proposal he sent me?"

"What proposal?"

"Really? A bad day for assumptions. Unless you're lying."

"I'm ignorant of a proposal," I said.

"Hmm. The President discussed establishing a colony in West Africa to which we can send freed slaves. Undo the slave trade's legacy."

"Do they wish to return to Africa?"

"They will if it's the only way to coax the South to free them and to escape white domination."

"Is it a way? The richest slaveholders might become the wealthiest men on Earth. What if they say *no* regardless of colonization?"

"Their only alternative would be secession, which would deny them access to the northern banking which funds them."

"Or expanding slavery northward, which they're doing in Missouri."

"Do you have a better idea?"

"No, that's why I came to you. Your premise is rooted in people being rational and embracing moderation so everyone gets something, but history tells us we're an emotional species. The South is motivated by spite as much as by financial interest and the three-fifths clause enables them."

"You're challenging the Constitution now?"

"Why should I appreciate a clause which enabled Mr. Jefferson to defeat my father?"

He snorted and glanced at the Jefferson portrait on his wall. He said without restoring eye contact, "Do you have anything else to say on this matter?"

"Not unless we discuss Missouri."

"I must decline, sir. Congress is mired in negotiations and I can't have my thoughts circling Washington."

"I understand." I stood and gestured to the door with my mostly unsmoked cigar. "Good day, Mr. Clay." He nodded and I left, contemplating our relationship's prospect for change but discarded the improbability from my thoughts.

XXVII

I SPENT MY day working at the department building and had Maury deliver a note to Calhoun, inquiring his interest in walking home together. He sent a return note bearing a positive answer. We left the office shortly after five, each having evening plans. Calhoun and his wife were to dine with the Wirts while Mrs. Adams and I were expected at Colonel Tayloe's ball. Mr. Tucker, another prospective guest, sought a rematch after I trounced him at chess last week.

Awkwardness saturated the first minutes as we walked toward his home. Then I said, "I apologize for my behavior at your party."

A moment. "Oh, it's not a concern."

"You know I struggle in conversation."

"The rest of us only sleep soundly by knowing your brilliance bears an Achilles' heel." He paused. "One attends and hosts so many gatherings in this city that each memory replaces another. They all merge together."

"I appreciate your forgiveness."

"There's nothing to forgive. Truly."

I shifted topics. One more stepping stone before the main subject. "I received a letter from Mr. Gallatin. He asked to resign as minister to France."

"Oh? Did he say why?"

"He's tired of working with the Bourbons, who of course serve Metternich."

"Who do you have in mind to succeed him?"

"Would you be interested?"

"Me?" he asked.

"Yes. Time in Europe would enlarge your sphere of usefulness."

"And keep me from Washington."

"To my misfortune. You're my partner. This won't impact future elections. The President will win a second term and your term would end before 1824. This posting will increase your diplomatic experience and make you a more attractive candidate."

"An interesting case, but I must decline. Ministers' salaries are too low and my wife would protest." A pause. "I hope I've not given offense."

"Of course not. It occurs to me, Mr. Calhoun, that despite our partnership, we've yet to discuss Missouri."

I watched him at an angle. The intensity I'd not seen since Jackson invaded Florida returned and was stronger than I remembered. His eyes felt darker, his posture even straighter, his jaw locked like a swamp reptile. "I've speculated about where this crisis might lead," he said. "I don't expect it to trigger the Union's dissolution."

"You don't?"

"No. Though if it does, the South will likely ally with Britain against the North."

"Would that not return the South to colonial status?" I asked.

"Yes, but it would be forced upon them by Northern aggression and demographic size."

"Would the alliance be offensive or defensive in nature?"

"Both."

"In that scenario, Northerners would either move inland to avoid the British Navy and starve or move southward by land and rebuild."

"I cannot speak to that, but I foresee every Southern locality expanding its military."

"If the slave question dissolves the Union, it will obviously be followed by the universal emancipation of the slaves. A more remote but not less certain consequence is the extirpation of the African race from this continent. We'd have to bleach areas that have intermixed, but like all great reformations it will be terrible in its means and glorious in its ends."

"You favor disunion then?" he asked.

"I'm not sure I *favor* it, but my conclusion is it's the only solution to the slavery issue. Even a temporary disunion would allow for emancipation."

"I disagree. The Constitution allows for free and non-slave states to coexist. We only need to respect that."

"But the slave powers wish to expand into the North."

"Which the Constitution allows."

"That is aggression against the free states. Slave states will outnumber them and enforce their will. Especially through the three-fifths clause."

"It's their defense against Northern aggression, which has European support."

"Either way, the Constitution doesn't protect the North from slavery's encroachment."

"You wish to abandon the Constitution?"

"What I wish is to fulfill the Declaration of Independence," I said. "It's the Constitution's foundational purpose."

"Was the Declaration not fulfilled when Cornwallis surrendered at Yorktown?"

"Not the introduction. Where it reads that all men are created equal and have certain rights the government must protect and not violate." I looked at his face. "Those ideals are incompatible with slavery."

"That's a noble sentiment, but in the South, whenever those words are mentioned they're understood as only applying to white men."

"How can that be? Skin color isn't mentioned."

"It's implied."

"You're perverting the document. My father was one of its architects and I know Mr. Jefferson. I am telling you what they meant."

"In that case, the clause that *all men are created equal* is the most false and dangerous of all political errors," he said. "If the prior generation intended for slavery to die then the prior generation was wrong. It's a natural fit for the Negroes. Any man in South Carolina who tried subjugating a fellow white man to domestic servitude would lose his reputation."

"Conflating servitude with labor is one of slavery's worst legacies."

"It is not needed for all labor. I man my own plow, as did my father. Manufacturing and mechanical labor are also not degrading. But menial labor is the proper work of slaves, of Negroes. No white person could descend to that because it would enhance inequality between whites and lead to them dominating one another. The current system is better."

"How can you say that? This Missouri crisis has shown me the Southern soul."

"Which is?"

"Southerners admit slavery is evil in the abstract," I said. "They disclaim participation in its introduction and cast blame on Britain's shoulders. But there's pride at the bottom of their souls. A vain glory in their masterdom. They fancy themselves more generous and noble-hearted than the freemen who labor for subsistence and look down on us yankees for not treating Negroes like dogs." I paused. "Slavery taints moral principle. What could be more false than claiming that humanity's rights are dependent on skin color? It perverts reason. Worst of all, it claims that Christianity sanctions slavery."

His jaw was set, ready to drown a zebra in the Nile. "Be it good or bad, it is so interwoven in our society that to destroy it would destroy us as a people. But don't think, even by implication, that the existing race relations are evil."

"*No*? Slavery is not evil?"

"No more so than the conditions which men labor under in Northern factories." He spoke with Mark Antony's quiet fury. "Masters care for their slaves, unlike Northern money men and their workers."

"The South's philosophy hurts our character in Europe's eyes more than all other causes combined. They call us liars and hypocrites."

"Why should any Southerner care what Europeans think of us? They've conquered most of the planet and murdered six million of their own people in the recent war. Plus much of that continent is ruled by the Holy Alliance."

"How soon until we rule Mexico, the West Indies, the Bahamas, Cuba—"

"Make your point."

"I'm not done. Puerto Rico, Jamaica, California—the entire Caribbean. How long until we've conquered all those regions to spread slavery? All because the South is convinced expansion is necessary for slavery's survival. Always adding, never ceding. A foreign policy of perpetual war."

"Why not?" he asked.

"Why not? Do you want the Union to become a colonizing, slave-tainted monarchy? To extinguish freedom rather than defend it?"

"There's nothing wrong with spreading slavery. Some races are destined to rule others. It's part of nature. And yes, it's in the Bible and the history of our species."

"Our revolution was meant to improve upon earlier forms of government." We'd stopped walking. "Do you realize that promoting slavery will make Britain your enemy, not your ally?"

"Please. She'd prioritize the Union's destruction to remove her rival."

"Then why have we worked so hard to befriend London? You and me? My endless meetings with Mr. Canning, our—"

"To acquire Florida," he said. "Britain is the enemy. Any cooperation with her is temporary."

"Don't you support Bolivar? If you're comfortable with tyranny, why not back Spain?"

"So we can expand at Spain's expense, and since British support makes rebel victory inevitable, it's only logical to side with the winner."

"So you support monarchy?"

"You know I don't."

"Do I? You see slavery as a positive and it's no less despotic."

"There's no reason for white men to be ruled by a king. Your question forgets that I support equality among those to whom it is granted."

"Then I'll ask a different one. What if you were born a Negro?"

"What?"

"What if you were colored? Would you feel the same way about slavery?"

A moment. "But I'm not colored, so the question is irrelevant."

"Only by coincidence," I said. "You easily could have been."

"Then nature would have dictated that I be a slave." He nodded along to his answer.

"Really?"

"Yes."

"You expect me to believe you'd embrace the role?"

"I would. If I were a dog I would bark. If I were a snake I would slither. And if I were a Negro I would serve."

"Then why fear slave revolts?"

"Does the deer enjoy being prey to the alligator?"

We argued for another hour. Calhoun missed his dinner and Mrs. Adams and I were tardy for the ball. I lost at chess.

I could barely look at Calhoun when we separated. How far our partnership had fallen. I once viewed him as the most talented man in Washington and felt blessed to collaborate. No more. He used his gifts to defend evil. His selfishness astounded me. He thought it a good thing to wield total power over others and deny them the liberty needed for the fullest life.

That freedom and slavery were both enshrined in the Constitution was morally and politically vicious. Freedom was left to perpetuate tyranny. It condemned slavery as evil but doubled the masters' representation.

Our conversation made it plain that our fathers' gamble had failed. Slavery not only lived but mushroomed and it was incompatible with the Revolution and was attacking. If it captured Missouri, the Northern states would secede from the Union to remain unpolluted.

No amount of mental energy that I invested could find a solution to check this existential threat. My anxiety returned.

PART FIVE

THE PROPHET
1820

XXVIII

"I'M GRATEFUL FOR the opportunity to finally congratulate you in person," the President said. "The university's inauguration is the seminal achievement of any man following departure from the office."

"Your words mean more to me than you could know, sir," Mr. Jefferson said. The former President's light gray eyes darted to me. I nodded, too stressed about Missouri to formulate platitudes. His eyes shifted back. "It's a fitting end to my career. William and Mary provided a pompous curriculum and I want the next generations to have access to modern schooling. If I accomplished anything worth remembering—"

"It's irrefutable," the President said. "Authoring the Declaration of Independence, acquiring the Louisi—"

"I've purged those eight years from my memory," Jefferson said. A hint of a smile sat within his lips. Like Father, his mind remained sharp. His outward appearance was less flattering. The presidency had aged him. Especially the embargo, which ended his administration on a poor note.

The Monticello mansion reflected its owner's mental powers and foibles. We sat on chairs with pink cushions around a hexagonal table. Piles of woodwork resembled the Appalachians along the room's flank, showing Jefferson's lifelong obsession with transforming the mansion into a neoclassical masterpiece. Portraits of Isaac Newton, John Locke, and Francis Bacon hung behind him. He told me he considered them the three greatest men to ever live for their roles in modern physical and moral science. He'd placed busts of himself and Hamilton, his adversary, facing one another in the Entrance Hall—locked in their mutually suspicious gaze for all time.

Mr. Easton Hemings, Jefferson's 12 year old slave, stood behind him and fanned. Jefferson was warm from inspecting his garden on horseback that morning.

Over 100 slaves worked the Monticello plantation. Most were in the field growing wheat and tobacco while others built woodwork and nails for the home's neverending construction and reconstruction. Hemings was lighter than most Negro slaves I'd seen. I recalled an old rumor. While President, Jefferson's Federalist enemies accused him of an affair with a slave and fathering her children. His family denied the claim but Jefferson stayed silent.

He sipped from his glass of Château Haut-Brion. A luxury I doubted he could afford. It wasn't difficult to determine that Jefferson spent beyond his means, especially in this economy. Most expensive was the rebuilding of his library. He bestowed its prior incarnation to the Library of Congress after Britain burned it and used his slaves as collateral to repurchase his books. Unless I misunderstood the situation.

It was comforting to be in Jefferson's presence again. He'd become a substitute uncle after we met in Paris during the War of Independence. He was capable of in-depth conversations about any topic. Were I ignorant I'd have thought he'd dedicated his life to agriculture or medicine, given his knowledge. He endeared himself to me by being gentler than my parents. Our relationship strained when he opposed President Washington and Father but it survived and I supported his foreign policy in the Senate.

He said to me, "Your letter was a work of genius."

"The one on Florida?" I asked. He nodded. "Thank you, sir."

"It was vital to our navigating the aftermath of General Jackson's invasion," the President said. His warmth felt bizarre. Jefferson aroused an unusual side of him.

"You should translate it into French and Spanish," Jefferson said.

"To make our case?" I asked.

"So those who speak the languages can appreciate the letter's perfect construction."

"Oh. Our control of Florida shall remain controversial until King Ferdinand ratifies the treaty."

"He's taking a long time. Do we know what's keeping him?"

"He fears making such a large concession will be unpopular and, along with his imminent defeat in South America, will cause uprisings within Spain. Despite my leaving his control of Texas and Mexico intact."

"I thought that a strange decision. Why *did* you let Spain keep Texas?"

I stole a sidelong glance at the President to see if he wanted to answer. He didn't. I wondered if he felt insecure in our company.

"A minor concession was necessary to secure Mr. Onís' agreement," I said. "Ferdinand will lose it as he has the rest of this hemisphere. I'm aware our critics are better negotiators than us. They've apparently learned how to obtain everything while granting nothing."

"Annexing Texas would have denied us any hope of finding a solution for Missouri," the President said. Ah, I'd forgotten what his voice sounded like.

"True," I said.

"Texas would be a slave state," the President said, "so no regional balance would be possible."

"I suppose that's fair," Jefferson said.

The President continued, "Finding and maintaining regional balance should be the priority for the next few years. We ought to be content with Florida until Northern opinion is reconciled to future change and tensions settle."

An interesting point. The Missouri crisis made additional expansion unwise, dooming my mission. I would lack the record to become President. Should I even serve another term in my post?

Jefferson was contemplative. "Do you disagree?" the President asked.

A moment, then, "I am of the opposite opinion of you gentlemen. Rather than inflaming the regions, diffusing slavery over a greater area would facilitate emancipation."

I exchanged a look with the President. "Would spreading slavery end it?" I asked. "It would increase the number of slave states."

"Yes," Jefferson said, "but it would also make the Negro population in every locality so small that whites wouldn't fear reprisal."

His claim reminded me of Clay's. I decided to raise the Speaker's proposal after glancing at Hemings. "One idea I heard is sending the Negroes elsewhere. That keeping their population consistent as the white population expands will reduce fear that they'd rebel. Is that plausible?"

Jefferson sipped his wine. "My concern with colonization is the vast distance required to travel. There's enough controversy over moving the Indians beyond the Mississippi. Sending the Negroes across the Atlantic dwarfs that a thousand-fold. Still, it will prove necessary, either with emancipation or after. Whites and Negroes will never coexist in peace. There's too much mutual animosity."

I wondered if that was true. I'd pictured America becoming a republic for all races, but I was learning many new things about my country.

"The Missouri question absorbs my every thought," the President said. "I was unable to follow the closing stage of Mr. Adams' Florida negotiations. It looks to me that those who proposed the Tallmadge amendment sought greater power in Congress and the Electoral College, so as to take back control of the federal government from the South."

Jefferson nodded. "That's right. This isn't a moral question but one of power. We defeated the Federalist scheme to transform this country into a monarchy and now they pander to extremists who demonize slavery. They must be thwarted if our citizens in Missouri are to have their rights protected."

"Do the Northern states not share similar concerns about the slave states expanding their numbers?" I asked. I sensed the President disapproved of my question but Jefferson didn't mind.

"Self-preservation is vital for both regions. But the South expanding slavery will result in slavery fading away. The North enforcing abolition would bring apocalypse. That's why Missouri's fate is a momentous question, like a fire bell in the night. I'm filled with terror. It could be the knell of the Union."

"Because it reveals the North's aggression?" the President asked.

"Precisely."

"You'd blame those who oppose slavery over those who profit from it?" I asked. Again, I felt the President's disapproval.

Jefferson smiled. "I assume you're aware that I correspond with your father?"

"Yes."

"One reason I appreciate him is, whatever his misgivings about slavery, he doesn't preach to me about it. He understands the South must resolve this problem on its own." He sipped wine. "Northern-enforced emancipation would destroy Southern civilization and the North wants this because it will capture the federal government for the first time since 1800." He paused, looking tired. "These Northern politicians are this generation's George III, its Hamilton."

I'd thought that Jefferson was a high authority for abolitionism. He was hardly the great man I once knew. He'd pandered to his indulgences and inner weaknesses for so long he'd lost his judgment. More charitably, he'd given up on the issue after decades of fighting.

"What if expanding slavery to new states and granting it control of the government doesn't end it? What if the plantation owners are too greedy?" I asked. I assumed the President wouldn't fire me for insulting his mentor.

"Then I suppose the sacrifice made by the 1776 generation was useless." He stared at his glass. "We acquired self-government and happiness for this country and our sons have thrown it away. There's nothing left for me to do but weep." He raised his eyes. "The North destroying the South would be evil and the perpetuation of slavery corrodes justice."

"If it comes down to one or the other…"

A moment to think. This discussion exhausted him at his age. "If it came to that, the South would have to secede from the Union."

I hid my disappointment. The President was stoic. We sat silently. Jefferson knew I disagreed and the President opposed disunion, but he made no effort to retract his comment. His evolution was yet another tragedy. I'd thought I knew my country, her people, her architects, but she was gray, if that bright.

"Afternoon leaves us," Jefferson said. "Do you plan to stay for dinner?"

"I'm afraid that must wait until a future visit," the President said. "I'm meeting with congressional leaders in the morning and must return to Washington."

I felt awkward and wondered if other Cabinet officers were invited to the meeting.

"Sorry to hear that," Jefferson said. "Martha and the grandchildren will be joining me."

"You know I'd stay if it were possible."

"Of course." Jefferson said to Hemings, "Notify their carriage driver to prepare for their departure." Hemings nodded and left. "We have time." He finished his wine. "Tell me, James, whether it be next year or in five years, who do you hope will follow you in office?"

"I suppose it would be banal if I said that I'm only focused on my present duties. The truth is I suspect several men covet the presidency and I don't have a strong preference between them."

"What if it were General Jackson?"

"You believe he would serve?"

"Unquestionably. He's a fox on a hunt. A bear might be a more apt analogy. The sons of the men who promoted me now support him. Another sign of a lesser generation."

"You dislike the General?" I asked.

"Yes. He operates only through force. One more threat to the republic. He's unfit for office."

"Do you have a preference for my successor?" the President asked. My stomach clenched.

"My choice is Mr. Crawford," Jefferson said. My heart sank. "He was born in Virginia, and it would be best to place another Virginian in the Executive Mansion."

XXIX

CLOP. CLOP. CLOP.

We returned to Washington in an open carriage. I sat toward the front and was pulled backward. I did not care for how this affected my stomach. The President was opposite me, enjoying Virginia's foggy evening air. I studied him. Was he angry at how I spoke to his mentor? I hoped not. I'd known Jefferson longer but their relationship was closer and he didn't want to be seen tolerating an unruly subordinate.

I doubted his thoughts were anywhere but Missouri. Did he have a plan? How could he? How could anyone? Jefferson and Madison would fail. Father, obnoxious and unpopular, would die trying. Only General Washington might have succeeded for he had the best grand vision, though like everyone he was wrong in predicting slavery's death.

Missouri, and thanks to me, Florida, would give the South the Senate. The three-fifths clause granted them disproportionate power in the House and the Electoral College. The Supreme Court was the final refuge at the federal level but Marshall and his followers couldn't live forever and it would fall eventually, resulting in the slave powers dominating the government and chains strangling American potential and hope.

Illinois was admitted as a free state in 1818 but no other Northern territory could join fast enough. I had to know the President's thinking. Could he save the Union? I'd thought him slow and uncreative but if— that was the key word—he'd sent Jackson deliberately vague instructions then it was an act. Had the President blundered or masterfully hidden his hand?

I leaned forward and put my arms on my knees but the carriage's momentum threw me back. I regained my breath.

"Do you regret that we're not stopping at Highland?"

It took him a moment to process that I'd spoken. He blinked and raised his chin from his fist. "Can you repeat?"

I spoke louder. "Are you disappointed we're not visiting Highland? Given its proximity to Monticello?"

"Between the Missouri crisis and the upcoming election, my attention is needed in Washington."

I nodded. "Are you satisfied with our chat with Mr. Jefferson?"

"I suppose so. He's elegant with his pen but not his voice. I recall his instructions when I was to negotiate New Orleans' sale from Napoleon and Tallyrand. He told me the republic's fate was in the balance."

"Was he wrong?"

"At the time, yes. Remember Tallyrand's offer to sell the entire Louisiana Territory was a surprise."

"Mr. Jefferson feared Napoleon wanted to build a North American empire," I said.

"I know. I was there." He blew air on his lips to warm them.

"Can we discuss Missouri?"

"What about it?"

"Do you have a plan?"

He sighed. "I wish to keep my thinking in as tight a circle as possible."

"I'm the Secretary of State."

"Meaning foreign affairs is your purview. I asked you to attend today only because Mr. Jefferson wished to praise your Florida letter." A pause. "Focus on Spanish ratification of your treaty. Request a meeting with Mr. Onís." Another pause. "All I'll say is that the two crucial outcomes are that Missouri maintains the autonomy afforded to all states and that the Union is preserved."

"But are those goals contradictory?"

"We wouldn't have a crisis if we knew the answer. I've received proposals from every state legislature but none are satisfactory. Both chambers of Congress have at least half a dozen pending bills that will go nowhere."

"Are there any hopeful glimmers?"

He hesitated. "I suspect an answer will come from the Northwest. Or the old Northwest, since we've moved our boundary. Ohio, Indiana, Illinois. They're settled by Northerners but have many Southern-born politicians, so they have a nuanced view of regional antagonisms."

"Are you in touch with their congressmen?"

"I've said all I care to."

I shifted issues. He must have a weak point. "Do you agree with Mr. Jefferson that spreading slavery would end it?"

He appeared disappointed that I gave him no rest. "I don't wish to insult him, for he's done more for this country than anyone. But no, I don't agree." He admired a robin's nest within an elm tree on the trail. "Slavery can't end without pacifying white trepidation. Colonization is the answer."

"Is it true you wish to establish a colony in West Africa and build a home for free Negroes?"

His face shifted slightly toward me, though he still would not make eye contact. "Who told you?"

"I'd like to keep my source private, if that's all right."

"You're telling the President *no*? That's fine. I know it was Mr. Clay." I tried hiding my reaction but he smiled. He knew from my eyes that he was right. "Don't worry, we can discuss this. It affects foreign affairs. I've spoken to a handful of congressmen and they insist on appropriating 100,000 dollars which I told them was insufficient and gives the project a weak start. I'm attracted to this plan because it bridges the gap between abolitionists and slave owners. The slave owners will enjoy ridding the country of colored people at the public's expense. They'll try to gauge us but I'm going to minimize that where I can. The Virginia legislature told me it's considering gradual emancipation and I hope other Southern states will follow. State-led emancipation will receive less hostility than if the federal government takes the lead. The problem is that many men freed their slaves after the Revolution, creating a class of free Negroes who pilfer and corrupt those still enslaved. The South prohibited the practice, but sending the free Negroes to a foreign colony will woo Virginia into considering my request."

"Will the South cooperate with emancipation under any circumstances?" I asked. "I spoke with Mr. Calhoun after the Tallmadge amendment's defeat and he took a more positive view of slavery than I expected. He implied—"

"It's rude to discuss a man behind his back, Mr. Adams."

"I'm sorry, Mr. President."

"That's all right." Now he studied me. He wanted to know the state of my partnership with Calhoun and what that meant for his administration.

XXX

WOE WAS ME, for I was responsible for simultaneous moves. I've already described my surroundings once, so I'll keep this brief. I'd complained enough for Congress to authorize the construction of new buildings to house the executive agencies. Four new Georgian structures surrounded the Executive Mansion. The Department of State settled in the Northeast Executive Building while the Department of War was to the west.

Each building was 160 feet long and 55 feet wide. It contained a wooden staircase in the center that was flanked by rooms and offices. We made our largest room a library and I claimed an office in the southeast corner that was far superior to the closet I'd previously inhabited. An anteroom, a room for Brent, three for the Diplomatic Bureau, two for the Consular Bureau, one for the Bureau of Archives and Laws, one for the translator, and some others. I appreciated its proximity to the Executive Mansion but every morning its drab coloring dragged me to the depths of depression like a beige kraken.

I bought a three story house on F Street. The President and Madison each lived there when they served in my post. Mrs. Adams made a contract with a mason named Van Coble to build an addition to the house, a measure to which I acquiesced in as much as I didn't prevent it. She wanted the house to have four entertainment rooms and myriad bedrooms for the family who came and left weekly. I spent many evenings arguing with Coble to stone the cellar after he'd used brick without my approval. My wife did not wait for completion to inaugurate our new estate into Washington's foremost social hub.

Charles stayed with us that summer and one day I saw him holding Mary's hand. This confused me because George had said he and the girl were engaged but I didn't pry.

If the Northeast Executive Building's color was a leviathan lurking under the waves, the slavery in our community continued to pull my heart through the seabed and deep into the Earth. The Thorntons, our neighbors, owned several, and the saloon we patronized was a favorite establishment for traders. A Negro woman purchased there leapt from the third floor, though I didn't witness this.

♦ ♦ ♦ ♦ ♦ ♦ ♦

I met with Chief Justice Marshall at *Gadsby's*, a lovely restaurant in Northern Virginia. He brought his copy of *Emma* and sat under a windowsill bearing roses and a candle that aided the sunlight. Behind me was an unlit fireplace and a sailboat painting on the wall. I felt honored by any opportunity to speak with him. He was Father's key advisor as President and helped the old man navigate the Quasi War with France. Father returned the favor by naming him to his current position as he walked out the Executive Mansion's door.

He was pleased the Court's term was over, not least because the associate justices had left their home to ride the circuit. I asked him about *the* interesting case from this term and he joked that all the cases are interesting and special in their own way. I clarified that I meant *McCulloch v Maryland* and he gave a generic summary of the state taxing a federal bank and how that allowed states to weaken federal entities. He explained why the Necessary and Proper Clause made such action illegal. I noted how the case reflected the surge of rhetoric targeting the federal government and he said the rhetoric was comparable to Father's heyday. I then asked about his 150 slaves and he gave an opinion on colonization similar to Clay, Jefferson, and the President. He inveigled if the President had a plan for Missouri and I replied I didn't know and reversed the question to whether the Court could settle the issue. He said he couldn't comment about the law in advance and the Court couldn't prevent either region from seceding. That turned the conversation toward whether the President would resist secession and I concluded that was also unknowable in advance.

Our gathering ended on that upsetting note.

♦ ♦ ♦ ♦ ♦ ♦

A few days later, I rode a steamship to Massachusetts. Mrs. Adams complained of physical discomfort and stayed behind. This was for the best. I was to visit George and John at Harvard and didn't need her coddling them. Happy to leave Washington and escape the Missouri crisis gnawing on my spine and shoulders. I spent the voyage drafting my letter to Onís. It was better than anything I'd written in weeks and I felt grateful.

I stopped in Braintree to check on Father, Tom, Nancy, and their children. They looked good and said they argued less. The next day I learned that Harvard admitted Charles on condition of his passing a satisfactory examination in Sallust. This excited Father and I and we celebrated with cider that evening.

A letter from Brent soured the mood. Mr. John Dodge, a merchant residing in Haiti, again pestered him to urge a formal acknowledgement of the mulatto government there. Dodge had met with me before my trip and I'd given my objections. I had no intention of advising the President to recognize a mulatto republic during a national debate on slavery. Dodge hadn't considered this and then forgot my answer. I needed time to write to Brent so he could respond to Dodge and pass along my thoughts to the President, though that was a polite gesture and nothing more.

I left for Cambridge and stopped at Mr. Jaques' house. A virtuoso in breeding cattle. I saw several remarkable animals, particularly a bull and an English Dray Horse.

I found the boys. George was in good spirits but looked unhealthy. He again insisted that cousin Mary accepted his proposal. This confused me and I felt it premature because he had no prospects but John said George lived in a distorted reality. George said he and Mary were not engaged and when I asked for clarification he couldn't give it. More confusion.

We started the next day with Luke 18:18. *And a certain ruler asked him, saying, Good Master, what shall I do to inherit eternal life?* We read Proverbs 2:11 that afternoon. *Discretion shall preserve thee, understanding shall keep thee.*

We bathed in a creek behind Mrs. Black's and then I had breakfast with Justice Story. We spoke for an hour about the Supreme Court and the Department of State. He mentioned a rumor that commissioners under the Onís treaty decided not to receive insurance company claims. I'd have thought his report incredible had Crawford not said something similar. I opted to not indulge my own suspicions for there was danger of doing injustice by listening too much to suspicion.

My boys were half-shot when we reunited, though they swore they'd not had whiskey. We attended a service near the university and heard Mr. Edward Everett, the Greek language professor at Harvard. A young man of illustrious promise. George insisted I see him. His text was 1 Corinthians 7:29. *Brethren, the time is short.* It was the most splendid sermon composition I'd ever heard. More rich, more varied, more copious, and more magnificent than those of Buckminister. Some passages reminded me too much of Massillon. He spoke slowly and with distinct articulation. A still greater defect was a want of unity in his subject. The house was full but not crowded.

The boys were to give me a tour of the campus but a temperance advocate intercepted us beforehand. I opted to speak with her to validate her feelings. We discussed alcohol consumption within education. Students and teachers often arrived drunk to class. I asked about the temperance campaign's use of Christianity as the faith historically tolerated drinking and she made an unenlightened comment about how excess separates us from God. I mentioned moderation and she agreed and she asked me to add the letter T at my name's end and pledge abstinence. I declined.

The tour resumed and I saw the new divinity school. I left them in their college yard and entered the philosophy chamber and library. I met many friends and acquaintances, including Senator King, who was there offering his youngest son for admission.

I went by the President's House and found President Kirkland. He showed me the list of the students' standing. George stood 30th in his class and John was 45th in his, near the bottom. Both were unacceptable. I wished to speak to Kirkland but he was busy. I tracked down my boys and took them behind the Meeting House so we could have privacy.

"What will you do about this?" I asked them.

They looked at each other. "What is there to do?" John asked. "We study as well as we can. Or at least *I* do."

George's look of betrayal mirrored the expression the Lord gave Judas. To me, "I have something more important to discuss."

"More important than your grades?" I asked. "Have you impregnated a girl?"

"I wouldn't do that."

"Then what is it?"

"I need my next stipend in advance."

I processed this. "Why? Did you spend it on alcohol?"

"No, I lent my last 35 dollars to Bracket."

"Who?"

"He's a midshipman on the *Columbus*."

"Why did you give him the money?"

"Claudius, my friend, said Bracket would repay me."

"Did you know Bracket?"

"No."

"So you gave a stranger what money you had on your friend's word?"

"Yes."

I sighed. "Do you know where Bracket is?"

"No."

I sighed louder. "George—" He blanched. "George, the loss of the money doesn't concern me. I can give you 35 dollars. It's the heedlessness and want of consideration that—"

"Don't lecture me—"

"You need to hear this, son." I paused. "If you don't want a lecture, I won't lecture. But you should attempt to recover the money before I compensate you. Get a certificate from Bracket. If you can't, notify an officer on the *Columbus* and write a letter to its commodore requesting an inquiry."

"That's mortifying."

"You'd rather our family accept the loss? It was your mistake."

A moment. "Fine." His tone contained deliberate anger.

"Good." I looked at John and returned to George. "Now, let's discuss your grades." George broke eye contact. "How do you approach your studies?"

"Well."

"That's meaningless. What do you do when you're not in class? Assuming you attend class."

"I attend them. Usually. I do nothing but study."

"While drinking? When you study, or do anything, do you slow down and think through your actions or do you act and think later?"

He turned to John but spoke to me, "Perhaps if you'd not spent our childhoods in Europe—"

"Your floundering isn't my fault. My one failing as a father is that I indulge you too much," I said. George turned so he faced the opposite direction from me. John watched us, scared for his brother. I said to George, "You don't have to become the Secretary of State, son, but don't you want a career in public service?"

He snorted. "Why would I?"

"I thought my boys would follow in my footsteps."

"I'd rather die."

"Don't speak that way. What *do* you want?" A pause. "Tell me. Please."

"To dedicate my life to literature."

I took a breath. "Did your mother give you this idea?"

"Yes." He faced me.

"All right. That's all right. Can you be more specific? Do you wish to write? That won't provide a stable income but we can find a solution. Or to teach the subject? Become a professor? Because that won't happen with these grades."

"Neither."

"What then?"

"I just want to read. Read and enjoy."

"That's not a job, son. How will you earn a living?"

"I don't care. I want to be rich without working hard."

Slap!

He stepped back and rubbed his cheek. "Father," John said.

I ignored him. "Mediocrity will not be tolerated in this family. Weakness, laziness, sluggishness. You're an Adams. There are standards you must meet. You have potential and a gift coming from—"

"Do you understand—"

"Do *you* understand? You're throwing away an opportunity *anyone* would kill for. Think of the poor, of the slaves, who will never —"

"I don't care. That's not my problem."

"Stop your nonsense."

He ran around the building's corner. "Father," John said. I thought of my younger brothers. Was George on the same path? Was history repeating itself? How could I prev—no, I couldn't tolerate idleness. He was an Adams and that meant something. "Must you be cruel?" John asked.

"I am not cruel," I said. "You and all my children know that while my speech is sometimes harsh, my temper is not bad."

We fetched George. He calmed down and I dropped the subject, for now. We returned to their home and had a pleasant evening. I dined with Mr. Webster.

A sleepless night. Cares for my children's future prospects, mortification at how much time in Cambridge they wasted, George's health. I couldn't close my eyes. I hoped at least one of my sons had the ambition to excel but they came into manhood with indolent minds. They flinched from study. 30th and 45th in their classes. Incapable of exertion. Disappointment. Bitter disappointment. A blast of mediocrity is the lightest of evils. The night's reflection led me to direct John and Charles to stay with Father when on vacation. He'd mentor them. I would take George with me to Washington and keep him under my eye. Upon the others I could operate only indirectly.

XXXI

"I KNOW YOUR game, Mr. President. You're appeasing the Northern states so they won't nominate a challenger this autumn," Clay said. "You're jeopardizing our Union to win another term."

"Why come to my home and spout guff, sir?" the President asked. "You know me well enough to dismiss the notion that I'd place politics over the nation's safety."

I never saw Clay challenge the President in this manner and reconsidered any thought of a partnership with the Speaker. I'd be on the President's bad side, though this was irrelevant if we faced imminent disunion.

The President met with Clay and four other congressmen in his office. Senator King and Mr. Taylor represented the free states and Mr. Randolph and Senator Smith, a friend of Jackson, spoke for the slave powers. I sat in the corner next to the mass of cloth and wool containing the coat rack. Crawford was to my left. I thought his alliance with Clay had expired after the Speaker's investigation of Jackson failed yet it endured. Judge Hay, the President's son-in-law and closest advisor, was in the opposite corner from Crawford, the globe squishing him.

"What I know," Clay said, "is that you seek to restore the Tallmadge amendment and—"

"That's a lie, wh—"

"—you would deprive the citizens of Missouri the rights guaranteed to other states—"

"No—"

"—to choose whether they be slave or free, denying citizens their property, and harming Negroes concurrently."

"How's that?" Taylor asked.

"They'll be given greater material care—food and shelter, for example—if their masters are enriched, instead of living in lesser conditions in the South," Clay said.

This wasn't the same man with whom I'd recently spoken. Did he support slavery's expansion or not? He appeared sincere in our meeting, meaning he pandered to Southerners today. He played with fire while degrading his virtue and making him untrustworthy.

"I thought you governed by no vulgar prejudices," Taylor said, "but you'd have the North submit to the slave interests. It's ludicrous to suggest we'll heal slavery's sins by expanding it."

"What's ludicrous is the North subjugating the first state formed from the Louisiana Territory," Clay said. To Randolph and Smith, "I shall return to Kentucky and raise an army to defend Missouri's rights before I let that happen." I watched the President. He made no visual response to the Speaker's rebellious threat. He looked fatigued and likely knew Clay was pontificating to win the Southerners' favor. Clay continued, focusing on the President. "My sources tell me you've dined with most Northern congressmen."

"To learn what will satisfy them and to form a compromise that will save the Union. I've no intention of robbing Missouri's citizens of their rights."

"Ah," Clay said. "What is the compromise? What must the South lose to be treated fairly?"

The President nodded at Taylor. The New Yorker said, "I propose we use the Mason-Dixon line as the barrier between free and slave states in the future."

Randolph sneered. "An unserious idea."

"It is serious."

"You'd rip away rights from all future states above the 39th parallel?"

"We'd have a policy to prevent this crisis from reoccurring. It would preempt applications from future states."

"Why should the South make this concession?" Smith asked. "Why not let the states make their own choices?"

"Because the slave states would capture the federal government," King said. "Mr. Taylor's idea will preserve the North's vital interests."

"By robbing the states and the people of their rights," Randolph said.

Clay said to the President, "You support this idea?"

"It's a reasonable concession to keep the North in the Union," the President said. "My only concern is whether it's constitutional to preemptively determine whether new states will be slave or free but I can instruct Mr. Wirt to ask Chief Justice Marshall."

"So you *are* buckling to the North," Clay said. "Just differently than I anticipated. More boldly."

"This is a surrender to the South," King said. "The slave powers will still have a majority in the Senate. A true compromise would include another concession."

"Such as?"

"An amendment to nullify the three-fifths clause," King said. Smith jumped to the door and exited. "Why should the South have an unfair advantage in the House and Electoral College?"

"Mentioning that idea publicly would trigger secession," Clay said.

"Which is why it's not part of our proposal."

"Does the North wish to destroy the South?" Randolph asked. "Such ideas are Eden's apple for the slaves."

"No, no," Clay said, placing his hand on Randolph's arm. "The North is not so vile. It's obvious that Senator King wants to rebuild the Federalist Party and run against the President again this November."

"That's false." King turned to the President.

"This is immaterial," Taylor said. "We're not asking to nullify the three-fifths clause, only for a division—"

"Maybe we should ask to nullify it," King said.

"There it is," Randolph said. He exited through the door Smith had left open.

"Rufus, the South will secede if we make that proposal," Taylor said.

"The North will secede if we don't," King replied.

The New Yorkers bickered, shouting across the table. Clay looked at the empty seats beside him and at the chaos surrounding the President. "I'm sorry we couldn't make more progress," he said.

Many times I've felt a listlessness which, without extinguishing the love of life, affects the mind with the sentiment that life is worthless. This was such a time. The Union was doomed. Doomed. There existed no compromise to preserve it. My mind was my best and only weapon and it was empty. I hated the sensation but months of thought had gone nowhere. What I witnessed gave me no reason to think the President was the devious operator who'd rise to the occasion and Clay, in his arrogance, fiddled while America burned.

Damn him!

XXXII

HE WILL WIPE away every tear from their eyes, and death shall be no more, neither shall there be mourning, nor crying, nor pain anymore, for the former things have passed away.

I reread Revelation 21:4 thrice. I navigated myself so I knelt by my bed. Eyes shut but I couldn't focus. Chills and goosebumps and sweat. I locked onto my breathing which felt arduous and wondered whether my face was red or pale. I noticed the spit in my mouth. Was it always this much? Did I make salivary noises when I spoke? Another flaw. Why did bodily fluids afflict me so? This and my eye fluid, would urine be next? I ought to read the passage on the Flood.

No joking. Focus.

Who was I kidding? I couldn't. This felt worse than normal because it was. Father was as important as any man to creating this country and he'd watch her dissolve with me as Secretary of State. A crushing end to his life. It would kill him, of that I knew. At least Mother wouldn't have to endure the sight. A terrible thought.

I heard a melody. My stress' source? It tugged strings within my conscience. I stood and exited the bedroom and followed the sonic sound to the rightward entertainment room, which my wife called the music room. There she was, performing Bach's *Come, Sweet Death* on her harp.

Her body was locked, her head down, her molars grinding, her fingers vibrating, her breathing cycling. I watched her for several minutes until she paused. Her eyes opened, bloodshot. A tear sat at her duct's edge and I moved to wipe it but she got it first. We stared at each other.

"Did I disturb you?" she asked.

"No."

"Were you sleeping?"

"No."

Silence. "I take it you're equally desolate?" she asked. I nodded. She turned to her harp. "The state of this Union—the nation, I mean— I'm trying to ward off another fainting spell."

"Did you think of Baby Louisa?"

"I couldn't stop it. The tiniest thought consumes a day." She returned to me. "Please don't be angry."

I saw her fear. That's what I produced in her. That was our marriage. "I'm not."

She sighed and shifted posture and winced. I didn't know why. "I take it that the meeting at the Executive Mansion went as poorly as expected?" she asked.

"Worse."

She grunted. "Lovely."

"The only thing missing was a duel." A pause. "I don't foresee the President or Clay resolving this."

"Are you surprised?"

"Disappointed."

"I suppose I thought the President would know what to do, given the experience he brought to the office. Mr. Clay's failure is predictable."

"I thought you liked him. You enjoy verbally combating him at parties."

"Yes, but he's your chief adversary. Or one of them. It shifts by the day." She smiled. "He's domineering and usurps a greater proportion of discourse than is earned. Always offending one person or another."

I smiled too. "Do you mind if I join you?" I gestured to her piano bench. She moved and I sat beside my bride. More silence. "Why must your family own slaves?"

"I don't know, John. The world's changed so quickly." She glanced at me. "You have my word that a slave will never step foot in this house. Not to serve."

She knew just what to say. "You promise?" I asked.

"I just did."

I kissed her cheek. Should do that more. "Am I unlikable?"

"John, your intellect could overpower anyone."

"But not befriend them. Not rally them. I lack the skill of a Jefferson or a Clay—"

"You wield more substance than either. More than anyone since your father and General Washington. Public service is your destiny."

"There may not be a public to serve much longer."

"That's fair." She giggled but then suppressed this. "I suppose you could always work in Massachusetts. I'm sure they've forgotten the embargo by now."

I touched her hand. "Thank you, my dear."

"Of course, John." She stared at me. "Still striking."

"Oh, please." I stood up.

"What?" she asked, her voice crackling with laughter.

"I'm grotesque."

"Don't you dare say that. I see the handsome man I fell in love with."

"You were a naive 20 year old."

"Perhaps on other topics. Not that. You were naive too."

"Is that a fact?"

"Oh, yes. You didn't know I came with a brain. Do you remember when I complimented you for dressing decently for once and you said it wasn't my business?"

"Yes. You said, in that case, I should marry a different girl." I smiled. "I should have known what trouble you'd cause me." The smile dissolved. "The future appeared so bright back then. There's something sweet and something sad in the remembrance of ancient enjoyments."

She stood and took my hand. "Not all joy is ancient." She guided me back to our bedroom.

XXXIII

BRENT LED ONIS on a tour through the Northeast Executive Building and brought him to my office. I know how thrilled you must be to see him again. I ate crackers and had two cigars on my desk but one was already pinched between the Spanish minister's lips. "Thank you, Daniel," I said. Brent nodded and closed the door behind him.

Onís probed my office. Red was its defining color, symbolizing our valor but he joked I used my victims' remains as paint. A crimson couch and matching armchair with cherry wood legs. Ample windows granted access to light from both the falling sun and rising moon while bookshelves lining the walls contained our department's secondary library. I'd restrained their unrivaled primacy to leave room for file cabinets, my maps, and my desk.

"Impressive," he said in English. "Much nicer than the surrogate."

"How is crossing the Atlantic these days?" I asked.

"It is less troubled than it was five or six years ago when Britain and France fought to the death on the high seas."

"The United States remember. Trust me."

He snorted. "Yes, I suppose both our nations suffered, as General Martín's command of the Pacific attests. With George III's passing that era recedes deeper into the past."

He turned toward me and I gestured to the cigars. "Do you mind if I start mine? You can take the spare with you."

"Do as you wish. I've no intent to impose."

"Of course not." I lit the cigar in a candle that stood in the corner. "I'm ready if you are." He motioned in the affirmative. "Why hasn't your king ratified our treaty? Why refuse his engagements, perform his word, do justice to those whom he acknowledged Spain has done wrong? The only logical conclusion is that he believes that delaying ratification prevents us from recognizing the rebels."

"In part. Much has happened, Mr. Adams, since our agreement in the carriage. Back then your country was strong. Now the economy retracts and your internal disputes raise the question of whether the Union will survive the year."

"Your master is waiting to see if we'll collapse before ratifying?"

"In effect."

"Did the Holy Alliance instruct him to delay?"

"No. Prince Metternich encourages him to ratify because he hopes adding Florida to the Union will exacerbate the slavery crisis. Alexander accepts ratification as inevitable. It was his Catholic Majesty's advisors who convinced him the treaty failed to defend Spain's honor."

I moved the cigar further from my face so smoke wouldn't cling to my eyes and nostrils and lips. Had I forced too many concessions from Spain that they wouldn't ratify? Onís was right. I was arrogant. The President had warned me.

"Conveying this to you is only one reason I'm here," he said. "I bring a more important message."

"Yes?" I had trouble maintaining eye contact. He enjoyed seeing me frail.

"My master authorized the transfer of his claims in Florida to—" searched for the words "—his wealthy friends."

A cannon went off in my chest. "What?"

"It is no longer within his Catholic Majesty's power to give Florida to your country. Under the Law of Nations, your government must respect our citizens' private holdings."

I snapped my cigar and tossed it aside. "Does your master not care about the Spanish monarchy, and all kingly governments, being held up to the world in an odious light?"

"Ratification triggers his overthrow. This saves his throne."

"And you. I suppose you think that by preserving Spain's North American holdings your king will grant you the Cross of Isabella," I said. He was silent and blew smoke through his nostrils. "I knew you lacked virtue, but—"

"Your actions have not guaranteed you a desirable afterlife either, Mr. Adams, and no priest can cleanse you. You took advantage of our weakness. The favor is returned."

Onís had his elbow on my desk and his cigar covered part of his face. I stood, knowing it was a retreat but failing to control myself. I stared out a window. "Why cling to this continent?" I asked. "The war in

South America is in its closing stage. Bolivar has liberated Venezuela and Martín did the same for Peru. Spanish reinforcements under General Riego mutinied and captured Andalusia for the liberals. Your master's colonies are lost."

"Must I repeat that both our countries are weak?"

I searched for a place to counterattack, but he was right. The last thing we needed was another slave state. Ferdinand's delay let Crawford and his partisans insult my performance and delight in my failure. I had to try something, anything.

"Communicate this to your master," I said. "If he does not ratify before the year's end, the President will ask Congress to unilaterally annex everything owed to us under the treaty and to place our southwestern border at the Colorado River, not the Sabine. And we'll recognize the rebels."

"That is an empty threat. Congress has never been less functional. The treaty increases pressure on your country's windpipe as it chokes on its own hypocrisy. I will enjoy watching the Holy Alliance carve up the Union's remains even more than I'll enjoy watching General Jackson vacate Florida."

"You're wrong. If we don't act with promptitude and vigor we will lose consideration in the world's eyes. *That* is when other nations will take advantage of us. As this government's senior diplomat, I instruct you to send your king this message."

"Very well. I'll send it to him and he'll laugh." He dropped his cigar's rump on the floor. "I believe we're done." I nodded and he left, leaving the spare cigar.

I stewed for the next days. Four years. All that work. The treaty was dead. My enemies would scorn me, but it was not they who beat me but the slave powers. Perhaps they were my true bête noire.

Nothing to look forward to but disunion and its aftermath.

XXXIV

MRS. ADAMS, MARY, and I attended church at the Capitol that Sunday. Services had been held there since President Washington's day. The House was overflowing and it was with great difficulty that we obtained seats. John England was our visiting preacher, the Bishop of Charleston and the first Catholic to preach there. He read a few prayers and delivered an extemporaneous sermon of nearly two hours' duration. He closed by reading an admirable prayer and then he spoke to me after the service and said he'd call and take leave of me tomorrow.

We exited and waded through the crowd. Many representatives attended every Sunday when divine service was performed in the Hall. Some considered it their public duty but that day saw more than usual. Most feared for the Union's survival. I felt gloomy both for disunion and for my treaty, though its breakdown wasn't yet public knowledge.

By 1820's end I would witness these undoings and by the 1820s' I'd endure their effects if this course proved inexorable. The rest of our lives in disunion's wake. I felt ill thinking about it but supposed we'd rebuild in Massachusetts.

"Mr. Adams!" I was so lost in my concerns that my name didn't register. "Mr. Adams!" We turned and saw Mr. and Mrs. Clay scurrying toward us, masterfully maneuvering through the crowd. They slowed as they approached us. "Mr. Adams." Out of breath.

"Mr. Clay." I made a short nod. "Good to see you both."

"You as well, sir." He turned to my wife and bowed. "How are you, Louisa?"

"Fine, fine. Lovely service."

"I agree entirely."

I nodded to Mrs. Clay and gestured to my niece. "This is—"

"Mary, of course!" Clay said. He bowed to her and said, "Would you ladies mind if I stole Mr. Adams from you? I promise to return him in a few minutes."

"What do you require of me?" I asked.

"Just a walk around the block. Once or twice."

"Do return him in one piece," Mrs. Adams said.

"He'll be in prime condition!" Clay said. My wife laughed. He looked at me. "Or—I'll see what I can do." The ladies laughed together.

Clay guided me until we were alone. What was he up to? His performance in the Executive Mansion made me think I needed my head examined for respecting him. My meeting with Onís fed this for it reminded me of Clay's conduct during the Florida crisis. He'd pushed the President to quarrel with Spain and hadn't played his game skillfully and so inadvertently promoted the treaty because calling for action independent of the President had alarmed Spain and gave us an argument to bring her to reasonable terms. I knew he'd seize upon Ferdinand's land transfers once they became public. Perhaps he knew and that's why he wished to speak. He bore dark rings under his eyes as textured as Saturn's.

He glanced behind us. No one near. "What's this about?" I asked.

"I need you to speak to the President."

"Why?" I injected anger into my voice.

He looked at me. "Do you care for the Union or not? Are you aware that every sentence spoken within Congress these days is of disunion and civil war?"

"Civil war?" I asked. He nodded as though it were obvious. "I assumed disunion would come peacefully."

"It's impossible to know until the Rubicon has been crossed and I'd rather not cross it."

I sighed. "Do you support slavery's spread?"

"What?" He giggled. "Oh—the meeting? That was a show. I assumed you knew. I need the South to trust me."

"You're taking a huge risk."

"I have no other choice. Now, what I'm going to tell you must be held in the strictest confidence. You mustn't tell anyone before you speak with the President. Not even Louisa."

"What is it?"

"I believe I've found a compromise to defuse the Missouri issue." He waited for me to speak but I didn't. "I've spoken to some Maine representatives and I think they're interested in separating from Massachusetts. We could bring them into the Union simultaneously with Missouri as a free state. That would preserve the Senate's balance."

I couldn't believe it. Maine was part of Massachusetts long before I was born. A fixture of reality, even more than the Union. "You mean to trade Maine for Missouri?" I asked.

"Yes, exactly. Also, Senator Thompson spoke to me about establishing the Mason-Dixon line as the northernmost barrier for new slave states. The same proposal as Mr. Taylor's. That will protect the North from slavery's encroachment and prevent this crisis from reoccurring."

"Why are you telling me this?"

"I need you to tell the President. Pushing this through Congress will be my ultimate test and I want to know he'll sign it once I'm done. His support will encourage members in both chambers."

"But why me?"

"Despite our differences, I know you're a principled man. Too principled for your own good. You'll execute this task with care and win the President's favor."

"But why not ask Mr. Crawford? He's your partner."

"*Temporary* partner. I don't trust him. He'd stab my back for a minor short-term gain."

My opinion of Clay changed every time we met. I wanted to test his openness. "Do you already have a plan for passing this?"

A moment. "I'll tell the Southerners this is the price they must pay for admitting Missouri as a slave state. They'll divide into moderates and zealots, as always, but by my count we'll have enough moderates if the President signals his endorsement. The North I'm less worried about because the President has already met with most of their representatives. My biggest concern is that Southerners in the House will accuse me of shenanigans over Maine and Mason-Dixon and will vote against the bill if all the sections are introduced as one piece of legislation. I'd break it into thirds but the Senate prefers combining related bills. That means a standoff between the chambers but I'll appoint a joint committee of moderates from both regions and they'll figure it out."

A light shone in the dark, a flickering candle flame in damp catacombs. The Union—the treaty—the future—would live. Most importantly, liberty's advancement—wait.

"Another slave state," I muttered. "Guarantees of new ones south of Mason-Dixon. Are we delaying the inevitable by compromising with slavery?"

"What are our alternatives?"

"Secede with the 13 or 14 states that are unpopulated with slavery and form a new union that stands for emancipation. A union that's true to its word."

"*The* Union is sacred, Mr. Adams. I'm not ready to give up on it. Not yet. Are you?"

"I suppose not."

"We'll work on your attitude. When can you speak to the President?"

"There's a Cabinet Meeting scheduled for tomorrow. Are you comfortable if I raise it there? He'll want to speak to the Cabinet anyway before making a decision."

He considered this. "Yes, that will do." A faint glimmer in his eyes, a step toward tranquility. "Let us return to the ladies if we've no more business to discuss."

XXXV

I KEPT MY eyes on the table. I didn't want my colleagues to see the nerves waltzing across my face. Needed to anticipate Calhoun's position. Was our partnership wounded at Austerlitz or had I consigned it to a mass grave along with my many other failed alliances?

I was the only Cabinet officer who wasn't a Southern slave owner. I hoped they knew this was the one chance to forge a compromise but I feared their passions ruled them. My eye liquid returned that morning and it disrupted my focus and I knew Crawford used it to highlight my defects. If he opposed Clay's scheme it would only be because I supported it and I would fight him until all that remained of one of us was a blood stain on the carpet. My other enemies were wrong but were motivated by more than their own interest. The river basin of Crawford's ambition lacked a drop of virtue.

The door opened and we stood as the President entered. Judge Hay shadowed him. "That's all for now, George," the President said. "Let's continue our discussion this evening." Hay left and the President went to his chair. "Be seated." We did as commanded. A stilted confidence failed to hide his voice. "I've learned of a potential compromise to resolve the Missouri crisis. Today's meeting will center around that proposal." I'd told him that morning of Clay's message so he could think it over before the others placed their harpoons in him. He put five cards on the table. I retrieved one and saw it bore two questions. The first read:

Does Congress have a constitutional right to
prohibit slavery within a territory?

Perhaps I should have spoken to Calhoun and given him time to consider this issue but I'd judged the risk too great. Crawford, the leader of the Southern block, went first.

"Article 1, Clause 2 is the relevant provision." He looked at Wirt for confirmation. To the President, "It says Congress can regulate the territories but can't prejudice the federal government or the states."

198

"Meaning what?" the President asked. "What is being regulated? The land that comprises the territories or the people living there?"

"I read that to mean the land, not the people."

Of course he chose that path. He wouldn't have been an affront not just to man and to the class Mammalia but to vertebrates if he hadn't. The President turned to me but I restrained myself. Instead he asked, "What say you, Mr. Wirt?"

The Attorney General cleared his throat. "The Constitution grants Congress the power to create needful regulations in the territories. *Needful* is the key. We'd have to determine if that word contains issues pertaining to slavery."

"There's the rub," the President said. "A ban on new slave states north of Mason-Dixon, aside from Missouri, is the piece of the proposal I find most troubling."

"I for one don't see anything in the Constitution implying slavery is needful."

Heinous yet predictable. I remembered Randolph's argument months before. My, how these Virginians all thought alike.

"Does the clause not say that Congress may regulate property within the territories?" the President asked.

"Property belonging to the United States, not their citizens," Wirt said.

"Federal property then?"

"Precisely."

"Your thoughts, Mr. Adams?"

"I disagree with the Attorney General. I've no doubt of Congress' right to interdict slavery. I urge us to remember that Congress may *dispose* of needful regulations for the territories. Dispose in this context means to transfer legal control over. That tells me Congress may set regulations regarding the territories' transfer to separate bodies. A new state government, for instance."

"But would prohibiting slavery be such a needful regulation for transfer?" Wirt asked.

"If the people and their property within the territories were not connected to powers to regulate the land, the powers would be meaningless."

"What suggests slavery is needful?"

"It's needful if it addresses why the Constitution was formed. The Constitution's preamble mentions establishing justice. How could justice not include the interdiction of slavery where it doesn't exist?"

"You're stretching the Constitution," Crawford said.

"I am not, sir. I am not. I am making proper inferences based on its wording and logical implications."

"Who defines justice?"

"I just spelled it out. Shall I do it again?"

"Enough gentlemen," the President said. "An opinion, Mr. Calhoun?"

The Secretary of War's intensity was not what it had been when he first joined the Cabinet. His tobacco-colored eyes were stale and his skill at knifing through conundrums had dulled. Most likely he was never what I'd thought, never the most competent man in Washington. He'd worn the costume and I wished it true. He'd done nothing but disappoint me. I waited for him to speak to learn if he'd do it again.

"I see no reason to think the power is implied."

Yes, again. He wouldn't share my voice but I couldn't let that stop me. "Does Congress lack the power to preserve the Union?" I asked.

"At the expense of the states?" Crawford asked. "The states that voluntarily formed the Union?"

"*Territories*, sir. Details matter."

"I'm only interested in legal analysis today," the President said. "Policy and philosophy can wait."

"Our discussion underpins legal analysis," Crawford said. "Our priorities shape the extent to which we're willing to read into the document whatever we please, to connect dots that are separate."

"Do you—do any of you—have a substantive critique of Mr. Adams' argument?"

Crawford nodded to Calhoun. "A plain reading of the clause grants a narrower interpretation than Mr. Adams' reading," my partner said.

I said, "Does the clause exist alone or under—"

"That will do," the President said. "I'm sorry no consensus was reached." His expression was that of a Prussian officer beneath Napoleon's cannonfire. If he accepted my argument, it was not on its face but because he was desperate for the compromise to be constitutional. "Turn your attention to question two." It read:

Does Congress' right to ban slavery from a territory carry over to when that territory becomes a state?

"Let's take a vote," the President said. "Who believes that, assuming Congress can ban slavery from a territory, that ban would *not* carry over into the state resulting from that territory?" My colleagues signaled in the affirmative and I stood alone, again. The President said to me, "Would you like to begin?"

"Yes, sir. Congress' interdiction of slavery would bind the state as well as the territory." Crawford shook his head and I spoke louder. "The interdiction in the territory means the people, when they form a constitution, have no right to sanction slavery."

"You grant the people no rights, do you?" Crawford asked. "State legislatures could of course alter their constitutions. Nothing in the federal Constitution prohibits that. The Northern states could restore slavery tomorrow if they wished."

"A state legislature cannot by any rightful exercise of power establish slavery. The Declaration of Independence not only asserts the natural equality of all men but that just powers of government are derived from the consent of the governed. A power for one part of the people to make slaves of the other can never be derived from consent and is therefore not a just power."

"The Declaration isn't legally binding."

"It states the goals that the Constitution is meant to achieve."

"Where is that written?"

"Gentlemen…" the President said.

"Nevermind," Crawford said. "I see Mr. Adams lets Senator King do his thinking for him."

"It *is* King's opinion," I said, "and it is mine and also the opinion of those who live in the states where there are no slaves, and of those members of Congress who voted for the Tallmadge Amendment, and of many of those who voted against it."

"You're exaggerating."

"You sicken my soul. Your view implies that a compact to secure sacred rights is a nullity which state legislatures may disregard and trample under foot."

"Yes."

"Let us not bring into the executive flames which rage in Congress," the President said.

"I agree with the Secretary of State," Wirt said, rushing the words from his mouth. We froze and I enjoyed Crawford's confusion at this disobedience. "There can't be a rightful power to establish slavery where it's never existed before. Congress must allow the state to make its decision but its decision, once made, cannot be reversed."

"What justifies the inconsistency?" Crawford asked.

The President spoke first: "It's impossible to exclude the implied powers that the Constitution grants to Congress. Remember a few years ago when Congress appropriated relief to Caracas after the earthquake. There was no express grant of authority but *we* decided it was an implied power. I agree with Mr. Adams. Regulations Congress authorizes for the territories must extend to their inhabitants." He paused. "If this policy isn't in direct violation of the Constitution it is still repugnant to its principles. It harms every state by narrowing their jurisdictions and attacks the generous spirit which always existed and was cherished by the states toward each other." Another pause and his eyes broke from their neutrality to meet mine. "But I intend to sign the compromise if it comes to me. I have no desire to preside over disunion."

I tried to see Crawford's look of defeat from an angle. His opinions were so unaccountable that they surprised even him by their absurdity. He didn't appear aware of the feelings which inspired them and occasionally threw out opinions for the sake of an argument. In such cases I tried avoiding taking them up but often couldn't help myself.

"The South shall be angry its reach is limited," he said.

"The North shall feel similarly that slavery has penetrated its side of Mason-Dixon," I said, "and that we've changed the Declaration's meaning."

The President said to Crawford and Calhoun, "Tell the Southern members of Congress that I'll support the compromise." To me, "Mr. Adams, you do the same for the Northern members."

"Yes, Mr. President."

Crawford had the last word before we shifted topics. "I wish I could toast the future states as they join the Union. May they vote Republican."

XXXVI

THE COLD WEATHER cleared in October but I expected frigidity to return as December approached. I spent an evening hiking the outskirts of Paris, Virginia, snatching a final opportunity to admire the stars. The growth on the trees—oak, ash, pine—extended two-thirds of the way to the top. The rest was shrubbery and the line separating the large and small woods went around the hill at the same elevation as though it were drawn with compasses. My journey gave me time to reflect.

That morning, I went with Mrs. Adams, Charles, and Mary to the Capitol to view Mr. Sully's portrait of Washington crossing the Delaware on Christmas 1776. A picture of men and especially of horses. It was large as life and had merit but there was nothing that marked the scene of the crisis. The principal figure was the worst. Badly drawn, badly colored, without likeness, and without character.

In the autumn months I completed my report on weights and measurements. The document was my great literary achievement—it contained the entire history of measurement systems, starting with Athens and Jerusalem. I concluded that the metric system was best and I wanted America's adoption of it as part of my legacy. I summarized my report to Canning and he said he'd speak to Lord Castlereagh about my proposal. A global alignment around the metric system would expand knowledge's reach and solidify world peace. My family was particularly excited about my report's completion. My wife encapsulated their feelings as, "Thank goodness I don't have to listen about measurements anymore."

Oh, Mrs. Adams. She entered another rough period in the year's latter half. I noticed her wincing and wondered if she'd become pregnant and miscarried again. She insisted that wasn't the case. Her plight worsened when she awoke one night in agony. I provided her 25 drops of laudanum and she confined to our room for the following four days and every time I checked on her she spoke of Baby Louisa. She said she wished for suicide and, had our daughter been older when she left us, there'd be nothing I or anyone could do to stop her. She calmed after emerging from her burrow and said her life was so uncomfortable that the wisest action was to retire to where she could spend her remaining years in peace. How strange was her mind constructed.

The President's backing gave Clay the leverage needed for his magnum opus. The process went as he predicted. The House split the bill into three segments—Missouri as a slave state, Maine as a free state, and codifying the Mason-Dixon line as a barrier. Moderates passed all three while zealots voted for the parts they liked. This led to a joint committee of both chambers which Clay stacked with moderates. The committee haggled for weeks on whether to merge the bills. Randolph fought the compromise at every step and proposed Southerners protest the final vote but they ignored him and he proposed reinstating the Tallmadge amendment. Clay used House procedures to thwart this chaos by ending debate and when Randolph complained the Speaker ruled him out of order. The compromise narrowly passed. 18 Northerners voted in favor or abstained. The President signed it and Clay, a spent force, received a deserved break as Congress recessed. The Union was saved, for now.

The nation sighed in relief and turned its attention to the election. The Federalists failed to nominate a candidate—the party of Father and Hamilton was dead. The President ran unopposed and won the Electoral College unanimously but for one vote. A Mr. Plumber from New Hampshire released a statement attacking the President's character and voted for me. I worried this could poison the President's feelings toward me but he asked that I remain by his side for his second term. I accepted, as did all my Cabinet colleagues. Let the good feelings continue.

There was no question the President would honor Washington's precedent and step down after two terms. Eyes shifted to 1824. Virtue instructed that I let the office come to me and I hoped securing control of North America would draw interest but Clay's compromise overshadowed my effort. He'd transformed himself from a failed Speaker humiliated by Jackson into the nation's savior. The leader in the middle and northern states, though New England was loyal to me. Crawford led in the South. I wondered if my partnership with Calhoun would recover now that the Missouri question was history but Clay offered an unexpected alternative. His views on slavery aligned with mine in a way Calhoun's did not and the Speaker's surge in popularity could only benefit me if we joined forces. That would threaten my partnership with Jackson but he languished in Florida as Clay became the most popular man in American politics.

The year's end also saw positive developments in Spain. King Ferdinand buckled as an uprising marched on Madrid. He pledged to restore the liberal 1812 constitution but this failed to appease the revolt. They stormed the palace, overthrew him, and imprisoned him in the Cortes Generales parliamentary building. A liberal government took over and recalled Mr. Onís, ridding me of that pest. It nullified Ferdinand's Florida grants and said it would ratify the treaty next year. I went to the President and he told Congress.

The new Spanish government also worked to end the war in South America. Bolivar, now President of Columbia, signed an armistice with General Morillo and opened negotiations for a peace deal. I instructed my clerks to draft reciprocal agreements for the new republics but the President wanted peace to be at hand before granting recognition.

All these developments were minor compared to my deliberations on slavery. I favored this Missouri Compromise, it was all that could be effected under the Constitution and I was unwilling to put the Union at hazard. But it would have been wiser and bolder to persist in restricting Missouri until it terminated in a convention of the states to revise and amend the Constitution. If the Union must dissolve, slavery was precisely the question upon which it ought to break. For the present the contest laid asleep.

I hardened my belief that colonization was a false middle option. The cotton surge guaranteed such fortunes that slave masters would never emancipate via bribe. Expanding slavery, as Jefferson proposed, would diffuse it and nullify white anxiety. His intent was to foster removal but it abolished any such incentive. These men I respected— Jefferson, Clay, the President, Marshall—were wrong. Liberty and slavery couldn't coexist and there was no center on this issue. It could serve as my life's purpose had I not held office. I'd spent decades fearing I was doomed to mediocrity but now I knew Father's generation delayed action on the greatest issue of all.

The Missouri Compromise bought time before the cataclysm. Slavery's expansion was checked for now but it would grow until it took over the central government. Then America would become a slavery-ruled monarchy and it would spread into Mexico and South America.

This was the likely outcome. There was one narrow, vain, horrible scenario to redeem the country. One way to keep the Union without slavery. The election of an antislavery President would trigger the South's secession, bringing a servile war in the slaveholding states combined with a war between the two portions of the Union. The President would end slavery through executive order as a war measure and pulverize the South into submission. I did not know who this man would be, or if I'd meet him, but I expected he was already born because otherwise he'd appear too late before slavery's victory. Somewhere in the Union lived our only hope.

I arrived. The Milky Way was the most magnificent image in the universe and it shone upon me as it never could in a city. A masterpiece, simplicity and complexity intertwined. I raised my spyglass and saw thousands of luminous bodies in every direction, increasing every moment in a most extraordinary brilliancy. I saw Orion the Hunter fighting Taurus with Canis Major, his loyal canine, beside him. My inner light, crushed by decades of argument and grief amidst politics and war, grew to levels that let me love life and appreciate the miracle of existence. The stress calcified in my muscles dissolved. Joy. True joy swelling. I felt like who I was meant to be instead of an imposter. I felt my destiny. I felt peace.

PART SIX

THE ALLIANCE STRIKES BACK
1821

XXXVII

THE FIRST TIME Brent knocked on my door, the sound whistled through my sleep as a musket through a coat. If I dreamt it was unworthy of attention. I clung to the relaxed state, resisting the threat to my delicate pleasure. The bubble held and I returned to slumber. His second knock breached my defenses. Walls tumbled and enemies invaded. My head sprung up and my arms covered my torso. I blinked until my vision regained focus. Noticed the puddle on my desk and prayed it was saliva and not eye liquid. I wiped it and rubbed my temples as a headache emerged. He knocked a third time and I shouted for him to cease.

My door opened and Brent made way for Senator King. I offered him the chair across my desk but he preferred standing. My hands squeezed to increase my energy. He joked that people usually waited for him to speak before dozing and I begged his forgiveness and informed him I'd woken before three the past several nights. I asked if Congress' term ended in March this year and he said it expired in May and that he'd narrowly escape the capital's humidity. This was amusing because I'd visited his home on Jamaica, Long Island, a few times and during my last trip the road there was overtaken by a heavy rain shower.

The reason I asked was to inquire about his interest in serving as minister to the Court of St. James for the President's second term. Rush could not endure eight years in that post. King declined, saying he wouldn't represent a pro-slavery administration, his tone one of restrained judgment for he didn't wish to offend me. I told him he wouldn't get to wear the blue uniforms the President mandated for our ministers. Included a fluffy hat and golden embroidery. He asked if they were silk and I said the inner lining was but the outside was cotton.

He asked for any changes from Gallatin on French restitution and I said they compromised on one claim, that Napoleon seized our property on the Isle of France. He then shifted the conversation to the 1824 election and before he finished his sentence I said any man plotting for 1824 was unfit for the office. He asked if I was worried about a President Crawford and said I must stop him. I was touched by his sentiment. King had himself been, and wished to again be, a candidate for the presidency, but knew his chances were slim. He was not, as Clay said during the Missouri debates, a hollow-hearted, insincere man. He was upright in principle if occasionally frail in practice.

I asked why me and he said that as Secretary of State I carried national attention and had the most foreign policy experience of any man who might win. I said he risked turning me into Macbeth, that unhallowed ambition would win me the crown but lose me my soul. I considered *Macbeth* Shakespeare's most moral play.

I said I wouldn't sacrifice my virtue, that the presidency must be assigned to the most able and worthy and if I were a candidate, it must be by others' wishes and of the public interest. He said stopping Crawford was in the public's interest. His brother, William, led Crawford's campaign in the North. William was based in Maine, showing the slave powers already took advantage of the compromise. He called the compromise a disgraceful affair. I asked if he preferred disunion and he said I spoke of virtue but appeased the South. That the compromise was sold as settling the issue yet nothing was less true for Missouri already banned free Negroes. He said the problem was that the best speakers were in the South and asked if I'd return to Congress if I did not stand for President and I said I didn't foresee that as likely.

He resented how the slave powers attacked his motives, accusing him of ambition. It was a common weapon in politics, originally coming from the Devil saying, "Doth Job fear God for nought." Undoubtedly there were hypocrites of humanity as well as of religion, but there wasn't a man in the Union of purer integrity than Rufus King. He was the wisest and the best of us. That we never formed a partnership was a missed opportunity but such an arrangement would fail to expand our constituencies as we were both Northern and critical of slavery.

◆ ◆ ◆ ◆ ◆ ◆

"Please raise your right hand and repeat after me. I, James Spence Monroe, do solemnly swear…"

"I, James Spence Monroe, do solemnly swear…"

"…That I will faithfully execute…"

"…That I will faithfully execute…"

"…The office of President of the United States…"

"…The office of President of the United States…"

"…And will, to the best of my ability…"

"…And will, to the best of my ability…"

"…Preserve, protect, and defend…"

"…Preserve, protect, and defend…"

"…The Constitution of the United States…"

"…The Constitution of the United States…"

"…So help you God."

"…So help me God."

"Congratulations, Mr. President."

3,000 voices roared their approval as the President lifted his hand from the Bible and shook Chief Justice Marshall's. I applauded with the rest of the Cabinet, who stood to the side. We'd arrived with the President in his carriage. Vice President Tompkins held his inauguration in New York and was absent.

The House chamber was crammed. Finally refurbished from the war. The inauguration was to be outside, like its predecessor, but a snowstorm struck Washington the prior day. I felt chilly despite squishing between Calhoun and Wirt. It worried me that the entire government was clustered together and vulnerable to foreign malfeasance. The President delivered his address once the volume dissipated. I'll try to make this painless.

"I shall not attempt to describe the grateful emotions which the new and distinguished proof of my fellow-citizens' confidence, evinced by my reelection to this high trust, has excited in my bosom. Having no pretensions to the commanding claims of my predecessors, whose names are so much more conspicuously identified with our Revolution, and who contributed so preeminently to promote its success, I consider myself rather as the instrument than the cause of the union which has prevailed in the late election.

"Just before the commencement of the last term the United States concluded a war with a very powerful nation on conditions equal and honorable to both parties. Our commerce had been driven from the sea, our Atlantic and inland frontiers invaded in almost every part, the waste of life along our coast and on some parts of our inland frontiers was immense, and not less than 120,000,000 dollars were added to the public debt.

"As soon as the war terminated, the nation resolved to place itself in a situation which should prevent the recurrence of a like evil, and, in case it should recur, to mitigate its calamities. With this view, after reducing our land force to the basis of a peace establishment, provision was made to construct fortifications at proper points through our coast and we augmented our naval force to be well adapted to both purposes.

"It need scarcely be remarked that these measures have not been resorted to in a spirit of hostility to other powers. Such a disposition does not exist toward any power. Peace and good will have been cultivated with all, and by the most faithful regard to justice. They have been dictated by a love of peace, of economy, and an earnest desire to save the lives of our citizens from the destruction and our country from the devastation which are inseparable from war when it finds us unprepared. It is believed, and experience has shown, that such preparation is the best expedient to prevent war.

"Europe is again unsettled and the prospect of war increases. Should the flame light in any quarter, how far it may extend is impossible to foresee. With every power we are in perfect amity, and it is our interest to remain so if it be practicable on just conditions. I see no reasonable cause to apprehend variance with any power, unless it proceeds from a violation of our maritime rights. In these contests, should they occur, and to whatever extent they may be carried, we shall be neutral, but as a neutral power we have rights which it is our duty to maintain.

"Entering with these views the office which I have just sworn to execute with fidelity and to the utmost of my ability, I derive great satisfaction from a knowledge that I shall be assisted in the several Departments by the enlightened and upright citizens from whom I received so much aid in the preceding term. With full confidence in the continuance of that candor and generous indulgence from my fellow-citizens which I have heretofore experienced, and with a firm reliance on the protection of Almighty God, I shall forthwith commence the duties of the high trust to which you have called me."

He concluded and the crowd granted polite praise. I ignored them, my thoughts on his omitting the Missouri crisis and the economy. Typical that he'd avoid issues rather than confront them. Anything to preserve good feelings and his republic that transcended parties.

The ceremony ended and that evening the President hosted a ball at Brown's Hotel.

♦ ♦ ♦ ♦ ♦ ♦

Another party was held at the Executive Mansion the following week. Mrs. Adams happily ceded responsibility. I admired my wife's performance as Washington's chief hostess when it wasn't her job. Her skin, blanched from her illness, clashed with her burgundy gown. Every wince saddened me. I could weaken Spain's empire but was powerless to alleviate her suffering. Her cheeks puffed and exhalation scattered.

"How do you feel?"

A moment. "Smaller attendance than normal. Still clawing out of the wedding fiasco."

The Monroes' infighting recast 1820's defining social event into a polarizing episode. Maria, the President's youngest daughter, married her first cousin at the Mansion after the President signed the Missouri Compromise. He hoped to lighten the national mood before an election amidst the crisis and economic woes. But Eliza, Washington's secondary host, directed the affair and shrunk the guest list. She snubbed most of Washington society, including the Cabinet. Crawford complained at a Meeting and the President spent an hour consoling us. I was happy for one less night away from my books. Now the Monroes pursued peace with the city's elite. The night's boycott included the diplomatic corps, telling me wider groveling was needed.

"Many 'ill' wives and sympathetic husbands tonight," Mrs. Adams said. "Yet I am *actually* ill and here I am promoting you. I expect you to dote on me later."

"I'll fulfill that expectation. Has the pain worsened?"

"There's been no improvement. I'll contact Thomas later." She referred to her brother. "He wants to ask me about watching his children anyway."

"More youngsters."

"I wish Eliza and I collaborated, but she is so proud and mean that I've scarcely met such a compound." She paused. "I know Elizabeth is restricted but she should be grateful we fill her void." Her eyes fused onto the First Lady. "She's dressed as a goddess, though."

"Be easy on Elizabeth. She braved the Atlantic at wartime and saved La Fayette's family from Parisian mobs."

She nodded. "Should we mingle?" I scoured the room, hoping to find Calhoun. I did not see him that night. Purposeless small talk for me.

Clang! Clang!

I turned toward the noise, which was easy to find as guests imitated the Red Sea. Canning and Hyde pointed swords at each other. Hyde's face informed me this was genuine. Neither moved, each anticipated the other's next strike. They studied every tick. A shark wandering into a crocodile's territory, circling each other. Too dramatic? What about a hog trampling through chicken feed, provoking outraged poultry?

"Do you bite your thumb at me, sir?" Canning asked.

"I do," Hyde said.

I placed my arm around Mrs. Adams and stepped back. I wanted to know who'd win but I had productive relationships with both men and preferred neither be recalled due to injury or to prematurely depart from the world.

The President swung his hunting sword between their blades. Both retreated and he stood between them. "Cease at once, gentlemen." He looked at each. "I'll not tolerate this behavior in my house." He surveyed them as they lowered their weapons and then he mediated a mutual apology. I'd never seen him act so decisively, like he was at Trenton as a young man. Where was this gladiator when we confronted Onís?

Awkwardness hung over the remainder of the evening, punctuated by Mrs. Adams' uncontrollable giggles, for no one enjoyed the scene more than she.

XXXVIII

"THE EMPEROR AUTHORIZED me to make the following proposal to your government," the Baron de Tuyll, Russia's minister, said, "though I request you inform me in advance of declination. In that case, it shall remain informal." A dark figure, wearing black with a red collar and gold tassels on his shoulders, the medals won fighting Napoleon's Grande Armée pinned to his uniform. His accent was a baritone deeper than any I'd ever heard, the croak of a man broken from lifelong service to his sire. Other voices modified via emotion—happiness, tenderness, hatred, vexation, and so on. Not the Baron's. His was the voice of a man who hated the world and everyone in it, including his master.

"What proposal?" I asked. We spoke in English.

"He wants the United States to ratify the Holy Alliance Treaty."

A moment. "He's sincere?"

"Yes. The Alliance is a league of peace. The United States would strengthen their ties to its members by joining."

"But the treaty is a collection of sovereigns' autographs. It excludes republics."

"The Swiss cantons were invited and acceded."

"I thought the Alliance was hostile to the United States."

"The Alliance is hostile to anarchy."

"We're not responsible for the French Revolution. The President and I interpret the Alliance as promoting the divine right of kings to rule over humanity. Our constitution is incompatible with such a view."

"Will you communicate his proposal to the President?"

"Yes. Though two-thirds of the Senate must vote for our joining."

"I see," he said. "Do you believe they will?"

"No."

"That is unfortunate. The Emperor wishes for your country and for Britain to join."

"He invited Britain?" I asked. He nodded. "The same problem, King George can't sign it without Parliament. I don't grasp why the Alliance invites our countries. Britain has a monarchy but elects her legislature. The Alliance recently crushed republican efforts in Naples and the Piedmont. Why would we join such an entity?"

"The Emperor is optimistic that Britain will join. It will be to the world's benefit if London and Washington adhere to the Alliance's influence. The treaty contains no specific points but sets an ideal for global peace."

"A peace built on despotism."

"You'll communicate his proposal to the President?"

"Yes. Is that all?"

"No. We must discuss the South American war."

"Why? Last year's armistice is stable and peace talks are ongoing. Royalist rebels harass the republics like gnats do elephants, but I expect the war to end by 1822."

"That cannot happen under current conditions. The continent's revolution insults Europe's monarchs and threatens her security. The guilty continent must return, through peaceful means or through arms, into the Alliance's protection."

Lines so wide that Noah's animals could walk through them with not just their mate but their whole menagerie. "The Alliance wants to conquer South America?"

"The Alliance will restore Spain's dominion. South America will receive greater autonomy than it did previously and will have open trade with all nations." A pause. "American independence caused the French Revolution. South American independence cannot bring a similar catastrophe to Europe."

"So your invitation to join the Alliance is meant to nullify objection to aggression toward this hemisphere?"

"To cooperate for the good of the world. The Emperor is anxious that a general peace be built. Embers burn in Europe that must not flame again."

"Embers of men and women who yearn for freedom. His route toward peace involves *destroying* an entire hemisphere. You must know we'll never agree to this and neither will Britain. She's invested enormous resources into supporting the South American rebels."

"We have ways of persuading her."

"Why alert us to your intent?"

"To reduce your government's anxiety so it will not attempt to stop what it cannot."

"What cannot be stopped is the inevitable doom of Europe's masters," I said. "Its people have been taught to inquire why certain men possess enjoyment at their expense. Civil wars shall rage in Europe until the total ruin of feudal constitutions has been achieved."

"The Emperor bears no hostility toward the United States or their institutions. You know this because you worked with him as a minister. I'm saddened to learn you do not reciprocate his respect. He views South American independence as a coming apocalypse that threatens man's connection to Christ through divine rulers. Your country will lose much and gain nothing by resisting what is necessary for a lasting peace. I pray your government takes his proposal seriously."

"I'll confer what we've discussed to the President."

"Thank you."

I escorted him from my office and Maury led him out of the building. Then I returned to my desk and analyzed his words. I'd feared the Holy Alliance's intentions for six years and finally its intervention was upon us. America had no choice but to resist and we had no hope of defeating Europe's combined might.

I remembered when Mother and I watched the Battle of Bunker Hill. The first major battle for independence. I was six and my principal memory was of Dr. Warren blunting the Red Coats as the Patriots escaped. Mother's tears mixed with mine as our family friend and physician died for freedom.

This William Collins poem came to me:

How sleep the brave, who sink to rest
By all their country's wishes blessed!
When spring, with dewy fingers cold,
Returns to deck their hallowed mould,
She there shall dress a sweeter sod
Than fancy's feet have ever trod.

By fairy hands their knell is rung,
By forms unseen their dirge is sung,
There Honour comes, a pilgrim grey,

To bless the turf that wraps their clay,
And Freedom shall awhile repair,
To dwell, a weeping hermit, there!

War. What it's always been and always would be. Heroism yes, but barbarism as men fight for their lives and for their friends and families and who'd stop at nothing to avoid the next world while granting those wearing a different uniform the same fate. One in every hundred Americans died in that war. That blood was mere drops compared to the rivers of the coming conflict. An existential conflagration between the hemispheres. A repeat of the conquistadors and the 40 million dead in their wake. Europe annihilating this hemisphere for the second time in half-a-millennium.

The Union would rupture within a year. The South's oppression finding common cause with the Alliance and the North fighting to the last man and woman. By evening I wore a coat of sweat and couldn't grasp coherent thoughts. No way out, a feeling I despised. My only talent, useless. I'd go mad if I didn't speak with another. I gathered my strength and exited my office and controlled myself on my journey to Brent's room. The door was closed but I'd no patience and entered. He sat with Ironside.

"These sorts of mistakes are understandable in your first week on the job, but—Good Day, Mr. Adams."

"Greetings, Daniel." I bobbed my head to Ironside. "Are you available?"

"Uh—yes."

"Good. Come to my office." We went there. "Shut the door."

Brent did so and sat on my couch. "Is everything all right, Mr. Adams?" I looked at my desk. A cigar? No, crackers. Grabbed several.

"The Holy Alliance intends to invade South America and reinstate the Spanish Empire."

I watched him for over a minute as his eyes darted about. The noise of carriage traffic along Pennsylvania Avenue built through the closed windows. His open hands pressed down his standing hair without his knowing. He returned to me.

"The Baron said this?"

"Yes. He also invited us to join the Alliance, but that's a trick so we'll concede to their will."

"Right. Are they capable of this? Of crossing the Atlantic? I don't question their armies—Russia and France—but their navies—"

"Russia has the second most powerful navy in the world. I don't remember the details, but yes, I think it's doable." I ate a cracker. "Let's think this through. Emperor Alexander is a god to his people." Another cracker.

"He's also your friend."

"Professional friend." The crackers helped. A little. "We negotiated a trade deal, socialized—he admires this country. That he would provoke war—"

"What about his faith? His praying has left an indention within St. Petersburg. He wants to return Europe to a Christian empire under his rule. The other Alliance members resist his ambition. Perhaps—"

"The other Alliance members are the ones who worry me," I said. "Alexander is the muscle and Prince Metternich is the brain." I crushed my crackers as his name left my lips. "Alexander takes orders from him. As does Prussia and the Bourbons in Paris. The man runs Europe out of Vienna. He's going to instruct France to return Ferdinand to the Spanish throne while it's still warm."

"How long will that take?"

"A year? I can't know with certainty."

"That gives us time."

"Some, to prepare for our doom." I paced a bit, dropping crumbs. "Remember his record so we know what to expect. Napoleon had Europe at his mercy and Metternich engineered his downfall. He brokered Napoleon's marriage to Marie Louise, Austria's princess, to convince the French tyrant that Austria was his ally. With Austria no longer a threat, Napoleon invaded Russia in 1812. Metternich anticipated his failure and organized a coalition to strike at France's moment of weakness, forcing Napoleon's abdication."

"What's the lesson? That he'll lull us into a fake complacency?"

"Perhaps." I closed my eyes. "He thinks our rejection of monarchy is heresy and has caused continuous wars across the Atlantic for 45 years. No one awaits our disunion more." My eyes opened and saw my mess. I flung my crumbs across the ruby carpet.

"You said Russia has the second largest navy. We've yet to discuss Britain. Will Lord Castlereagh tolerate this?"

"Originally I thought not, that he'd worked too hard supporting the rebels. But the Baron said something about persuasion."

"A repeat of Napoleon's Continental System?"

"A bribe. Castlereagh backed the rebels to remove Spain's monopoly on South American commerce. The Baron said the continent's trade will be left open and the Alliance can offer to join Britain's suppression of the slave trade, which we can't reciprocate because of the South. That includes acting against the Barbary Pirates in the eastern Mediterranean." I referred to the Ottoman Empire's agents.

"That's placing a lot of trust in Metternich. I know they're friends, but British neutrality might be more likely."

"Hmm." I paced about, smushing the crumbs deeper. "That's our best option."

"Why? We should ally with Britain and South America if—"

"No, Daniel. Remember President Washington: no permanent alliances. The United States are tied to no one but each other."

"But—"

"*That's* Metternich's ploy! He wants us to run back to Britain. To tell the world we can't defend this hemisphere on our own and we need mommy Britain to save us. It will break our credibility and reduce us to semi-colonial status."

"And rejecting Britain pushes her toward the Alliance, because she can't oppose the Alliance on her own."

"Exactly. We lose either way."

"What's the best course? Asking Britain to stay neutral? That risks an Alliance invasion, even though I still question how far it'd get."

"It's a better gamble than the alternatives. Let's think about South America. Allying with them restricts our foreign policy and that's what Metternich wants. It also pulls us toward war. Not doing so results in their relying on Britain. Castlereagh will create a monopoly in that continent and take Cuba."

"We should recognize them as soon as possible. This changes things and we have to expedite the process. It also creates the option for alliances without a commitment and keeps them from getting too close to London."

"I agree. I'll convey all of this to the other Cabinet officers and to Forsyth and the Committee on Foreign Relations. But not yet."

XXXIX

"THE GENTLEMAN FROM Massachusetts speaks falsehoods," Mr. Baldwin, a congressman from Pennsylvania, declared on the House floor. "The bill would only cause an eight per cent increase in the cost of —"

"Eight per cent?" Mr. Otis said. "You betr—"

"It is my turn, Mr. Speaker," Baldwin said to Clay.

Tariffs replaced Missouri as the dominant congressional issue. I sat on the balcony, which was crowded but not overflowing, as it regularly was in 1820. Calhoun was among the mass but I didn't know where. His presence explained mine.

Clay banged his gavel. "Allow Mr. Otis to make his point, Mr. Baldwin."

Baldwin shook his head in disgust. Otis grinned and said, "On one side are the pro-tariff economists and cyclopedists, and on the other are Adam Smith's disciples." He gestured to himself.

Mr. Alexander of Virginia stood. "I brought my copy of *The Wealth of Nations*." He opened it to a marked page. "'In general, if any branch of trade, or any division of labor, be advantageous to the public, the freer and more general the competition, it will always be the more so.'" Tariff opponents, mostly from New England and the South—a peculiar entente—cheered. "The great man warned us about restricting competition and building monopolies, and this bill will tax the South for the North's gain."

"Not all of the North," Otis said. Tariff opponents cheered again.

"Do you want Northern workers to riot?" Baldwin asked. "This is their third year of unemployment. Mr. Crawford has already bailed out western farmers through federal land sales. It's the North's turn."

"Those sales didn't harm the other regions," Otis said. "Your bill creates a new manufacturing interest at the expense of agriculture and commerce." Cheering and jeering.

I saw a tall and thin silhouette with wide hair rise across the balcony. It had to be him. He departed and I followed. It took several minutes to exit the Capitol but I found Calhoun in an introspective mood on the building's steps. He was enveloped by sunlight and appeared secure, a similar portrait to our early days together.

"Are you free to speak?" I asked.

I expected to startle him but I saw the rationality I admired. His eyes contained apprehension as though I'd spied on him. "Mr. Adams, of course."

We descended the stairs together and stood at their base. "Any thoughts on Baldwin's proposal?" I asked.

"None in particular. Greater issues occupy my mind."

"Such as?"

"My allies in South Carolina inform me of local anger about the Missouri Compromise. There's talk of secession."

"Still?"

"Yes. They don't feel slavery is safe in the Union."

I didn't wish to sink into that topic. "Is it true baby Elizabeth has passed?"

"Yes." His eyes were steady but I knew it was an act. He wasn't less human than the rest of us, even if he strove to be.

"You have my deepest sympathy."

"Thank you. The city's outpouring of support during this trial softened our grief. Pass along my thanks to Mrs. Adams for her sizable contribution."

"I will."

"This was our third daughter lost since I assumed my position. Perhaps it is unlucky." He paused. "I'm glad you found me. There's something we need to discuss."

"I have a topic in mind as well. Let's do yours first."

"I've spoken with the President and Mr. Jefferson. Acquiring Florida was the foreign policy goal for the administration's first term. Cuba should be next."

"Why?"

"It will define the President's second term and it removes two potential problems—that Britain wants the island and that it can be revolutionized by Negroes." His real motive was he needed this to win in 1824 since the Missouri crisis divided his followers along regional lines.

"Now is not the time to risk war with Britain."

"Jefferson disagrees."

"He does?"

"He says it's a necessary gamble to secure importations of coffee and sugar. Spain has lost South America and we should push her from the Caribbean as well. I have a contact on the island who says he can start an uprising. We won't even have to ask Congress."

"You will if you want to admit Cuba as a state. The President can't promise admission."

"A confidential communication then. Stealthy action will preserve our relationship with Spain."

"Congressional secrecy is neither possible nor proper. The whole business will be divulged in a week, maybe even a day. You intend it as a slave state?"

"Yes. It's only fair since the institution's expansion northward was checked by federal—"

"Let's not go there," I said. "War with Britain will result in her possessing the island. The Royal Navy will eviscerate our maritime forces. We'll absorb Cuba eventually."

"We can absorb her now. You surprise me, sir. I thought you'd fancy this idea, given how hard you fought for Florida."

"It's critical we do not push Spain and Britain together and to the Holy Alliance. Especially now."

"What does that mean?"

"It relates to my topic. We face our biggest threat since independence. The Baron de Tuyll told me the Alliance plans to invade South America and return it to Spain."

A moment. His mask did not move an inch. "Do they not face enough problems in Europe? Republicanism confronts them in Spain and Italy. Equality is replacing feudalism and lords and vassals. Even if the Alliance defeats these movements the spirit will triumph at some other point. It is not easy to control."

His separation of monarchy and slavery amazed me. "I told the Baron as much."

"When was this meeting?" he asked. "Why haven't you sent us a memorandum?"

"My analysis is incomplete. That's why I wanted to speak with you."

"How can I help?"

"Does the Alliance have the requisite naval power to attack across the Atlantic?"

A moment. "I suppose it's possible, though not without difficulty. The French Revolution slaughtered that country's officer corps and Lord Nelson's victory at Trafalgar finished what was left. Her fleet is limited to frigates and some privately-owned vessels."

"What about Russia?"

"The Emperor built a powerful navy to battle Napoleon. She has dozens of battleships and ships of the line, and hundreds of frigates. Russia has conducted over a dozen world tours since the start of this century."

"I see."

"But their fleets are in the Baltic, the Black Sea, the Caspian, the White Sea, and the Okhotsk. Do you know what they have in common? None has a warm water port. They freeze in winter. That means any offensive or reinforcements could only depart in spring or summer."

"It sounds like you don't take their threat seriously."

"It's mixed, so long as Britain doesn't join them." He paused. "Have you anticipated her response?"

"I expect her to pursue her interest, as always."

"She aims to dominate this hemisphere and transform it into another India. Though that would be better than Metternich."

I did not want to discuss this further until I knew I could trust him. "I've missed our strategy sessions."

"As have I, Mr. Adams."

"Missouri dampened our partnership, but that's behind us."

He broke eye contact and stared at the Capitol. "Our partnership was built on our common viewpoint. We now know of the differences between us. Slavery shall remain a contentious issue and so our strains will recur. Let us collaborate where we can and battle when we must."

I couldn't appear weak. "Very well."

XL

THAT EVENING I returned home to find Mrs. Adams with her brother Thomas and Lucy, her chambermaid, in the central entertainment room. I yearned to set a cheerful tone and pacify my nerves. I found that obsessing over work before bed followed me into my dreams and ruined my sleep. I greeted everyone and handed Lucy my bag.

"Place these with the other articles to be washed, dear."

"They're damp," she said.

"I wore them in the Potomac during my morning swim. I lasted 80 minutes." I turned to Mrs. Adams. "A new record while clothed."

"Are they folded?" Lucy asked.

"In my way."

Her nostrils flared and her eyebrows cocked like a knife, she glared like a cornered leopard. She took my bag and I turned to my wife and brother-in-law, who sat on adjacent couches along the room's back left corner. They provided extra seats as the dining table ruled the room's center. Our furniture had low backs and was light so we could move it for parties. A fire burned low and cast shadows over their dour faces.

"I didn't mean to inconvenience her," I said.

"You never *mean* to do anything, do you, John?" Mrs. Adams said. She looked weaker than normal, a rose deprived of sun. "Yet you trample over us every day." Not yelling but her voice was shrill.

"Who do you think you're talking to? Do you know the responsibilities I carry? They'd break a lesser man. I have to maintain my daily routine to survive."

"Is something happening?" Thomas asked. "Something the government isn't telling us?"

"You know I can't answer that."

"Then can you answer why you deliberately hurt me?" Mrs. Adams asked. "What if you'd drowned? Did you think of that? What would happen to us if your clothes dragged you under the surface?"

"I have to think about more than our family," I said. "More than our country. I—"

228

"Don't pretend you think about our family at all. I know how your—"

"Our family has bled me dr—"

"John!" Thomas stood and grabbed my arm, which I'd placed between my wife and myself, and guided me across the room to the closed door separating that room from the overflow room. "John, you mustn't antagonize Louisa. She's not well."

A moment. "Is it lethal?"

Mrs. Adams turned toward us. Thomas grabbed me tighter and took us to the upper left corner. "Not inherently," he whispered. "Her rectum has inflamed veins. It could be caused by irregularities in the female anatomy, but I suspect she's not the first member of the Johnson family to be vexed by this condition." He glanced at her. She watched us. He returned to me. "I'm taking her to Philadelphia. Dr. Physick has a new surgery that he insists can cure her."

I sighed at the thought of an untried treatment. But if she and Thomas were decided I would support them. "Do you need me to accompany you? It will be difficult for me to leave Washington."

"Mary will assist me. Don't worry, I'll have her back in a month."

I sighed again, this time with relief. "Thank you, Thomas." I returned to my wife. "Would my reading the Bible soothe you?"

◆ ◆ ◆ ◆ ◆ ◆

"Is it all right if Mr. Wirt joins us?" the President asked. He and the Attorney General were in their traditional seats at the Cabinet table.

"Of course, Mr. President," I said and placed my papers down.

"I read your memorandum with great interest," the President said. Wirt nodded. "Though I noticed you only described the problem and made no recommendations."

"That's correct. I'm still contemplating our response to future contingencies."

"One contingency that is beyond debate is that we shall treat an Alliance attack on South America as an attack on the United States. Congress will agree, but I would commit us even without their permission, regardless of the political consequences." Wirt and I concurred. "I'd hoped to avoid a war during my administration and I thought I had once the Florida Treaty was ratified." He touched his left shoulder. "The Hessians at Trenton made war real to me. I stood at the Paradiso's edge. A war with the Holy Alliance will be to the bitter end. No American will be left untouched."

"Amen," Wirt said.

"My memorandum mentioned that we should expect the Alliance to return Ferdinand to power," I said. "They'll then break the armistice. The Department of State is already preparing trade proposals for the new South American republics. We should move forward with recognizing them and do it as fast as possible."

"I am pleased to hear you say that," the President said.

"Are we including the Brazilian Empire?" Wirt asked.

"Ought we?" the President asked.

"Yes. Brazil is a monarchy and including her will soften the Alliance's response. It shows we're not favoring a single form of government, that the republics aren't banning together against them."

The President smiled. "I agree. Declining to recognize her independence from Portugal because she's monarchical departs from our policy of noninterference in other nations' internal politics."

"Brazil would also make a valuable trading partner, more valuable than the rest of South America," I said.

"True," Wirt said.

"But—" I said. Wirt sighed. "—though the Portuguese King declared her independent when he hid there from Napoleon, he's since returned to Portugal and has not yet notified us of Brazil's status. I'd like proper documentation before acting."

The President said to Wirt, "That's reasonable." Wirt nodded. The President said to me, "Should our intention to defend South America be made public?"

"No, sir. It binds us to commitments in the future and guarantees we'll be engaged in two or three wars at any given time. We must prioritize our goal of controlling North America."

"It's foolish to place our selfish expansion over mutual protection," Wirt said.

"A powerful America will become this hemisphere's greatest defense."

"If she survives long enough."

"What about Britain?" the President asked me.

"Short of becoming Metternich's serfs, declaring our desperation for British help is the worst possible outcome. A great nation does not need others to save it."

"Has Metternich bought your loyalty," Wirt asked, "because you'd have us lay naked before the world. Let's swallow our pride and use the Royal Navy as our shield."

"He has a point, Mr. Adams," the President said. "Your memorandum questioned the Alliance's nautical strength. A compact with Britain promises our safety."

"Their limited ability reduces the likelihood of attack," I said, "whereas turning to Britain ensures a new dependency."

"So you'd gamble the New World's survival?" Wirt asked.

"Questions of war and peace always involve gambles."

Wirt said to the President, "Lord Castlereagh is close to Europe and that means he's close to Metternich, whereas our dispatches must cross the Atlantic. We mustn't waste a moment before aligning ourselves with London. I advise you to instruct Mr. Adams to contact Mr. Canning *immediately.*"

"*No*, Mr. President," I said. "Metternich hopes that we'll subordinate ourselves to Britain. That's his real game. He knows there's little chance Ferdinand will ever rule South America again. Even if Castlereagh *did* reverse his support for the rebels, the British public would force him from office."

"Your argument is built on assumptions," Wirt said.

"Enough," the President said. "A decision isn't needed today. Let's proceed slowly and keep our options open."

XLI

"I SEE THAT the money the House appropriated was well spent," Clay said as he circled my office. "I expect gratitude."

"A well-funded Department of State is in the nation's interest." I stood behind my desk.

"One day you'll learn my words contain infinite jest." I ignored his comments for I needed to test our relationship's fertility during a world crisis as foreign affairs had long been our starkest disagreement. He spent several minutes analyzing the abundance of cherry wood, part of a crimson motif from which I'd hoped to draw strength but that proved a touch too sanguinary.

He came to me and I gestured to a chair opposite mine. "What can I do for you, Mr. Speaker?"

A moment. "The economic contraction has struck Kentucky worse than most. It hasn't spared my family. Do you remember that I visited London and negotiated a commercial convention after leaving Ghent?"

"Yes. 3 July 1815."

"The government never compensated me and the payment would be most helpful."

"Why are you asking me? That action requires a special appropriation by Congress. I'm confident they wouldn't object."

"No, but it's embarrassing and takes time. I need the money now." He paused. "If you can't arrange this through the Department of State I'll have to leave public service for a few years." Another pause. "*Please*, Mr. Adams."

I thought it over. "I'm sorry, but our rules tie my hands." His expressiveness was the antipode to Calhoun's mask. Heartache resided in even the lowest expectations. "I could offer you the next vacancy for a mission abroad, if that helps," I said.

"Thank you, but there won't be an opening for two to three years. I spoke to Mr. Cheves and he said the job of Counsel to the Bank in Kentucky and Ohio is mine if I wish it. I suppose I do, though *wish* mocks me in this case. I hate to leave public service at this critical juncture though, when the administration's weakness—"

"The President was reelected with virtual unanimity."

"Yet he hasn't the slightest influence in Congress," he said. "We know he'll retire after this term and so nothing further is expected by him or from him."

"He still has vast public support. His budget proposal, for instance—"

"We'll approve his request to cut the military. It's a logical move in this economy. I spoke with Crawford and we agreed a reduction from 25 million dollars to five million would be best."

A moment. "You wish to destroy Calhoun."

"The government's revenue is a barren lake and such a large cut is necessary." He smiled. "This reduction has the added benefit of decommissioning Jackson."

"Expect the President to reverse his proposal," I said. "I assume Forsyth showed you my memorandum?" He nodded. "The Allies' aggression does not alter the administration's plan to recognize the new republics."

"Really?" Energy supplanted vindictive-laced disappointment.

"We can't let Metternich interfere with our diplomacy. Congress should pass a resolution denouncing the aggression. Such a statement will be better coming from Congress as it will provoke less hostile attitudes from foreign powers."

"I can arrange it. In exchange—"

"We're not bargaining. This is a crisis with few, if any, parallels."

"Hear my proposal. The New World should form its own alliance to counterpose the Holy Alliance. One that favors independence and liberty. We can lead republicanism's opposition to monarchy."

"*Please*, Mr. Clay. We helped each other during the Missouri crisis. I don't wish us to be enemies again. But I must prioritize the administration's foreign policy and we're determined to maintain our independence from other countries since they'd lead us into unnecessary wars and restrict our goal of mastering the continent."

He sighed. "You're right regarding Missouri. Let us strive for civility." A pause. "I take it that the President would defend South

America if the Alliance *does* attack?" I nodded. "Then an alert to the united resistance they'd face deters them."

"That would be included in the congressional resolution."

"It's better coming from the executive as it's our face to the world. Passing an unofficial declaration of war will be difficult."

"I'm confident that you can do it," I said. "Imagine if we align both branches to a common goal, unlike our bickering during the Florida episode."

"But with what am I to align? You invite aggression by leaving the republics divided when monarchism is unified and obsess over the long view while bringing immediate catastrophe."

"I will not have America eternally a secondary power by tying it to states who oppose our rise. Doing so drops us into the Alliance's trap. Let's search for the root of our different views. You claim that I'm ignoring the next few years in favor of—"

"I'm claiming that your leadership cannot be trusted," he said, "and if the President follows your course then I do not trust him either."

I hit the table. The next hour bore witness to our angriest encounter. Clay once more proved to me who he was and I'd been a fool to think him otherwise. He was eloquent with proper manners and his school was the world. Loose morals and the most distinguished man the West presented as a statesman to the Union. Impetuous temper and impatient ambition. He'd long marked me as his principal rival and took no more pains to disguise his hostility than was necessary for decorum. Our fortunes were in wiser hands than ours. Clay had liberal views on our public affairs and that generosity attracted support. As President, his administration would be one of perpetual intrigue and management with the legislature, sectional in spirit and a sacrifice of all other interests to the West and, given his middle views, to slaveholders.

XLII

CLAY PUBLISHED A piece in the *Edinburgh Review* the following week. An evisceration of the administration's foreign policy and our reluctance to engage with South America. His influence was never greater and his piece threatened to turn the public against the President during the emerging crisis.

I had to respond, though I'd never defensively repelled his attacks before. The country didn't need the Speaker of the House and the Secretary of State arguing through newspapers and I decided not to publish a counter argument in the *Intelligencer*. An alternative revealed itself. Every fourth of July, the House invited a guest to read the Declaration of Independence and speak about its importance. That year it chose me. An ideal framing to assert the simultaneous autonomy of our nation and our hemisphere.

I arrived in my Harvard gown, reminding my audience and myself that I'd served as a rhetoric professor back when the future looked bright and I'd thought myself capable of anything, before compromises and mistakes led me to greet reality during sleepless nights.

Cobb, chairman of the Military Affairs Committee, introduced me as I surveyed the room. I was encircled by congressmen, including Clay in the Speaker's chair. Vice President Tompkins was on the balcony with the other Cabinet officers, senators, journalists, Washington socialites, and foreign ministers. Canning and Hyde—their swords absent—and most importantly, the Baron de Tuyll. We locked eyes. I'd never answered his invitation to join the Alliance. His stare said the terms offered were the best we'd get and if I did as he expected I'd mourn the memory of his generosity. I turned to friendlier faces. The vice usually in my throat before speaking was absent and I'd never felt more assured while standing center stage.

"Fellow citizens, until within a few days before that which we have assembled to commemorate, our fathers, the people of this Union, had constituted a portion of the British nation. A nation, renowned in arts and arms, who, from a small island in the Atlantic, had extended their dominion over considerable parts of the globe. Governed themselves by a race of kings whose sovereignty was founded on conquest and for a period of seven hundred years they exhibited a conflict almost continued between the oppressions of power and the claims of right. In the theories of the crown and the mitre, man had no rights. Neither body nor the soul of the individual was his own. From the impenetrable gloom of this intellectual darkness and the deep degradation of this servitude, the British nation had partially emerged."

A glowing response to my introduction, for nothing pleased Americans more than pillorying the British. You're right that Canning felt differently, though that's an easy prediction and you shouldn't feel proud.

"From the earliest age of their recorded history, the inhabitants of the British islands have been distinguished for their intelligence and their spirit. How much of these two qualities, the fountains of all amelioration in the condition of men, was stifled by subserviency to usurpation and of holding rights as the dominions of kings? When in spite of these persecutions, by the natural vigor of their constitution, they attained the maturity of political manhood, a British parliament, in contempt of the clearest maxims of natural equity, in defiance of the fundamental principle upon which British freedom itself had been cemented with British blood, on the naked, unblushing allegation of absolute and uncontrollable power, undertook by their act to levy, without representation and without consent, taxes upon the people of America for the benefit of the people of Britain. This project of public robbery was no sooner made known, than it excited throughout the colonies, one general burst of indignant resistance. It was abandoned, reasserted and resumed, until fleets and armies were transported, to record in the characters of fire, famine, and desolation, the transatlantic wisdom of British legislation, and the tender mercies of British consanguinity."

Applause, primarily of canes striking the ground. A music that rejected harmony or structure or rhythm, a magnification of rain pelting glass.

"Long before the Declaration of Independence, the great mass of people of America and of Britain had become strangers to one another. Here and there, a man of letters and a statesman, conversant with all history, knew something of the colonies, as he knew something of China

236

and Japan. Yet the Prime Minister, urging upon his omnipotent Parliament laws for grinding the colonies to submission, could talk, without amazing or diverting his hearers, of the island of Virginia. Even Edmund Burke, a man of more ethereal mind, apologizing for the offense of sympathizing with the distresses of our country, ravaged by the fire and sword of Britons, asked indulgence for his feelings and expressly declared that the Americans were a nation of strangers to him, and among whom he was not sure of having a single acquaintance. The sympathies most essential to the communion of country were, between the British and American people, extinct."

I reviewed the origins of the War of Independence and read the Declaration. Jefferson's prose reaching heights in our language unseen since *Hamlet* and *Paradise Lost*. Life, liberty, and the pursuit of happiness, grievances toward Britain's monarchy, Father's compatriots pledging their lives and sacred honor.

"That pledge has been redeemed. Through six years of devastating but heroic war, through nearly forty years of more heroic peace, the principles of this declaration have been supported by the toils, by the vigils, by the blood of your fathers and of yourselves. The conflict of war had begun with fearful odds of human power on the side of the oppressor. He wielded the collective force of the mightiest nation in Europe. He with more than poetic truth asserted the dominion of the waves. It was with a sling and a stone, that your fathers went forth to encounter the massive vigor of this Goliath. They slung the Heaven-directed stone, and 'With heaviest sound, the giant monster fell.'"

My eyes returned to the Baron as I approached my climax. My words were for him and Clay alike.

"And now, friends and countrymen, if the wise and learned philosophers of the older world, the first observers of mutation and aberration, the discoverers of maddening ether and invisible planets, the inventors of Congreve rockets and shrapnel shells, should find their hearts disposed to inquire, what has America done for the benefit of mankind? Let our answer be this—America, with the same voice which spoke herself into existence as a nation, proclaimed to mankind the inextinguishable rights of human nature, and the only lawful foundations of government. She has uniformly spoken, though often to heedless and often to disdainful ears, the language of equal liberty, equal justice, and equal rights. She has, in the lapse of nearly half a century, without a single exception, respected the independence of other nations, while asserting and maintaining her own. She has abstained from interference in the concerns of others, even when the conflict has been for principles to which she clings, as to the last vital drop that visits the heart. She has seen that probably for centuries to come, all the contests of that Aceldama, the European World, will be contests between inveterate power, and emerging right. Wherever the standard of freedom and independence has been or shall be unfurled, there will her heart, her benedictions, and her prayers be. *But she goes not abroad in search of monsters to destroy.* She is the well-wisher to the freedom and independence of all. She is the champion and vindicator only of her own. She will recommend the general cause, by the countenance of her voice, and the benignant sympathy of her example. She well knows that by once enlisting under other banners than her own, were they even the banners of foreign independence, she would involve herself, beyond the power of extrication, in all the wars of interest and intrigue, of individual avarice, envy, and ambition, which assume the colors and usurp the standard of freedom. The fundamental maxims of her policy would insensibly change from liberty to force. The frontlet upon her brows would no longer beam with the ineffable splendor of freedom and independence, but in its stead would soon be substituted an imperial diadem, flashing in false and tarnished luster the murky radiance of dominion and power. She might become the dictatress of the world, she would be no longer the ruler of her own spirit.

"Nor even is her purpose the glory of Roman ambition, nor 'tu regere imperio populosa' her memento to her sons. Her glory is not dominion, but liberty. Her march is the march of mind. She has a spear and a shield, but the motto upon her shield is Freedom, Independence, Peace. This has been her declaration: this has been, as far as her necessary intercourse with the rest of mankind would permit, her practice.

"My countrymen, fellow-citizens, and friends, could that Spirit, which dictated the Declaration we have this day read, that Spirit, which 'prefers before all temples the upright heart and pure,' at this moment descend from his habitation in the skies, and within this hall, in language audible to mortal ears, address each one of us, here assembled, our beloved country, Britannia ruler of the waves, and every individual among the sceptered lords of humankind, his words would be, 'Go thou and do likewise!'"

I finished and became a great fish in a vast sea of applause. This time the Baron played Jonah. We stared into each other and I knew he'd received my message and would convey it to Metternich and his emperor. The United States of America rejected the Holy Alliance's offer. We stood for independence, including and especially, this hemisphere's. Sword would meet sword.

I wished I could see Clay. If he clapped it was performative. Newspapers would carry my speech across America and Europe. Its substance was American policy and there was nothing he could do about it. But a goal was different than a strategy and advising the President toward that goal was my ultimate challenge. Nothing could prepare me for what was coming.

PART SEVEN

APOCALYPSE OF DIPLOMACY
LATE 1821

XLIII

At one O'Clock, I went to the President's and presented to him Mr. Canning, the British minister, who gave him a letter from the King of Great Britain, announcing the decease of the Queen. The President told him he received the communication with all the sympathy which the event was calculated to inspire. This was gravely said. The rest of the interview savored of dullness and was rather long, Mr. Canning waiting for the nod to be dismissed. Something was said about the Turks and the Greeks, something about the harvest in England wet or dry, and something about the British king's visits to Ireland and Hanover. As we retired, Mr. Canning reminded me that I owed him four notes. I asked him if that about the Newfoundland Pirates was one. He seemed as if suddenly to recollect himself that this was fifth. I told him the papers had been with the Attorney General for an opinion, which I hoped—

Knock knock.

"Come in." I pushed my diary further onto my home desk and Lucy entered my study. "What is it, dear?"

"Mrs. Adams is awake if you'd like to see her." She looked grateful. "She's in the music room."

Anger coursed through my thoughts as an alligator rolling through a lake. "Why is she up?"

"She's comfortable. See for yourself, sir."

Lucy led me to my wife, who lounged on a couch under a sapphire blanket she'd brought from London. She held a book, tea sat on the table nearby. Her weak appearance since her surgery scared me. She'd gone in and out of consciousness for weeks. This burden led me to anger and then to guilt.

"What are you reading?" I asked.

Her eyes halted their advance across the page. "*Ivanhoe*."

"Is it good?"

"Might be Scott's best."

"Wonderful. Is there anything I can get for you?"

She shook her head, her nose gently cutting about. "Just sit with me." I pulled a chair. "We've something to discuss."

"Yes?"

She turned to me. "Adelaide wants to send Johnson to us." She referred to her sister and nephew. "Are you all right hosting another relative?"

"What's one more?"

"There's a complication: Johnson has a slave named Holzey he wishes to bring with him. Now I—"

I leaned back. "You gave me your word—"

"I know, John."

"Your *word*, that we'd never have a slave in this house. Does your word mean nothing?"

"I don't have energy for this."

"Energy? Do you know how deprived of consciousness I feel, and in our most perilous moment in forty years you ask me to betray everything in which I believe?"

Her head sank into her pillow. "What would you have me do? Refuse my family?"

A moment. "Yes. Tell them *no*. Our answer is *no*."

"I've already said the opposite."

"Then you'll correct your error."

"I will not." An exacerbated mumble.

"You will." I leaned forward. "How *dare* you force this on me when—"

"What I've forced on you? I spend my days fearing for our family's safety. Metternich will kill you."

A moment. "Where did you hear this?"

"It's obvious. He wouldn't hurt the President, but—"

"You mustn't see murderers within shadows."

Her eyes widened, panicked. "We must hide you or else give him what he wants." Emotion incarnate.

Knock knock. Our front door.

"Not even Metternich would do such a thing," I said. "Not even he—" Lucy opened the door "—What now?" Brent entered. "Oh, Daniel, it's you."

"Hospitable as always," he said. He carried a file. To Mrs. Adams, "How are you, Louisa?"

She smiled like a young girl, a dozen sweat droplets on her forehead. "As well as can be expected. Thank you for checking."

"Of course. Get some rest," he said. She nodded and fell asleep upon his command. He turned to me. "Can we speak in your study?" I nodded. I saw Lucy's routine anger before I closed the door, furious that I'd argued with Mrs. Adams in her current state.

I gestured to Brent's file and asked, "Is that for me?"

"Yes, but we've something to discuss first."

"Spain?"

"No. I haven't heard anything since the French Third Corps defeated General Morillo."

I shook my head. "The Spanish Army's attempt to fortify northern cities at the countryside's expense will not stop Metternich from returning Ferdinand to his throne within a year."

"Will Britain intervene?"

"Castlereagh won't cross the Allies over Spain." I paused and looked at my diary. "A hundred thousand French soldiers. I'm amazed Napoleon left that many in this world. The Europeans never tire of war."

"Sir?" He got my attention. "The Mexican congress has elected Iturbide as emperor."

I snorted. "All that time I wasted negotiating with Onís. The concessions I made. My critics still accuse me of surrendering Texas. And now New Spain is an independent monarchy. This is why Clay tortures me."

"You can tell him that many Mexicans question the vote's legality. They demand a constitution."

"It doesn't matter. Ferdinand will rescind the liberals' recognition of Mexican independence and the Alliance will crucify Iturbide. Literally, for all I know."

"I added Mexico to the list of countries for which to choose ministers, just to be optimistic."

"I was at the President's yesterday, reviewing applications."

"Did he make any choices?"

"Indecisive as always. He can't pick between four men for Lima, though I believe he wants Forsyth for Angostura."

"I see." He raised the file. "If we're finished, I'll leave this with you. The Baron brought it this morning."

I opened it on my desk. I'd rather Brent had brought a battery to my house.

XLIV

"EMPEROR ALEXANDER HAS claimed for his subjects an exclusive right to enter the Northwest coast of North America, beginning from the Bering Straits to 51 degrees North and from the Aleutian Islands to the eastern coast of Siberia, as well as along the Kuril Islands to the south cape of Urup Island. This means vessels departing from our ports or European ports not only can't dock within this zone, but his navy will seize such vessels if they come within 100 Italian miles of these land masses. That's 115 English miles. With this edict, the Emperor has granted the Russian-American Company a monopoly over the Northwest fur trade. The United States and the British Empire are the nations chiefly affected by this move for it nullifies our claims to the region and the treaty I negotiated with Canning in 1818."

The President and the Cabinet's silent contemplation offered a study of each man. Calhoun projected the logic he cultivated as his signature at these meetings. Crawford restrained a panic of rightly receiving blame for inviting this to pass. Wirt and Crowninshield, always the weakest among us, shared looks of defeat and hopelessness, the kind that doomed the greatest and least of causes. The President, as during Amelia Island, Florida, and Missouri, unveiled his inner strength.

"I don't see how this edict—this *ukase*—can be seen any way other than the Holy Alliance invading North America," he said. "It is a direct challenge to test if we can resist. The clouds of war gather over us." To Calhoun, "Am I correct in believing the Army would need months to reach the Northwest in large numbers?"

"Yes, Mr. President. Such an expedition would be a nightmare to arrange. The Army would have to cross the continent and our supply lines would be vulnerable to Indians. We'd be sending our men into an abyss, unable to contact them as they confronted the Russian Army."

Somberness spoke to each of us individually before forging a rare consensus. Wirt said, "The Army would be far away while the Alliance threatens this coast. Both our country's and this hemisphere's. We'd be defenseless."

"That is their intent," the President said. "To make us choose between the Northwest and resisting an attack. Either choice reveals our weakness."

"We stepped too far," Crawford said. "We're unready to claim the Northwest. We should cede the territory to Russia until later this century."

"Why must you undermine our growth at every opportunity?" I asked.

"I'm being pragmatic. *You've* led us into a claim we cannot maintain and from which we must retreat. You are the architect of our humiliation."

"No, I—"

"It will take decades for our reputation to recover from what you —"

"Stop it," the President said. "I will not tolerate bickering this time." To Crowninshield, "Would deploying the Navy be as troublesome?"

He looked down. "Our ships will have to sail around South America, which will take months, and they'll confront the Russian fleet when they arrive."

"And again, they won't be able to defend our coast simultaneously," Crawford said. The President nodded.

"Remember that the Russian military also has limits," I said. "She too must decide between deploying her forces to the Northwest or against the New World's eastern flank."

"What does that mean?" Crowninshield asked.

"Drawing them into the Northwest could save South America. The Allies lack another fleet to—"

"We are not making such a gamble," the President said. His manner said to me, *I can't believe that came from you.* "I'm hearing that the Northwest is indefensible." Crawford nodded and Wirt and Crowninshield copied him. Calhoun did not.

"That may be true for the United States, but not for Britain, and the edict undermines her claim too," the Secretary of War said. "I suspect that Alexander acted on a whim. Metternich has lost any chance of luring London into joining him, or even into remaining neutral. Alexander has given us a powerful ally."

Their mood lightened but mine did not. I feared Britain more than the Alliance and I disagreed with Calhoun. I saw Metternich's hand behind Alexander. The Prince knew that forcing us to rely on the Royal Navy was easier than convincing Castlereagh to reverse his stance on South America. I'd hoped to keep Britain neutral by insulting her in my Fourth of July speech. Metternich knew this and thwarted me.

"I agree that Britain's interests overlap with ours, but we should open independent talks with Russia," I said. "I plan to tell Canning this when we meet the day after tomorrow."

"You'd reject the way out of this mess?" Crawford asked. "Your mess?"

"Begging Britain to save us will kill any chance of our controlling North America."

"You claim that I undermine the country yet you lead us toward suicide. You'd have us oppose Russia alone when we can't use our military as leverage."

"He's right, Mr. Adams," the President said. "How would you approach negotiations with the Baron under these circumstances?"

"I'd prefer to not discuss my plan," I said.

Crawford scoffed. "Is it a secret or does it not exist?"

"It's a secret from you, because you would inform Clay."

"My Cabinet officers must trust each other," the President said. "We're a team and we must stay unified if we're to resist our enemies."

"This type of diplomacy is delicate, Mr. President. It will adjust as circumstances change. I'd rather keep my thoughts in as small a circle as possible."

A moment. Then, "Write me a memorandum with your plan by the end of the day."

"Thank you, sir."

"Why should so much trust be placed in Mr. Adams?" Crawford asked. "He created this crisis and rejects the clearest way out of it." To me, "Why do you hate Britain?"

"I don't."

"You denounced her on the Fourth of July when you knew of Metternich's intentions toward South America."

"My speech was directed at the Holy Alliance."

"Most of it targeted Britain. Do you want Castlereagh to join the Allies?"

"I must say, as a New Englander, being accused of prejudice *against* Britain is refreshing."

Crawford leaned over the table, controlling its center the way a tortoise claimed a boulder. But I insult the reptile. "Let's address the biggest issue. You believe that placing the United States in control of North America will convince our citizens to elect you President. Don't bother arguing, I know I'm right. That's why you want to control the Northwest and why you don't want to ally with Britain. You care about your advancement, not the country."

"How dare *you* of all people attack my virtue."

"Your virtue is a mask for ambition. It signals a fake morality so others will elevate you through society. You say what you think sounds virtuous, not—"

"This is impertinent, Mr. Crawford," the President said. He leaned away from Crawford's tabletop ascendancy. "What is your goal for the negotiations, Mr. Adams?"

"We leave Russia in control of some islands in the North Pacific so they can partake in the fur trade and whaling, but nothing more."

"That's too ambitious. Mr. Crawford is right that resisting Russia and rejecting Britain appear incompatible. Tell the Baron we'll accept a claim at the 55th parallel but nothing south of that point."

"We'd still be tolerating Russian—"

The President signaled for my silence. "We've yet to discuss that Alexander is the chosen arbitrator for the dispute over Britain's theft of our slaves during the war. Negotiating separately risks prejudicing either party and lets Russia use the dispute as leverage."

Crawford said, "As though Adams doesn't hope that the Emperor rules for—"

"What say you, Mr. Calhoun?" the President asked.

"On what subject?"

"On whether Mr. Adams is up to the task." His gaze on me. I met it.

"Mr. Adams managed the Florida annexation with great skill. We should give him the opportunity to prove himself again."

"Very well," the President said. To me, "You've assigned yourself quite a task. I await your memorandum this evening."

XLV

YOU'VE LIKELY DETECTED my dislike for Crawford and so you know how painful it is for me to admit that he was right. Negotiating separately from Britain prevented us from using military power as leverage and I had yet to compose a substitute. The President's demand for a memorandum forced me to concentrate. The idea came to me, as always, from somewhere beyond my reach, as though a ghost chose me to unveil it to the world.

Restore our friendship with Russia. Use honey and not vinegar. Draw Russia away from Metternich and remove the Prince's muscle. Alexander feared that republicanism threatened monarchy but we could make friendship worth his while with generous trade terms and by siding with him against Ottoman Turkey, Russia's historic enemy. The risk was upsetting Britain. Russia replaced France as Britain's rival after Waterloo and antagonizing her jeopardized our international trade and a return to London's pre-1818 hostility. I had to balance relations with both countries and foster a competition between them for our affection. I wanted us to be closer with Britain and Russia than they were with each other or with Metternich. That would secure our interests for a decade or more.

My proposal enticed the President. He called me to the Mansion the next day to discuss it and suggested I should delay meeting Canning because he feared Britain would send our communication to Russia. I asked if I should meet with the Baron first but we agreed Britain had too large an interest in the Northwest to not be consulted. I kept my schedule.

◆◆◆◆◆◆

"Your speech on the Fourth of July turned our press against you," Canning said. "The *Times* ran a series of articles portraying you as a French partisan."

"You're not the first to tell me my address was ill-received." I leaned back in my chair and ate crackers while glimpsing the autumn rain as it battered my windows. "I had no intent to offend."

"Did you clear it with the President beforehand?" he asked. I shook my head. "You're lucky Parliament is distracted by Alexander transforming the North Pacific into a Russian lake." He looked at his notes. "He insists his claim is grounded in Article XII of the Treaty of Utrecht. He argues the Russian government is claiming less than is its right and we should be grateful the claim is so narrow and that restricting foreign shipping within spheres of influence is common practice for sea powers."

I listened to him but my hands swelled and I focused on how the raindrops splattered against the glass. How their angle of impact determined the direction they burst.

"Should I repeat?" he asked.

"Has Lord Castlereagh written to you about this?"

"He has. He called the edict unacceptable aggression but he believes it threatens British interests less than American claims to the region."

"Why?" I asked, still watching the rain. Crumbs built upon my lap. "Our treaty agreement for joint control of the area doesn't expire for seven years."

"Your Congress is debating a bill to open the Columbia River for settlement and to admit the area as a state."

"You needn't worry until 1828."

"Your government would win Castlereagh's favor by cooperating with the Royal Navy's suppression of the slave trade. Our officers in Sierra Leone reported Spanish, Portuguese, and Dutch colors off the African coast. Your navy could help police the region."

"Not this again," I said. It was obvious how Britain planned to exploit this situation. Perhaps I could use this to show my Southern colleagues why they should hesitate before submitting to London. "Every time you raise this subject we repeat the same points. Do you not recall that the slavery debate almost ruptured the Union last year?"

"France has joined us."

"Louis is king in title only. Castlereagh will let Alexander nullify British access to the fur trade over an unrelated matter?"

"Your country's hypocrisy lessens the British public's pressure on Castlereagh to side with America against the Allies. Are you comfortable that the Holy Alliance is better on this issue than the United States?"

"What does the British public think of Metternich?"

"It doesn't trust him. He personifies the continent."

"So when the time for decision arrives, will it accept Castlereagh doing Metternich's bidding, as Alexander does? Most of your people admire mine. They dislike slavery but they admire what America represents. The ideal, if not the reality. Whereas Metternich is the archenemy of liberty and Russia is their competitor and is challenging their access to the fur trade. Castlereagh will have to override the public to side with the Allies and undermine the principles your country shares with mine, both at home and around the world."

A moment. I brushed some crumbs off me. He said, "I take it that Rush keeps you informed on British public opinion?"

"Yes, that's why I know Parliament will force Castlereagh from office if he tolerates Russia's aggression."

He sighed. "I fear that may occur regardless."

"Would George, your cousin, not succeed him?"

"That's true, and given their competition I ask you to never inform him that I said this, but Castlereagh was instrumental in Napoleon's defeat and building Europe's peace and it's tragic that there are entire novels written that only exist to attack him."

"Thomas Moore."

"His leading critic, yes. Moore blamed him for the calvary suppressing the Peterloo mob and said he'll impose the Alliance's oppression on Britain. Madness. That's how they see his diplomacy with the continent, as though talking to Europeans is worse than preventing wars. He has no good options available to him."

"I know the feeling. Let's return to Russia. Negotiating jointly with Alexander is too complicated. We'd have to build a team of diplomats from both countries that could advance our common interests and choose a leader."

"Castlereagh could negotiate with Mr. Levin, Alexander's minister in London, with Rush present. Would that work?"

"No," I said. "Rush is an able man but I will see to this myself."

"We're amenable to that. Have you a goal?"

"The President wants Alexander to withdraw his claim to the 55th parallel," I said. He wrote that down, his eyes wide. "Let's not allow Russia to use the arbitration as leverage. She mustn't divide us."

He nodded. "With what will you bargain?"

"That's for me to know, not Castlereagh."

"But what influence does America have if she acts without our support? Russia is not Spain and you only defeated Onís because the Royal Navy kept the Allies at bay."

"I will speak to the Baron about Turkey."

"Ah. I imagine Lord Castlereagh will do something similar."

XLVI

JUDGE HAY OPENED the door. I entered the President's office and the Baron followed me. "Mr. President," I said, "I present to you the Baron de Tuyll." I stepped aside so they could meet. The President stood behind his chair at the head of the Cabinet table.

"Mr. President, I am honored by your hospitality. I bring to you abundant professions of good will, both of Emperor Alexander and myself, toward the United States of America and to you."

"And to the people of the United States?" the President asked.

"Yes. The Emperor did not intend to suspend or harm relations between Russia and the United States. He has at heart friendly relations with them and sees nothing in present events or in future prospects which would in any manner impair them."

"Hearing of your majesty's warmth pleases me. I consider him to be one of the most forward-looking men of our time. His leadership saved Europe during the war and his dedication to preventing similar wars wins the hearts of all caring souls."

"Thank you for your sentiments, sir."

"Please, sit." The President gestured to where Crowninshield ordinarily perched. He and I went to our normal chairs. "I wish to discuss the Emperor's edict."

"May I say a few words on the topic?" the Baron asked. The President nodded. "Thank you." His clasped hands on the table, left of his papers. "General Speransky asked me to clarify the edict to ensure the Emperor's intent is not confused. He initially wanted to declare the Northern Pacific Ocean a Mare Clausum, but later took the 100 Italian miles from the 30 leagues in the Treaty of Utrecht, which excludes fishery and not navigation."

I turned to the President and found his pupils waiting for mine. He said to the Baron, "Thank you for informing me of this detail."

He'd told me in advance to say: "The Russian claim on the Northwest coast of this continent is groundless. The Emperor has committed himself, before the world, to pretensions he cannot sustain.

His only option now is to obtain by negotiations a part of the wrong by renouncing the remainder."

Not a muscle in the Baron's face moved, as though he wore a mask of bronze or metal. Was this a negotiating tactic or rooted in his nation's power? The President continued my thought, "I know the Emperor will be satisfied if we adjust the boundary to 55 degrees latitude. This adaptation will respect the mutual interests of Russia and America."

"The Emperor is not interested in retreating," the Baron said. "His concern is that Americans in the region sell whiskey and weapons to the local—" looked at his forms "—Indians. This makes the Indians dangerous. They harass our merchants."

"Our government cannot police our citizens from so great a distance," I said.

"That is why the Emperor banned them from the area."

"Russia's claim violates our own claim to the region. We are open to conceding to Russian entry at the 55 degree boundary, but any more is unacceptable." I still thought the President was wrong for offering that concession. "The United States are adopting the principle that the American continents are no longer subjects for any new European colonial establishments. The remainder of both the American continents must henceforth be left to management of American hands."

"Why should the Emperor accept such a policy?"

"Because it's vital to preserving a good relationship with this country."

"The Emperor desires a good relationship but he must prioritize his people's interests."

"If I may," the President said. The Baron looked at him but I kept my focus on the Russian minister. "America is open to making additional concessions to maintain and strengthen the Emperor's friendship, if he will adjust the boundary."

"What concessions?"

"Unrest stirs in Greece. We can deploy a squadron to the Mediterranean to aid the Greek cause. It will weaken Turkey's grip on the Balkans."

"The Emperor will need our help," I said. "Britain and Austria will side with Turkey."

"Such a pledge would please the Emperor," the Baron said. "What else will you offer him?"

"A new commercial treaty," the President said.

"The Emperor is adverse to commercial treaties." To me, "You know this." I nodded. To the President, "Russia has no discriminating duties, no colonial monopolies to remove."

"Aside from the edict?" I asked.

"Yes. Aside from the edict."

"We appreciate Russia's generous trade policy. We're locked in a trade dispute over the West Indies because Britain discriminates against goods stored on our ships. Whereas our trade with Russia is conducted only through our vessels."

"What do you offer the Emperor?"

"We're aware of his anger toward British opposition to his acquiring a warm water port. We, likewise, resent British arrogance and history of supporting our enemies. Perhaps we could increase our trade at London's expense."

"I see." No other man in Washington unnerved me so. Every crisis left me feeling less the master of events but my insecurity was never greater than when in his presence. Knowing he was in the city, waiting, gave me cause for concern. That this man was another's slave— imagine if he were the monarch. The Baron was not interested in appearances. I envisioned him crushing entire populations to maintain control. He was ill suited for a throne.

"It is in neither of our countries' interests to let Britain solely control the Northwest, which is her aspiration," the President said.

"Are you submitting that Russia moves her claim to the 55th parallel, and in exchange, America will help Russia banish Britain from the region?" the Baron asked.

"Yes," I said. I felt the President's eyes on the back of my head but I watched the Baron.

"Interesting. Perhaps America can also lend her navy to help Russia counter Britain's global naval superiority."

"Perhaps," the President said. "But we don't wish to sever our relationship with Britain. We don't want a third war."

"Certainly." To me, "You explained this to Canning?"

"I have to act strong toward you so he'll trust me," I said.

"How do I know you're not doing the reverse?"

"Closer relations with Russia will remove British competition in the Northwest and protect us from Metternich. Britain can't offer a comparable outcome."

"You'd break your 1818 treaty to win the Emperor's devotion?"

He'd caught me. The President said, "An American-Russian alliance discourages British retaliation."

"Excellent. You should know that my latest report from St. Petersburg contained the Emperor's decision upon the question given to him by Washington and London as to the construction of the Treaty of Ghent's article which provides for the slaves evacuated from your territories."

"Oh?"

"This is not yet official, but the decision is in your favor."

I said to the President, "We should publish the Emperor's decision in the *National Intelligencer* once it's announced."

"An excellent idea," he said.

The Baron said to me, "Let us meet soon to flesh out the agreements between our countries."

"I'll be in touch."

The Baron left and the President kept me for another hour. He inflicted harsh words for stepping beyond what he'd decided in advance of the meeting and said I risked our relations with both Britain and Russia. I told him I could negotiate a mutual sharing of the Northwest between the three countries. He said I'd better succeed or else failure would be my cross to bear.

XLVII

ANTOINE AND I left for my Potomac swim after my morning routine of reading the Bible and writing in my diary. We intercepted Mary and John, my son. They held hands and journeyed to watch the sunrise. Like a spider, Mary had insinuated herself in my home, plucking the strings of each of my sons and picking the one most scrumptious to her tastes. I extracted myself from the situation.

I congratulated Mary on making her pick among my boys and told them to put their affairs in order before announcing a public engagement. I instructed them to bless God for marriage and for the enjoyment of a portion of felicity resulting from this relation in society, greater than falls on the generality of mankind, and far beyond anything that I deserved. Its greatest alloy arose from my wife's constitution, the ill health which affected her, and the misfortune she suffered from it. I reminded them our union wasn't without its trials nor dissensions. We both had frailties of temper. But she'd always been a faithful and affectionate wife and a careful, tender, and watchful mother to our children. They thanked me for my advice.

After the Potomac I went to the office. I played with the notion that the Holy Alliance targeted not only America's rise but my political ascension. I flattered myself that they feared a new Adams presidency and favored Crawford, an incompetent, or Clay, a zealot. Brent found me and said the President had summoned me. My stomach tightened and I left for the Executive Mansion.

I feared news on the Northwest. Had Canning and the Baron learned of my contradictory promises? Anxiety became confusion as I found Calhoun and Wirt waiting with the President in his office.

"Morning," I said. To Calhoun, "I hear Yale granted you an honorary legal doctorate. My congratulations." He nodded and the President and Wirt drummed the table.

"Mr. Wirt," the President said, "please inform Mr. Adams on developments in Florida." Ah, Florida. I should have guessed. One of my many faults is losing focus on issues that don't concern me.

"Are you familiar with the saga of General Jackson, Judge Fromentin, and Commissioner Callava?" Wirt asked.

"For the most part," I said. "Jackson jailed Callava and Fromentin issued a writ of Habeas Corpus to discharge him and Jackson summoned Fromentin to answer for challenging his authority. Fromentin complied, not in obedience, but to offer his reasoning."

"Correct. The *Enquirer* is publishing a report on the newest details later today." The *Enquirer* was the Virginia faction's organ and Wirt worshiped its backer, Spenser Roane.

"How damaging will it be?" the President asked. I had trouble focusing, the Northwest crisis and family troubles drained my energy.

"I expect them to call for Jackson's removal as Florida's governor," Wirt said. The President's cheeks sank. "I propose we ask the *Intelligencer* to defend the administration. They can argue Judge Fromentin issued the writ irregularly and possibly illegally."

"The root of the question is Jackson's current status," the President said. "He was discharged from the Army when Congress reduced the military last term."

"He's a civilian governor but still issues orders to the troops as he did before," Wirt said. "The military obeys and this is what Callava protested. Now, what's tricky here is that Colonel Brooke, the commander of Pensacola, wrote to General Brown inquiring whether he is subject to Jackson's orders. Brown not only answered negatively but was surprised the question was asked."

"Brown's letter passed through the Department of War," Calhoun said. "We've yet to send it to Brooke."

"That's true," Wirt said. "Thank you for mentioning." Why was Wirt so deferential to Calhoun? Why did he respect everyone in the Cabinet but me?

"Who thinks Brown is right?" the President asked. "That Jackson has no authority to issue military commands?"

"I do," Wirt said. "I mean I agree with Brown." Calhoun nodded. The President was relieved until he saw me.

"I don't," I said. Wirt's head fell. "Jackson's commission grants him the powers not only of governor but of the Captain General of Cuba, which means he's the province's military chief. The military is the province's only executive power and if the government has no military command it has no effective authority. No means of executing either administrative or judicial decrees."

The President smirked, as though saying, *You always side with Jackson.*

"What if Jackson employed the militia?" Wirt asked.

"There is no Florida militia," I said.

"He introduced juries. Why not constitute a militia?"

"How would he arm them or establish officers? Who would pay the expense? It is a question of form. If Jackson cannot, as governor, issue orders as a military commander, he can still issue requisitions to the same effect which the troops are bound to obey."

"They *are* obeyed," Calhoun said. "They'll continue to be obeyed until counter-orders are received." I was delighted he agreed with me. We collaborated so well on security matters that it was tragic that slavery divided us.

"Let's return to the controversy between Jackson and Fromentin," the President said. "Did Fromentin have the right to issue the writ of Habeas Corpus to liberate Callava?"

I wanted to shape the discussion. "The only federal laws extended to the territory are those of revenue and the slave trade and Fromentin's jurisdiction is confined to them, so he had no right to issue the writ."

"That's a reasonable argument," Wirt said, "but though he issued it erroneously, his judicial capacity means Jackson had no right to summon him. They were both wrong."

"But the writ resisted Jackson's lawful authority. That grants Jackson authority to summon Fromentin to answer for his contempt." They all looked skeptical.

"What prevents Jackson from abusing his power," the President asked, "like when he removed the remaining Spanish officers from their positions without permission?"

"It's a binary choice," I said. "If we hold that Jackson lacks the right to issue military orders we ought to inform him and Colonel Brooke before cases arise where the legality of his orders are of infinite importance. We haven't yet mentioned that Callava threatened resistance by force and Butler's soldiers loaded their muskets in front of Callava's house. If violence occurs under illegal orders the administration shall be blamed."

"Jackson's powers are those exercised by provincial governors," Wirt said. "The object of the powers conferred upon him was to maintain the liberty enjoyed by the Spanish inhabitants until they can be admitted as American citizens. This was stipulated in the treaty you negotiated with Onís. How then can Jackson exercise authority over Americans?"

I couldn't fault the Attorney General's legal reasoning, but that didn't mean I agreed with him. "You're taking guidance from the Constitution, but our principles restricting power aren't suited to this occasion. We acquired a Spanish province, heretofore governed by military rule. Congress deferred separating powers in Florida during their last session, so all powers formerly exercised by the Supreme Rulers of the province are now vested in the governor."

"An outrageous argument."

"The military was its only executive. Denying the governor the right to command the soldiers strips him of effective power. If our citizens enter the province, they must respect its laws."

"You raised the episode where Jackson removed Spanish officers," Calhoun said to the President. To me, "In that context, I'm not sure he has the power you suggest." Wirt nodded. "I don't want to hear of some tragedy happening there. Jackson's disposition is to exercise every particle of power given to him. He disregards our institutions and popular opinion. Remember that almost every newspaper has sided against Jackson in this episode, even those who supported him in the Seminole War."

"Our institutions, popular opinion, and comments by newspapers do not bear weight in this case," I said. "Jackson's commission gives him the power of the Spanish governor. He exercised it for justice. It's absurd to grant him absolute power and to then blame him for using it."

"Jackson ought to respect popular opinion," Wirt said. "It affects the administration's influence."

"Mr. Adams is right," the President said. Divine words, the best our language ever produced. "Congress extended to Florida only laws relating to revenue and the slave trade. The Spanish system is continued until the next session in all other respects. The problem is the two systems are of opposite character but are in operation in the same territory. American law supports Fromentin and Spanish law supports Jackson."

"In that case, you, as President, can send Jackson instructions to exercise no authority incompatible with our institutions."

"He should exercise as little authority as possible."

"Would such an order not be dangerous?" I asked. "It would suspend all government in the province."

"Under the current system, we must consider every light in which Jackson's actions are susceptible," Wirt said, "and anticipate every objection that can be made."

"I agree."

"Jackson's reign isn't worth that," the President said. "Fromentin was wrong to issue the writ but he had pure motives."

"Perhaps we should write to Jackson to learn his version of events."

"And repeat the 1818 crisis?" Calhoun asked.

"I have no interest in reliving that experience," the President said. "What if we relieved Jackson of his post and issued a public statement thanking him for his service? That way we'd be rid of him while pacifying his followers?"

Wirt and I nodded, but Calhoun said, "We'd only be rid of him for a time. Jackson will seek power elsewhere, likely in Washington."

"I cannot risk losing public support while the Holy Alliance threatens this hemisphere."

Calhoun turned to me. *The President is passing Jackson off to his successors.* I was comfortable with this. Jackson was my partner and could prove useful in 1824. He could become my protégé.

"If that's decided," Wirt said, "let's discuss the extent of Callava's immunities."

XLVIII

MRS. ADAMS ASKED to attend George's commencement as we'd not heard from him since he graduated Harvard months prior. Her health remained frail and I questioned the wisdom of her taking the trip but I complied, scheduling my meeting with the Baron for after my return to Washington. Hope deluded me: no valedictory oration, no performances in Hebrew or Greek and the only performance for a master's degree was in English. They said it was about genius but from what I heard it was upon love. We dined at Smith's Tavern that night with Tom's family.

I awoke the next day with a poem in mind. It read:

Ambition, when she seeks a certain end,
Deceives herself with hypocritic art:
That end obtain'd, her purposes to bend
Because a means, another end to start.
Such, of the plumless biped is the fashion:
Ambition is a never ending passion.

I didn't know if I'd written it in a dream or remembered it but I asked my wife and she said it was unfamiliar. The notion that I'd penned while asleep melted my concerns and I enjoyed my enthusiasm for a short while.

I walked with George through Quincy. I noticed him shivering. Winter approached but he contorted more than I thought reasonable. Was he so vulnerable, so lacking in basic hardiness? Even a few months ago he'd looked more adroit. While in Washington with me he said he wished to become an early riser and requested I wake him each morning. I did so after making a fire. He'd come to my chamber and read the *Federalist* for class. This routine died after nine days.

I glanced at the shops and allowed nostalgia to alleviate the stress of Metternich and Jackson. Then, to George, "Are you ready to talk?" Silence. "Your mother and I worry about you. Why don't you write to me anymore?"

More contortions. "Why should I? So you can rip my life apart?"

"That's what you think of me?"

"You've only ever treated me bitterly."

"How much of this is Mary choosing John?"

A Shakespearian epic played across his face. "I don't care about her." He saw my reaction. "I don't. She can be unhappy if she wants."

"Do you have other romantic prospects? You're 20, are you thinking about—"

"There's another girl. Since Mary."

"What's her name?"

"It doesn't matter. Our relationship was stillborn."

"What happened?"

He sighed. "I dreamt of kissing her and of you criticizing me for doing so."

"Why would I—"

"Because you criticize me for everything. Don't deny it, Father, you do, and it's my life's seed. Every decision leads to criticism. So I won't make them. Romance and marriage are for fools."

"*That* is a decision."

"No it isn't."

"Son—"

"Don't call me that."

A pause. "That's what you are to me."

"Regrettably."

I wanted to strike him but I resisted. I watched him. Face pale, his cheekbones all but bursting through his skin. "Are you using opium?" His eyes wouldn't look into mine. "Be h—"

"It helps." A pause. "I'm not ashamed. You judge me but you use religion for the same purpose."

"Do not pre—"

He laughed. "The letters you wrote to me about the Bible made it obvious even when I was young."

More temptation for violence, but it would end the conversation. Digging was wiser. "I take it you've put no more thought into your life's purpose? Do you remain committed to dedicating yourself to literature?"

His posture softened. "That's still my preference."

"Where will you live?"

"With Grandfather."

"Tom and his family already fill his home."

"He said he has room for me. He does not judge me as you do."

"He's softer on you after what happened to Uncle Charles but he shares a similar disappointment."

"You're lying."

"I'm *not*, son." We stopped walking. "My parents' most important gift to my life, beyond even the Revolution, was setting virtue and ambition as my creed. Each exists because of the other and they are the source of my success." His lips thinner than straw. "I fear you haven't absorbed either, despite my efforts." He moved away but I grabbed his arm and overpowered him. I held him as I would a disobedient dog. "You've little time left to reverse your fortunes. You have the same capacity to succeed as your grandfather and I. Come to Washington." He shook his head. "Yes, son. Come with us. Your mother can nurture you. She'd love that." He cried and I felt my eyes swell too. "Try rising before the sun again. Don't indulge in despondency. Failure is a choice. It's a choice. Life is hard and everything comes with a tax but you *fight* through it. You—"

"I can't."

"You must."

"I lost every investment you entrusted to me," he said. "I didn't follow them. Wasn't even during the hard times."

I bit my lip. "That's all right, son. We'll begin again. You and me. *You* will begin again."

"Doing what?"

"You'll become a lawyer."

"So I can fail at that?"

"You won't fail," I said. He nodded. "Do you know how hard I fought to fulfill my duty as my parents' eldest son? The sacrifices I made? I bled for them. I denied myself happiness for them. I still do, and you won't even try. You—"

He threw his weight against me and I lost my grip. Then he pushed and fell, rolling before rising and running away.

"George!"

He didn't look back. I walked alone for another hour. I concluded he was beyond redemption and any effort made to help him was effort wasted. I said this to Mrs. Adams and we held each other and cried and mourned deep into the night.

XLIX

I SET TWO chairs and a table near the Anacostia River's bank, where Father's administration established the Washington Navy Yard. The Navy destroyed the base to thwart British capture in the late war but Congress authorized its reconstruction early in the President's tenure. Snowfall that morning transitioned the scenery. White joined the brown and green and gold. I wiped specks off the chess board I'd put on the table. I felt cold even in my coat but I wanted to meet the Baron outside. I feared one or more of my clerks was giving Canning information and felt insecure hosting this discussion in my office.

I circled the furniture a few times and decided it was ready. I sat on black's side, my back to the river. Saw more people than I expected walking about but none were interested in my presence. I bought this chess set while minister to Russia, a standout in my collection. Memories of St. Petersburg were not just of another era but another life and someone told them to me and they became mine. Meals Mrs. Adams and I shared with Alexander and his wife. They were our friends, we laughed and we discussed the world. Faith, leadership, parenthood. Now we were adversaries. How could he let Metternich manipulate him? That must have been the case, or else Napoleon's 1812 invasion unleashed a paranoia greater than I knew. I fooled myself thinking our friendship influenced his foreign policy, that he cared I served as chief diplomat and bore responsibility for countering his actions.

At ten, a black speck in the distance caught my attention. I wondered if the precipitation produced a mirage but then I was certain he was upon me. I studied the way he navigated the foliage with precision and had an insight. The Baron often paused before speaking. I'd thought he did this to intimidate but really he listened to others more deeply than most, giving himself time to analyze before acting.

"Good morning." That deep monotone.

"To you as well," I said. "Care to join me?"

"You wish to decide North America's fate with a game?"

"I hoped to produce a jovial atmosphere."

He stared at the pieces. "That is acceptable."

"Good." I lifted both kings and swallowed them in my fists and shuffled them behind my back and then raised them. He tapped my left fist. I opened it. Black, of course. "Help me rotate the board."

"It would be simpler to switch seats."

He wanted to see the woods, not the river. The broader field of vision. I hesitated but had no reason to argue. "As you wish." We each circled the table to our right and I restored the kings.

"Move when you are ready," he said.

I built a pawn fortress, staggering them along the board's center. It was not my usual opening but was something I'd toyed with in the prior months. My intention was to constrict his movement but he didn't comply. The Baron punctured my right flank with his queen and rook. I castled my king on the queen's side and my rightward bishop and knight leapt into action.

"Does the 1818 treaty have a rescission clause?" he asked.

Chess was a mistake. I'd hoped to lighten the mood by proving we could play while negotiating but he pursued a checkmate and I feared his rapid victory would set a dominant tone. I had to stabilize the match. I lost a rook and both knights and needed my queen and white squared bishop to hinder—

"Well?"

I blinked. "Rescission clause?"

"Yes, for the 1818 treaty. Our discussion must be our focus."

My eyes on the board. A whisper: "Yes, we can rescind the treaty."

"Good. I do not believe that America will risk British retaliation for the Emperor's goodwill."

"We told you—"

"I know what the President said. That a Russian-American alliance deters British aggression. But Castlereagh cannot allow a minor power to betray him without punishment. It makes London look weak."

Of course we had no intention of betraying Castlereagh. I planned to write to Rush about whatever framework the Baron and I reached to pressure Castlereagh to enter these talks on my terms. I advanced three pawns on the left side.

"Let's address the merger between the Montreal North West Company and Hudson's Bay Company," I said. "Castlereagh wants to build an entity to rule the Northwest as the East India Company rules the subcontinent. It's already issued its own currency."

"That reinforces my point. How would we impose this ban short of war?"

"Castlereagh cares more about free navigation in the North Pacific than the fur trade. Would the Emperor relinquish Prince of Wales Island from the Russian sphere?"

"No, and he makes no distinction between the island and the ten leagues of water past its southern tip."

"He must know the British will never tolerate such a claim nor reward bad behavior via concession."

"War with Russia means war with the Holy Alliance. Castlereagh will accept Russia's action to avoid this."

"The action still severs your ties to Washington and London, likely for years."

"Not necessarily," he said. "Your proposal convinced me that the Northwest is better shared by two than by three, and if Levin and Castlereagh can reach a deal to divide it between Russia and Britain, I don't see what America can do about it." I looked up from the board. He said, "Britain offers us what America cannot."

"What about the Greeks? Castlereagh supports the Turks."

"You will not even align with South America. You expect me to believe Washington will intervene in the Balkans but not its own hemisphere?" A pause. "This solves the problem of your people selling the local Indians weapons and whiskey."

I returned to the board. Both of us had lost most of our pieces, a Borodino on 64 squares, but he held an extra pawn and knight so every exchange was advantageous. He knew the game distracted me. I had to stop thinking about it.

"Did Britain reject the Emperor's offer to join the Alliance?" I asked.

"How is that relevant?"

"It's obvious the edict is meant to focus us on the Northwest while the Alliance invades South America. So the question is whether Castlereagh will tolerate restoration of the Spanish Empire after funding its ruin in exchange for your proposed arrangement."

"I've told you South America will remain open to trade. London will have access to this hemisphere and better relations with Europe, all while containing America's growth. It's ideal."

"The British people will remove Castlereagh before he'd allow for South America's subjugation. Not every country rejects its people's voices."

"Which is why the world has become so turbulent," he said. "You're conflating two issues. Russia and Britain can decide the fate of both continents without American input."

"Russia would spare South America?"

"I will not speak to that at this time."

His arrangement was for London to surrender the Northwest in exchange for South America. This left us reliant on British and Russian mercy for a generation. Canning had said Castlereagh feared our encroachment in the region more than Russia's so I couldn't threaten to ally with Britain.

"It's your move." He gestured to the board. Ending the game showed weakness. I had my king, a bishop, and some pawns. He had the same, plus the extra knight and pawn. I had to stop his pawns from reaching my end of the board.

He'd seen through my strategy the moment the President and I made our proposal and knew how to use it against me. Look at him: his nose and cheeks were red but I'd not seen him shiver once whereas my endurance unraveled by the minute. I'd grown up in Massachusetts but my New England hide couldn't match his Russian blood.

Minutes passed.

"There's no guarantee that Castlereagh and Levin will divide the Northwest," I said.

"Correct."

"We should continue negotiating. The three powers can share the region."

"That is your true goal?"

"Yes."

"Then make a proposal. A real one."

"What about a commercial treaty?"

"I'm listening."

We discussed how Britain would complicate our access to the Atlantic if we prioritized Russian trade. Charm replaced menace and I relaxed, though the cold still pricked my shoulders.

"The problem is that the Emperor's trade policies are so generous that we have little to gain from a treaty," I said.

"True."

"Will he renew his treaty with Britain next year?"

I felt the urge to turn around but the Baron placed his bishop on a vulnerable square. Why sacrifice it? I considered various contingencies. Did he hope I'd move my king toward his pawns?

"Could America compensate Russia in coffee and sugar if the Emperor does not renew the treaty?" he asked.

I didn't answer and he rose from his seat. I took a moment to break my focus and face the other way. Canning stood behind me. My muscles contracted, making my skin uncomfortable. What had he heard? Did it matter?

"What a surprise," the Baron said. "Wonderful for you to join us."

Canning nodded. To me, "Why are we meeting out here? It's freezing."

L

"*HOW* DID THIS happen?" the President asked. We were in his office, me in my chair while he paced. The pain in my hands was worse than ever and I felt a new stinging in my eyes. I feared my body shattering. "I thought I could trust you."

"I'm sorry."

He turned to me, hand raised and fingers extended, a knife to sever my throat. "What *exactly* did Canning hear?"

"I can't know with certainty. We were discussing Russia signing a commercial treaty with us in lieu of renewing the one with Britain."

Do you remember my saying that Mrs. Adams' expression won Plato's contest for the ideal image of dread? The President won the fury category. "So he thinks you were convincing the Baron to undermine British interests?" He turned from me. "What happened next?"

I pictured what transpired. "We were both confused and irritated from the cold. There was a terse exchange of words and he said my office had invited him. Then he left."

"Did you pursue him?"

"I called for him but it was unbecoming to look desperate. Plus, I didn't want to abandon my chess set."

He shook his head. "At least your game made it home safely." He looked out the window. The sun departed Washington. "Did the Baron say anything?"

"Just that he needed time to assess this development." I paused. "At first I thought Canning had spies in my department. Now I'm convinced the Baron sent him a letter in my office's name. He never took our proposal seriously and used it to fool us. To waste our time as France defeats the Spanish liberals."

"And to drive a wedge between you and Canning, and between us and Britain. You *know* Canning will report this to Castlereagh, which will make London suspicious of us."

"I've started drafting a letter to Canning. I'll meet with him as soon as I can to smooth this over."

He sighed. "Frayed relations with the British and the Russians. Now of all times." I wondered how badly his confidence in me was damaged. Was I a liability, were my days numbered? "What happens next?"

"Everything depends on Castlereagh's negotiations with Levin," I said. "If Britain and Russia agree to share the Northwest without us, we'll be powerless to stop them."

A moment. "We'll renounce our claim to the region."

"No, Mr. President—"

"The decision is made." He turned to me. "Better to relinquish it voluntarily than being forced out."

"We ought not do anything rash."

"Then what's our way out of this one?"

As during the Missouri crisis, my mind was empty. "I don't know."

"Maybe you *were* lucky with Florida."

"That's not fair."

"No? Had Castlereagh not tolerated Jackson's invasion, would we be in this mansion today?"

"My plan was a good one but the Baron lured me into a trap. My fear after the edict was that the Allies were driving us toward Britain but he saw it could foster an accord against us." A pause. "I still doubt the British public will accept that outcome."

"Which means our fate is in their hands and it's true that we can't defend this hemisphere on our own," he said. "You overestimate your abilities."

"We must rid the Americas of European control. That's been our goal all these years."

He turned from me again. "We weren't ready."

"Mr. President, it has to be now."

He shook his head, disbelieving that I stood my ground after today. He exited.

◆ ◆ ◆ ◆ ◆ ◆

My status diminished within both the Cabinet and the Department of State. Crawford saluted the apparent destruction of my presidential prospects. Calhoun convinced the President not to renounce our Northwest claim until we learned of European developments. I felt sad that my word now caused more harm than good and couldn't even complain to Brent because he'd replace me after my fall from power. I sent Canning my note, explaining I'd not conspired against Britain. His reply was barely a page long, he asked for time before meeting again but assured me he wouldn't be recalled.

A milestone. The President asked Congress to authorize funds for diplomatic postings in Mexico, Chile, Gran Colombia, and the United Provinces in his end of year message. We finally recognized the stable Spanish American republics. Joaquín de Anduaga, Spain's new minister, sent me a protest. I wrote back that the Spanish war on South America was over and nothing could disrupt the continent's independence.

I told the President we had to meet a South American official. Manuel Torres of Colombia was the only available authorized agent. An interesting man. Born in Colombia, he fled to Philadelphia and dedicated his life to Spanish American independence. He spent the war advocating for weapons and money for Bolivar, which I resisted to remain neutral. Onís recruited a team to destroy Torres and King Ferdinand directed his forces to sack his Colombian home and murder his wife and daughter. Torres kept fighting.

His vision achieved, his health failed. He asked to delay the meeting and arrived at the Executive Mansion in early 1822. I thought he would die by summer's end. I introduced him to the President, who was joined by Calhoun and Clay. The latter had rebuilt his finances and returned to Washington to plot his return to Congress and the Speakership. The President felt he deserved to attend given the years he spent advocating for South America. I respected that the President could overlook Clay's opposition to his administration, though I felt uncomfortable seeing my rival in my weakened stature.

The President, Calhoun, and I were in our standard seats while Torres took Wirt's spot and Clay took Crawford's, replacing his ally.

"You look well, sir," the President said.

"No, I don't," Torres said. Blunt and smiling. "I need a good climate where there are no books, paper, or pencils and I can speak of politics through words."

"I take it you won't settle in Washington?" Clay asked.

"Certainly not." We laughed. "I want a garden and a horse to ride. Perhaps I could convalesce." To the President, "Colombia is a free and independent nation. A sister republic. We've vanquished our Spanish oppressors and are ready to unite two oceans which nature separated. Our proximity to the United States and to Europe destines us by the Author of Nature as the center and empire of the human family."

"You needn't convince me," the President said. "The United States take great interest in your country's welfare and success."

Torres cried for a few minutes. "I am honored you opened your home to me after our prior interactions."

"What are those?"

"That I, along with others, commissioned the rebel capture of Amelia Island." The President turning to me was an event for the ears, not the eyes. Another failing. I knew of Torres' involvement in the Amelia Island episode but still believed him the best representative to meet the President. Torres said, "Britain supported our cause, but my people will remember that the United States were first to recognize our sovereignty." The President relaxed. "Britain has recalled loans we've already paid." To me, "She wants to place us in her debt. Permanently. British settlers seize Venezuelan land. If you look at the recent treaties between Spain and the Dutch—"

"We should spend our time on more sensitive subjects," Calhoun said. "How does your government view the Holy Alliance's intentions toward South America?"

"The Alliance will not rob Colombia of her independence and our army will be grateful for another war." Torres paused. "Our people will suffer most severely but our spirit cannot be put down by Europe's united power." Clay slapped the table. The President and Calhoun followed. Finally I capitulated, too awkward to resist. "Colombia and the United States should join together against the Alliance," Torres said.

Silence as they waited for my response. "We must prioritize our growth. Coalitions restrict us," I said.

"Can you defend yourselves on your own?" Torres asked. "I read today that Russia captured several of your vessels near Nova Scotia."

"What of Britain?" Clay asked. "We could form a rival, temporary faction with Britain and South America." Clay was happy for me to portray Claudius and I felt the President's glare.

"I would advise the President to maintain our independence," I said.

Torres shifted from disappointment to anger. "Britain will stand with us if you will not."

"How is it in our interest to allow London to join with our southern neighbors in our place?" Clay asked the President. "To establish defensive and commercial ties. To earn benevolence. I haven't understood this for the past five years."

The President leaned back in his chair, his arms crossed, his mind reconsidering his foreign policy. Torres spent the next hour speaking with Clay and Calhoun on less contentious issues. He departed before dark and gave me a copy of Colombia's constitution as he left. He wanted me to know his country was stable.

PART EIGHT

IS VIRTUE ENOUGH?
1822

LI

HAD THE TITLE *president* become associated with yellow and I'd not been told? That notion danced within my secondary thoughts as I sat in Kirkland's office at Harvard. Yellow-painted walls while curtains imitating rays from the celestial ball 93 million miles away draped the windows. A carpet with overlapping red and green borders surrounding white flowers. It was superior to that other presidential office in Washington, though in fairness, the British army hadn't incinerated this one.

"I take it you're here to discuss John?" he asked, a stack of papers at the ready.

"I wanted to learn of any news on the university's observatory. We can discuss the end of his schooling and his next step if we have time." My secondary thoughts now pictured if he'd look better without the wavy red hair dispersed on his scalp's rim. They ruled affirmatively.

"I see." He looked down, contemplating. "I'm afraid there's been no progress since our last discussion."

"That's disheartening. Why not take this task seriously? Harvard voted to consider the subject seven years—"

"You needn't remind me, Mr. Adams. The economy—"

"Has recovered."

A pause. "Mostly. I'll phrase this differently. No one wants to lead a fundraising effort."

"No one cares about Harvard's honor or science's advancement?" I really needed a small victory after months of diplomatic limbo. My eyes and hands perpetually stung and on the bad days they felt far worse. "No progress at all?"

He didn't hide his annoyance and skimmed hastily through the stack. He retrieved a title deed. "Here. A widow—who asked to remain anonymous while living—pledged 20,000 dollars upon her death."

"For the observatory specifically?"

"Yes."

"Good for her," I said, "though of course more is needed for the new professorship."

"What professorship?"

"An expert to work alongside the institution. Otherwise it won't fulfill its potential."

"You're talking about a lot of money. Harvard has other concerns and I'm not sure it's in the university's interest to prioritize this project right now."

"What if I took the lead on raising funds?"

"How much?"

A moment. "One thousand? It's a sum more suited to my circumstances than my inclination."

"This is a public donation?"

"Yes. It's my obligation as chief diplomat to foster learning."

"Your office's prestige will aid the cause. Anything else on this topic?"

"I suppose not. You mentioned John. Unfortunately, Mrs. Adams and I must return to Washington before commencement, but—" His expression butchered my sentence.

"You really don't know?" he asked. I shrugged. "Mr. Adams, your son is expelled. He led the student rebellion before exam period."

Mounting disappointments. "I don't know what to say. I'm mortified. At his behavior, at what it means for his future, and for our reputation."

"I'm sorry you had to hear this from me."

"Can he still receive his diploma? His grades improved last term."

"Your son violated our policies. Showing him mercy is unfair to the other students. The ones he led."

"You understand this news will embarrass me as Secretary of State?" I calculated how this could make my stature even worse in shaping diplomacy and the election.

"I know, and I hope this doesn't affect our friendship. Or your donation." A pause. "Does it?"

I took a moment. Giving Harvard money made me look weak. But John's immaturity was at fault and did looking weak matter anymore, given recent events? I had to think of how it affected my virtue, instead of my ambitions.

"No, it doesn't," I said. He smiled, too smug for my liking. "Let's make it contingent on Harvard raising the sufficient funds within two years."

◆ ◆ ◆ ◆ ◆ ◆

I returned to Peacefield and found Mrs. Adams, Nancy, and John lounging around the sitting area. I overheard my wife explaining that we planned to vacate Washington for Philadelphia that summer. Every day her recovery from surgery became clearer. She saw me and slowed her words. I constrained myself but surely the anger was still flush in my cheeks. She returned to Nancy and finished her thought and then all six eyes were on me.

"Take a walk with me, John," I said.

The boy turned to his mother. "You stay here," she said.

"In that case, I ask you ladies to excuse us."

"I'll not draw back."

Nancy rose. "I'll give you all privacy." I nodded but Mrs. Adams scowled.

I waited until we were alone. "Did you know Harvard expelled him?"

"What?" She turned to John, who closed his eyes. He must have known Kirkland would tell me. If he didn't he clearly didn't belong at the university, or any university.

"He led the student rebellion," I said. "What were you thinking?"

His eyes ajar. "President Kirkland's restrictions were unreasonable."

"You hosted battles, dropped cannon balls—"

"Why must we tolerate strictness?"

"He was the authority and you must show him respect."

"Like how Grandfather respected King George?"

"You know that's different and you insult the Continental Army by suggesting a comparison." I paused. "How many students were expelled? 30?"

"Must be over 40 by now," John said. My wife shook her head. "They started with four but we decided as a group to resist until our friends were reinstated."

"Which clearly worked," I said. I fought the urge to compare my son's actions to my own recent missteps. "When Kirkland said you were expelled, I assumed it was because you spent too much time with Mary. Have you thought of how you'll support her?"

"I'll go into business. Perhaps you'll invest in me."

The arrogance of this boy. "You've no experience at business. You must think as an adult, son. I'll find you a position as a lawyer's apprentice."

"You hated practicing law."

"It's an option in reserve." I looked at Mrs. Adams and said to John, "Can you let your mother and I speak alone?" He turned to my wife, who nodded. His eyes widened and he left. Mrs. Adams and I watched each other from across the room. I stood with my hands in my coat pockets while she leaned back in her seat, her arms dangling over the sides.

"What words do you have for me?" she asked.

"We know you're too soft on the boys."

"That's the problem?"

"What's your theory?"

"That you've placed the country above our family for longer than any of us have been alive."

"That's the only road consistent with virtue."

"Not this again."

"Yes, this. Only this. Deeds fade and ambitions disappoint. Our virtue is all we have. It's who we are."

"You expect me to believe it isn't an obsession with legacy, like your father?"

"*Shh*. He'll hear you."

"He wouldn't hear me if he were in the room. Besides, Nancy is distracting him."

"Don't speak that way about him in his own home."

"Fine, but you kept me in Russia away from our sons for two years. You knew there'd be consequences for their growth."

"We must look past our desires and—"

"That's impossible. Even for you."

"Cicero. Washington."

"Maybe in myth. Not in reality."

"Not everyone has *your* limitations, Louisa." I shouldn't have said that. Apologizing was proper but you know it's hard expressing regret to someone who irritates you little by little everyday for so many years. She turned and I followed her gaze. Charles stood at the entrance, our youngest son wearing a tricorn hat and smoking a cigar.

"Remove that from your lips this instant," she said.

"Why?" he asked. "I see Father and Grandfather do it. And George and John."

Mrs. Adams said to me, "Do you see the effect you have on the boys?" To Charles, "Son, cigars are the enemies of sobriety. You'll ruin your health and peace of mind and your mother, who loves you, will rue the day you were born."

Charles said to me, "Do you object?"

"I'm your mother and you must listen to me," Mrs. Adams said. "Eat fresh vegetables and avoid meat. Drink as much milk as your stomach can bear. Fresh from a cow every morning, if you can. Or find a woman to supply you. You'll never find a woman if you smoke cigars. My sex detests the smell."

"Enough of your self-pity, Mother."

"Do not speak to her that way," I said. I wondered if his attitude was from Mary's rejection.

"Pandering to irrational sadness is not a virtue, Father. It's selfishness."

"At least word it more gently."

"It's important to know that Mother indulges her desires and that you pride yourself in denying yourself of yours."

"Since when do you know our hearts?"

"How else do you justify your career?"

"The community's interests—"

"What about our family's interests?" Mrs. Adams asked. "We have needs that must be met too."

"We just discussed this, Louisa," I said. "Virtue is the only stable identity and it commands—"

"It is not virtuous to lead your family into unhappiness, John. No matter the cause."

"Denial—"

"How do we differentiate virtue from self-righteousness?" Charles asked.

"Regarding what?" I asked.

"Regarding public service."

"Your grades better excuse that remark, son."

"Why? There are few duties that truly call upon a man to serve his country."

"Do you hope to come home for Christmas this year?"

"Am I wrong? There are many who will fill the roles, so they won't be neglected."

"Can you continue arguing elsewhere?" my wife asked. "I want a break." Her eyes barely open.

"I'm going to write in my diary and then go for a walk," I said. "I need to think." To Charles, "Go study."

"Exams are over for this term," he said.

"Then go find another way to improve yourself."

LII

MRS. ADAMS AND I returned to Washington. I spent the voyage thinking about my sons. Were they destined to fail? I instructed their studies from a young age, supervising their education in language, the classics, and mathematics, but they retained little. A weakness within Adams men defeated some, like my brothers, while others, principally Father and myself, overcame it. Father was an ambitious man and propelled himself from humble origins to become Boston's most prominent lawyer and a new nation's architect. He and Mother endowed me with a similar drive to reach the zenith of that nation as a two-term President. I honed my focus in every moment to maximize my improvement and utility. That was my mistake, my failing as a parent—I pushed my sons toward professional success but had placed the bar too low. They'd have resisted their familial weakness to reach ultimate apotheosis.

In fairness, Alexander's edict concealed my destiny. News of Castlereagh and Levin agreeing to share the Northwest would doom my 1824 prospects. My fate depended on the British public and you can imagine how comfortable I felt.

For months I analyzed my insistence that we act independently of Britain. The edict made her neutrality impossible. Wirt asked if a Castlereagh-Levin compact meant sharing the Northwest in exchange for Alexander renouncing his intent toward South America. I said the Baron implied such terms. He said cooperating with Britain could have led to a trilateral deal and I reiterated that Metternich hoped we'd surrender our independence in that manner and that I rejected the notion that becoming an appendage to the British Empire was our best option. Yet an alternate path alluded me despite countless discussions with Brent. Metternich had crafted a scheme where we lost no matter the outcome. Should the compact come, and Britain and the Alliance decide our hemisphere's portion without our input, I'd resign my post, abandon hopes of the presidency, and return to Massachusetts a broken man where I'd find an early grave.

Washington climbers made their inevitable proposals. John Floyd, a Virginia congressman and flaunting canvasser, brought my biggest headache. His bill required the President to occupy the Columbia River and surrounding land north of the 42nd parallel and admit this *Oregon Territory* as a state once it had 2,000 residents. It would solidify our claim and make us harder to dislodge. I feared this move would provoke a British and Russian military response. I explained this to the administration's allies and the House defeated Floyd's bill.

He retaliated instead of accepting his defeat with dignity and called for the administration to give the House all records from the Treaty of Ghent. He hoped to embarrass me with damaging evidence from the negotiations. Obviously, Floyd was Clay and Crawford's proxy. They smelled blood and showed their willingness to destroy the Secretary of State during a global crisis so long as they devoured my 1824 electability. Calhoun told me that Crawford's plot to destroy the administration, for which we'd predicted for years, was upon us.

The President opted to comply and not risk Floyd forming a committee and subpoenaing his administration. I worried he was ready to dispense with me should anything inglorious be discovered. I couldn't rely on anyone else to save me. Floyd filed his petition the day after my return and so I catalogued the Department of State's records from Ghent while also organizing my office and resetting my mind for work.

I scrutinized every document and letter to find anything my enemies could use. Nothing, but I was troubled by a letter that Jonathan Russell, the junior member of our negotiating team, had written the President when he served as Madison's Secretary of State. Russell made a vague reference to a follow-up letter where he'd list his concerns about us. I sifted through the documents twice more and concluded its absence.

The President was the letter's recipient. He must have forgotten to leave it with the Department of State. I wanted to avoid raising this with him and sent Russell a note instead. I barely remembered Russell at Ghent but recalled Madison appointing him as interim minister to Sweden. I dismissed him in 1818 but doubted he held a grudge since he'd fallen upward, replacing Forsyth as the new chairman of the Committee on Foreign Relations. Plus Russell was from Massachusetts and so my election could only benefit him.

♦ ♦ ♦ ♦ ♦ ♦

He came to my office. "What can I do for you, Mr. Adams?" He showed his nervousness by placing his elbows on his knees and hunching his back like a turtle shell.

"I asked you here because of Floyd's request that my department surrender its files on the Ghent negotiations to the House."

"I see."

"Are you surprised?"

"No. I thought you might contact those of us who served with you."

"You're the first. I found a letter you wrote the President when he held my office, dated 24 December 1814. You said you'd send another regarding concerns you had at the time. Do you remember this?"

"A letter?" He looked down, likely afraid I was angry to learn he'd complained of me behind my back. Turning the other cheek could make him an ally. "Yes, I believe I do."

"Excellent. Would you have a copy, by chance? If I don't include it in my report my critics will claim I'm withholding it."

"Mr. Adams, it's been years since I've thought or seen—"

"Could you look? You'd earn the administration's goodwill. And mine."

A moment and then he nodded. "I can look. If I find it, I'll have my daughter produce a copy and I'll deliver it to the Department."

"That's perfect, sir. Thank you." Stress lifted, but only a miniscule. "Would you care to discuss the 11th District?"

He followed through, leading me to think I'd underestimated him at Ghent. I sat behind my desk and read the letter. Its contents were a prelude to my political obituary.

LIII

I WENT TO the Executive Mansion the next day. It was no longer a choice, I had to ask the President for his copy of the letter. I prayed he had it. Literally, I prayed at church that morning. The sermon—delivered by Mr. Little, the Unitarian preacher at the Capitol—focused on Acts 5:38. *And now, I say unto you, Refrain from these men, and let them alone: for if this counsel or this work be of men it will come to nought—but if it be of God, ye cannot overthrow it.* There's a certain persecution carried on against these doctrines which alone justifies this polemic style in Congress. I placed my thoughts on this subject and my breathing to remain calm.

I found Judge Hay in the Mansion. "Where is the President?" I asked. "I have an urgent matter to discuss with him."

"He's occupied with his wife. Her condition is worse than normal."

"I wrote him last night that—"

"Yes, and he instructed me to speak to you." He raised a file. "I believe this is what you seek." I opened it. A letter from Russell dated 11 February 1815. "The President grants you permission to read it."

I unveiled the letter Russell delivered yesterday. "You'll find this interesting. Russell claims this is his copy of the letter, but I have a strong suspicion it's a duplicate, not the original. It's formed of seven folio sheets directed to little less than a denunciation of the Ghent mission. Russell charges that I offered the British an exclusive right to navigate the Mississippi River."

"I take it you didn't?"

"I would never. Russell hopes I'll have no choice but to include this in my report to Congress and that the western states will accuse me of betraying their interests to secure New England fishing rights. It's clear that Clay and Crawford promised him a job in their administrations if he helps them destroy me."

A moment. "If that's true it is one of the basest things I've ever heard," he said. I appreciated the confirmation that I wasn't mad.

"Is the President comfortable with me taking his letter home? I can compare them tonight and return tomorrow."

"I'd rather set you in my office. How long do you expect to take?"

"A few hours if I'm not distracted."

"Perfect. The President will be available this afternoon."

I smiled. "Thank you for helping me, George."

"Of course, Mr. Adams." He led me to his office, which was adjacent to the President's. He cleared his desk and even readied his chair for me. I thanked him and he left.

I read the President's copy and was stunned by its differences from Russell's. Russell's version claimed I violated the Department of State's instructions, no such charge existed in the original. It did vent about the rest of the team—Clay, Gallatin, Bayard, and myself, but the duplicate existed to attack my character. My virtue was all I had left and Russell, Floyd, Clay, and Crawford would suffer the consequences for this strike.

I listed the differences between the letters and outlined remarks refuting the duplicate. I paused before writing a first draft, tired and angry, but noticed the sun setting. Gathered my materials and left Hay's office and entered the President's without knocking. I found the President sitting and Hay standing.

"*Welcome*, Mr. Adams," the President said. "I've been expecting you."

"Has George told you of our conversation?"

"He has."

"Clay is behind this. Behind Russell and Floyd. He knows I'm vulnerable and is delivering the coup de grâce."

"Did you find any differences between the letters?"

"172." I lifted my list and the President smiled. "The main ones portray me as disobeying your orders and offering Britain control of the Miss—"

"What's your plan?" I detected suspicion in his tone. His chance to be rid of me.

"I'll insert both letters into the report to Congress and include remarks giving them context."

His posture shifted, a wall between us. "Including the 1815 letter brings me into this mess." Saving himself at my expense, after all I'd done for him.

"Withholding it supposes I'm afraid of its appearance when I'm not."

"It ruins us both to appear prejudiced toward the next election's outcome."

"You must judge how this affects you and what course to pursue. But it concerns me and I'm convinced the course most desirable for me is to communicate the letter."

"I'm happy to send a statement saying you followed my directions at Ghent and I was pleased with the outcome. But nothing further."

"Mr. President, Russell gave me the duplicate at my office and I'm obligated to include it in the report. It differs from your letter and alters the understanding of what transpired at Ghent. Only by including your letter will the misunderstanding be resolved."

"Let's slow down. Russell's conduct is reprehensible and his motives are to influence the next election. The problem is it's my duty to take no part in that election and if I send this letter an acrimonious controversy will ensue and all parties can make me the vehicle of their anger."

"I understand, sir. Really, I do. The course you propose is the proper one in your situation. But I cannot hesitate nor doubt so far as my own interests are concerned. I wish both letters to be transmitted to the House with my remarks upon them. This plot is a deadly thrust at my character and I wish to grapple with those who've schemed against me. In the face of the country, the attack on me has been made. In the face of the country, I wish to make my defense."

"I know, Mr. Adams."

"I have no wish to prostrate or expose Russell's character. My only object is to defend myself."

The President sighed. "I can consider the subject further. I'll ask the Cabinet—"

"No, I wouldn't wish—"

"Mr. Wirt, at least. I should consult the Attorney General. If you came to me before going to Russell, I could have told the House that such a letter existed." He adjusted his weight in his chair. "A statement of facts would do you justice. I could say that Mr. Madison and I had approved of your actions at Ghent."

"I appreciate this approbation, but I wish for the conduct to stand on its own grounds, not a testimonial."

Hay said, "It seems to me there's a difference of opinion between you two as to the proper course to be taken."

"The only difference of opinion is to the course most expedient to my concern in the affair," I said. "I know the President wishes to uphold neutrality. In this I acquiesce and it is all I've asked of him. He must judge what is required of him and if he declines to send the letters I will cheerfully submit to his determination, even though Russell aims to dishonor me." To the President, "I repeat sir—if the letter is withheld, a vague and indefinite charge will hang over me. I can never conquer every prejudice against me, but I can satisfy every responsible person that Russell's imputations of my offering to sacrifice the West's interest were groundle—"

Knock knock.

The President said to Hay, "Go answer it." Hay did so.

"Is the President available?" Russell's voice, soft and tense.

"Enter," the President said. Hay stepped aside and Russell angled himself toward the President until he saw me at the table's other end. He shed his skin like a lizard. "What do you want, sir?"

"I came to discuss—uh—your letter to the Chinese emperor." Russell convinced no one, not even the termites beneath us.

"The letter you left at the Department is an extraordinary paper," I said. "Your conduct in this whole transaction has been equally extraordinary." His eyes closed for he knew he'd been caught. "I recall we were in Paris together when you wrote this." I raised the real one. "That you wrote it without your colleagues' notice when their conduct is arranged is strange, sir. That you've furnished a materially different duplicate is still more so."

His eyes opened. He spoke with the strongest voice he could, an octave above squeaking. "Remember that I wrote the letter because you, Gallatin, and Bayard voted to trade Mississippi navigation to the British in exchange for fisheries to—"

"That's a lie."

He spoke louder. "That was not Clay's desire, nor mine. So I thought it necessary to justify my conduct to the government. Floyd called for the Ghent papers without consulting me, but upon his call my letter became necessary. I'd written my daughter at Mendon for my old draft and she sent it all but the last two sheets."

"That's—"

"So there may be *some* variations between the two versions but there are no alterations of facts."

"You're mistaken," I said. "There was an alteration in the form of an accusation that the mission's majority violated instructions."

"The original refers to different instructions."

"The original has no reference to the instructions cited. I can show it was impossible that you should have thought we violated—"

"Did the Status ante Bellum include a British right to navigate the Mississippi?" Russell decomposed and every minute alternated between being flush and pale.

"Do you recall, Mr. Russell, when the Department of State sent us instructions in October 1814 authorizing us to offer Britain access or control of the Mississippi?" I asked.

A moment. "I have no recollection of our receiving such an instruction."

"I do."

"Well—then there is no question it was so."

"There'd be no question if you paid attention." I leaned my weight on the table with my right hand. "My question is whether this was a genuine misunderstanding, or—"

"I've not acted in concert with your enemies. I've never written or published a word against you in the newspapers. Nor have I acted from hostile motives toward—"

"I wish not to inquire into your motives." I felt greater energy than I'd had for months. "Henceforth, as a public man, if upon any occasion I can serve your constituents, it will afford me as much pleasure as if nothing ever occurred between us, but—" His head fell "—but of private intercourse, the less there is between us, the more agreeable it will be to me."

A vanquished man. The President watched our interaction with interest, Hay with terror. "I told Brent, when I delivered my letter, that

I'm indifferent to whether it's communicated to Congress," Russell said. "Did he tell you this?"

"No."

"I see."

Knock knock.

"George?" the President said.

"I'm on it." Hay opened the door and Crowninshield entered.

"Are you ready to discuss boats?" Crowninshield's words lost momentum as he saw Russell withholding tears and my triumphant stance. "I'll come back later." The President nodded.

"I'll come with you," Russell said. To me, "I wish you well." They left. I held the table tighter to avoid collapse. I felt exhausted and sat in Wirt's chair. Wiped sweat from my brow and let my mind relax.

The President waited a moment, then, "I don't believe his claim that he didn't act in concert with Clay and Floyd."

"I don't either," I said.

"My takeaway from what I just witnessed is that we should tell Congress we've found none of Russell's letters. It's the only way to save you *both* from public deaths."

"Mr. President, Floyd called on the Department of State to report its files and Russell delivering the letter makes it an official record. It must be included. That means yours must be too. A message to the House that no such letter is at the Department risks a strong public animadversion. It's impossible the letter's existence won't become notorious and when it doesn't appear in my report—"

"*Your* report? It's *my* report. It is no report at all until I've accepted it."

I was tired of his selfishness and how he'd treated me since the edict. My feeling wound up to a pitch and it was difficult to preserve my temper and command my expressions.

"Sir, it *is* your report to do what you please when it is received," I said. "But so far as I understand the Constitution of this country, it is my report to make and I am the responsible person in making it."

"When I was Secretary of State, I considered the reports made to Madison subject to his control. I felt bound to make any alteration in a report that he required."

"I observe the same rule. I've never, in a single instance, written a public paper without making every alteration that you suggested. I'm willing to make any alteration to this one that you desire—once I present it to you."

"Floyd means to influence the next election and it's my duty to have no part. Producing these letters will cause controversy in Congress and the newspapers."

"You said this alr—"

"Then allow my point to stand," he said.

Whatever control of my words I still possessed went through my fingers like grains. "I ask no favor. Nothing but a hearing. But to suppress facts—that Russell has delivered to the Department a paper to be communicated to the House—as the duplicate of a letter called for—that this letter differed from the letter he really wrote—in a charge against the Ghent mission—takes sides with Russell and against the other Ghent negotiators."

I knew I'd overstepped. The President folded his arms higher than I'd previously seen. The veil of anger that was all too familiar during the prior months. Hay stared at the President and we both wondered if these were my final seconds as Secretary of State.

"I have no intention of sending the letter," the President said. Then, as an afterthought, "Unless the House calls for them, of course."

A lifeline. "If that is your decision, sir, it has my respect," I said.

LIV

I INVITED TIMOTHY Fuller, the representative for Massachusetts'
Fourth District and my closest congressional ally, to my office. He only
knew of Floyd's request so I made him comfortable, cigar in hand, and
gave a brief synopsis of the Russell quagmire.

"Am I prejudiced for or against Britain?" I asked rhetorically.
"My adversaries must make up their minds."

"You're certain that Clay is behind this?"

"He has Russell playing the Jackall to set the West and South
against me."

He shook his head. "Disgraceful behavior from a former
Speaker."

"He won't be *former* once he holds the position again after this
autumn's elections."

"Is there no way to stop him?"

"He holds great sway over your colleagues. Especially after the
Missouri Compromise."

"I was in awe of his leadership at the time. Tragic to learn he's
capable of such duplicity." He raised the cigar to his lips but paused.
"What do you require of me?"

I injected regret into my voice. "I find myself in the most painful
situation of my life. I'm compelled to renounce all friendship with a man
whom I had esteemed and with whom I'd been associated in a trust of
the highest public importance. The work we did together was to the
nation's satisfaction. But I must expose him to shame. This hasn't
happened to me with any other man but Russell brought this upon
himself. Such is the nature of the charge that if the letter gave a true
representation of the facts which it alleges, it would be the House's duty,
even now, to impeach the surviving members of the Ghent mission's
majority. Therefore, it is indispensable to defend myself, which I cannot
do without exposing him."

"I agree. It's your only option."

"You're the only member of Congress to whom I've spoken
upon this subject. I'm aware Russell is your colleague and I don't wish

for any member to side with me and against him. But the President hesitates whether to send the House the letters or withhold them. I requested he send them, with or without my remarks upon them. He said a call from the House for the letters is the only action that would convince him." A pause to let him absorb my request. "If Floyd or Russell call for the Ghent papers again—including the letters—I need my friends in Congress to support the motion."

"And if they don't call for them?"

"Then I wish for some *other* member to do so. I desire it be known that I don't wish for the letters to be withheld. I want them to be public."

"I'll look into this for you, Mr. Adams, and I'm confident I'll get the votes. Congressmen don't like it when the President withholds secrets. Makes them feel like a lesser branch."

"I ask for neither favors nor affection from any in this conflict. The facts will speak for themselves."

"I'll draft a resolution calling for the letters tonight. The clerk will have it in the morning and it'll be on the President's desk by tomorrow evening."

A smile clawed through my tepid resistance, a frontal attack on a thin line. "Wonderful, Mr. Fuller. Wonderful. I can't remember a more productive meeting I've had with a member of your body."

◆ ◆ ◆ ◆ ◆ ◆

I visited the Executive Mansion two days later, after work, and found the President and Hay preparing the carriage. "Ah, Mr. Adams," the President said, "how convenient for you to arrive."

"What does that mean?"

"We're off to the Capitol to deliver the Ghent report, including the Russell letters and your remarks upon them. Come with us."

"Are you sure?"

"Yes, it's fitting. Besides, we have something to discuss." He gestured to the carriage door. I climbed aboard and sat beside Hay. We faced the President. "George and I made a few alterations to your remarks." He handed me the new version and I skimmed it. Gone were harsh expressions made in a hurried indignation.

"You've read this?" I asked.

"Briefly. The pressure of other business stops me from focusing on any one subject. But George read it very attentively. Isn't that right, George?"

"Yes," Hay said.

"George told me that, having perused both letters—the real and the spurious one—that your paper is so unanswerable in substance that the less severe its manner the more powerful it will be."

"It was only six lines," Hay said. "The paper, in fact and argument, is the most overwhelming thing I've ever read."

"Thank you, sir," I said. "I'm not offended by your edits. You could have marked more passages for alteration if they're objectionable."

At the Capitol we found Floyd speaking with Crawford and Crowninshield. A coincidence, I'm sure. The President told them he was delivering the report to the clerk. Floyd thanked the President for complying with his request, though I was certain he and Crawford damned this outcome.

The President told me he planned to stay and sign a few dozen recently passed bills. He said I could depart if I wished. I waited in the Hall of the House instead and watched the evening session dissolve. The President and Hay found me after dark and took me home.

I went to bed delighted and questioned whether the President resented my actions. My last thought of the day was that I had to prioritize my virtue even above his amity.

♦ ♦ ♦ ♦ ♦ ♦

"Is now a convenient time?"

"One moment."

I completed a paragraph and inspected it before pushing the sheet further up my desk, next to a large and growing stack but not joining it. I turned to face my wife, standing in my home office's doorway. I was eager to write and felt more energy than any time since falling into the Baron's trap.

"Yes, Louisa?"

"I'll have the children—ours, Tom's, Adelaide's, the others—packed and ready by Thursday."

"Good," I said. "Good. Philadelphia will be a pleasant vacation site this summer. Other families we know will be there."

"Then I ask you again—"

"Louisa—"

"—to please come with us."

"I can't."

"Washington is vacated. You'll be alone and miserable with only the humidity to accompany you."

"Hay is staying to administer the Executive Mansion while the President is in Highland and I await the lack of distraction."

"You've already defeated Russell. Your task is complete."

"He refuses to admit defeat." I raised a copy of the *Kentucky Reporter*. "Clay and Crawford's newspapers published his piece making new arguments about the letters. They're still trying to ruin me with this dribble."

"How's the piece?"

"It's empty but Russell's a good writer for such a dull man. It misrepresents facts in a sophisticated and subtle way. The President and Hay think it might make an impression on the public mind."

She sighed. "Will your pamphlet end this?"

"Yes. It's the most thorough argument I've ever made. He'll only have peace with me by waiving the white flag." I paused. "It's going to be a book, by the way."

Another sigh. "Is that necessary?"

"Yes, Louisa. It will contain the President's message to the House, the various Ghent Treaty documents, Russell's note, and my new argument that will be 100 pages long. This shall end the debate for all time."

"Who will publish it? They'll be taking a great risk if it doesn't sell."

"I've spoken to a Mr. Force about it. He expressed interest. If he declines, I'll publish it myself."

"We can't afford that, John."

"Defending virtue is worth any price."

Her head and shoulders fell. "Your every sentence for the past year has held that word. You care for it more than life itself."

"That's correct. We live in a world separated from God, Louisa. Our strength, glory, and happiness, both as people and as a community, are centered in our moral purity. Monarchy can survive without virtue but republics cannot."

"But must it outweigh circumstances in every decision? Your declining to join us is only one example."

"We can't control outcomes and ought not build our identities around them."

She shook her head and leaned toward the door but came back. "What's your new opus titled?"

"*The Duplicate Letters, Fisheries, and the Mississippi.*"

"It rolls off the tongue." She lifted the page from earlier. "Is this worded correctly?"

"What's wrong?"

"You wrote that Russell's letter, *trumped beforehand throughout the Union, as fraught with disclosures, which were to blast a reputation, worthless in the estimation of its possessor if not unsullied.*"

I took the paper and read the line a couple times. "It still needs to be edited," I said. She smiled. "Allow me to reword it."

LV

I ENTERED THE tavern within Brown's Hotel on Pennsylvania Avenue, where the President held both of his inaugural balls. The hotel was expanding and I saw a new Pocahontas painting at its entrance. A group of off-duty marines, stationed in the capital, occupied half the room. Some played cards while others sang an old tune. An unutilized bastion of recreation and alcohol, the room felt curious, like miles of blue ocean without a fish or crustacean in sight.

Clay sat alone, sipping his signature mint julep, a cocktail of three shots of bourbon and two shots of dark coffee. He waved to me and I approached.

"Thank you for joining me." How did he manufacture a pleasant tone at will? A talent I lacked and one of the few traits of his I'd have admired had it not been rooted in ingenuity. "Care for a drink?"

"Not now. I'm going back to work once we're done."

"So am I."

"Campaigning, I assume?"

"Until November. Then I'll return to the Speakership. My finances are in order, no thanks to you."

"What you asked of me violated our internal rules," I said. "Don't moan or feign moral superiority. I know you picked up a stone, slipped it into Russell's hand, and whispered, *there, throw this stone at that pane of glass, break the window, and then I will get in, and you after me*." He smiled. "I know you're at the bottom of this, that from the day the Treaty of Ghent was signed, you've worked like a mole to undermine me in the West and misrepresented the transactions at Ghent to suit your purpose. That you pulled the strings holding Floyd and Russell, that you —"

"Obviously it was me, Mr. Adams. We both know that. The denials I gave the newspapers are a routine of the lives we lead. I reject your moral claim too. Your book so obliterated Russell that he resigned his congressional seat and may even flee Massachusetts. Your supporters are chasing him out of town."

"He deserves it for he was your tool. Did you not think I would defend myself? You knew I'd notice the duplicity of Russell's letter. Or did you think my position precluded me from providing an antidote to your poison? You were wrong and Russell's mismanagement blew up the plot. Floyd continues embarrassing himself in the *Enquirer* by pretending I battered him."

He studied my face as I did the stars. "How have you survived so long in this profession if you take machinations personally?"

"Individuals esteemed with public trust owe their community virtuous—"

"That's true when holding an office, but one cannot be acquired without defeating rivals. A person with your attitude ought to be a reverend."

"You'd have the sort of treachery you attempted become a mainstay of our republic's politics?"

"It already is. Not just in our country but in every hierarchy that's ever existed. You've only avoided it because of your name."

"I weep for the future if it reflects your image. How selfish must one be to sabotage the Secretary of State during a crisis?"

"I attempted the country a favor by removing you from the President's ear."

"Why do you desire war?"

"I don't," he said, "but you've led us into isolation and weakness as the Holy Alliance threatens this hemisphere's survival. Freedom's cause would be better served with *anyone* else as our chief diplomat."

"So this was about foreign policy? You weren't thinking about the next election?"

"Oh, I was. Your bungling of the Russian edict and South America proves you can't be trusted with the presidency."

"In your mind no one but you deserves that trust."

"I'm not going to answer that."

"Know that your ploy backfired. I've not been this popular since completing the Onís treaty. Letters come to my home and office every day."

"That won't matter. As many as half a dozen men may run, too many for anyone to win the Electoral College. That will send the top three candidates to the House under the Twelfth Amendment. We and Crawford will be the three, but only one of us will be Speaker."

"So you'll steal the presidency?"

"I'll use the amendment as it's intended."

"My observation is that congressional loyalty is divided between Crawford, you, and Calhoun, in that order. You're too sanguine about your chances."

"I believe most congressmen, when asked to vote between Crawford and myself, will view me as the more attractive choice. Don't you?"

"I did before the Russell episode," I said. "Not anymore. You're both cobras in the grass."

"The most formidable of the world's serpents."

"That wasn't a compliment."

"I know, Mr. Adams." He had half a glass left and finished it in a gulp. He leaned forward. "You should appreciate my generosity in implying you'll be in the top three candidates. That you'll even stand for office. My plan's success didn't matter, and do you know why? Because your handling of the Alliance and the edict is the worst statecraft since Pericles exacerbated the Athenian Plague. You're unlikely to survive in your post through your term's conclusion and the President dismissing you will save the country from another Adams presidency. My scheme was just a way to pass time until I return to the Speakership."

Words were an inadequate response and I did not envision a duel ending in victory. After a moment I stood and whispered in his ear, "Your tragedy, Mr. Clay, is that you are a talented man. You have the potential to be a great leader of our age. Instead you squander it with a lack of character. In that way your waste makes you even worse than Crawford." I straightened my posture.

He smiled and said, "Have a good day, Mr. Adams."

LVI

MY OFFICE FAILED as a haven from my clerks' commotion. I stupidly left my door ajar, not predicting that my brother-in-law's visit was an excuse for neglecting responsibility. I had trouble concentrating on the *Intelligencer* despite its coverage of the year's main event.

A court in Charleston, South Carolina, ruled Denmark Vesey and his 34 followers guilty of plotting an uprising to seize the local arsenal and lead slaves to freedom in Haiti. Someone betrayed Vesey and the militia arrested him. The court sentenced the rebels to death and ordered the raising of the African Methodist Emanuel where Vesey preached.

My conclusion: Missouri worsened sectionalism. Both sides pointed to it to support their arguments. Vesey said it showed slavery's end was near while the city claimed it as proof that Northern hostility provoked a new era of resistance. That Vesey saw Haiti as a new Jerusalem gave me insight into the Negro viewpoint. Its Negro majority and origins as a slave revolt that bested Napoleon made it the only hemispheric nation the President had no intent to recognize for fear of Southern secession.

Intolerable ruckus. "Enough! Back to work!" Silence. One part of my mind questioned how long until the clerks were productive and another returned to the article but nowhere was it ready for Thomas to enter uninvited.

"Good day, John."

I nodded. "What brings you here?"

"Louisa sent you a letter." He raised it.

"Could it not wait until this evening?"

"I haven't opened it."

"Summarize it for me. Make yourself useful."

"Are you sure? What if it contains—"

"It won't, I assure you."

He opened and read the letter while I cut out the Vesey article for my records. "Brent! Daniel! Where is he?"

"He's out," Thomas said. "You know, it's hard to concentrate when you're noisy."

I restrained the urge to imitate Robespierre. I placed the article apart from the newspapers to form a new pile and then turned to the international section of the *Intelligencer*. The administration helped emancipated Negroes buy sixty miles of land in West Africa and establish Monrovia, named for the President. Colonization's test. I remained pessimistic.

Next I read about the growing Greek rebellion against Ottoman Turkey. Greek Admiral Konstantinos Kanaris destroyed the Turkish flagship near Chios. Nasuhzade Ali Pasha, second-in-command of the Turkish Navy, was among the dead. The Turks executed 20,000 Greek prisoners on Chios and exiled 23,000. Oh, the massacre was in March, so the Greek naval victory was retaliation.

Greece was the newest factor in the world crisis. Our citizens supported her and Clay and others called for our intervention. The Cabinet had yet to debate the issue but I expected the parley to follow the established pattern. The difference being I was weaker than ever. I didn't think helping the Greeks to be in our interest, while Crawford would argue we could win Alexander's sympathy while Metternich—

"She asks you to join the family in Philadelphia, now that you finished your book," Thomas said. "She's met supporters who can arrange campaign events."

I snorted. "Publicly pursuing the presidency is unseemly and I can't leave Washington now. Not when the President or Canning might ask to discuss Greece or the Allies." A moment. "You don't have to stay with me if you'd like to go."

"No." Another moment. "You shouldn't be alone. You're stressed. Besides, I have business in the capital."

"Whatever you wish." I turned to the *Intelligencer*'s advertisements. One caught my attention. Edward Dyer, an auctioneer, arranged a sale for that afternoon. A woman named Dorcas Allen and her two children were the available item. She'd murdered her other two children and was acquitted as insane when the crime occurred. Birch, her owner, offered the family for 475 dollars as damaged goods.

"Thomas, have you heard of this?" I showed him the ad.

"Oh, yes. Terrible story."

"Do you believe she was insane?"

"Wouldn't someone have to be to do that? A parent?" He paused. "A court ruled as such."

"I know, but something feels awry." I stared at the ad. This woman called to me. A stranger I could help. Perhaps… "The auction's at four."

He frowned. "You don't want to buy her, do you?"

"Certainly not." The Holy Alliance. The Northwest. The election. All slipped from my control. Getting caught helping this woman would be my Waterloo, my enemies' triumph, and the hemisphere's downfall. But how could I claim virtuosity if I ignored something like this? "Let's go."

"Really?" Thomas asked. "Isn't it controversial for you?"

"Yes, but I must help her if it's in my power to do so."

He smiled. "Why leave now? Alexandria's not far and the auction isn't for several hours."

"Exactly."

◆ ◆ ◆ ◆ ◆ ◆

Thomas and I arrived after 11. We asked around and found Dyer's shop. A dull and perverse circus complex, eliciting a fear of unpredictability. Some threats, say a monarch, destroy you for threatening their power, but that's rational and less disturbing than a danger with which negotiating is meaningless and survival rests on whims.

Dorcas and her children sat in a small pen. She wept most piteously. I approached.

"Greetings, ma'am." She wailed, her head dropped to her chest, her arms around her legs. "How has he treated you?" No response or acknowledgement of my presence. I noticed a wound on her left wrist. Looked at her daughters, sitting along the wall, away from their mother —ages nine and seven—they watched me as though I intended them harm. "It's all right, little ones. I won't hurt you." Dorcas' screaming made it difficult to speak or think. "Ma'am, can you tell me—" I couldn't complete the thought. "You're going to be all right, ma'am. I—" The howl escalated and my focus dissipated. I watched the girls again and nodded, hoping to convey I was there to help. Their stares said that notion wasn't an ingredient of the realm they inhabited.

I rejoined Thomas and we waited by the circus' entrance. Dyer returned and our presence startled him.

"Edward Dyer?" I asked. He nodded. "I'm—"

"Mr. Adams. I've seen your portrait. What brings a *Northerner* to my auction?" We made ourselves heard over Dorcas' crying. He looked at Thomas. "I'm sorry, I forgot to ask your name."

"Thomas Hellen. I'm his brother-in-law."

"A pleasure." They shook hands. "I'm sorry, I can't think over her noise."

"Let's step outside," I said. They followed. "Is that better?"

Dyer nodded. "Where was—ah, yeah. Why's a Northerner at my auction? You wanna purchase her?"

"Something like that."

"Your reputation goes a different way."

"Has anyone procured her?"

"Not officially."

"Meaning what?"

"Meaning I made a deal with a man for 475 dollars, but I doubt he'll have it in time and so here we are." He paused. "It's her husband."

"I didn't know she was married."

He laughed. "He works at *Gadsby's*. Tryin' to raise the money. I lost patience with him."

"How is she married as a slave?"

"That's where it gets tricky. Her owner married a War Department clerk named Davis and when the woman died she had Davis promise to free Dorcas here." He gestured to her. "Davis did so and that's when Dorcas married. They were together for—it was either 12 or 15 years, I don't remember. Had four children. The issue—" Dorcas' loudest shriek yet. "*Goddammit*, woman! Keep it down over there! Where was I?"

"You mentioned a problem," I said.

"Right, right. The problem was Davis never drafted papers for her freedom. Or he never gave them to her. But Davis remarried and died and that widow married a man named Orme and Orme realized Dorcas lacked freedom papers. Sold her and the children to Mr. Birch, my client, for 700 dollars."

"Wait." I turned to Thomas, then to Dorcas, and then back to Dyer. "She's a free woman. You can't—"

"Yes, I can." He straightened his posture. "I read about this. Without the papers she was never free. Birch owns her and I've the right to arrange her sale. Look it up." He acted like he'd discovered my secret intent.

I turned to the Allen family. Dorcas maintained her state and the girls stared at me. "What happened next?" I asked. Kept my eyes on the children. "After Birch bought them?"

"They spent a night in a slave prison in Alexandria so he could fetch them the next day," Dyer said. "The prison visible from the Capitol Building."

"Is that when—"

"Yes. That's the night she killed the young two."

"Their ages?"

"The boy was four," he said. "The girl under a year." I thought of Baby Louisa and felt a thunderclap upon me but refused to cry. "She tried killing these two but they fought and yelled until other slaves stopped her. Then she tried ending herself and failed. You read about the trial in the advertisement?"

"Yes," Thomas said. "Acquitted for insanity."

"You can see why." Dyer gestured to her.

I studied Dorcas. I couldn't begin to empathize with what she'd endured. Our lives were too different but I pictured myself undergoing similar hardships. I hated the feeling of events beyond my control shaping my life and she confronted this at its maximum extent. To be a slave, worse, a slave who'd known freedom and had it stripped away, to know her children's fate. What spirit could withstand such torture? What society asked to find out?

"She isn't insane," I said. "Her action was a response to slavery's character."

Dyer snorted. "Believe what you want."

I kept my eyes on Dorcas. "You won't delay the auction?"

"Why should I?"

"How about this: if you fail to sell her, ask her husband to visit my home tomorrow night."

Thomas grabbed my arm. "John, are you—"

"Yes," I said. To Dyer, "Will you do that?"

A moment as Dyer watched me. "You're gonna help him buy her?"

"If I can. The outcome is the same for you and Birch. Money is money."

"Why do you care?" He pointed at Dorcas. "About them?"

I paused to find an answer to satisfy both Dyer and myself. "Some are slaves to others. The rest of us are lucky to only serve our own souls."

Another moment. "I'll do it."

"Thank you," I said. "Do you have a paper so I can write my address?"

I reorganized the furniture in the central entertainment room. Thomas and Antoine helped me move the couches in the back left corner so they faced one another and we placed a segment of the dining table within arm's reach. Antoine prepared small dishes if the Negro arrived hungry. My eyes swelled and my hands stung at the slightest provocation. I told them *no, at least not tonight*.

He came around 7 and brought Dorcas. Antoine led them to me. He appeared nervous and she looked down but her head wasn't limp as though she lacked conscious control. Eyes closed, or almost closed, she followed her husband's movements. I pondered why she existed internally and couldn't interact with the world around her. Did she reject the outside for what it had done or was she so ashamed that her mind collapsed?

I shook his hand. "Welcome to my home, sir. What's your name?"

"Nathaniel. Nathaniel Allen."

"Honored to meet you, Nathaniel." I gestured to the couches. We sat opposite each other. Thomas beside me, Dorcas beside him. "Do you know who I am?"

"Yes, sir. Adams."

"Did Dyer tell you?"

"Yes, but I knew you." His face softened. "You're a good man."

"As are you, Nathaniel." To Dorcas, "Speak whenever you wish, ma'am."

"We know, sir," Nathaniel said. To Thomas, "You too."

Thomas laughed. "I'm here if needed."

Nathaniel and I leaned toward each other. I inferred him to be an ignorant but active man. I used a more serious tone. "How have you been? Since this started?"

His eyes sank. He looked at his wife and then back to me. "I don't know if we can survive."

"I can only express my deepest regrets that this happened and I wish I could say the same on the government's behalf." I paused. "Where are your children? Does Dyer have them?"

"Birch has them. So we don't run."

"How much of the 475 have you raised?"

"Are you familiar with General Smith?"

A moment. "Yes, General Walter Smith. He served in the late war."

"He offered 330 if we raised the rest."

"And how much have you raised?"

"Not much."

"Dyer said you work at *Gadsby's*."

"Yes, sir, but I make little. I have less than 20. We had money. But Dorcas gets sick. Badly sick. Ten or more days each time."

"Sounds like epilepsy," Thomas said.

Nathaniel nodded. "Her owners—they make me pay." He lost control of himself and cried, which made me uncomfortable. I looked at Dorcas but she appeared unaffected.

"I'm willing to write you a 50 dollar check, Mr. Allen," I said. "Tonight."

He coughed and attempted to compose himself. "50? That's all?"

"That's all I can afford."

"Can you even afford *that*?" Thomas asked. "You couldn't afford to publish the book, and—"

"I'll figure it out."

"But Louisa—"

"Won't know."

"You know Birch will take our children if we don't pay?" Nathaniel asked.

"50 is the best I can do," I said. "Honestly."

"What about your friends?"

I was afraid he would ask this but I'd prepared an answer. "None of my friends in this city will help you. Most support slavery." A pause. "Don't be discouraged. You have less than 100 dollars to go."

From sadness to anger. Then, "I have a question. How did Orme get her? Some say he doesn't own her."

"Dyer told me that her owner instructed Davis—"

"Emery."

"That was her owner's name?"

"Yes, sir. Emery from Baltimore married Gideon Davis."

"I see. I wrote to Francis Key with a similar question. Have you heard of him?" I asked. He shook his head. "He's Washington City's District Attorney. He supports slavery but he sent me an answer. Orme left the District after selling your wife to Birch and can't be found. Now, Dyer takes Birch at his word that he has ownership of Dorcas and when I asked for proof he said Birch's word was enough. Additionally, the record shows that Davis died destitute and so his creditors have a claim to Dorcas. Orme and Birch can say they're creditors."

"If they're creditors, would paying the 475 protect Dorcas from reclamation?" Thomas asked.

"That's my concern. It's possible Birch and Dyer are conspiring to wring the 475 from you before letting Davis' creditors take Dorcas and the children anyway." I paused to let Nathaniel process this. He cried more than before and I again ignored my feelings about this. "I advise you to push forward. It's unlikely Birch and the others have thought this far ahead." I looked at an advanced note. "Key sent me the papers from Dorcas' trial. A murder indictment was filed for each slayed child but she was only tried for the boy. The prosecutor had complete evidence but the jury acquitted her as insane and so the prosecutor entered a nolle prosequi for the second indictment. Key implied, as I expected, that there was no evidence for insanity when the killings occurred. There was evidence of hour-long fits, but despite occasional violent language—"

Dorcas elevated her face. Her eyes were unchanged. I wondered if she was struggling against the python constricting her conscience. She breathed loudly, the loudest sound in the room, building energy for over a minute.

"They in Heaven, now. They in Heaven. If they lived, I don't know what become of them."

A pause as I waited for her to continue. Then I said, "I understand. You—"

"My mistress was wrong. She wrong. She was Methodist and so am I."

Another pause. I changed tactics. "Yes, ma'am. The Bible's proclamation that we're all created in God's image is the origin of equality." To Nathaniel, "Does what I'm saying make sense? Your only legal option is paying Birch and hoping that's enough. Even disproving his title wouldn't discharge Dorcas."

He squeezed her hand. She still leaned forward and he stared at her, his ducts not yet dry. He said after a few minutes, "What about the rest, Adams? 50 is not enough."

"Here's what I recommend: Notify General Smith of my pledge and ask if he'll cover the balance. The remaining 95 dollars may be within his means."

Dorcas corrected her posture. Nathaniel's smile flickered. "We are grateful, Adams."

"Don't be. None of this should have happened. But make me this promise: if we succeed, and your family becomes free again, make the most of your lives. Live at peace, with yourselves, if not with the world."

I watched Nathaniel, wondering if he could fulfill my request and love Dorcas after what she'd done. How would I react if Mrs. Adams killed Charles to prevent his capture by French soldiers? I'd understand it rationally but emotionally she'd have wrecked me. I'd never see light again, our marriage an untied yarn. I might even desire retribution. So I considered what it said about this man if they rebuilt their connection. I felt urged to raise this but knew better than to pry.

I wrote a 50 dollar check to Walter Smith Esquire at the Bank of Washington. The Allens hadn't eaten their food and I invited them to take it. They never contacted me again. I visited Dyer's auction a week later. He was absent and Dorcas and her children were gone.

I chose to believe they'd prevailed.

LVII

CHARLES AND I walked around Washington that August, before he returned to school. Both running through the rye of our thoughts and not focused on each other. He was 15 and on the cusp of manhood. Did he have a vision for the future or was he like my other sons? Had Mary's withdrawal from that vision left him desolate? I was afraid to ask.

I appreciated autumn, though summer became winter within a week and I felt robbed. My patience for the cold, endowed on all Massachusetts youngsters, must have dissolved in Europe.

Picking my way through the thicket of my thoughts, anxiety consumed me. Russell and Dorcas left bruises but were also a respite from the Alliance and impending doom. I felt my reckoning approaching.

I hated the idea of Metternich winning. He personified the world our era had meant to surpass. An aristocrat smug in his belief that he'd vanquished Napoleon and that subjugating our hemisphere would finish the job. The revolution which set men free reduced to relying on her former master for survival. The Age of Reason a historical errata. Metternich and Napoleon were twin evils, political opposites both imposing their views on the planet. I couldn't let him win. Couldn't let him outsmart this country, the cause, me.

Everyday I awoke fearing a Castlereagh-Levin breakthrough reaching our shore. Every. Day. I'd lost hope that the British public might save us. Castlereagh would reach a deal accommodating Russia that rejected our Northwest claim. I allowed myself to prepare for this inevitability, to step into my failure in advance and accustom myself to a terror worse than death. I told myself greatness lied in virtue but I was skeptical it would ever be enough.

Then there was Spain. Soon France would defeat the liberals and Ferdinand would be king once more and the Alliance would reimpose the Spanish Empire. I still didn't believe Castlereagh would tolerate it. The British public wouldn't let him. Right? Or Greece—the rest of Washington saw her as a wedge to push between Alexander and Metternich. I viewed her struggle as another unnecessary war, another distraction from investing in our future, from controlling the continent, from—

"Are you all right, Father?" Charles asked.

Good boy, saving me from my perennial overthinking. "What prompts your query?"

"Your iron mask is slipping."

"My what?"

"The iron mask you wear for the world. An image you wish us all to believe. The wise man who will guide America toward virtue."

"Am I not this person?" I asked satirically though secretly interested.

"You lack the prudence which gives knowledge its luster."

"I never spoke this way to my—"

"The mask is why you've so many enemies. It's aggressive and untruthful. You're good underneath but your pleas for higher motives and your feeling that you're denied credit separates you from your community."

"What of your mother?"

"She's the opposite. Her feelings take her to extremes. She repents but she never leaves them."

"What of yourself?"

"I'm sober."

"You've nothing left to learn?"

"On the contrary, Father, I await the proper moment to ask for your advice."

"Advice from an iron mask?"

"You are not your mask."

"How may I assist you, my child?"

"I must develop a compelling and unique literary style if I am to become a writer and academic. Where ought I begin?"

An ambitious child? Really? Had my parenting succeeded after all? "To write well you must read well," I said. "Start with the best. Pliny. Voltaire. Pascal. Cicero, of course."

"Ugh, Cicero."

"Watch your tongue. You are barely a man and you insult the greatest—"

"Have I?"

"He should be the study of your life. You know that he is central to my growth."

"For reasons that are beyond me. Cato is better."

"Cato? He's an inflexible moralist. Cicero was practical."

"Moral compromise is better than striving for perfection?"

"Listen here: We shall not always agree, but each of us may rectify his opinions by weighing those of the other. I'll have you read the *Treatise of Cicero de Claris Oratoribus* before I hear another flippant remark from one whom the world has yet to test. The last 18 or 20 sections are among the most interesting of Cicero's writings. They are introduced by Atticus' sarcastic remark upon the multitudes of speakers whom Cicero had included in his list of orators—many of whom Atticus insists were no orators at all. Atticus also laughs at him for comparing Cato the Censor as an orator with Lysias, but Cicero very seriously maintains the position…"

PART NINE

THE EARTH WAS DIVIDED
LATE 1823

LVIII

CANNING SENT ME a letter. We'd written to each other and met a few times since the Anacostia River incident but those interactions were unproductive. This note's pouncing prose conveyed urgency. What happened? Had the Castlereagh-Levin compact arrived—the Northwest for South America? I considered other possibilities. Had George IV died after three years on the throne? Would that require an immediate discussion? A Turkish victory in Greece? A personal issue? I rejected these options.

We'd known that France captured Cadiz for a week. Had Castlereagh sent a message on Britain's response to Ferdinand's return? I contemplated the worst and least likely scenario, that Castlereagh made a deal with the Devil—I mean Metternich—about this hemisphere's independence. I prepared written responses to all these contingencies.

I offered to meet in a restaurant, which would allow me to buy his favor by paying for the food and drink of his choice. He replied that his subject was so sensitive that only my office was sufficient.

Autumn rains washed the city that morning but the sun emerged for our joining. He declined a cigar and wine. I disliked knowing that he held the power and moved slowly, desperate to avoid mistakes.

"I bring two critical pieces of information for your government," he said. "They provide context for a third topic. I ask that you allow me to convey them with minimal interruption." Normally he'd make a joke about how I'd struggle with such a request but not this time and I respected his seriousness.

"Proceed." My hands clasped.

"Let's start with Spain. My government views France's invasion as having avoided the worst potential outcome. Yes, Ferdinand has hanged the liberal leaders and has asked the Alliance to restore his empire, but we feared a French defeat would revoke what little legitimacy the Bourbons have."

"So Castlereagh closed his eyes to avoid another Parisian revolution?"

I feared I provoked his ire at my violating his request so quickly. Instead he squirmed, closing his eyes for a moment to stabilize his thoughts. Something I said?

"The world crisis is delicate and we must manage every element without adversely impacting the others," he said. "I know a secondary country like America doesn't understand how a miscalculation could unleash another large war."

"We covet peace more than you. It's our hemisphere tilting at the abyss."

"Hundreds of thousands died in Wellington's campaign against Napoleon's marshals on the Peninsula, including 50,000 British soldiers and sailors. We take no pleasure in France controlling the region again. But the Allies saw the Spanish liberals as Jacobins and our intervention —"

"Has Castlereagh betrayed the Americas to maintain Metternich's illusion of peace?" I couldn't control myself.

His eyes closed again. I was right. That explained it. The Foreign Secretary agreed to what Ferdinand called the worthy object of upholding his legitimacy in South America and Canning was tasked with telling this government the apocalypse was upon us. My handling of the Russian edict was fatal. Some moments of gradual breathing and then eyes open.

"You force me to move to the second subject. It is more important than the first. You've made clear that Mr. Rush has not notified you and it is important your government learns this before it reaches your press so you know the situation, both in London and between our governments, is stable and any changes this means for British policy." He paused. "Lord Castlereagh ended his own life. He stabbed himself in his carotid artery while in Kent."

A moment. "I see. That's..." I searched for the word "...most unfortunate. We had a fruitful discourse and he had my respect."

"I know you'll indulge deeper mourning privately. It's the type of tragedy that Sophocles or Shakespeare might have written. The brilliant statesman who knows what's better for his people than they know themselves so he's torn apart until he breaks."

"Was there a specific incident?"

"No, but years of abuse from his enemies for the pattern he set in Greece, Spain, the Northwest, and elsewhere. It amazes me that a people who lost so many fathers and brothers and husbands fighting Napoleon couldn't grasp why he prioritized stability over liberty. Only he understood how each piece affected the whole."

I appreciated the affection Canning had for Castlereagh but Metternich had lost an ally and British foreign policy was in new hands.

"May I ask who replaces him?"

"George," he said.

"My congratulations to your family."

"Thank you. He sent me this news and notified me of the third item for our discussion. George lacks Castlereagh's warmth toward the Alliance and openly warned Paris against invading South America. Louis ignored him and a French army has begun crossing the Atlantic. It will land in either the Caribbean or the southern continent," he said. I suspected he lied to manipulate me. "George instructed me to offer a proposal I thought obvious since the Alliance announced its intention. He asked Rush to sign an accord whereby our countries will tell the world that we'll oppose an Alliance invasion of the Americas, through force if necessary."

"Rush cannot sign such a document without the President's approval."

"That's what he told George. Hence my urgency."

"What happens to the Northwest under this arrangement?"

"Our nations would jointly reject Russia's claim."

"Would Britain and America be equal partners?"

"It does not specify either nation as superior to the other."

That didn't matter. We'd have to follow London's direction and it would use this to block our ascendancy. Our rise would evaporate and we'd return to British servitude. Britain would have this hemisphere under her umbrella for over 50 years. I wondered if Metternich suggested this to George Canning. More likely Metternich took the exact steps to bring this about and the Cannings saw the opportunity. Two years and I was still mystified about how to avoid this outcome. Was I deluded in thinking I could stop the man who destroyed Napoleon?

"What troubles you?" he asked. "A transatlantic league will overpower any hand the Alliance might place on this hemisphere. The collision will end. South America, the Northwest—all of it."

"I appreciate that fact, but I have concerns."

"Such as?"

"Britain hasn't recognized the South American republics."

"True, Castlereagh didn't want to offend Metternich."

"How can our countries pledge to defend former colonies when your government doesn't wish to give its own colonies any ideas?"

"George will grant recognition when the circumstances are right."

"Which will be when?"

"You will not dictate our foreign policy."

"So this partnership isn't equal? Instruction goes one way?"

"Mr. Ad—"

"What about Cuba? It's no secret that both our countries hope to wrestle her from Spain."

"Britain renounced political interest in Cuba as long as her markets are open," he said, "and I thought the Missouri fiasco convinced America against adding any more states to the Union."

"You're asking the President to trust with our survival the same hands that razed this city not ten years ago."

"Do you not see what America is offered? There has seldom in world history required such a small effort of two friendly governments to produce such unequivocal good and prevent such extensive calamity. A new epoch. Europe will recognize America as a political and commercial power and Britain, the world's maritime leader, will grant mutual access between the two. But becoming such a state brings certain responsibilities."

"Responsibilities aligning with British interests."

"I cannot believe you fail to see what George is offering. Everything you seek can be yours."

"And can be taken away, depending on British kindness."

"May I trust you to notify the President of our offer or must I write to him?"

"No," I said, "I'll tell him about the accord."

"Thank you."

LIX

"IF WE'VE CONCLUDED our discussion of the Arikara attack, I'd like to hear Calhoun's report on the Balkan conflict." The President turned to the Secretary of War. "What do you have for us?"

Calhoun's report was placed between the President and himself on the Cabinet table, he had a one-page summary before him. "The key takeaway is that neither the Greeks nor the Turks are organized sufficiently to win the war. The Greeks are broke and depend on plunder and gifts. Their commanders' disregard for their new government resembles Caesar disrespecting the Senate. As for Turkey, the Sultan disbanded the Janissaries and executed over 6,000 of his elite troops. Now he relies on Egypt, the Armenians, and other outsiders. External involvement is necessary to avoid a stalemate."

"How are the Europeans reacting? Any surprises or impact on allegiances?"

I was hurt that the President didn't defer to me on this subject. Was he respecting Calhoun's authorship or signaling that I remained out of favor?

"I'll start with the Holy Alliance," Calhoun said. He looked at his summary. "Metternich is quiet but we know he doesn't consider either the Greeks or the Turks to be civilized and he places Turkey with monarchy and stability, even if they're Mohammedan, and the Greeks with the other revolts who threaten to return Europe to anarchy."

"Meaning France will side with Turkey as well," the President said. "And Russia?"

"I'm less certain of Alexander's thinking because so is he. The question is whether supporting his Eastern Orthodox brethren and weakening his Turkish foe outweighs convincing his Polish and Ukrainian subjects that the Greeks have the right idea."

"Is he deliberating about Alliance cohesion?"

"Alexander and Metternich were never affectionate. Metternich's flexibility is the only reason Europe is large enough for them both, but supporting opposite sides in this war might be more than he can tolerate."

"Should it happen, will they be too divided to attack this hemisphere?"

"I'd like to think so but I can't answer with confidence. They might treat the issues individually."

"Analyze how we can separate them." A pause. "Will Britain support Greece?"

"Castlereagh wants to but is afraid of offending millions of Mohammedans in India."

The President said to me, "Do you have anything to add?"

"No, Mr. President." I delayed mentioning Castlereagh's suicide for a moment. Calhoun nodded, thanking me for my endorsement.

The President looked at his notes. "In that case, let's discuss how we can invite Russian support for Greece. I received letters from Rush and Gallatin. Both support immediate recognition of Greek independence. Rush advocates recognizing Andreas Luriottis as the Greek leader and Gallatin suggests deploying a naval force to the Mediterranean and offering it to the Greeks for their use."

"A force consisting of what?" Calhoun asked.

"A frigate, a corvette, and a schooner. To start." The President paused, his eyes looking at us over his silver, rectangular glasses. Crawford nodded to Calhoun.

"Such a move would, of course, help the Greeks and likely convince Alexander to follow us," Calhoun said. "Supporting the winning side and earning Greek favor will outweigh preventing domestic uprising in Russia."

"It might even lead to a convergence between Alexander, Castlereagh, and us," Crowninshield said. "The three nations can then settle the Northwest dispute on reasonable terms." Such a naive vision from such an inexperienced strategist. It was endearing.

"How might Turkey retaliate?" Crawford asked.

"What do you mean?" the President asked.

"The Sultan won't appreciate our support for a rebellion against him. Could we provoke his hostility to justify our involvement?" Unbelievable. Only Crawford would entertain traitorous thoughts in the President's office.

"Turkey's in decline," Calhoun said. "Let's not worry about her response. Instead, we should discuss whether to write to Alexander and suggest a joint intervention before deploying our fleet. It would detach him from Metternich."

Crawford nodded. Was something afoot? Why did he want to remain in agreement with Calhoun? Was he trying to recruit him into a new partnership? He turned to me.

"I assume you're opposed, as is your habit?"

"*Yes*," I said. "We mustn't let our sentimentality for the Greeks blind us. Sending a fleet provokes a Turkish declaration of war and I cannot think of anything less needed. There's no reason to assume our involvement will invite Russian friendship. It's just as likely to drive Alexander toward Metternich and allows Metternich to proclaim us hypocrites for intervening in Europe when we're calling for an end to European conquest in the New World."

"You remain predictable and unbelievable at once. Opposing cooperation with Britain and Russia. You act as though we can resist the whole world on our own."

"We must prioritize—"

"Expansion, I know. I've heard you. For seven years I've heard you. How many times must you be proven wrong before you learn that it's better to have friends and not only enemies? I suppose your policy reflects your personal life."

"I'll be validated when—"

"Mr. President, please stop listening to this man. He's either corrupted or so headstrong that—"

"Cease this instant," the President said. He shook his head and his exhaustion was palpable. "What if I dispatch an agent to meet Luriottis who can report to us from Greece?" To Calhoun, "I'm certain your report is excellent but an agent can give us more details about European intentions." We all nodded. "Does anyone have a recommendation?"

"Mr. Edward Everett is a wonderful speaker and an able man," Calhoun said. He looked at me. "A Harvard man."

"Everett is a good choice," I said. "We should dissuade any notion that our agents will be secretive. They're always discovered and it usually doesn't take long."

The President frowned and wrote Everett's name into his notes. "I'll consider this." I wondered how sickened he was of our lack of consensus and speculated whether he regretted standing for reelection. "Does anyone have anything else to contribute on this or any other issue before we depart for—yes, Mr. Adams?"

"I have a rather large development."

"What is it?"

"Canning informed me that Lord Castlereagh destroyed himself." I paused to observe their reactions. Eyes blending sorrow, confusion, fear, rage, and hope. "George Canning, Stratford's older cousin, is now Foreign Minister. He appears, or pretends, to be more sympathetic to liberalism and more critical of the Allies than his predecessor. He's proposed that America and Britain make a joint proclamation opposing the Alliance's hostility toward this hemisphere."

They processed this. The President: "Have you an opinion on whether we should accept?"

"I'm skeptical," I said. Crawford scoffed. "Accepting places us back in Britain's care. We'd reverse the Revolution—London dictates terms, our credibility collapses, and our expansion freezes. Metternich wants us to accept because it breaks our independence."

"Has a more stubborn man ever served this government?" Crawford asked. "We're granted salvation, a second chance after your poor decisions offended Britain, and you *still* oppose it out of a misplaced sense of destiny. Yours and the country's."

My biggest mistake in those years was not forcing Crawford to give his opinion on topics before he knew mine. I wondered how much fuller my scalp would be if I'd taken that approach. Tragic how people cannot think of solutions to problems until they're free of them.

"You accuse me of sabotaging our policy, of obeying Metternich," I said. "Yet you're a worm preying on the administration's vitals. You—"

"I'll not be lectured—"

"The Treasury is empty with you at its head. You're unable to devise a source of revenue but loan upon loan."

"You're changing the subject. We've had ample chances to thwart the Alliance, but they require temporary concessions to Britain and Russia and you reach for perfection, your view of perfection, and have no ability to compromise."

"It's not a compromise when it's Metternich's—"

Bang!

The President struck the table. His composure worsened by the minute, hunched over like a critter. "Can barely think. The two of you…" Paused. "Would anyone else care to contribute? Wirt? Calhoun?"

Crowninshield sulked at his exclusion.

"I share Mr. Adams' suspicions," Calhoun said. "The Holy Alliance has crushed every vestige of liberty in Europe. Now they extend their efforts across the Atlantic. Britain will abuse our submission and extract Cuba. That she is ready to seize that island if an opportunity offers can hardly be doubted. Controlling Cuba lets Britain sever New Orleans from the rest of our country. Adams is right that acceptance stunts our growth. For years. We must consider this."

"I grant you that," Crawford said, "but how else are we to resist the Allies?"

"I don't know. We should explore every option before accepting servitude."

"I agree," the President said. "This meeting was longer and more contentious than I expected. You have an assignment. Let's meet in two days and until then, analyze the offer as Mr. Adams described it. We'll discuss every idea on its merits regardless of who introduced it." To me, "Did Canning say how his cousin's rise impacts the Northwest? Whether Alexander altered his edict now that he faces a confrontational British minister?"

"He did not."

"Obtain that information before our next meeting."

"Yes, Mr. President."

We separated. I was tempted to grab Calhoun but hesitated. Would he accept my olive branch? I opted to let him form his own opinion but regretted this upon reflection. No Cabinet Meeting was as important and my destiny was at stake.

LX

I DIDN'T SLEEP that night. The stakes heightened their upward trajectory, mirroring that of a cannonball fired over the corpses at Leipzig. The President's decision would reveal where it fell. Any detail could sway him and I studied every fabric of the world crisis to counter Crawford and his lackeys. I ignored Mrs. Adams and the children living with us. Energy, too much energy, couldn't focus. Everything that transpired since my return from Europe built to this.

The Baron came to my office the next morning at my request.

"I bring a dispatch from Count Nesselrode," he said. He raised it. "The Emperor has left St. Petersburg for a three month tour to inspect his troops."

"Is that it?"

"There's more, but my government wants the President to know that the sire's movement is not a hostile act. We are also informing the European Courts."

"I'll notify the President."

"Thank you."

"I asked you here to discuss alterations to British policy since Castlereagh's suicide."

"Has Canning announced alterations?"

"Stratford mentioned the direction we should expect his cousin to pursue."

"I see."

"He'll be less accommodating of the Alliance," I said. "I don't know if he ended negotiations with Levin, but I don't anticipate his withdrawal from the 1818 treaty. If that's correct, will the Emperor modify the edict?"

"No. He said the Northwest's future shall be decided in St. Petersburg. He has met with Sir Bagot regularly since the edict." He referred to Britain's minister in Russia.

"What about his hostility to South America? The Alliance will never coax Canning into accepting the restoration of Spanish colonies. Attempting so brings war, the exact war the Emperor wants to prevent."

"The Emperor has no intention of recognizing the South American ministers and does not acknowledge them as lawful states. Not in 1823, nor by 1923. He believes in the Alliance and its goal of guaranteeing tranquility within the civilized world. He takes pride in the Alliance's actions in Naples and Spain."

"An Au Io Triumphe for the fallen cause of revolutions. Does he seek revenge on liberalism for Moscow's destruction?"

"Yes. Napoleon's crime altered his view of politics."

"Napoleon hardly represented liberalism as—"

"It does not matter, Mr. Adams. Rejecting divinity made him possible and his successors must be prevented at all costs. Liberalism is arrogant to think it can reinvent society. The attitude will lead to movements to reinvent man himself that are even more violent. They will eradicate every tradition and institution you value and those who benefit from such practices shall defend themselves with savagery. That is the bloodsoaked future liberalism brings."

"Said without irony from one waging war on the New World."

He raised the dispatch again. "You'll deliver this to the President?"

"Yes."

"Thank you." He handed it to me. "Despite these disagreements, I hope you know the Emperor respects you. As do I."

I took a moment to choose my wording. "I assure you from my knowledge of the President's sentiments that he has great confidence in you."

"I shall endeavor to deserve it."

"Before you depart I'd like to ask: is it true that a French army is already bound for this hemisphere?"

"I am unaware of such an expedition." No hesitation and his voice provided no clues. He had no reason to tell me the truth and his government may have withheld facts from him. Perhaps his government didn't itself know. But it was more likely that Stratford Canning lied to scare us into accepting his cousin's offer. I chose to operate under this assumption.

LXI

All gracious Parent! on my bended knee
This dawning day I consecrate to thee.
With humble heart, and fervent voice to raise
The suppliant prayer, and ever grateful praise.
To thee, the past its various blessings owes,
Its soothing pleasures, its chastising woes.
To thee, the future, with imploring eye
Looks up, for health, for Virtue, for the Sky.
However the tides of Joy or Sorrow roll,
Still grant me, Lord, possession of my Soul,
Life's checker'd Scenes, with stedfast mind to share,
As thou shalt doom, to gladden, or to bear.
And Oh! be mine, when clos'd this brief career,
The crown of Glory's Everlasting Year.

MY ENDEAVOR FAILED and I felt demoralized. My creation was joyful but I'd read enough good poetry to know what it looked like and this wasn't it. I considered rewriting it into Latin. Why bother? Did other species have dead languages?

My poems, always with a flash of genius at conception, emerged stillborn. Reality can never fulfill the expectations of our thoughts. If only it were pliable to the will. But it couldn't bend for everyone because scarcity begot value. Thus hierarchy.

The pain of my eyes and hands forestalled another night of sleep. It wore on me, my mind dull, my mastery of detail to be absent from the meeting where I needed it most. The critical decision of the President's tenure. His legacy and mine. If he accepted the offer the last seven years were wasted and I ought to have stayed in Europe writing mediocre poetry. My parents' trials, a life of separation, squandered. Father better off staying a lawyer, the Revolution for naught.

These United States
1776-1823
Killed by cowardice

I drafted a letter to Calhoun making my argument for rejecting the offer. It felt unconvincing and I threw it away. Showed my reasoning was hollow. Winning him meant winning the President. Yes. The partnership, the triumvirate. *There shall not be another President from the Revolutionary generation. The torch is passing. If we stick together, Mr. Adams, we shall triumph over our adversaries and define the coming era of American politics.* So long ago. Optimistic then, despairing now. We three were to produce victories that earned the public's support. Then Congress would support us or suffer electoral defeat. Now our national independence looked doubtful.

I retrieved Antoine and we departed for the Potomac. Wait. So many children bunched around the fireplace in the music room. John, Mary—the Hellens hadn't copulated so numerously and we hadn't housed all their youngsters. I observed until I recognized all *seven* pubescent suspects. I saw Mrs. Adams resting in a chair beside her harp. Caught her attention and pointed for her to join me. She obliged and we stood near the front door.

"John, the river will be freezing."

I kept my papers under my coat, protected from the November snow. "Nevermind that. It will wake me and I have a very important meeting today. Are Tom's children here?"

"Yes."

"I thought I saw Liz, Isaac, and the others. Why wasn't I consulted?"

"You were busy and I decided to help Nancy."

"Not *this* busy."

"How many years have we been married?"

"25."

"26."

"Since w—"

"There you are."

"Why didn't you say anything in July?"

"I didn't dare."

"How are we to afford sponsoring all these—forget it. I don't have time for this."

"Before you go..." She lifted a treatise. "You received this letter."

I was tempted to say I'd read it later but then I saw it was from Joseph Hopkinson, a former congressman and ally. Opened and scanned and snorted.

"Affability?" she asked. "I thought you left my husband."

"He asks me to cultivate newspapers who will support my candidacy and compares my insistence that I don't desire the office to Macbeth saying he'll only be king if chance crowned him. He forgets that if Macbeth had maintained that code there'd be no tragedy."

I remembered speaking to Senator King about the play, about how ambition robbed men of their souls. Digging through my stone of ambition revealed a virtuous core. I couldn't pursue service contracts with the press without being obliged to provide suitable returns.

"Do you desire the presidency?" she asked.

"Louisa—"

"It's a simple question."

"Then *no* is my simple answer. Half a dozen men are being considered and the country can do without me."

"I don't believe you. You crave attention more than you admit, even to yourself. Remember this spring in New York when you spoke to citizens for so long we missed our ship—"

"Why are you—"

"Our luggage was already loaded."

"Enough, Louisa. You've no idea of the strain upon me."

"Because you won't speak to me. Pursuing public office is beneath you, John. Your intellect is greater than the rest of this city combined."

"Now is not the time to discuss this." Snarls. She was revolted but that was her reward for pestering me at this most stressful of times. "Come, Antoine."

"Y-yes, sir." He held himself, though he'd yet to leave the house.

LXII

WE WALKED A mile and a half to my usual spot by the canal at Tiber Creek. I ignored the frigid water and bathed for half an hour. Found it, as always, conducive to my health, my cleanliness, and my comfort. It was essential that I never buckled to weakness if I was to succeed in life. That didn't mean I'd never feel pain but that I'd rise above it.

I left my clothes on the same rock I always did and attached my green goggles and began my swim. Antoine rowed behind me. I swam for two hours, a mile out. The tide caught me but I clawed out of it without Antoine's aid. The experience cleared my thoughts, refreshing me and readying me for the most important Cabinet Meeting of my tenure.

I returned to the Tiber and found a woman—early to mid 50s—sitting on my clothes. She held a quill and parchment. A hood over her curly black hair and a bow around her neck.

"Mr. Adams?" She raised her voice. My first instinct was to lunge for my clothes but I couldn't exit the creek without exposing my nakedness. A Clay proxy? Or did Crawford mean to prevent my attendance?

"What is the meaning of this, ma'am?" I asked.

"Are you Mr. Adams?"

"Yes, but—"

"I'm Anne Royall. I write for *The Huntress*."

A moment. "Oh. I know you. You've written to my office requesting an interview."

"More than once. And your office rejected my requests, when it replied at all."

"I happen to be quite busy, ma'am. Are you aware of events overseas that require my focus?"

"Of which my readers would like their leaders' opinions."

"*Antoine.*"

From his boat, "Yes, sir?"

"Retrieve my clothes."

"Is a story of the Secretary of State's guard bullying a reporter—and a woman—preferable to granting an interview?" she asked.

"I don't intend to capitulate to one who behaves so unprofessionally," I said.

"Just one small capitulation to avoid a scandal. With the election a year away."

I paused. "If I agree to an interview will you return my clothes?"

"Yes."

"I must be at the Executive Mansion by two. My presence is critical." Another pause. "You're costing me a stop at the Department of State."

"I'm sure that Mr. Brent will manage." She stood.

"Antoine." He returned to shore and recovered my outfit. Royall looked away as I dressed and then returned to her rock as I stood. "What's your first question?"

"Are you not past the age for such strenuous exercise?"

"I'm thin."

"Which doesn't help with the cold."

"Do you have an actual question?"

"Yes, sir." She looked at her parchment. "Do you believe the Holy Alliance *truly* intends to invade South America?"

I tried framing an answer but couldn't. Agitated from work, from the cold, from my wife, and from this reporter's audacity. Nuance beyond my reach.

"I can't answer that," I said.

"That question is the basis for all the others."

"Then this shall be a fast interview."

"Can you tell me whether the administration accepts that premise?"

"I can't answer that either."

Her nostrils flared. "What impact do you think Lord Castlereagh's death will have on the world?"

I had to give her something. "Lord Castlereagh was one of the great men of our time. As Foreign Secretary he was vital to the Coalition's victory against Napoleon and to building Europe's peace. I worked with him while minister to the Court of St. James. We had an excellent professional relationship and enjoyed each other's company very much."

"That doesn't answer my question. How do you foresee his death altering British foreign policy?"

"I expect Mr. George Canning to be less belligerent toward revolutionary causes."

"So he won't appease the Alliance?"

"Correct."

"How far will he go in opposing an Alliance invasion?"

I'd shifted from agitation to pleasure in fulfilling her requirement. My mind relaxed and speaking without thinking, I made my largest misstep since the Anacostia River incident. No. This was larger.

LXIII

I RODE A whirlwind to the Executive Mansion. Too unsettled to organize my papers in the President's office. Crawford entered, restraining his jubilation. We both knew the President was the final arbiter of our struggle. One more reason I could accept no outcome save victory. If I held office next I'd appoint Crawford minister to the United Provinces he loved so much. Or the moon.

Focus.

Royall would inform all of Washington about Canning's offer by evening and most of the country within weeks, elevating Britain's popularity to its peak since before the Proclamation of 1763. I'd withheld my opinion about our acceptance, which her readers could interpret however they wished. My mind empty of contingency plans. Cicero and General Washington would know what to do, but I was not them.

The other Cabinet officers joined us. Crawford bowed his head to Calhoun and Calhoun nodded in return. Unusual. At last the President graced us with his presence. Our attention swirled toward him in a vortex. He was downcast, his jawline puffing. He reached the table's head and passed around notecards. They read:

The subject for consideration is British Secretary of State George Canning's proposal relating to the Holy Alliance's projects upon South America.

"Sit," he said. We did. "Let's move directly into discussion, unless anyone holds an urgent thought." No one did. "I wish to state this point before opening the floor: Canning's object, in my view, is to obtain a public pledge from this government which looks like a statement about the Holy Alliance's interference between Spain and South America, but really or especially is against our acquisition of any Spanish American possessions."

An ounce of stress lifted, only an ounce.

Everyone hesitated to speak first. Then, Calhoun: "I'm happy to give my position if you're willing to accommodate me." We affirmed.

"I've spent the past two days thinking of nothing else and I've concluded that we ought to grant Mr. Rush discretionary power to join the declaration against the Alliance. Even if this pledge prevents our absorbing Cuba or Texas, British power is greater than ours and it is to our benefit to join with it."

A radical departure in his views.

"The case is not parallel," I said. "We have no intention of seizing either Texas or Cuba, but the inhabitants of either may exercise their rights and solicit a union with us. They won't request this of Britain. Joining the proposal gives Britain a substantial and inconvenient pledge against ourselves and obtains nothing in return. We must keep our freedom to act in emergencies and not tie ourselves to principles which might thereafter be brought to bear against us."

Crowninshield clapped on the table. Unexpected but welcome.

"I am averse to any course which subordinates us to Britain," the President said. Was this not to be a battle after all? "What if we established a special minister to communicate with the Alliance and protest their aggression?"

"That's an excellent idea," I said. "Such a minister could attend any future congresses the Alliance holds."

"Attending future congresses is a mistake," Calhoun said. "We ought not validate their claims."

"We could establish the revocation of Alliance claims on South America as a condition for our attendance," the President said.

"That defeats the purpose of our sending a minister," I said. "Unless you mean a congress focused on fostering recognition of South American independence. But I don't foresee such a congress occurring for years."

"Fair point, Mr. Adams."

I lifted a document. "The Baron visited me yesterday. He delivered a dispatch from Count Nesselrode and repeated the Emperor's refusal to accept South American ministers." I lifted another document. "I've drafted this response. It is meant to oppose the Allies while declining the British overture."

"May I?" Calhoun asked, his hand extended. He read it. "Insinuating the Alliance is unChristian is sarcastic and fruitless."

"That is the main point of my note."

"Then I suggest rewriting it."

"A verbal response to the Baron is best," the President said. "We've digressed. Mr. Adams, have the Cannings indicated an intention to recognize the South American states?"

"Just the opposite. Stratford told me his cousin will grant recognition when he chooses and we have no say over the matter."

"Why would London still object to granting recognition?" Calhoun asked.

"Two reasons. It doesn't wish to fly in the Alliance's face and such an action involves breaking treaties with Spain. Particularly that of July 1814." I discovered this in the Department of State's files yesterday.

"That's unfortunate." Calhoun said to the President, "This is my principal point: if we reject Canning's offer and Britain is unsure of our cooperation, I don't believe Britain will oppose the Holy Alliance. Not even she can defeat the Allies in a war alone. Therefore Britain will fall into Metternich's views to save herself. I foresee Canning gifting Metternich and Alexander the Royal Navy to subdue South America. Their next step will be demolishing the world's first successful rebellion."

Everyone knew what that meant. I saw Crowninshield nodding.

"That framing is a false choice," I said.

"No, it needs voicing," Calhoun said. "You expect British neutrality, but the world's greatest power cannot stay impartial when so many of her interests are threatened. She'll defend them with the most favorable option. That will either be through us or through the Alliance."

"You once told me you believed Britain wanted a monopoly over South American trade and to transform this hemisphere into another India. What changed your mind?"

"Nothing, but becoming India is superior to becoming Poland."

"You're content with our being a second-rate country? Settling for a return to the British imperium?"

Crawford cleared his throat. "That's a reasonable segue. After our last meeting I thought it wise to seek advice from our nation's best minds." He raised two dispatches. "I wrote to them as soon as I returned to my office. Jefferson sent his answer last night. I received Madison's this morning."

He handed the President his notes. I understood his plot. Crawford was untrustworthy so he borrowed the authority of better men. He'd partnered with Calhoun and instructed him to take the lead in debating me since the President trusted the Secretary of War. Then he deployed the men whom the President held in highest regard. I wondered if Crawford had made an accurate description of Canning's offer in his letters.

I watched the President's eyes and saw as he reconsidered his analysis. So malleable. At that moment I knew it was impossible that he'd sent Jackson deliberately vague instructions in Florida to hide his hand. He didn't contain such cleverness. He lowered the papers and I anticipated the worst.

"They both think we should accept," he said. "Mr. Jefferson thinks that no President in our history has faced a greater challenge and passionately argues for pledging with Britain. Mr. Madison notes that Britain is more impelled by her interests than by the principle of liberty, but advises the same."

I said, "How far Jefferson, who has viewed Britain as his antagonist all his life, has come from advising against entangling alliances in his Inaug—"

"This is ludicrous," Calhoun said. "Do you even have an alternate idea? The French vanquished the Spanish liberals and before the next election they'll take Mexico with 10,000 men. Then the rest of South America shall return to Ferdinand's dominion."

I wondered if Stratford Canning had told Calhoun about the French army already sailing. "I don't deny Britain might join the Alliance and invade. They might make a temporary impression for three, four, or five years. But I no more believe that the Holy Alliance will restore the Spanish Empire upon the American continents than that Chimborazo will sink beneath the ocean."

"So you agree that rejecting the offer guarantees war?"

"We should be wary of involving ourselves in the South Americans' fate if they can be so easily subdued. You'd embark our lives and fortunes in a ship which you've declared that rats have abandoned."

The President said, "Mr. Ad—"

"We can test whether Canning's proposal is right or wrong. If we consider the South Americans as independent nations, they themselves, and no one else has the right to dispose of—"

"Do you realize violent parties shall arise in this country and we will have to fight within our own shores when the invasion comes?" Calhoun asked. He meant slaves rising up for their freedom amidst the chaos.

"You're hallucinating, sir. You've joined an extravaganza. You —"

"That is enough, Mr. Adams," the President said. "Does anyone else have anything to add?"

"I for one don't see why this is controversial," Crawford said. "Canning has warned us of a coming crusade and is correct that Britain and America can withstand it by joining together. We should thank him for his foresight, not curse him. It is fortunate that British policy, though guided by a different calculation than ours, has presented a cooperation for the same object as ours. With that cooperation we have nothing to fear from Metternich or Europe. Yes, we'll rely on her, but she'll rely on us too and we'll gain influence over her."

I said to the President, "I tell you, sir, with greater weight than any advice I've given you since your administration's inception, these men are mistaken and it's not in our interest—"

"I have heard your case," the President said.

"Crawford is not a serious advisor. He cares nothing for you or the country. He cares—"

"You can't accept standing alone, can you?" Crawford asked.

"I've spent my life standing alone."

"Yet you never question why. You never speculate that if everyone else agrees maybe they're right? Maybe they have a point?"

"Majorities are not infallible."

"True, but they're right more often than they're wrong. That's why they're majorities. But that doesn't matter to the brilliant John Quincy Adams, who knows better than the rest of us but who's only here because of his father."

I jumped to my feet and looked for how to maneuver around the table.

"Sit down!" the President said.

the South? I hoped they lived long enough to see their legacy, to know what they'd done to man's bastion of liberty in exchange for power.

I entered our house and wanted a drink. Debated whether to write to Stratford Canning to request a meeting or drown my sorrows and write to him in the morning. Obviously I chose the latter. Have I described the new kitchen yet? It was less claustrophobic than the last. More space for Ellen and Lucy between the counters and we kept the round three-legged table despite its inadequacy when hosting the children. So many children. I ignored them and prepared my Madeira.

Mrs. Adams joined me. "Can we speak?"

I kept my eyes on my glass. "Must we? I'd rather not think until tomorrow."

"I never expected such words from you."

"Today's different."

I looked at her. She bit her bottom lip. "My subject is important for our family."

"*Fine*." We exited to the music room and I sat on the piano bench. "What can't wait?" She sighed at my tone but I didn't care.

"Charles informed me that Mary stole his innocence some years ago," she said. "I believe she's done the same with John and that they engage in this regularly. You must speak with John."

"He won't listen to me if I tell him to stop."

"I know. You must tell him to propose."

"I will not."

"He mustn't impregnate her before wedding her. It would ruin them both and bring shame upon us."

"John's an adult. He's studying law and I've arranged mentorships that will bring him into the field. He'll afford a family."

"They must bear the consequences for their decisions."

"I said *no*, Louisa."

I saw muscles tighten across her face, neck, and arms. "What's wrong with you? You are more disagreeable than usual, which says much."

"I had the most dreadful day. It would be a lie to say my future is uncertain. I know it and it's grim."

She took a breath. "The presidency is unattainable." She looked at her hands and we were silent as the sound of Tom's children frolicking in the central entertainment room pattered through the wall. "Go to Braintree."

"To tell Father of my failure?"

"To escape from Washington. You'll think better there."

I sipped my drink. The President would be angry if I left before writing to Canning, but my career was over so his anger was irrelevant. I yearned for my home, my real home. Felt lighter already.

"Thank you, Louisa."

"You're welcome, John."

"Do you want to come with me?"

"I'll watch the house. Besides, this feels like a journey you should take alone."

LXV

Alas! How swift the moments fly!
How flash the years along!
Scarce here, yet gone already by,
The burden of a song.
See childhood, youth, and manhood pass,
And age, with furrowed brow, rime was.

IDEAS WOULDN'T COME. My mind's impotency growing with time. Its nectar squeezed dry from crisis after crisis. For seven years every episode eroded my spirit. I missed my youth, the conversations with Jefferson and La Fayette, the absorption of language after language. I'd wasted my potential and had no excuse, considering where I started in life.

I put my pencil and diary away. Couldn't even commit platitudes to verse. Should get some air outside my cabin but the New England coast in November wasn't hospitable for, as Royall implied, a man my age. I'd bought a last minute steamship ticket when their office opened. Such an innovative country, so much potential, returning to London's tendrils.

Potential. *Wasted.*

Another thought, validating the darkness. Step outside the cabin and jump into the Atlantic. No, a virtuous—forget it—no—yes. Was Lord Castlereagh's fate any different? Britain rejected his foreign policy and he stabbed his carotid artery. The President and America rejected mine. Was I stronger than he, stronger than an architect of Napoleon's defeat? Of course not. Follow his example. Our doing the deed back-to-back was my last hope for entering the historical record. My life wasted time, mine and everyone else's. Losing my soul was worse than death and to spend my life a failure, looking Father in the eye and seeing his disappointment, watching my country return to where it started at my birth, was an unacceptable existence. Do it. Do it now. It would be fast. No more pain. Peace, like swimming in the wintry Potomac. Troubles gone. Troubles outweighed joys. Joys? Don't make me laugh. Structure and productivity defined my life and look where they got me. Do it. Do it. Do—

Wait.

See Father and Braintree one last time. Return to your origins before departing. Yes. Tell Father of my failure and see him and home. A Braintree miracle. Like always.

A calm remainder to my journey.

♦ ♦ ♦ ♦ ♦ ♦

I reached Peacefield the following evening. Tom opened the door. "John?" His eyes wide, innocent.

"Good to see you, Tom."

"Come in. Come in."

I entered, holding my bags. Father and Nancy were in their normal sitting room spots by the fire. I greeted them.

"Sit, Johnny." Father pointed to a chair opposite him. I obliged and brushed snow off my coat. His eyes clouded with smoke as they watched me. "Why have you come? Does the President not require your counsel?"

"A break was in order if I am to give him my best work." I leaned toward the heat.

"But did you desert your duty?"

I didn't answer and Nancy asked, "Did Louisa join you?"

"She's watching the children. Yours, the Hellens, and ours."

"How—"

"Walk with me, Johnny," Father said. No interest in mindless chatting.

"John just sat down," Tom said. "He came such a—"

"*Now*, Johnny."

"It's all right," I said to Tom. I helped Father balance himself with his cane and we waddled to the front door.

"You're crazy," Nancy said. "Don't freeze yourselves."

"She's right," I said. "Let's speak here."

"Fine," Father said. I saw Tom and Nancy one last time across the room before joining Father in facing the door. "Why are you here, Johnny?"

"I wanted a respite from Washington."

"I follow the news enough to know the topics in your office. I'm in the midst of writing Thomas about them, about the Spanish patriots, and I know your being here means something is wrong."

A moment. "Can we discuss the world crisis?"

"Oh, Johnny. Don't come to me for counsel. I am too old and have been out of action too long to be useful."

"That's not true, Father."

"J—"

"I don't know the way forward. You told me I must become President but that route—"

"Find a way, Johnny."

"You don't understand."

"Find a way."

"Then can we—"

"It's your burden, not mine."

I stared at my boots. "It can't be done." I felt his judgment.

"Step outside."

"Why?"

"Come back once you've found a solution."

"It's too cold."

"That will motivate you. Do as I've instructed."

I nodded and opened the door, stepped through it, and heard him close it behind me. Thank goodness I hadn't removed my coat. I stepped away from the house. Why this? I'd spent two years trying to outsmart Metternich and failed. Freezing to death wasn't helpful. My mental resources were exhausted and shriveled, my best and only weapon drier than ever.

That was it. *I* was drained, but a better man might see through the vapor enveloping the jungle to behold the life it contained. I spent an hour weaving a conversation with Washington and Cicero. Washington reminded me of how the Jay Treaty prevented war with Britain but I told him that agreement hadn't proclaimed the world too dangerous for American independence or given London control of our foreign policy. Cicero said that he'd elevated Octavian to stop Mark Antony, creating 2,000 years of living gods in Europe. Useless. Then I heard Mother instruct me to *expel the mist*.

347

I screamed. Of anger, of frustration, of disappointment, of failure. I tore at my sleeves. My joints buckled and I clutched my legs in the snow. This hadn't helped. Nothing did. Nothing. Unsolvable. Metternich had won. He'd beaten me. I should have dove into the Atlantic. More useful as shark food. Can't even do that right. Nothing went right. Nothing. Noth—

"Son." I looked up. Father stood on his porch with his cane. "I take it you've not found the answer."

"There isn't one."

"That's not acceptable." He turned back. "Stay out here until you've found it."

"But Father, it's dark."

"Do as I've said." He entered the house.

I growled. More of a beast than a man as my mind became primitive. *Improvement was a better goal than specific outcomes. It allowed me to become my best possible self.* A lie. *Improvement meant working toward virtue. Perfection was possible for only the divine and the insane but our duty was to aim for it anyway and slow progress over time bettered our nature.* Yet I sat as a creature, not a man, perfect or otherwise. Improvement undone, a popped bubble. No future. No forward path.

Waited. The great bear above me at its zenith. Jupiter near Libra. I grew tired of the cold and stood. Something within me ordered me to walk. And walk. And walk. I circled the farm. Then I did it again. And again. And again.

Around. Around. Around.

I did this for hours. Blackness and wind threatened me to retreat inside and I laughed in their faces. Plodded and thought. Hour after hour. The stars, faint but visible, were my company. Joy. Swelling. I felt like who I was meant to be instead of an imposter. I felt my destiny. My inner light not extinguished any longer. I relived every world event of my lifetime. The Declaration of Independence. The war. Franklin and Paris. Yorktown. Victory. France's revolution. Washington and Father keeping the peace. Transfers of power. Napoleon. Pitt and Nelson and Castlereagh and Alexander and Kutuzov and Metternich and Wellington. The late war. The Congress of Vienna. South America. The Seminoles. Florida and Onís. Missouri. The Holy Alliance. The Cannings.

My body needed a break. I granted it. My mind didn't and I'd have denied the request. I thought. And thought. And thought.

Dawn came. I heard the door open. Footsteps. Gasps. Father and Nancy. I sat on the ground, my hands fists, covered in dirt and sweat, eyes down.

"John!" Nancy said. "This is madness! Come inside." She grabbed my shoulder. "I'll make you soup and tea."

"You weren't meant to stay out all night," Father said. "Do you mean to catch pneumonia?"

I looked at him. "Father?"

"Yes, Johnny?"

"I have it."

He smiled. "You mean…"

"*I have it.*"

LXVI

"THE PRESIDENT WILL see you now."

"Thank you, George," I said to Hay. I entered the President's office. The President was at the table's head with three paper stacks taller than his forearms as he scribbled on the sheet before him.

"One moment," he said. I nodded, though his eyes were too narrow and too low to see me. He completed the thought, dropped his quill, and looked up. He removed his glasses. "Yes, Mr. Adams?"

"Your son-in-law said you were ready."

"My last point became longer than I anticipated."

"Is that your annual message to Congress?"

"A draft." He looked at it for a moment. "You've been gone. Brent managed the Department in your absence." A pause. "He was adequate."

"There's no one in this city I trust more."

"He said Louisa told him that you'd gone to Massachusetts."

"That's right."

"I assume your family wrote of a quandary." He paused. "Did you notify Canning of our accepting his cousin's proposal?"

"No."

I saw his last iota of goodwill toward me die. The final nail dropping toward our relationship's coffin. "I received a report informing me that an Alliance army is already on its way." He gestured to it. I saw *Department of War* written across the top. "Really, Mr. Adams, accepting this offer is the only thing that Mr. Clay and Senator Jackson have ever agreed upon. I considered asking Brent to write to Canning but I trusted you and feared his receiving two letters for the same purpose. You've made clear you don't deserve such generosity."

"We shouldn't accept it, s—"

"The decision—"

"I have an alternative." We stared at each other. His eyes exuded blackness, mine hope. "Please hear it."

"Quickly." My final chance. The nail hovering.

350

"We should write to the Allies that it is our policy to oppose any future European colonization of this hemisphere. In exchange, the United States will refrain from intervening in Europe or the Old World. The hemispheres shall remain separate for a generation or more."

Warmth blossomed. He broke eye contact. I saw that he grasped my idea's power. "We'd make this statement on our own, separate from London?"

"Yes."

"We could never enforce it. That's the entire problem. We can't resist the Alliance without Britain's help."

"The Cannings will support the statement," I said, "but by making it alone first, we avoid appearing to rely on Britain for our defense."

"There's no guarantee of their support."

"There's no guarantee of anything in diplomacy. But I believe it to be much more likely than not that they'll endorse it."

"What if our individual statement offends them?"

"George Canning won't appreciate it, but his preference is preventing an Alliance invasion. It'd be absurd for him to join Metternich over our individual statement."

"I'd want us to send this statement before rejecting his offer."

"Exactly. Britain wants to commercially dominate this hemisphere, but not politically. Under this scheme, she and the United States can compete for South American markets without London controlling our foreign policy—and she won't be able to limit our expansion."

He thought for a few minutes. Then, "You call it a statement, but it's more like a *principle*. I'd need to rewrite the foreign policy section of my message to Congress. Oh—this principle means I'll have to remove my request to recognize Greek independence."

"When did you make that decision?"

"In your absence. Clay visited and pressed the case."

"It's a mistake, sir. Intervening in the Balkans justifies Alliance involvement in South America. We shouldn't give Metternich pretext for his aggression. Your term is drawing to a close and I believe Americans will remember it as the republic's golden age. I feel a solicitude for its end to correspond with its character, that the administration hands to its successor a peace and amity with all the world. If this cannot be, if the Holy Alliance is determined to make issue with us, we'll meet them in battle, but let us not invite or justify such action."

"I hoped to bring Clay closer to the administration in its final year."

I remembered my last exchange with Clay and shuddered. "Remember, Mr. President, that when Clay pushed for South American independence, he cared less about her freedom than about his own popularity and embarrassing the administration."

"We made a tentative agreement. How can I minimize his anger?"

Always testing me. "Congress can pass a resolution supporting Greece. Congress is responsible for its own actions and foreign powers don't pay the same attention to it that they do the executive. Let the Holy Alliance be outraged at Congress, not you." I chuckled. "They might even sympathize with Americans."

"It feels wrong to not mention Greece."

"You can say that we support the Greek cause without recognizing them."

"I'll think about it." He paused. "A lot to think about."

"The Principle is a mutual remonstrance against interference. The Allies don't use force in South America and we disclaim involvement in Europe."

"I know. But I hesitate to make it our policy during this crisis." Another few minutes. "How about this—let's have a Cabinet Meeting where you make your case to the other officers. The best argument will reveal itself."

"I look forward to it."

"I know you do. But you must promise me that no matter how contentious the meeting becomes, it will not devolve into violence again."

"You have my word."

"Good. I'll see you then," he said. I nodded and turned to exit. "Mr. Adams?" I paused. "You look well. Better than you have of late."

"Thank you, sir."

LXVII

THE CABINET MET three days later and I enjoyed my colleagues' confusion. It was impossible that we'd already heard from George Canning about our acceptance. Had Stratford said something so crucial that a memorandum wouldn't suffice?

Eyes darted between Crawford and myself. I read my notes but he watched me as though I'd returned from death. I suppose I had. This left his victory incomplete and uncertain. I hoped he feared me and my plan.

My bodily pain lessened since returning to Washington.

Calhoun was handsome when we first met but these seven years had aged him. He once was lissome, his hair full and groomed, his eyes resembling the color of tobacco. Now he was cadaverous, his eyes faded into clouded orbs, his mask a perpetual scowl. Those orbs had lightened again, which I read to mean that he was more curious than suspicious. I prayed I was right. Where Calhoun went so went the President—or so it seemed since I'd fallen from favor. We were no longer partners but we had to align one final time.

"Don't get up," the President said before he was through the door. He lacked the animation I expected, vexed that another debate was required. He organized his files and sat. It was time. "During my tenure I've tried to avoid discussing settled questions. I find it unproductive to interrogate our collective judgment and have no interest in becoming Hamlet. But an exception must be made regarding Canning's—"

"Why, sir?"

"Do not interrupt, Mr. Crawford. Mr. Adams, our esteemed colleague, articulated a principle to me that may suit our interests and make our acceptance unnecessary." To me, "I ask that you now state the Principle and that we discuss it in good faith. Let us make the best decision for our country, regardless of personality."

"Thank you, Mr. President." I lifted a letter. "This is my newest draft in response to the Baron's dispatch. My purpose is to act both moderately and firmly in declaring our dissent from Russian objects. To assert, instead, the republicanism upon which our government is founded

353

while disclaiming the intent of propagating it by force and declaring our hope the European powers will equally abstain from spreading into the American Hemisphere." I paused but they were silent. "Framed another way, we'd set as government policy a principle of mutual non-interference between the Old World and the New. We will keep out of their affairs, in Greece for example. In exchange, we ask that Europe never again claim new territory in the Americas. We will enforce this if necessary. Delivering this message to the Baron and other European governments avoids our admission of weakness by declining Canning's offer without actually declining it and invites his support for a principle that suits British interests. No compromises on our part are required aside from staying out of European affairs but that is in our interest anyway."

I paused again. They were still silent but I wanted their commentary before expounding further. They needed the President's opinion to know the boundaries of their thoughts. The President deduced this:

"I believe this idea has great potential, but disagree, primarily, with one point." He continued before I could analyze my remark for weaknesses. "It is better to announce the Principle as a section of my annual message to Congress than in dispatches to foreign governments." I relaxed. "My message's theme is the solemnity and alarm gripping the country. It is menaced by imminent and formidable dangers. I've written about the French victory in Spain and the Greek war. Including this Principle frames our response to these events and shall capture national and global attention."

"This is an excellent idea," Calhoun said. "More than that, it's exciting. Our foreign policy henceforth is ending. We embark on a new chapter, one of independence not just for our country but for our hemisphere."

The triumvirate revisited? "I appreciate your enthusiasm, gentlemen. I ask, Mr. President, that you reconsider including the Principle in your message. Introducing it so publicly will take the nation by surprise and may alarm them like a thunderclap. We've never enjoyed a period of such calm and tranquility and have never been in a peace so profound and secure as at this time. This message could summon arms against Europe."

"I thought you'd be honored at its inclusion," the President said.

"I am. But Europe has had 30 years of convulsions. Every nation within it has been alternatively invading and invaded. Empires and kingdoms overthrown. Revolutionized and counter-revolutionized. This message buckles the harness and throws down the gauntlet. Spain, France, and Russia may break relations with us and we'd no longer enjoy the quiet of the past seven years. Communicating it through dispatches is softer and less provocative."

"I'm stunned, Mr. Adams, to hear you describe the past seven years as tranquil," Calhoun said. "We've worked under the expectation that the Holy Alliance will invade South America. The President ought to sound the nation's alarm. We'll need all our energy to prepare the public mind."

"That's right," the President said. "The Allies support Spain in recovering her colonies and this message frames our response for both our citizens and the world."

"If I may speak…" Crowninshield said.

"Yes?"

"Mr. Adams is right, sir. Overreacting is more common than underreacting."

"I didn't mean to cause such a long discussion about my message to Congress. I'll write two separate versions and we can discuss the completed drafts." He paused. "I reject the notion that this era is benign. The Alliance attacks the very concept of popular rule."

"Perfectly put, Mr. President," Calhoun said.

"The choice is yours, of course, Mr. President," I said. "I'd still like to communicate the Principle to the Baron directly, given how essential Russian power is to Alliance aggression. You'll win Clay's favor by highlighting the Principle's support for republicanism in these lands."

"Too ostentatious a display of republicanism will offend the Russian government and perhaps even the British government," Calhoun said. "Giving the Baron a copy of the message's relevant section is sufficient. If even that is necessary. The message is for our countrymen, not foreigners."

"If I may," Wirt said, "the Holy Alliance has come to our house and proclaimed the virtues of despotism. The President's message is our answer."

"The Principle goes beyond what the Alliance asserted."

"The Baron bearded us to our faces upon the Holy Alliance's monarchical assumptions," I said. "This is a cause to be pleaded before mankind. Emperor Alexander is wedded to his system but I believe, if given the opportunity, he will disclaim any hostility toward us, the Northwest, and even South America. If not, he will at least make plain his intentions for the world."

"I agree with Mr. Adams and Mr. Wirt," the President said. Calhoun nodded, conceding the point.

"I've another concern," Wirt said. "The Principle sets vital interests that the Alliance cannot cross, and if they do, implies we will wage war to defend them. The executive cannot assert such a guarantee without a congressional resolution purporting the same. We should alert Clay and congressional leaders before sending the message."

"Hear hear!" Crawford said. The first peep from that cretin.

"That isn't necessary," I said. "Clay will support the Principle for its republican nature. I'd rather deny Congress influence over the President's message." The President nodded.

"Are we sure its republican nature isn't a problem?" Calhoun asked. "It reduces the likelihood of British support and risks building kinship between London and the Allies."

"That's a good point," the President said. "Britain is trapped between her anti-Jacobin policy, which builds sympathy for the Alliance, and the pressure of her debt and taxes which led to her supporting the South American rebels to open trade with that continent. I believe she'll side with us but if we alarm her the Alliance will give anything to appease British commercial cravings and create common cause. Leaving us in the lurch."

"Yet if we revoke the Principle's republican emphasis, we'll have to speak with Clay to secure its congressional support," Crawford said. The number of arguments he found in his posterior explained its size.

"The Principle avows republicanism but disclaims propagandism," I said. "The Cannings will recognize this distinction. It upholds existing independence to which Britain is already pledged and reaches the same conclusion as Canning's offer." Wirt and Crowninshield nodded. "As for the Allies enticing Britain, Cuba is the only object which might interest her but Spain would never consent."

"Gambling congressional rejection hurts the President."

"It's hardly a gamble. Most of Congress will embrace it, with or without Clay."

"Disregarding the Speaker." Crawford faked astoundment. "The Principle cannot satisfy both Clay and Canning. We should reconsider its viability, Mr. President. Canning's offer is a safer choice."

The President's eyes narrowed. "You're aware that accepting Canning's offer also requires congressional approval?"

Crawford made his attack: "If anything, Mr. President, we should ask whether the people would even support a war for South American independence. Some of the people are warm toward them but it's never been the general opinion. That makes the Principle and Canning's offer empty threats and betrays our honor. Metternich may have even arranged the Canning offer as a trap to ensnare us into denouncing the Holy Alliance without taking part in a war against them—meaning you'd pledge our country to war without support from Britain, Congress, or the people. That would destroy your administration. That's it, Mr. President. You have no power to oppose the Alliance. South America is on its own."

This finally achieved the unanimity the President had long sought, all right eyebrows raising into the same demeanor. My chance to isolate Crawford. I turned to Calhoun.

"Do you recall, back in your first Cabinet Meeting, when Mr. Crawford viewed provoking war with the Alliance as an acceptable risk for recognizing the United Provinces?"

"I do."

I said to Crawford, "How has your thinking evolved during your tenure? Why the change?"

"How would I—"

"I remember when you said relations with South America justified weighing the Allies' naval power."

"Recollecting such debates is worthless. I'm protecting the President's interests. Unlike you."

"Your analysis is flawed," Calhoun said. "Our purpose is detaching Britain from the Alliance. Britain will not and cannot resist them alone and our neutrality guarantees Britain will accommodate them. The President standing against them guarantees otherwise."

Crawford scoffed. "I'm sad to see you—"

"As for our people's wisdom, if the exigency requires it and we properly explain it to them, they will stay the course. The Alliance ultimately eyes us and if we don't resist their conquest of South America, they shall subdue this country through force." To me, "That is why I support the President's message proclaiming this Principle."

I felt as though our partnership had never ended. Time for what I hoped to be the fatal strike on Crawford.

"It's good that Mr. Crawford raised such objections for the President's consideration. I know he'll give them weight before coming to his decision. If they prevail, neither the Principle nor Canning's offer will be proper. But I believe the Principle to be proper and necessary, even if the Alliance never restores Spain's empire. Spain will never again maintain her dominion. It's absurd to imagine the Alliance will waste its blood and treasure on such nonsense. No, the Alliance wants this hemisphere for itself. Russia will take California, Peru, and Chile. France will take Mexico and perhaps Buenos Aires. Britain will settle for Cuba. Therefore we must act. The President is not pledging the nation to war. Canning said from the outset that the compact is meant to avert war and I reject the notion that the Principle offends Europe or Alexander. I resided in his Court and have a higher opinion of him than any of you. Not one word I have uttered will give him offense. The Principle merely acknowledges that monarchical government is different from ours but it states no reason why we can't live in peace with each other. It shows we desire peace. I expect the Emperor to say that he equally desires peace. He may even clarify his support for Alliance action in Spain and suggest that he only opposed mutiny from a faction he didn't recognize. He will say this because the Principle benefits all men tired of war."

Silence.

The President banged the table. Calhoun. Crowninshield. Wirt. A ring of support built around me and against Crawford. He matched my smirk, defiant. He could resist all he wanted. He'd lost. The standoff ended when Crawford leaned back and grabbed his left arm. His eyes narrowed. The President stopped and the others followed.

"Let's move on," the President said, not wanting to embarrass his Cabinet officer further.

"You explained that wonderfully, Mr. Adams," Wirt said, "but I fear Calhoun is right about lecturing Europe on republicanism. As a Virginian, I'm used to the man who flips his nose getting struck by a brickbat."

"I'll defer to the President," I said.

"A wise policy."

"I'll decide by the morning," the President said. "I want Canning to know—" Crawford groaned and he started converting into a ghost. He sank and, had Wirt not caught him, would have fallen from his chair. The President: "Get a doctor!"

I opened the door. Crowninshield left to find the nearest physician. Calhoun and Wirt lifted Crawford and guided him from the office. The President followed. I paused for a moment, my help not needed. I reflected on the seven years which led to this moment and my eyes settled on the President's chair.

Who'd sit in it next?

LXVIII

I RETURNED TO the President's office the following morning. My spirits were higher than any time since learning of Alexander's refusal to recognize the South American republics, possibly since arriving in Washington in September 1817.

"Good day, sir." I shut the door. "Any news on Crawford?"

"Yes, but nothing good. His heart sped out of control and so his health may be irrecoverable."

"Oh dear. Do we know why?"

"George told me the physician believes Mr. Crawford returned to Georgia sick this summer and a local doctor prescribed digitalis as a cure."

I shook my head. Some people were so irresponsible that relying on anyone was folly. Considered saying I'd pray for him but the President would have rightly questioned my sincerity. He saw the paper I held.

"Is that the latest draft?"

"Yes." I handed it to him. "I stayed up all night working on it." He began reading. "I included the feedback I received from yesterday's meeting. Or at least the relevant feedback. It should reflect the choices you requested. I cheerfully gave up all the passages you marked for omission, except one, which contained—"

"May I finish?"

"Yes, sir. Sorry, sir."

"That's all right." He smiled. Then, "I'd like to hold this for the rest of the day and write to you tomorrow if I have any more changes. I can't think of any."

"Even the paragraph on republicanism?"

"Yes. It's the paper's heart."

"That mirrors my thoughts. The rest is a series of deductions from it. The Baron's dispatch contains observations on monarchism that require an answer. An answer of liberty. Independence. Peace."

"Right."

"I cannot imagine that it will offend anyone." I reiterated my point from yesterday. "It will only offend Emperor Alexander if he's decided to invade South America and if he has this paper will become our protest."

"I agree."

"My hope is to persuade him. If it doesn't it shall be our manifesto to the world. Our stand against the Holy Alliance before mankind." I paused. "Sorry for my solicitude, but I consider this to be the most important paper that ever went from my hands."

"You needn't apologize, Mr. Adams. I know you've born a peculiar responsibility to craft the Principle and write this paper. I remain hesitant to offend Canning or the Emperor. Allow me to give you my answer tomorrow. The republicanism paragraph will likely remain. Once this is finalized, I'll rewrite the foreign affairs section of my message to Congress."

"Clay won't like our lack of action for Greece but I suspect the Cannings will support the Principle. That an empowered America threatens British interests less than the Alliance has been my key contention throughout my service as Secretary of State."

"Everything depends on their reaction. I hope you're right."

"I believe I am. And when proven so, the Era of Good Feelings will end as it began—in peace."

◆ ◆ ◆ ◆ ◆ ◆

Three months later.

"You must admit the President's message was insolent," Stratford Canning said.

"Why?" I asked.

"Issuing an independent, unified statement that your country cannot enforce alone when we hoped to form a joint one? That does not appear insolent to you?"

"What did cousin George say?"

"He called it *insolent*."

"Sorry to hear that." I leaned back, my elbows on armrests and hands clasped under my chin.

"You're convinced of your cleverness."

"Are you asking a question?"

"No. Do you remember when Burke wrote that the peasants who ask the government for bread bite its hand on the first scarcity? That's what your government has done to mine."

"Except we didn't—"

"Do not pretend your government can defend this hemisphere without us. You want—need—our help without being seen asking for it."

"Has George decided his response to the President's insolent message?"

"He endorsed it in an open letter." That was it. The last piece. "How certain were you of this outcome? Despite insulting us?"

"I had little doubt."

He laughed. "Inseparable from youth. I hope you know that America has lost her opportunity to access European politics."

"We will be treated as a great power when the world cannot deny such reality. We won't rely on British permission."

"A powerful America. With luck I won't live to see it." He looked at his notes. "How have the South Americans reacted?"

"I received a stream of letters and visitors for weeks after the President's message. A spectrum of opinion. Some thanked us, others asked if they'd exchanged one master for another."

"They will adjust to the new order. George sent information from Europe he wants your government to know before it reaches your press."

"Such as?"

"King Louis endorsed George's endorsement of the President's message."

"Really? As in France won't support an Alliance effort to restore the Spanish Empire? I don't see how it could mean anything else."

"Correct, Mr. Adams. George and Chateaubriand are negotiating a compact disclaiming new territorial conquest or commercial monopolies in the region." He referred to France's Foreign Minister.

"Will George recognize the South American republics?"

"He's working on it."

"I look forward to our becoming trade competitors. Did he mention Cuba?"

"Yes, actually. He asked for your thoughts on whether Ferdinand would accept an arrangement where he recognizes his former colonies' independence and London recognizes Cuba as Spain's."

"Such a proposal would only anger Madrid."

"I suspect he knows that. Ferdinand will have no choice but to accept the new status quo. So will Metternich and Alexander. They were contemptuous toward the President's message until George's endorsement but Greece absorbs their time now."

"Any developments there?"

"George recognized the Greeks as a belligerent party. Metternich called him a *Jacobin*, because that's the only insult he knows. Then Alexander followed George." He paused. "I know how badly you must feel for Metternich." Canning explained how his cousin feared that Russian intervention risked the Ottoman Empire's collapse and that Britain needed to prop it up but my mind wandered elsewhere.

"Alexander broke with Metternich?" I asked.

He stopped mid-sentence. "Yes, he said Metternich prioritized stability over Christian independence from Turkish rule. Metternich responded that Alexander's action threatened the Sultan's legitimacy. That's when Alexander threatened war with Austria."

"Where does that leave the Holy Alliance?"

"An unhappy marriage? I suspect they'll resolve their dispute but that Alexander will not follow Metternich's orders again. It's the end of Metternich's reign as Prime Minister of Europe."

I was unused to this much optimism. It made me uncomfortable and I closed my eyes. Oh no. Had the liquid returned? Why, my stress— wait. Tears. Still embarrassing. Resist them for now.

I beat him. He couldn't hurt us anymore. The New World was free and the first part of my mission was over.

My eyes opened and I saw Canning smiling. "What?" I asked.

"Congratulations, Mr. Adams." He paused. "Let's break for now. You have my memorandum and may read it at your leisure."

"Thank you."

He rose. "Before I depart, I'd like to say something—our terms in office aligning provided me with the most educational experience of my diplomatic career. You taught me more than either George or Lord

Castlereagh by making decisions I'd have never predicted. I shall spend years studying them."

I reached over my desk and we clasped hands. "Thank you for your kind words, Mr. Canning."

LXIX

"COME IN." BRENT guided the Baron into my office. "Have you given our guest a drink?" I asked.

"No, Mr. Adams."

"Get him a drink."

"That is unnecessary," the Baron said. He fronted stoicism but I heard his wheezing, as though his lungs contained embers smoldering from a lightning strike.

"Are you sure?"

"Yes."

"Very well. Is the door closed, Daniel?"

Brent checked, it was. He remained standing while the Baron sat across from me. I was going to enjoy this.

"Why do you think I requested to see you?" I asked.

"To discuss Canning's statement about the President's message to Congress," the Baron said.

"We'll get to that. The House Committee on Foreign Relations asked us to submit both of our notes to them. Do you object?"

A moment. "No."

"I am also considering submitting a summary of our verbal communication."

Another moment. "I am not sure my government wishes for such material to become public. It will produce excitement directed at both the Emperor and the President."

"Do not worry about the effect such publication will have for this government. If you change your mind, know that this country has freedom for its press and even you, as a minister, may use it."

"May we now discuss Canning's statement?"

"Yes. Has the Emperor's thinking changed?"

"It has, but because of Greece, not Canning."

"I believe you."

"The Emperor sees an opportunity to remove Turkish control of the Balkans. He remains uninterested in recognizing the South American republics but his attention is elsewhere."

"His decision will improve relations between our governments."

"Such a development is obvious, Mr. Adams. To clarify for my Court, the President's message is that the United States support Greek independence but will not act on its behalf?"

"That's right. It is part of our new policy to minimize political involvement between the hemispheres."

"I do not know what led to this new policy, but the Emperor has only a friendly disposition toward the United States. Of this I am certain. The United States are a republic and republican principles must prevail within them. The difference between republics and monarchies need not involve hostile collisions between them. The Emperor distinguishes between republics like the United States and rebellions founded on revolts against legitimate authority. I fear that you and your people have not given him the credit he is due for making this distinction."

"Perhaps we haven't." I looked at Brent, who shook his head behind the Baron. To the Baron, "For our part, the American government supports other countries choosing whatever political system is best for them. Our decision to recognize the South American states did not hinge on their becoming republics. We merely treated their independence from Spain as a fact."

"I will communicate this to my Court."

"Are there any other subjects you'd like to discuss regarding Canning's endorsement of the President's message?"

"None occur to me."

"One does to me. Daniel?" I asked. Brent froze his pacing. "Do you mind excusing us?" He nodded. "Shut the door on your way out." He exited and I looked at the Baron. I leaned onto my desk and smiled. "Let's discuss the Emperor's edict."

♦ ♦ ♦ ♦ ♦ ♦

1823 drained my energy and 1824 contained the election. I held no tolerance for any more surprises connected to my tenure as Secretary of State until I received an unexpected message. The President invited me to dinner at the Executive Mansion. Just us. Rare but not unheard of. A sign that I was back in his good graces and he thanked me for devising the Principle and recognized what we'd accomplished.

During our first course, the President instructed me to prepare a report about my discussions with the Baron, regardless of his permission. I said I'd do so and would show it to him before submitting it to the Committee on Foreign Relations. I informed him the Baron and I established a framework for the Northwest: the territorial boundary at 54-40, Russian ports opened for our ships, and Americans permitted to enter the Russian zone on the condition that they didn't sell guns and whiskey to the Indians. The President approved and said the treaty could be completed and ratified either that year or by the subsequent administration.

Thus ended our political talk. We spent the evening enjoying each other's company. I smoked a cigar and the President smoked hashish. It dawned on me that Europe's supremacy over the New World, which began with Columbus, was over due to our actions. A historical milestone which, in my opinion, rivaled the achievement of Father's generation. An independent hemisphere.

The age of monarchy—of Caesar and Augustus—was ending. Metternich was wrong to think that monarchs could rule through force and disregard their people. Our example unsettled Europe's ancient governments and would overthrow them without a single exception. I held this revolution to be as infallible as that the Earth would perform a revolution around the sun in a year.

I felt gratified having contributed to this worthy movement.

PART TEN

BAD FEELINGS
1824 - 1825

LXX

1824. THE YEAR I'd dreaded since the President's letter asking me to serve as his Secretary of State arrived at the Court of St. James. The year that would determine if I'd fulfill my parents' expectations or if I'd die a failure—worse, if I'd live as one. I spent New Years reflecting on my tenure as the Department's head. Any success to which history honored the administration was due to the Department of State but I couldn't analyze my actions regarding Florida, Missouri, or the Alliance, and not conclude my skills were imperfect. I doubted my capacity to capture the presidency.

Crawford remained in the lead, despite his illness. He insulated himself from the press by hiding in Virginia and Georgia. Clay and Calhoun built followings in the middle states and the South, respectively, the former loudly, the latter covertly. New England was my base, though its leaders remained angry that I supported Jefferson's embargo over 15 years ago. I had no way to win support in other regions. That I saved the American Hemisphere was irrelevant. Men supported their regional favorites because they couldn't see past their noses. Crawford, that debilitated ingrate, was unstoppable.

I had an idea. General Jackson had a large following in the middle and southern states, and I held the North, so our partnership could defeat the three Cs. *Adams can write and Jackson can fight* could be our slogan. 8 January was the ninth anniversary of his victory at New Orleans and I instructed Mrs. Adams to prepare our home for a party in Jackson's honor. She rose to the challenge, the climax of her role as Washington's secretary of soirée. I saw the woman I'd married as her passion returned. I'd missed her.

I sent invitations to all congressmen and senators except Alexander Smyth and John Floyd. Called upon the President but he excused himself, as I suspected. He'd refused to visit Crawford during his recovery because of an emerging tension between them and feared attending my party showed favoritism. I told him I wasn't the least offended.

Mrs. Adams' weekly tea party fell two days before the big night. Company of 50 people, less than normal. Dancing with piano music. Ira Hill, a geologist, appeared and asked about the larger event. I invited him.

Our boys, the Hellen children, and Tom's rascals were deployed on the eighth. Furniture removed, including the carpets. A dance area on the first floor and a buffet on the third. We served meats, pies, and Florida oranges to remind the General and all of Washington about our joint achievements. Mrs. Adams feared the second and third floors couldn't bear so much weight so we rented extra pillars. The children decorated the walls with paper eagles and flowers. I feared the city's elite might find this silly so my wife added rose wreaths.

500 invitations. 1,000 guests. Carriages flooded the snowy F Street. Congressmen, reporters, diplomats, the Cabinet—minus Crawford—mingled in our home with their wives. Mrs. Adams and I stood at our entrance and greeted our guests. Most of the names that I've mentioned to you crossed us: Justice Story, Senator King, and Mr. Hyde, for example. Stratford Canning congratulated me on marrying my superior and Calhoun and Clay looked apprehensive. I went inside because some Jackson supporters ran around while carrying candles. The flames were dim from the lack of air in the packed space. I questioned them and they said they were reenacting the British inferno during the war and this showed the importance of Jackson's victory. I asked them to refrain should they cause a literal reenactment. Returned to my spot. The Baron de Tuyll arrived and we exchanged pleasantries. He was surprisingly gracious about the world crisis' outcome.

A black coach arrived at 9:30. It opened, revealing a blood red interior. Jackson exited with his wife. Newton would have studied how eyes pulled to him. First the ones outside and then layer by layer within our house as word of his arrival spread. He approached and we each bowed our heads.

"Good evening, Mr. Adams."

"Good evening. Do you prefer *Senator* or *General* as your prefix?"

"General. The title I spent my life earning." He paused and I expected him to turn to my wife but he remained fixed on me with a sapphire twinkle in his eyes. "Thank you for hosting this celebration. I'm honored, as are, I am certain, the veterans of that fateful day."

"Nay, sir, it's my honor to acknowledge such patriotism."

Jackson nodded, a minimal acknowledgement. He released his wife and extended his arm to Mrs. Adams. "Shall we?"

"Let's."

They entered and toured the first floor. Jackson spoke to every man and woman and each felt his sincerity as though his words were fresh every time and only meant for he or she. Each bore a similar look of awe. I restrained my glee. Recruiting him as Vice President made my triumph inevitable. Plus he couldn't hang anyone from the vice presidency. Right?

Clay stared at Jackson and then turned to me and shook his head. We'd not had a meaningful conversation since he predicted my destruction at Brown's Hotel. I cared not for his thoughts but I was curious if my joining with Jackson prompted hysteria. Jackson ignored Clay but spoke to his wife. The enemies avoided eye contact and Clay folded his arms like a child dragged to church.

Jackson *did* speak to Calhoun and his wife. I remembered when Calhoun and I recruited Jackson in front of the Executive Mansion. Just after the Florida invasion and it appeared we three would vanquish Spain and define the era. Then slavery drove Calhoun and I apart and I had to outwit Metternich alone. I wished to renew the partnership after my election. I as President, Jackson as Vice President, Calhoun continuing as Secretary of War, and Brent as Secretary of State. Calhoun looked perplexed and I wondered why. I decided I must speak with him, one of my most frequent thoughts in recent years.

Charles came from the second floor, interrupting Jackson's excursion. "The buffet's next course is ready for those interested." Jackson may be the night's star but my youngest son was apparently Moses as he led so many guests to the third floor that I feared our stairs couldn't stand the weight. That's where Jackson made his main statement. Mrs. Adams on his right arm, lifting champagne with his left.

"As I hold your attention, I would like to take this opportunity to thank the lovely Louisa Catherine Adams, our host this evening." Applause. "She does honor to me and to the Tennessee militia, the Regiment of Tennessee Volunteers, the Kentucky militia, the Lou—"

Plop!

An oil lamp hanging from the ceiling landed on Mrs. Adams. Jackson released her and jumped, dodging the splatter. The crowd gasped and stared and then looked at me before returning to her. Was she hurt? What ought I do? She leaned to the buffet table and grabbed a cloth she knew was there. She wiped her face and revealed a smile.

The room relaxed and a cheer began first as a trickle and then as a wave. My wife giggled. Our guests quieted, presuming she had a remark. She did, so much better than I.

"The one thing to be sure of in a rented house is you'll end up with a spoilt gown." The women laughed, the men followed. I walked to her. Oil covered her hair and dripped down her neck, shoulders, and back.

"Are you all right?" I asked.

"Yes. We mustn't be rattled, as you've always told me."

I saw John. "Find Mary." He nodded and left.

"Please don't worry," Mrs. Adams said.

"I'm not."

"You've been anointed with sacred oil," Mrs. Jackson joked. I ignored her. John and Mary appeared.

"Take my wife and change her into fresh clothes," I said. Mary nodded, took Mrs. Adams' hand, and departed. I turned to General Jackson. "Can we speak?" I looked for a quiet place and concluded none existed. He followed me down the stairs and outside behind the building. I caught my breath and lit a cigar. He was half a foot taller than me.

"You look well, General." I tried to be innocuous. "You dress well."

"Did you expect a tomahawk in my hand? That I'd be covered in my enemies' blood?"

"I did not mean to offend."

"None was taken. I jest." His lips held their downcast slant.

"I hope you know that Mrs. Adams achieved the feminine equivalent of our greatest deeds tonight."

"It was the finest event I've attended in this city. It shall be spoken of for years."

"I thank you. As does my family."

"What is its purpose, sir? What is yours?"

"Why—"

"This is an election year and you wouldn't honor me without a reason. I want to know that reason."

I sighed. "I think we should form a ticket. Crawford leads for now and even if he weren't sick, we both know he lacks the virtue to be President. He'd be a disaster in his current condition. I predict he'll ally with Clay or Calhoun to place the Electoral College in his pocket. Our partnership would stop him. I'll bring New England and you'll undermine my competition in the West and South. We'd win, it's unquestionable."

A moment. "You're right, especially since most states have altered their voting laws to allow the people to direct their electors. But it'll only work if I am President and you are Vice President."

"Be reasonable, General. I have more experience in this city and in foreign—"

"Hardly an appropriate claim for the people's leader, Mr. Adams. This election pits the people against this city's corruption. The people do not like professional politicians and don't trust those connected to Europe."

"This is what you think of the guests who took time to see you tonight? To applaud you?"

"These people…" He turned to my house. "They mean well but they'll always put themselves first. They didn't care when the Bank erased years of working effort. Years we'll never have back. Because it didn't affect them other than its impact on some elections. This city looks down on the people."

"Do I?"

He turned back. "I don't know you. Not well enough to say."

"I hoped to avoid mentioning this, but I expected gratitude after defending your invasion."

"As though *I* owe *you*? Your negotiations would have failed if not for me."

"And I rescued you from Clay. That incident showed—"

"I was born for the storm, Mr. Adams. The calm of the vice presidency does not suit me. I must rid this country of corruption before it enslaves the people to monied interests. No one but myself is willing or able to adhere to the people's wisdom, certainly no one entrenched in Washington."

"How do you plan to accomplish your goals if you've made Congress and the department clerks your enemies?"

"Congress will bow to the people's will. They'll have to."

"Is that a threat?"

"It needn't be. My election will make this city appreciate the need to respect others' desires."

I thought back to when Clay called on Congress to censure Jackson. The Speaker warned of Jackson becoming our Alexander, our Caesar, our Cromwell, our Napoleon. I'd dismissed him, but the General sounded as though he was ready to overthrow our constitutional order in the people's name.

"What does removing corruption look like?" I asked. "What policies?"

"Standing up to the Bank. Freeing the local Indians from our government by moving them further west. Our presence leaves them discontent in their ancient home and we'll grant them new territory." A pause. "Does that adequately answer your question?"

"I suppose. You know the Constitution restricts the various branches?"

"I'll embody the people's general will. Any act I commit in their interest cannot threaten them. We mustn't fear the people's virtue. Now, unless you have any original points to make, I think it best that we return to your guests."

"Lead the way."

"As is my custom."

I followed him inside. The crowd roared and sucked Jackson into its embrace while leaving me on its perimeter. He'd accepted my aid over the years, saving his career repeatedly, using me. I watched him charm hundreds into drunkenly following his every tick and swelled with terror. He rejected constraints or questions to his power. Why was I surprised? He did not constrain his own temper. He destroyed his opposition, never negotiating or considering alternate points of view. He had the trappings of a military dictator and posed a more immediate threat than Metternich ever could.

And I launched his campaign for President.

LXXI

O Lord, I know that the way of man is not in himself:
It is not in man that walketh to direct his steps.

I REPEATED THIS passage several times over the subsequent days. God, not I, controlled my destiny. The election was in His hands, it was His decision if Father would die disappointed and Mother's last wish went unfulfilled. My actions couldn't alter His chosen outcome. This comforted me.

Yet I had to make decisions. The Tennessee and Pennsylvania legislatures endorsed Jackson after my party. An unprecedented movement swelled with the General at its head. The people had never spoken with such thunder but their substance, and not their volume, worried me. Jackson's old military subordinates coordinated his campaign and spread his message. Senator Eaton, a major at New Orleans, was his right hand. He instructed friendly newspapers to write glowing pieces. Jackson's denial of involvement fooled nobody but let him claim he was honorable. This contrasted with Clay, who spoke to anyone who'd listen, mostly in near-empty taverns across the West.

Virtue dictated that I say and do nothing to advance myself. Stand for office, nothing more. Such constraints ensured my defeat. I had to campaign, publicly or quietly, to have a chance. Explain to the people what I'd done for them. But losing after campaigning was the worst ending, one I'd deserve. Too great a risk. So why stand at all? Forfeit. Spare myself. Yes. But would Father, or Mother's memory, accept that? Would they accept anything but victory?

How strange to lose to Jackson, a man whose defining achievement was winning a single, daylong battle where he held every advantage. Whereas I'd saved the New World and no one cared. I wondered if Clay, who thwarted disunion, felt likewise. In a sane world we'd be in the lead instead of Jackson and Crawford.

Fear of failure made work impossible and reciting Jeremiah 10:23 ad nauseam didn't help. Eating, sleeping, and thinking all became as difficult as at the height of the world crisis. I was miserable analyzing every contingency over and over and had to speak to someone and there was only one person who could relate.

April was Calhoun's month for Charles Bird King to portrait him. The first candidate's turn. I traveled to King's office in Georgetown one day after work. He'd painted my wife some years before so I knew the way. Crossed the old bridge at Rock Creek. He'd made a small warehouse his studio. Might as well have been an Indian hut amidst the grandest cathedrals in Europe when compared to Washington's larger buildings.

I entered and the door creaked but neither man looked at me. Calhoun faced the other way and King stood behind his canvas. He shivered, finished his immediate task, and lowered his brush. "Mr. Adams?" King asked. "You're scheduled for May."

"Excuse the interruption. I require a minute of Mr. Calhoun's time, if that is acceptable."

As a poet, I knew King's anger well at having his artistic focus broken. To Calhoun, "The choice is yours."

"I will speak with him," Calhoun said. King nodded, frowning. "We'll only be a moment."

King nodded again. "Get me when you're finished." He exited his studio.

I approached Calhoun. He remained sitting. "Do you mind telling me how it looks? He asked that I not see it until completion but you've provided a loophole."

I walked around the easel. "He's made your hair effeminate, but you hold a strong jaw. Your coat buttons aren't symmetrical and your entire outfit has the air of a boy pretending to be a man."

His shoulders sank. "I suppose it will have to do for there's no time to begin again."

"I didn't say it was poor quality." I scanned the studio, a potpourri of ugly. A garish yellow and orange carpet reigned over the floor and the walls hid from it behind myriad paintings. Mostly Indian portraits but I noticed various literary and genre paintings and assumed, had money not mattered, that he'd focus on these efforts.

"I assume you're here to discuss the election," he said.

"Correct."

"Good. I have a question for you."

"Yes?"

"Why did you promote General Jackson? Between your party and Clay directing Tennessee to endorse him—"

"Do we know for a fact that Clay is responsible?"

"I trust the source who informed me."

I signed. "I hoped Jackson could undermine Crawford. Clay likely felt the same."

"Well you succeeded." He paused. "I thought you were offering to become his Vice President."

"I've no interest in that office."

"Even if Jackson or Crawford offered it?"

"I would never work for Crawford," I said. "Would you?" He hesitated. "Has he made an offer?"

"No," he said. "I've become close with Senator Taylor." This troubled me. Senator Taylor, unlike his counterpart in the House with the same name who sponsored the Missouri Compromise, was an extremist who wrote a pamphlet titled *Tyranny Unmasked* attacking the Compromise and federal power. Was he Calhoun's mentor? "He advised me to leave the contest after Pennsylvania endorsed Jackson. I needed that state to win and with its loss I've no path forward."

"Don't despair. You're—what?—42? You have ample time to become President. 42 is too young anyway, no President has been younger than his Cabinet officers, so you'd have few options."

You've likely noticed that I've referred to several men wearing masks. Confident facades they want others to believe. None was faker than Calhoun's. He was riddled with frailties and was the biggest disappointment of my tenure. A dour man, he never smiled, even if the moment demanded it. His gaze was strong and penetrating but it betrayed his thoughts. As disastrous for a politician as for a gambler. It told me he knew I spoke for my own advantage.

"I have a condition for my withdrawal," he said. "The remaining candidates must pledge they'll direct their electors to elect me Vice President."

No consideration was needed. "You have my word."

"Thank you. I'll write to the others."

"I would like to speak openly as we are no longer competitors. Do you foresee my chances being any better than yours?"

He calculated. "Yes. The others haven't stolen New England and are unlikely to do so, whereas my Southern support abandoned me."

"But I'm unable to reach elsewhere."

"Have you tried? We lack the draw of Jackson or Clay but we both know what you achieved as Secretary of State. Tell the country, no one else will."

"My business was to serve the public to the best of my abilities, not to intrigue for further advancement. I've never expressed a wish for any public office and I should not now ask for that which ought to be spontaneously bestowed."

"Times have changed, Mr. Adams. You must change with them to remain relevant."

"Is virtue a figment of the past? What leadership will we have if such practices become expected?"

"You're free to preach, but what will you do?"

I couldn't answer him.

LXXII

WE KNOW SO little of the future that whether I ought to wish for victory was among the election's greatest uncertainties. I aspired to look upon it indifferently, but who can hold fire while thinking of the frosty Caucasus? Suffering without feeling wasn't within human nature and when I considered that my success or failure was a vote of censure by the nation upon my past service I felt more at stake upon the result than any other individual in the Union. Yet a man qualified to be Chief Magistrate of tens of millions must be tempered to endure defeat. This is the principle that I impressed upon my own mind.

A break from my emotions came that summer. The President invited General La Fayette to tour the country, conclude the Era of Good Feelings, and endorse the Principle. La Fayette agreed and in exchange the President asked Congress to grant him 23,000 acres in Florida and a 200,000 dollar gift. It complied.

He arrived in New York. 80,000 people greeted him. He stayed at Vice President Tompkins' house on Staten Island and then trekked through the middle states. Mr. Ingersoll, one of his guides, invited me to join them in Baltimore. I accepted. We attended service at Christ Church and Bishop White read from Psalms 73:25-26.

Who have I in Heaven but thee? And there is none upon Earth that I desire beside thee. My flesh and my heart faileth: but God is the strength of my heart, and my portion forever.

It was a communion day sermon but the bishop made no adaptation for the occasion of La Fayette's presence. From there to Philadelphia. He asked to visit a school for the deaf and dumb. A young man named Wells was the teacher and I remembered meeting him on a steamboat. The pupils performed and their knowledge surprised me. Thence to the Pennsylvania Hospital for the sick and insane. Among the lunatics was Scott, from Boston, who wished to see me. He said he'd been president of the Phoenix Fire Club when I was a member and inquired about Father and my family. He exhibited no token of insanity. Followed us around several of the apartments and made remarks upon the picture of Christ healing the sick. We saw one bedridden woman. She died that day.

We proceeded to a meeting of the Washington Benevolent Society, who admitted La Fayette as an honorary member. I'd been warned against attending the ceremony because the Society was a Federalist political organization of violent character under a benign vizor but I couldn't avoid accompanying the General. Then we saw the Schuylkill Waterworks and viewed the dam, the wheels, and the pipes which ascended the water to the reservoir on the hilltop.

Our final stop was at the Hall of Independence, so called because it was where the Declaration of Independence was issued. The interior was altered. La Fayette surveyed the Children of the Schools. 2,250 girls and 1,800 boys, mostly from seven to 14. Several addresses and a song later, he shook many teachers' hands and many of the girls obtained the same, despite previously announced regulations. The event took three hours and the General declined to sit or use an umbrella.

We spoke afterward, for I had to return to Washington. He still refused an umbrella but I covered myself. It was odd seeing someone etched into memory as a teenager at 67. Few had done more to advance liberalism against its enemies, whether they be monarchs or Jacobins.

"Do you mind talking in French?" he asked. "I miss it here."

"Let's use English. I don't want to be overheard speaking a foreign language."

A chuckle. "So you *are* focused on the election. Will being seen with me remind Americans of your father?"

"Don't be cynical, I'd never abuse our friendship. Besides, I should do nothing to promote my candidacy. If the country wants my service she must ask for it."

"How is he? Your father?"

I shrugged. "The infirmities of old age are upon him. His sight has dimmed and he can neither read nor write. Nor can he walk without aid. But his memory remains strong, his judgment sound, his interest in conversation considerable."

"Has he recovered from your mother's passing?"

"I'm not sure he will until they've rejoined."

He frowned. "Can we discuss the election? I am pleased that republicanism endures here, unlike in France where they restored the monarchy. It gives me hope that our cause will survive the Alliance and return to Europe in future generations."

"What do you want to know?"

"Who do you expect to win?"

I groaned. "Crawford was the initial leader but General Jackson overtook him. He tried reviving his campaign in June by having the congressional Republicans nominate him but failed. That's how every President since Jefferson won the office and Crawford hoped to be the fourth but this election is unlike those of the past. The people seek greater say. Clay, Jackson, and I boycotted the meeting and our congressional allies followed suit. Only 66 of the 240 men in Congress attended so the event stunk of desperation and of muting the people. He then suffered another bout of his illness and the press say he can't feel his limbs. I don't expect him to live until the election but he refuses to exit. Now he claims to be the most pro-slavery candidate and the most devoted to shrinking federal supremacy over the states."

"Such a claim only helps him in the South."

"Yes, but he's trying to halt Jackson's lead in that region. No one will win a majority of the Electoral College if all four candidates remain and the top three will go to the House. I can't foresee who'll win a House contest but Clay is Speaker and engineering Crawford's victory is his preference if he can't win himself. They're partners and he can use the infirm President as his puppet."

He sighed and I girded my emotions like Caesar's fortress at Alesia. "Soliciting an office blunts the country's voice," I said. "You were closer to General Washington than anyone save his wife. You know he'd never approve of—"

"Standards have shifted."

"They've lowered."

"They'll lower further if the presidency becomes a farce." He paused. "Have you received inquisitors?"

"Hundreds since the spring. Most propose deals to secure my victory but I tell them I'd govern in national terms, not sectional ones. A cautious tariff, for example, which all regions can digest."

"Does that include slavery?"

"Unfortunately. I've not spoken of it publicly and Southerners don't trust me for having never owned a slave." I paused, he looked disappointed at both me and America. "Governor Clinton's allies offered me New York if I promised him a high Cabinet position. New York is one of six states that retains legislative control of its electoral votes. Senator Van Buren has repeatedly tried to give the state to Crawford but a political operative named Mr. Tweed resists him."

"Who does Tweed support?"

"Me. I've not met the man but he'd do anything to break Van Buren. The Little Magician is our most devious political operator." I wanted to end this conversation soon so I could get him inside. He mustn't become ill.

"You risk that man controlling the government? Along with Crawford and Clay?"

"Virtue informs my every decision. How can I skin an animal before it's caught? I'll not become Van Buren because a soiled man makes an unworthy President. He ought to be ashamed of pushing someone New Yorkers despise on their electors. They oppose all he stands for."

"Better a good leader than a perfect critic."

I insisted we find cover. My break ended the next day. The General's party left for Yorktown to acknowledge the battle that won our revolution. I braced myself for the election results that trickled in like the rain that poured upon our guest. They carried the outcome of my life's effort.

LXXIII

VOTES ARRIVED THROUGH the autumn months and the count finished in early December. The outcome:

General Jackson won 153,544 votes, 99 electoral votes, and carried Illinois, Indiana, New Jersey, Pennsylvania, Maryland, Tennessee, both Carolinas, Alabama, Mississippi, and Louisiana.

I won 108,740 votes, 84 electoral votes, and carried Maine, New Hampshire, Vermont, Massachusetts, Rhode Island, Connecticut, and New York.

Crawford won 46,618 votes, 41 electoral votes, and carried Delaware, Virginia, and Georgia.

Clay won 47,136 votes, 37 electoral votes, and carried Ohio, Kentucky, and Missouri.

Jackson won a plurality, but not a majority, of the Electoral College, so the election went to the House of Representatives. The top three candidates—Jackson, myself, and Crawford—were eligible and Clay was eliminated.

The Constitution gave each of the 24 states one vote. We needed 13—a simple majority—to win. Jackson had 11, I had seven, and Crawford and Clay each had three. I didn't know how Tweed got me New York, nor did I want to, but I was grateful.

My fate, future, and soul converged at one impasse. Jackson would have won had there been fewer candidates. Virtue and honoring our republic meant accepting the people's will. Right? The House contest was a viable option. Could I betray a system by utilizing contingencies built into it? The sinful three-fifths clause won Jackson his plurality. Otherwise it'd be 77 electoral votes for him and 83 for me. Was capitulating to the slave powers virtuous? Allowing them to elect their Napoleon? What if virtue dictated—

What was I thinking? No one would believe that I overruled the people for virtue's sake.

That implied others' affirmation determined virtuosity and it wasn't something I knew about myself regardless of others' opinions. Virtue said to not campaign and limited my electoral votes. Why combat Jackson and the slave powers in the House if virtue didn't permit it earlier? Conceding was the consistent choice. I shouldn't have stood for office at all. Virtue dictated my actions and I accepted what the world gave me. Right?

I reflected on Mother's words at my quest's genesis:

Remember to not look back or shrink from your duty, however arduous or dangerous the task assigned you. And never forget virtue. It's equally important. Purge any Old World values you absorbed from your soul. Your great intellect counts for little if virtue, honor, and integrity aren't added to it. I'd much rather you found your grave in the ocean while returning from Europe than see you an immoral profligate or a graceless man.

She mentioned duty but placed greater emphasis on virtue and grace. Prioritize virtue over outcomes. What Mother directed, my eternal practice. Accept the people's choice even if they were wrong. It was settled.

Then I reflected on my conversation with Father moments earlier:

"Realize where you started in life, Johnny. History won't give me my due. I won't be credited for my role in the Revolution. The parts performed by General Washington, Mr. Jefferson, and Dr. Franklin will be exaggerated instead. But we are still one of America's leading families. You came into life with advantages that will disgrace you if your success is mediocre."

"I am the Secretary of State."

"You must become President."

"My position makes me heir apparent. The last three Presidents all held my office before ascending to the Executive Mansion."

"That's not a guarantee."

"A guarantee is impossible."

"It was for General Washington. You are not he, but it can still be done."

"How?"

"Find a way, Johnny. And you must win two terms, to make up for my loss to Jefferson. Restore the family legacy."

"You once told me that you studied politics and war so I may study mathematics and philosophy, and I had to study mathematics and philosophy so my children could study painting and music."

"There will always be a need for politics, son. If men were angels no government would be necessary. I am not advising you. I'm telling you. You must achieve the presidency. For your own worth and for mine. For our family's. You must succeed."

"Yes, Father."

Ambition. Rising through society and achieving greatness. The other half of my creed. I was the eldest son to America's greatest family and was duty-bound to honor its name. Make something of myself. Become President: the destiny my parents chose for me.

But ambition robbed men of their souls. That's why it must go hand in hand with virtue. I'd walked this bridge for decades and it brought me to the presidency's edge. I thought that breaking Europe's grip and mastering the continent would woo the people. I was wrong. They were ungrateful for everything I'd done for them. Instead they idolatrized a barbarian who fought Indians and slaughtered some redcoats and who pretended he was the next General Washington. I, if anyone, was Washington's successor. I was not a soldier but my policies achieved his vision. America as a great power, internal improvements binding us together, a giant dwarfing all of Europe's empires. Jackson as Washington was superficial. Adams as Washington was substantive, but I'd thought too much of the people to see this.

Think of what I'd been through. What I'd endured as Secretary of State. Endless hours for eight years analyzing every factor involved in taking Florida and the Pacific coast from Spain, in defeating Metternich without yielding to Britain, all while keeping favor with the President, Congress, and the press as my enemies peeled the flesh off my bones any chance they could. Becoming President was my reward. Right? The people owed it to me.

Were these the thoughts of a virtuous man? Ambition alone made me no better than my enemies. Virtue told me to accept defeat, to spend my years reminding myself and others that my failure was justified. Could I live with that after what I'd done as Secretary of State?

No.

No. No. *No.*

I'd come too far to fail my parents now. That was the rub. They gave me two values and I'd spent my life pursuing both but now they were incompatible and I had to choose. I betrayed my parents either way. Lose the office or my humanity. Which would they rather? Mother left me and writing Father was unnecessary. It was for me to decide. Which value? Which path?

I read *Macbeth.* Shakespeare's masterpiece on ambition. It warned me of that option, of becoming like every other politician who quested after power.

Two truths are told
As happy prologues to the swelling act
Of the imperial theme
—Act 1, Scene 3

The prophecy. The witches were right about his becoming Thane of Cawdor and so he knew they were right about his becoming king. Likewise I deserved the presidency for achieving my goal as Secretary of State. But did I wish to be Macbeth? His story did not end well and Mrs. Adams was hardly a Lady Macbeth pushing me.

Nay, virtue was my excuse for failure. Father wouldn't accept that explanation upon my return to Braintree as a private citizen. Nor would Mother. I must succeed, for my worth, for Father's, for our family's. I could compensate for a failure of virtue but not of ambition. I could do good as President and build a better society all while acting purer than any before me. Even George Washington. Failing to win the office left me nowhere. Virtue without ambition was meaningless. I'd have nothing.

I made my choice: Ambition.

I had seven states and needed six more to win. Congressmen cycled through my office day after day until New Years. Illinois wanted a pledge that I wouldn't admit another slave state to the Union. Done. Maryland asked me to promise I'd not exclude Federalists when considering clerks. Done. Two of Louisiana's three congressmen, Gurley and William Brent, resented Jackson from when he served as governor and came to me with open arms.

Governor Clinton sent General Brown to speak on his behalf. He said New York might switch to Crawford if I didn't grant Clinton a prominent posting. A dangerous moment, losing New York was fatal. I envisioned Jackson and Crawford becoming partners. It had yet to happen but it might if they saw me collecting states. I told Brown to assure Clinton that I had the highest opinion of his talents. That left the situation stable for now.

Mr. Newton, congressman for Virginia's First District, talked with me for two hours. He said his state favored Crawford but felt he couldn't win and I was their second choice. He asked for my position on tariffs and internal improvements. I spoke with perfect candor, I wanted conciliation and not collision. I was satisfied with the current tariff rate and would rather reduce it than raise it because the economy prospered and federal revenue was abundant. My opinion on internal improvements was well known. Congress had the power and it depended on the elected franchise and good sense to prevent its abuse. He accepted these answers and said he'd speak with his colleagues.

I held ten, maybe eleven, states by the year's end. Not enough.

The deadlock continued and I walked above moral fire.

LXXIV

"MR. PRESIDENT, I present to you Mr. Rebello, Brazil's Secretary of Legation."

I stepped aside so Rebello could bow to the President, who said the gesture was unnecessary and they exchanged salutations. I scanned the Williamson's Hotel ballroom. Washington's elite were scattered in clumps, conversing and waiting for the clock to introduce 1825. La Fayette, Clay, and Senator King formed an unlikely trio by the fireplace on the room's right flank. Calhoun spoke to Van Buren—what did the Little Magician want with the presumptive Vice President? Justice Story with Senators Pickering, Fromentin, and Webster, McLane with Van Rensselaer, and Brent with Canning and Hyde—swords lowered, for now. Behind every rectangular column stood different combinations of congressmen, senators, diplomats, judges, and soldiers. Almost 200 elected, appointed, and military officials. My focus returned to Rebello.

"—that is why this year shall witness King Ferdinand's final defeat. I shouldn't even name him as such. No man should be king, especially that killer." I was confused as Brazil maintained a monarchy. "Spanish forts in Veracruz, Chiloé, and Callao will fall by next New Years and South America will be rid of Spain for the first time since 1491."

"Do you no longer fear the Holy Alliance?" the President asked.

"Why should I? Your message to Congress made them irrelevant. I doubt they'll be united by the decade's end. History shall forget that such an arrangement existed."

"I'm pleased our policy contributed to their downfall. Tell me, how has Brazil received it?"

A pause. "Opinion is divided. Most are grateful the Allies cannot help Ferdinand but others are suspicious of North America speaking for South."

"I assure you and your countrymen that this government hopes for long and friendly relationships with our sister republics and with your country."

"Your Secretary of State said the same."

"Do you feel Brazil's transition to independence from Portugal has gone smoothly?"

Another pause. "I've delayed your guests for too long. Wonderful seeing you, Mr. President." He stepped aside and the next member of the President's receiving line stepped forward. I walked past Eliza, the line's gatekeeper, and rejoined John and Charles. Mrs. Adams was ill and Mary helped Lucy nurse her.

"That was painless," I said. "Time to relax, enjoy the New Year." A lie. The election's stalemate subjugated every moment. Prolonged misery beyond my control decayed my thinking and demeanor. I occasionally wished Jackson would win to end the purgatory but then I rediscovered my judgment.

"Can we leave?" Charles asked.

"Not until after midnight," I said. "Then we'll endure toasts, hopefully fewer than a dozen." Charles wore his displeasure as though it was opera glasses. "Go make a friend."

"I don't need friends."

"John, help him." My second-eldest nodded and guided Charles into the mass. "Need a drink." I looked for a waiter and saw Mrs. Hayne, Mrs. Livingston, Mrs. Ticknor, and Miss Gardner forming a square in the room's center. Others orbited them and I envisioned the room as a galaxy, assigning celestial roles to everyone. I admired these ladies for how comfortable they looked. I envied women's superiority in these settings. Found a waiter. "Do you carry Madeira?"

"Only a French Rhine. If you'd like, Mr. Adams, I can check the kitchen."

"The Rhine will do." He arranged a glass and I thanked him. I looked for a companion to pass the time but gave up. Five chairs faced the fireplace and only one was occupied. I walked that way when Letcher, a Kentucky congressman, intercepted me.

"Mr. Adams." He was too excited. "I hoped to find you here."

"That makes one of us." I paused. "I refer to myself, not to you."

He ignored my remark. "I've received many letters regarding the election. Most want our state to vote for General Jackson."

"I see."

"Our legislature will pass a *nonbinding* resolution directing us to do so." A moment. "Do you appreciate my words?"

"What does Kentucky want in return?"

"That will come later. I just need to know you're open to our needs."

"I am."

"Wonderful. Happy New Years, Mr. Adams."

"Happy New Years."

He departed and I resumed my quest. The taken chair was the second from the right. I placed myself two seats further left. I absorbed some heat and turned to see whose lead I followed.

General Jackson.

I lacked any social sense, even the minimum to avoid embarrassing myself. I turned from him and he didn't acknowledge my arrival, making the affair even more degrading. Why couldn't I anticipate contingencies in public settings the way I did in foreign policy? Politics ought to be a less communal experience. Allow those who'd rather read than speak, the ones who make the most thoughtful decisions, to work within their element without attending such events.

Mrs. Adams would have avoided this. She'd know who sat by the fire or talk to him on my behalf. She'd prevent this pathetic standoff —no, sitoff. I stared at the fire. Eyes bored into the back of my head but I ignored them.

This went on. My mind wandered. Did Jackson know I made a mistake or did he think I sat to oppose him? Would the House vote hinge on who moved first? Most of that chamber was present so it was a rational concern. No way out? If neither conceded we'd be there in perpetuity and I'd die in that chair. I wished someone—the President, Brent, my sons—would call for my attention and grant me an excuse to exit. No one did.

New Years could free me. We'd have to join the others in toasts. I never felt so eager but that could be an hour or more in the future. Could I last that long? Had to. How many eyes stared? Ignore the world and study the dancing flames until 1825.

It was sad. Jackson understood my predicament more than anyone but he was the last person with whom I could discuss it. He told the world he was tougher than wood but I knew he felt lost in the fog. He'd be inhuman not to. I'd learned as Secretary of State not to sympathize with my opponents. Doing so was foolish. It wasted energy processing others' pain when I'd be better off exploiting it. All emotions had limits. Soft men objected to this but every successful leader knew it was true.

"Well, gentlemen, since you are both so near the chair, but neither can occupy it, I will slip between you and take it myself!"

Clay's arrival startled me. I restrained myself as he sat in the middle chair. Laughter spread as guests explained the Speaker's joke to others. For ten years he mocked me. I heard him sip his drink and wished he'd spill it on his lap. He didn't.

"Whoever brings me a refill becomes President!" Applause. "I enjoy the rare felicity, whilst alive, which is experienced by the dead." The same. "Come now, Mr. Adams, you're at a party, not a funeral. Smile." I refused. "What about you, General? A smile?" Cheers. "Voila! Our next President!"

I shut my eyes, waiting for the agony to end. Finally Clay knew he'd exploited his joke's potential and left. He told us we weren't fun. I rose a minute later, mumbling that I needed to find my sons.

Clay's ability to play a room was his foremost skill. I thought of the Russell episode, when Clay conspired to destroy my career during the world crisis. I heard what he said when I confronted him after defeating his scheme:

My plan's success didn't matter, and do you know why? Because your handling of the Alliance and the edict is the worst statecraft since Pericles exacerbated the Athenian Plague. You're unlikely to survive in your post through your term's conclusion and the President dismissing you will save the country from another Adams presidency. My scheme was just a way to pass time until I return to the Speakership.

New Years. Church bells rang and couples kissed. Resolutions and singing. Drinks finished and bottles popped. I said pleasantries to my sons and looked at snowfall through the window.

The President raised his glass. "To General La Fayette, a living symbol of freedom's resistance to tyrants and who reminds us of our nation's founder."

"To La Fayette!"

The Frenchman: "To the President of the United States, whose legacy is rescuing freedom from monarchy."

"To the President!"

Clay: "To General Bolivar, who has won his continent's liberty. May it have come sooner." The President glared.

"To General Bolivar!"

Clay said to me, "You should go next, Mr. Adams."

Why did this man hate me so? "I'm honored but I'll refrain, if that does not offend you."

"You've nothing to toast?"

"So it seems."

"What of you, Mr. Calhoun?"

"I second Mr. Adams' sentiment."

"A pity."

Over a dozen toasts followed, ending with applause for the administration which was closing without a successor in place. The President thanked his guests and said his achievement was won via collaboration with those better than he and even his critics deserved thanks for elevating his conduct.

The party dispersed and the river returned to individual conversational drops. I waited for a person or two to retire before departing to avoid appearing rude or pathetic. The coming constitutional crisis hung over us. The House was to vote on 9 February and no one had the requisite 13 votes for the first ballot. Then the House would fall into stalemate and argument. It had to choose a President by 4 March. I'd never surrender the office to Jackson or Crawford. Maybe they'd join against me, for together they had enough states. Could happen any time.

"Let's go," I told my sons. No one had set the precedent but I was disgusted with this city. I said goodbye to the President and La Fayette and the reigning ladies and we walked to the door.

"Mr. Adams." I turned around. Clay stood alone, holding a near-empty glass. Must he torture me further before the door hit me? "May we speak?"

"We were about to leave for the night," I said.

"I only ask for a moment." He looked at my sons. "Alone, if possible."

I sighed. To John, "Wait by the exit. I'll be back." Clay guided me to the opposite wall from the President. As far from his ears as possible while still in the room. "What do you require?"

Quiet. Then, "Let's meet a week from today," he said. "I wish to discuss public affairs."

"Where?"

"How about your home? Let's say six?"

"Shall I instruct my servants to arrange dinner? Louisa and Lucretia can join us." I referred to his wife.

"No. Your servants would have to shop for supplies and I'd like to keep this as confidential as possible. We mustn't risk news of our meeting leaking to the public or the press."

"I understand. I'm happy to accommodate you as best I can."

"Wonderful. I look forward to it. Have a good night, Mr. Adams, and please tell Louisa that I hope she feels better."

LXXV

THE WEEK PASSED. I attended two church services the morning of our meeting. Then I crouched by our fireplace to thaw the snow speckling my sleeves and cuffs. I felt as good spiritually and physically as the day permitted as I waited with no notes to study, no strategy to plot in advance. Mrs. Adams remembered that mint julep was his drink of choice and prepared it before his arrival.

Clay was 15 minutes late. My wife removed his coat and he gave her his straw hat. He smiled at my reaction. "It's about the style, not the insulating qualities. Helps maintain my western look." Mrs. Adams handed him his beverage. "Bless you, Louisa. You always know how to make me feel right at home."

"You flatter me, Mr. Clay."

"As you deserve." He took a sip. To me, "Shall we begin?"

"Let's." To Mrs. Adams, "Thank you for your help."

"I'll be in the bedroom if needed," she said.

Clay waited until she exited. Then, "I hope you realize she's far beyond what you merit."

"I thought we could sit by the fire." I led him to the overflow room and gestured to two chairs I'd set facing each other by the hearth. The flames crackled and bounced less elegantly than those at the Williamson. I confirmed the chairs were beyond their reach. We sat and he sipped his cocktail. "You asked for this meeting."

"True. Permit me to proceed." He crossed his legs but then unfolded them and leaned forward. He looked comfortable, studied me, then, "What do you think of me, Mr. Adams?"

A moment. "It's no secret that our relationship is one of contention and disagreement. But I feel no ill-will toward you, including for the Russell episode."

"You can imagine why I find that hard to believe. You're known to carry a grudge."

"Which I can move beyond."

"Where do you stand on internal improvements?"

"You know my position. Washington and Hamilton were correct. If building a cohesive Union and growing our power to resist foreign interference is the goal then investing in improvements is the means. Canals, roads, and ships—we'd never fear Europe again. Such a program is the next stage of the policies I implemented as Secretary of State."

"How would you fund it? The South resents tariffs."

"By letting our citizens purchase publicly-held lands in the West."

"Would that placate Southerners? They fear that an active federal government could become active enough to take their slaves."

"I'd appeal to their interests. A road linking New Orleans to Washington City, for example."

"Is that enough? After Missouri?"

"It's hard to know this far in advance."

"True." He took a swig of his drink. "I assume you don't share the President's view that an amendment is needed for this to be constitutional."

"Correct."

"Good. Good." He paused, then inhaled. "You can imagine my disappointment at failing to be among the top three candidates in the Electoral College. Took me a week to make peace with my defeat. But Crawford's friends banged on my door within five minutes of the results becoming clear. He expects me to transfer my states to him because of our partnership. But our partnership is dead. He has no morals and honestly, he disgusts me. He's presumptive in his expectations, he's openly pro-slavery, and, of course, he's in no condition to serve as President.

"Next is General Jackson. I know he won a plurality but I have no interest in electing a military chieftain. Killing 2,500 Englishmen doesn't qualify him for the complicated duties of the Chief Magistracy. The people made a mistake and the Constitution gives me the opportunity to correct it. Denying his election will hurt my popularity in the West but that's less objectionable than living under a Caesar. Do you know Mr. Buchanan, the Pennsylvania congressman? Of course you do. He told me Jackson will offer me Secretary of State if I make him President. I haven't declined yet but I'd sooner dig Napoleon out of his grave and elect *him*. They're the same political force and at least the French emperor is iam mortui.

"Which brings me to you, Mr. Adams. We've known each other for ten years. Sometimes friends, more often enemies. I don't yearn to see another Adams presidency but you are the only acceptable choice left. You'll even pursue the agenda I desire. Jackson cares for nothing but his own power and will crush anyone in his way to get it. You're the opposite. I believe your obsession with morality is genuine and though I find it unbearably irritating at times it is nonetheless an admirable trait. My only question is whether it inhibits accepting my aid to win the House vote."

Another moment. I predicted this meeting's purpose was offering the presidency and a new partnership. I was right.

"There's nothing unconstitutional, illegal, or dishonorable in accepting," I said.

He smiled. "I assumed you'd say that, given how you've wooed states away from Jackson and Crawford. How many do you have now?"

"Ten or 11, depending on Virginia."

"Hopefully it's 11. Ten gives us no wiggle room, no space for defectors." He paused. "I'll get you elected on the first ballot."

"Really? What do you need from me?"

"Let me worry about it. The House is my purview and this is my biggest challenge since the Missouri Compromise. It's going to be fun."

Thou wouldst be great
Art not without ambition, but without
The illness should attend it
—Act 1, Scene 5

LXXVI

LIMBO DEFINED THE next month. I kept myself busy and blocked 9 February from my thoughts but anxiety survived my new partnership with my bitterest rival. He controlled my destiny after fighting it harder than anyone. I doubted he'd succeed, I'd not won a single popular vote in Kentucky—not one—and their legislature instructed their delegation to vote for Jackson—yet Clay told his colleagues to support me instead. Was even *he* so persuasive? We sailed through dangerous waters and which of us was captain was unclear.

My sleep worsened by the week. A pattern developed. Mediocre sleep. Oversleep. No sleep. It made work difficult. I relied on twice as many cigars to focus and calm my nerves. I proposed a deal to God to accept any result if the day would pass. Never heard His answer.

Mrs. Adams hosted a tea party the night before the vote. 67 congressmen attended along with 400 others. I stayed at the office to avoid controversy, the most common outcome of my public appearances.

I sat by our fireplace the next day, failing to read the Book of Job. A snowstorm consumed Washington and I worried Congress couldn't convene. Failing to do so meant a constitutional crisis and I told myself that if Congress could survive the British Army it could endure the weather.

I thought I heard a noise and shouted for Antoine to check the door. "Yes, sir." Everett, my secretary from when I was minister to Russia and our current minister to the Netherlands, joined me in the overflow room. Antoine carried his coat and snow dropped from it onto my floor. Everett approached me, huffing.

"Am I the first here?" he asked. "I so desperately wish to be first."

"You are."

He smiled. "In that case, it's my pleasure to tell you congratulations, Mr. President Elect."

I absorbed his words. *Mr. President Elect*. I'd write to Father to tell him I'd fulfilled his expectation of me. Wished Mother was beside him so they could read my letter together. My destiny achieved, I'd celebrate upholding the family name before starting the next chapter.

"What was the count?" I asked. He went to his coat and dug a card from his pocket.

I won 13 states, carrying Maine, New Hampshire, Vermont, Massachusetts, Maryland, Rhode Island, Connecticut, New York, Ohio, Illinois, Kentucky, Missouri, and Louisiana.

General Jackson won seven states, carrying Indiana, Pennsylvania, New Jersey, Tennessee, Alabama, Mississippi, and South Carolina.

Crawford won four states, carrying Delaware, Virginia, North Carolina, and Georgia.

Disappointed that Virginia remained loyal to Crawford but it didn't matter.

"The Senate overwhelmingly elected Calhoun as Vice President," he said. "The House then submitted its ballots and Clay counted them. There was mostly cheering, with some ridicule, when he announced the result. Most were surprised it only took one round."

I was wrong to underestimate Clay. His legislative prowess was unmatched in the republic's history. Finally, I chose the right partner.

♦ ♦ ♦ ♦ ♦ ♦

Wyer arrived next. Then Bolton, Thomas, and Crowninshield. Brent brought our clerks. I received a procession of guests all afternoon but Senator Webster proved the most important. He brought an affectionate note from Rufus King. I poured him a glass of Bordeaux and myself some Madeira.

"You better appreciate what Clay did for you," he said. "No one, not even you, did more to win your election."

I evaded offense. "Did you help him?" I asked.

"Yes. Van Buren led the effort against us. He joined with Jackson while still directing Crawford's campaign and planted a rumor that Jackson's supporters would destroy the city if you won."

"Heavens."

"Clay defied the threat. Van Buren then tried pulling New York to Crawford. Several congressmen defected and Van Rensselaer became the deciding vote. We went to his office and told him the Union would dissolve unless someone, anyone, was elected on the first ballot."

"He's an old man."

"Did you want to win or not? Jackson and Crawford would have pooled their states if New York deserted. The first ballot would have stalemated and the plan would have collapsed."

"I know, but I hope you didn't upset him."

"He cried, but he'll be fine."

To be thus is nothing, but to be safely thus
—Act 3, Scene 1

Mrs. Adams organized an early supper. I told her the President arranged for an event celebrating my victory and I couldn't be late but she insisted. A cordial meal: John, Charles, and the other children praised my success. I thanked them but noticed my wife's pale, waxen complexion. She retired to bed early and I left for the Executive Mansion.

LXXVII

HER REQUEST PROVED beneficial, for I received so many visitors that I lacked time for hunger. The President's family had covered the State Dining Room's walls in green silk and Roman and French-inspired decor, including Italian marble mantels with Neoclassical caryatids on each side of the two fireplaces and scattered ornamental pieces around the room. The President seated me with Eliza and himself at a table isolated from the U-shaped arrangement containing his guests. The chair intended for Mrs. Adams remained open and I explained her sudden absence.

The President congratulated me but said little else. Nothing about how he'd hoped I'd succeed him, that he looked forward to witnessing my achievements, or even that I rightfully earned the honor through my service to his administration. A mere *congratulations*, a joke about how the country was my problem now—as though it wasn't already—and some banal advice about listening to others while trusting my own judgment. More than ever I felt his coldness toward everyone outside his family. He'd never been open with me or treated me as his friend. This was one relationship made estranged not from my seriousness but from his keeping me at a distance. He led from the shadows and never trusted anyone with his thoughts. A better President than Jefferson or Madison but his style wasn't for me. I'd be America's voice and articulate my vision for her future.

The Calhouns approached. I rose and stepped from the table to escape the President's ears. The room applauded as we shook hands.

"Congratulations, Mr. President Elect." His mask was tighter than ever and I doubted it'd ever slip again. Permanently vexed.

"And congratulations to you, Mr. Vice President Elect."

"I look forward to working with you." I heard his insincerity.

"I agree with everything you're saying. How would you feel about forming a partnership?"

"I'd like that. The President listens to us when we speak in unison. A partnership will mutually benefit us and the country."

We'd done it. We'd beaten Crawford and the Allies and held the power to define our generation. But our spark had fizzled. We never recovered from Missouri. I decided we should meet before the inauguration to discuss any concerns. We couldn't come all this way only to fail from our personal estrangement.

"I feel the same." I enhanced my enthusiasm as best I could. "It appears we've attained what we discussed all those years ago. Now we must implement our agenda."

"First we must learn if the country approves of your election."

"Ye—uh—yes. I mean after that." To his wife, "Floride, how are you?"

"Wonderful, Mr. Adams. Congratulations."

"Thank you, dear." I had nothing else to say to her. To her husband, "I hope to work closer together than our predecessors did."

"I'll serve the country to the best of my ability."

"I expect nothing less." A moment. "Thank you for stopping by."

"The pleasure was mine." They departed and I returned to my seat.

Clay and the Baron de Tuyll converged upon me. "Don't get up," Clay said, placing one hand on my shoulder and another across my back. "You've undoubtedly been congratulated enough times that the word's lost its potency."

"Senator Webster said I owe you a *thank you.*"

"Please, it was in the country's interest."

"Nonetheless, you have my gratitude."

He smiled and I saw his genuity. "You're quite welcome."

The Baron lingered behind him. "One moment," I said to Clay. He gestured to the open seat beside me and I nodded. The Baron clasped my hand. The same stern grip.

"Congratulations, sir. You deserve this."

His wording puzzled me. "Thank you, Baron." He released me and disappeared back into the crowd.

"I take it Louisa is unwell again?" Clay said.

"She is. It's strange because she was fine this morning."

"Tell her I wish her the best and I hope to see her soon."

"I will. Thank you."

He stayed put and watched the gathering. I wondered if he fantasized about being President Elect while speculating how long until it was real. Minutes rolled by as I waited for my next visitor but the guests kept their distance. Canning waved for me to come to him but then he remembered who outranked whom in protocol. Clay ignored him and I stood as he neared. He guided me from the table.

"What is it, Stratford?"

"Y—congratulations."

"Thank you. Continue."

"You should avoid sitting with Mr. Clay. It looks bad after he just won you the presidency."

"You're thinking too much."

"And you're not thinking enough. I overheard a reporter call you a *clay President*, meaning the Speaker can mold you as he wishes."

"Anyone who knows me knows I stand by my beliefs. Even if it costs me."

"The election may convince otherwise."

"Then I'll remind them."

"In the meantime—"

He paused as the room collectively watched Jackson rise. A handsome woman who was not his wife took his arm. He walked toward us, his strides slow and confident. I met his stare even before I saw the whites of his eyes. The room's focus was on him. Would he outshine me no matter what I accomplished or did the crowd think he'd slay me in the Mansion's biggest spectacle since the British assault?

His details became clearer. His lips conveyed neutrality but the sapphire glint in his eye indicated that I'd made an enemy, a great enemy. He extended his available hand.

"How do you do, Mr. Adams?" His voice was cheerful and I smelled whiskey on his breath. "I give you my left hand, for my right, as you see, is devoted to the fair. I hope you are very well, sir."

"Very well, sir. I hope General Jackson is well." I feared my tone was worse than I intended and that I appeared inglorious or defensive about my victory. "Is Mrs. Jackson indisposed this evening?"

"Unfortunately. I take it Mrs. Adams is as well?"

"Yes."

"May our wives recover."

I was tempted to say they'd feel better now that the election was over. We separated and he circled the room, delighting all. A natural leader. I questioned my recent actions but reminded myself I'd saved the republic from an autocrat.

Lingered through the next hour. Picked at my dish and spoke to Clay between visitors. The President turned to me—he'd mainly talked to his daughter all evening—and told me to deliver a toast. He would give me orders until he died.

I stood and dinged my glass. The crowd turned, tightening my stomach.

"Thank you all for attending this evening. As we look toward the peaceful transfer of power, the signature achievement of free government, I'd like to dedicate this evening to the 22nd of February and the sixth of September—the birthdays of Generals Washington and La Fayette."

La Fayette sat toward the U's rightward tip. He smiled as the room applauded him. Then he lifted his own glass. "Thank you, Mr. Adams. I would like to dedicate my own toast to the Fourth of July, liberty's birthday in both hemispheres."

He received greater acclaim, which I joined. I sat once it ended and Clay whispered, "He makes me want to join the Greeks."

"A great man," I said.

◆◆◆◆◆◆

I returned home shortly before midnight and wrote Father a note. Three lines: I asked for his blessings, told him the day was the most important of my life, and that I closed it as it began with pleas to the father of mercies for its consequences to rebound to His glory and to the country's welfare. Placed it with Senator King's note. I'd send them in the morning.

A band played outside our house to honor me. My wife awoke and congratulated me again. She meant it but I heard her pain.

LXXVIII

MRS. ADAMS FELT a little better some days later and I insisted we make a public appearance, my first since the President's dinner. We went to see *The Poor Soldier*, a British opera and, I believed, a favorite of General Washington.

I hoped dressing up would improve her demeanor but she was pale and hid from the candles in our theater box. If she could relax and enjoy the performance it might reverse her fortunes.

Jackson spoke to the press. He said Clay's rejection of the people's vote validated his claim about the capital. Compared our partnership to that of British monarchs and Parliament and then compared Clay to Judas. I cleared my thoughts of this rabble as Mr. Edmund Kean, a miniature Shakespearean actor set to play Patrick that night, came on stage. The audience hushed.

"Good evening, and thank you for taking the time to join us. We're going to perform a pair of Irish songs before we start the show. First though, I've been told that John Quincy Adams, the incoming President, is here tonight."

I stood so all could see. Faces turned. A smattering of pitiful applause. My wife looked away, embarrassed at both our reception and her appearance. I sat and expected Kean to move on. Instead he sang:

> "Ye gentlemen and ladies fair
> Who grace this famous city,
> Just listen, if you've time to spare,
> While I rehearse a ditty,
> And for the opportunity
> Conceive yourselves quite lucky,
> For 'tis not often that you see
> A hunter from Kentucky."

It was "The Hunters of Kentucky," a song written after Jackson's victory in New Orleans. It became his campaign's anthem and was synonymous with the General. Kean was pandering to his audience. They sang:

> "Oh Kentucky, the hunters of Kentucky!
> Oh Kentucky, the hunters of Kentucky!"

I was mortified. Mrs. Adams withheld tears. I was tempted to leave but I planted myself in my seat. Kean:

> "We are a hardy, free-born race,
> Each man to fear a stranger,
> Whatever the game, we join in chase,
> Despising toil and danger.
> And if a daring foe annoys,
> Whatever his strength and forces,
> We'll show him that Kentucky boys
> Are alligator horses."

We watched as hundreds sang to honor Jackson. Dozens faced us. No choice but to endure the humiliation.

> "Oh Kentucky, the hunters of Kentucky!
> Oh Kentucky, the hunters of Kentucky!"

On it went.

Clay came to my office. He hung his hat and coat on a rack by the door.

"Shall we sit?" I asked.

"If we must."

"We can stand if you'd rather."

"No, it's all right. What can I do for you, Mr. President Elect?"

"Let's use *Mr. Adams* for now. How have you been since the House vote?"

He shrugged. "Jackson's followers have behaved as I expected. Various threats and what not. Senator Van Buren wants to unseat me from the Speakership and once I beat him the storm shall pass."

"What if defending your position was unnecessary?"

"What does that mean?"

"I want this office to be yours, for you to serve as my Secretary of State."

A moment. "I thought the position was Mr. Brent's."

"Brent served me well for these eight years," I said. "The Department couldn't have achieved what it did without him."

"Then why not elevate him and leave me in Congress?"

"Because I trust your judgment and I want you as my closest advisor. Plus I hope you'll bring me greater Western support."

"The West favors Jackson. You know that his followers' anger toward us will double. They'll claim we exchanged promises in advance."

"Not if he becomes Secretary of War."

"Have you spoken to him?"

"No, but I hope he'll accept and that Crawford will choose to remain at Treasury. Such an arrangement will unify the country."

"Crawford would refuse even if he were healthy. He loathes you."

"In that case I'll recall Rush from the Court of St. James and give him the position."

"Who'd replace him in London?"

"Senator King. His term is ending."

"Rush and King are Federalists," he said, "and King led the anti-slavery faction during the Missouri crisis. You'll offend even the National Republicans."

"They have my confidence."

"But remember the political context. Jackson and his supporters will despise everyone in your administration and they'll be even more determined to destroy your presidency."

"Don't worry, I have a plan to rebuild my popularity."

"Oh? What plan?"

"I'll tell you *after* you take my offer."

His head fell and he leaned back. I felt confident of his answer. Secretary of State was the most powerful Cabinet post and the last four Presidents, including myself, held it before their election. He'd be my heir.

"I ask for time to speak with my friends, but I'll accept unless I hear a good objection," he said. "We mustn't allow Jackson to dictate appointments."

"Excellent."

"Is Brent your second choice?"

"Either he or Governor Clinton. I spoke to General Brown this morning. He believes I owe Clinton for delivering New York but I think you and Brent deserve it more."

"If we move forward you should announce my nomination as soon as possible so the criticism dissipates before your inauguration."

"That's not my intention. Our partnership does not end our disagreements but perhaps they'll be less frequent."

He looked apprehensive. "Can we discuss some of your priorities in foreign policy?"

I smiled.

LXXIX

THE PRESIDENT MADE his office available to me and my growing Cabinet. I was in my normal seat because I refused to assume the President's chair until after my inauguration. Calhoun and Wirt—who agreed to remain Attorney General—did the same. I told them my choice for Secretary of State was joining us but I'd not given a name.

Clay arrived. "Gentlemen, meet my successor," I said. They were surprised, especially Calhoun.

"I look forward to working together," Clay said. To me, "Where shall I sit?" I pointed to Crawford's old chair.

Calhoun said to me, "You're astonishing, sir. That you'd align with your enemy to seize power from the people."

"I hope you don't think that I promised Clay his position before the House vote," I said, "because that's untrue."

"Why wouldn't I believe it?"

"I'm telling you—"

"What is your word worth, Mr. Adams? You preached virtue throughout our tenures yet you robbed the people of their voice and rewarded your accomplice."

"The Constitution provided for our actions—"

"That doesn't—"

"—and Clay is the best man for the position."

Calhoun turned to Clay, judging him as Clay held a neutral expression. He returned to me. "My entire image of you was a lie," Calhoun said. "I'm disappointed."

How was I to respond to such a remark? "I'm sorry you feel that way. I hope you'll still help me govern the country so we can avoid duplicating my father's relationship with Jefferson when they served as President and Vice President."

A moment. "I'll serve the people as best I can." Similar to the answer he gave at the President's party, hardly a pledge of loyalty or cooperation.

"Thank you, Mr. Calhoun," I said. To everyone, "Can we proceed?" Dispassionate nods. "Good. I have some other developments on the new Cabinet: Crowninshield will continue as Secretary of the Navy and apologizes for his absence today. General Jackson declined to serve as Secretary of War and so I'll ask Senator Barbour. Another Virginian to endear us to the South. I've also drafted a letter for Rush, offering him Secretary of the Treasury."

"I've voiced my concern about adding a Federalist to the Cabinet," Clay said. "Your election satisfies New England's representation."

"I know, and your concern has been noted. Anything else on this topic?" No. "I asked for this meeting to summarize my agenda for the next four years. The closing administration broke Europe's preeminence in this hemisphere. I want to build on its triumph and place the country on a new trajectory."

"What does that entail?" Wirt asked.

"Internal improvements are its heart. Roads and canals to bind the regions and stretch across the continent. Tides of wealth will flow from the Atlantic to the Pacific."

"That's quite ambitious."

"It's only the start. I want Congress to establish a national university in Washington City and an observatory to study the universe. Europe has 130 and North America has none. We'll rectify this disgrace. We must also sponsor more expeditions modeled on Lewis and Clark's, both here and around the world. A Department of the Interior. A naval academy. A bankruptcy law. Adopt the metric system to better—"

Wirt and Clay both spoke. Clay deferred to the Attorney General. "Thank you, Mr. Speaker," Wirt said. To me, "How will we afford this?"

"Congress will open publicly-held western lands for private purchase."

"That will increase prices in the region," Calhoun said. "The West will hate you."

"They'll have greater access to goods and markets."

"That won't convince them or Southerners. Neither region wants such power concentrated into federal hands."

"It is the government's duty to foster improvement." I paused. "You used to believe this too. We discussed it in our early conversations."

"A lot has changed in the subsequent years."

Awkwardness. Then Clay said, "I'm unsure if it's wise to make such a large proposal. You're entering office in a weaker position than your predecessors and you lack influence in Congress."

"The agenda's potency will rebuild my popularity," I said.

"Was this the plan you referred to in our last meeting?" he asked. I nodded. "You're putting the cart before the horse. You can't beat Congress into submission, it isn't Onís or Metternich. You must convince its members. We should start smaller: a canal connecting the Ohio River to the Chesapeake Bay, for example. That will build momentum toward your loftier goals."

"Public attention on me will be highest after I take office and that will be my best opportunity for placing a seed within the national mind. The plant may come later, but the seed shall be sown. We'll be closer to God once the plant has blossomed."

Clay sighed. "Please reconsider. A President must guide public opinion but that can't be done if you're too far ahead of it. Jackson and Van Buren will fight us at every step and you're placing your neck on their guillotine."

I was excited to hear his proposal for engaging Congress. My idea was to ask Senator Webster to craft legislation and I thought he'd suggest something better. I was disappointed.

"Let's move on to foreign policy," I said.

"May I ask a question?" Clay asked. "Do you want the President or the Cabinet officers to be responsible for hiring new clerks?"

"I'd prefer to set that policy once openings occur."

"Won't they occur immediately? Most clerks favor Jackson. We need to remove them and reward your loyalists."

"I won't preside over a purge of government employees. We'll disregard our personnel's views as long as they perform competently."

"Do you want the departments to undermine you?"

"I—"

"We risk betraying our friends to curry our enemies' favor."

"Expelling our critics does nothing to heal sectional wounds from Missouri and the election. If anything, we should hire more Jackson-supporters to prove our virtue."

Clay said to Calhoun, "How prevalent is the belief that my partnership with Mr. Adams is forged by deceit?"

"Very," Calhoun said. "It will be universal once your appointment as Secretary of State is announced."

"That's my fear." Clay said to me, "Are you ashamed by being elected through the House vote? Because your proposals will lead to political disaster and if you could disavow—"

"I'd rather my presidency fail than be wicked," I said, "but my agenda will win the people's favor."

"You told me you trusted my judgment. I'm warning—"

"That's enough, Mr. Clay. Let's turn to foreign policy." I saw him reconsidering our partnership. "Explain what we discussed."

He took a breath. "General Bolivar called for a congress of all American nations to foster trade and pledge mutual defense against future European threats. We want to send a delegation."

Calhoun said to me, "How does this not violate the Principle and everything you argued for throughout your tenure?"

"It builds on the Principle," I said.

"Your new partnership has allowed Clay to influence your judgment. This idea displays his obsession with transforming the hemisphere into a cohesive system of republics."

"What's wrong with that?" Clay asked.

"It surrenders our independence. The very thing Mr. Adams fought to prevent."

"This is different," I said. "We'll strengthen our friendship with our neighbors while concurrently passing my agenda. Such policies are no longer incompatible."

Calhoun's features became more reptilian with every passing minute. Soon he'd have slit pupils and fangs. "Will Haiti attend?" he asked.

"I imagine so."

"Our meeting them as equals will encourage slave uprisings. The South will block Congress from approving your delegation."

"The Cannings will seize this opportunity if we snub it," Clay said. "London will monopolize South American markets and our sister republics will rely on Britain for defense. Will that please the South?"

"Speaking of Canning," I said, "I'd like you to prepare memos on the West Indies and Cuba."

Clay wrote a note. "I'll do so, but don't expect progress on either. Canning isn't inclined to open the West Indies to our trade after you embarrassed him by rejecting his accord and we're best leaving Cuba under Spain's rule for now. Adding another state to the Union is a mistake and the alternative is the British Empire absorbing her after the island implodes."

"Now you're mimicking me. My memo on Cuba last year argued the same position. Just touch up the relevant sections."

"Perhaps we're converging." He laughed.

"This isn't funny," Calhoun said. "This administration was conceived in corruption and now you two speak of radically altering our policies by putting the government in control of the economy and surrendering our sovereignty to Negroes and mulattoes. General Jackson is right that politicians in this city seek unlimited power. You're becoming no different than Metternich or Alexander."

"That's a foolish remark," I said.

"Everything you've proposed harms the South. Recent history, like Missouri and Vesey's rebellion, proves that we must never bow to outsiders."

"You're not bowing to the North. The South is disproportionately represented in Congress."

"That isn't enough. Your presidency threatens our liberty. The South will veto your legislation regardless of how Congress votes."

I was stunned. Clay shared my unease. "That policy returns us to the Articles of Confederation," I said. "It repeals the Constitution."

"Good. This is a confederation of states. Not a nation."

"Let me be blunt: I *won't* tolerate the South's hysteria. I *won't* compromise with nullification and I *will* enforce the law with all the power this office provides me."

Calhoun stared at me and completed his primordial transformation. Then he gathered his papers and stormed out.

LXXX

MRS. ADAMS WAS ill through the night and before dawn she suffered a violent fever and fainted. I sent for Dr. Huntt to attend to her. I entered upon the day with a supplication to Heaven for my country and for myself and for those connected with my good name and fortunes.

I hadn't slept since the 1st of March. The Department of State's pressure was always heavy as congressional sessions closed but this period was made worse by the end of my own service as Secretary and my excitement for the new condition I was to enter. Received multitudes of visitors, both for business and for my wife's health.

She'd be the first foreign-born First Lady of the United States. I stayed by her as Huntt bled her but come morning I dressed in a black suit and trousers. A simple outfit to contrast with the outgoing President and show that a new generation was in power.

Knock knock.

"Come in!" I evaluated my coat in the mirror.

Charles entered. "Mother is awake."

A mixed feeling: she could stand with me in my brightest hour but she'd also delay my departure. "Will she see me?" I asked.

"Yes." We left his bedroom and returned to mine. Mrs. Adams stood in a cream satin gown with short sleeves and dark green ruffles around her neck and with matching trim along the gown's bottom. Long cream gloves covered her arms and she looked pale but stronger than she'd been in a week.

"Louisa…"

"See, John?" she said. "I can be ready on a moment's notice when given incentive."

"Can you endure this?"

"Nothing shall stop me." A pause. "How do I look?"

"Divine."

She smiled.

◆◆◆◆◆◆

415

Drums cracked and trumpets buzzed at 11:30. I stepped outside and saw the First and Second Legions of the Washington and Georgetown militia occupying F Street. The calvary and two carriages stood among them. The front one white, the latter black, each strapped to four horses. Both were open despite the downcast, cloudy sky. The President, Elizabeth, and their daughters were in the black while Wirt and Crowninshield were in the white facing backward.

I left the door open and Mrs. Adams, John, and Charles joined me. We absorbed the sight. I noticed the citizens on the militias' other flank and they cheered when they spotted me looking at them.

Time to depart. I walked toward the black carriage but was blocked by militiamen. Caught the President's eye and nodded. He nodded back, stoic as ever.

I helped my family climb into the white carriage. John sat beside Crowninshield so Charles, my wife, and I could be together on the rear seat. The crowd had a better view of me and cheered.

"Morning, sir," Wirt said over the noise.

"Good morning. I didn't know you were joining us."

He leaned forward. "The President asked. We're happy to."

"I hope everyone is comfortable."

"What?"

"I said I hope—forget it. Thank you for being here."

"You're welcome." We shook hands and leaned back.

The militias parted and the carriages launched. *Clop. Clop. Clop.* Citizens lined the route to the Capitol. I waved to them. So did Mrs. Adams with what strength she had. I felt their admiration but reminded myself that they'd applaud any President. The militia band followed us and captured my ears.

I studied Washington City. It was unrecognizable from when I arrived in 1817. It had recovered from the war and held a scale and magnetism as great as anywhere in Europe. A testament to the outgoing President's success. Strange he was returning to Highland after reigning here for so long. I thought about our achievement. Europe had besieged this country since the Revolution and now America might not confront a foreign threat for 100 years because of what we did.

Thousands ringed the Capitol. It, too, was restored. A shallow dome on top. Congress discussed appropriating funds to raise it into a majestic structure. I hoped to sign such legislation into law. We slowed and the marine band performed "Hail Columbia" as both carriages emptied.

The marines opened the Capitol's doors. We entered, the cheers and music dimmed. Clay waited for us and we smiled at each other. "The Vice President is being sworn in in the Senate," he said. Mrs. Adams was to my left and my sons were behind me. Behind them stood the outgoing President and his family. The Supreme Court justices emerged and formed the group's tail, their robes donned.

Clay led us into the House chamber. A marshal wearing a blue scarf said, "Everyone, the President Elect of the United States: John Quincy Adams."

Applause.

Vice President Calhoun stood before the Speaker's chair. The oldest senator—General Jackson—had sworn him in and was now to his right. They looked comfortable, their torsos unguarded and facing each other. A new partnership. Calhoun had joined Jackson, Van Buren, and Crawford. Worry tomorrow and enjoy today. I shook their hands and we exchanged banal but affirming words.

The gallery overflowed with ladies. Some waved plumes but most sat respectfully. Army and Naval officers among them. The foreign ministers, including Canning, Hyde, and the Baron, sat on the House floor's left side. Congressmen, senators, and more military officers filled the remaining seats. The five Supreme Court associate justices went to chairs placed in a semicircle by the clerk's table.

My family, the President and his wife, and Clay joined Calhoun and Jackson near the associate justices. I faced the audience at the Speaker's chair. Applause. Enjoy it while it lasts. Guards held back the crowd at the doors. I glanced at my wife and the President and then turned to Chief Justice Marshall.

"Congratulations, Mr. Adams."

"Thank you, sir."

He raised a volume of laws and I set my right hand upon it while raising my left. The moment had arrived.

"Repeat after me. I, John Quincy Adams, do solemnly swear..."

"I, John Quincy Adams, do solemnly swear..."

"...That I will faithfully execute..."

"…That I will faithfully execute…"

"…The office of President of the United States…"

"…The office of President of the United States…"

"…And will, to the best of my ability…"

"…And will, to the best of my ability…"

"…Preserve, protect, and defend…"

"…Preserve, protect, and defend…"

"…The Constitution of the United States…"

"…The Constitution of the United States…"

"…So help you God."

"…So help me God."

"Congratulations, Mr. President."

We shook hands. The room thundered and when the crowd heard it joined the celebration. Approval. Denied to me for so long and now entrenched in my memory. Enjoy it while it lasts. I'd spent every day since receiving the letter asking me to serve as Secretary of State plotting toward the presidency, the summit of American power, and now it was mine.

The sixth President of the United States of America.

Look at the congressmen and senators applaud me. Would that expire in a day? Or when they received my legislative package? Enjoy it while it lasts.

I embraced or shook hands with Mrs. Adams, John, Charles, Monroe, Elizabeth, Calhoun, Clay, and Jackson. Monroe's was the most special. Finally equals.

"Congratulations, Mr. President," he said.

"Thank you, Mr. President."

Quiet returned after several minutes. Time for the day's most stressful event. I ascended the Speaker's chair. More applause. I unveiled my speech and waited for silence. My nerves launched a revolution, contracting muscles and making my skin tingle. Like George III, I proved powerless to stop it. Papers crinkled in my hands.

"In compliance with an usage coeval with the existence of our federal Constitution, and sanctioned by the example of my predecessors, I appear, my fellow citizens, in your presence and in that of Heaven to bind myself to the faithful performance of the duties allotted to me.

"In unfolding to my countrymen the principles by which *I* shall be governed in the fulfillment of those duties my first resort is that Constitution which I swore to the best of my ability to preserve, protect, and defend. That revered instrument enumerates the powers and prescribes the duties of the Executive Magistrate and in its first words declares the purposes to which the whole government instituted by it should be devoted—to secure the blessings of liberty to the people of this Union in their successive generations."

To Clay, my enemy who was now my friend:

"Since that period a population of four million has multiplied to 12. A territory bounded by the Mississippi has extended from sea to sea. New States have been admitted to the Union in numbers nearly equal to those of the first Confederation. Treaties of peace, amity, and commerce have been concluded with the principal dominions of the Earth. The forest has fallen by the ax of our woodsmen, the soil has been made to teem by the tillage of our farmers, our commerce has whitened every ocean. Such is our condition under a Constitution founded upon the republican principle of equal rights. To admit that this picture has its shades is but to say that it is still the condition of men upon earth. From evil—physical, moral, and political—it is not our claim to be exempt."

To Monroe, whose burden transferred onto me:

"I turn to the administration of my immediate predecessor. It has passed away in a period of profound peace. The great features of its policy have been to cherish peace while preparing for defensive war, to yield justice to other nations and maintain the rights of our own, to discharge with all possible promptitude the national debt, to reduce within the narrowest limits of efficiency the military force, and to extend equal protection to all the great interests of the nation. Under the pledge of these promises, made by that eminent citizen eight years ago, the Floridas have been peaceably acquired, our boundary has extended to the Pacific Ocean, and the independence of the southern nations of this hemisphere has been recognized."

To the entire audience:

"Fellow citizens, you are acquainted with the peculiar circumstances of the recent election which afforded me the opportunity of addressing you at this time. Less possessed of your confidence in advance than any of my predecessors, I am conscious of the prospect that

I shall stand more in need of your indulgence. Intentions upright and pure, a heart devoted to the welfare of our country, and the unceasing application of all the faculties allotted to me to her service are all the pledges that I can give for the performance of the duties I am to undertake. Knowing that *except the Lord keep the city the watchman waketh but in vain*, with fervent supplications for His favor, to His overruling providence I commit with humble but fearless confidence my own fate and the future destinies of my country."

A final applause. I defied the revolution and stress retreated from my bones. My reception felt genuine and lasted longer than I expected. When it finished I descended and received more congratulations. First from my inner circle and then from members of the various professions I mentioned earlier. This time Mrs. Adams' was the most special. She appeared brittle and I doubted she could host the ball that evening.

The marshal opened the door and the House chamber emptied. Those clogging the Capitol withdrew, bumping into each other, tripping and squishing against the walls until the path opened. Almost an hour passed before we stepped outside. Rain drizzled onto my face and clothes.

Felt alarmed upon finding what I assumed to be every citizen in Washington City, enough to fill the Atlantic, waiting for us. I held Mrs. Adams' hand and we walked down several stairs. Monroe, Clay, Calhoun, and our sons followed. The people saw us and I hoped for the largest cheer of the day. Instead I received a noisy concoction, mostly hissing and snickering. Jackson's accusation that I stole the election had worked. The presidency was to be a far greater challenge than the crises I confronted as Secretary of State.

The sound dissipated. A light *hurray* was the last to fall. Distinct. I searched for its source: a large cluster of Negroes with the happiest faces within view. This charmed me more than the unanimous adulation from the others ever could.

I stood alone. Always alone. It was my destiny to spend my life fighting to improve myself and everyone else. I was the President and I should have been proud. My mission succeeded, my parents' ambition fulfilled. The first and deepest of my wishes was satisfied but apprehension caused swelling in my arms, throat, and eyes. Was it the crowd? Or my family's dejection? No. It was me, knowing I would spend the rest of my life asking myself if this was worth it.

THE END

List of Principal Characters

The Adams Family

John Quincy Adams, Secretary of State
Louisa Catherine Adams, wife
George Washington Adams, son
John Adams II, son
Charles Francis Adams, son
John Adams, father and second President of the United States
Abigail Adams, mother
Thomas Adams, brother
Ann "Nancy" Adams, sister-in-law

The President and his Cabinet

James Monroe, fifth President of the United States
John Calhoun, Secretary of War
William Crawford, Secretary of the Treasury
William Wirt, Attorney General
Benjamin Crowninshield, Secretary of the Navy

The Europeans

Lord Castlereagh, British Foreign Minister
George Canning, British Foreign Office official
Stratford Canning, British minister to the United States
Ferdinand VII, King of Spain
Luis de Onís, Spanish minister to the United States
Klemens von Metternich, Austrian Foreign Minister
Alexander I, Emperor of Russia
Baron de Tuyll, Russian minister to the United States

Other Characters

Henry Clay, Speaker of the House
Andrew Jackson, Major General of the United States Army
Eliza Monroe Hay, President Monroe's daughter
George Hay, President Monroe's son-in-law
Daniel Brent, Chief Clerk at the Department of State

Author's Note

PRESIDENT ADAMS INSISTED that his agenda was constitutional under the General Welfare Clause but then waited for Congress to enact the legislation rather than prompting the legislature. General Jackson directed his followers to oppose Adams' efforts and the President only managed to pass a handful of internal improvement bills. When he left office the National Road stretched from Maryland to Ohio and the Chesapeake and Ohio Canal, the Louisville and Portland Canal, and the Dismal Swamp Canal in North Carolina were underway.

Van Buren led the effort against US participation in the hemispheric congress Bolivar called for in Panama, claiming it broke from Washington's Farewell Address and the Monroe Doctrine. The Senate did not authorize the American delegation until after the Congress ended. It was considered a failure, enabling Britain to become South America's largest trading partner for the rest of the century.

John and Louisa's marriage was at its lowest ebb in this period. They only saw each other at meals and Louisa lost interest in music and became obsessed with death. She wrote a ballad about a shipwreck and a play about a character who was a thinly disguised image of her husband, portraying him as a cold, even cruel, figure.

John Adams and Thomas Jefferson both died on July 4, 1826, the fiftieth anniversary of the Declaration of Independence and midway through the new Adams presidency. He called the event a "visible and palpable mark of divine favor" for the United States.

The Jacksonians captured both congressional chambers after the 1826 midterms, ending any hope for Adams to pass additional legislation. He faced Jackson again in the 1828 election, the ugliest election until 2016. Jackson won in a landslide, carrying 173 electoral votes to Adams' 83 and winning 56% of the popular vote, the largest percentage for any candidate until Theodore Roosevelt in 1904. Jackson's presidency redefined American politics, strengthening the executive branch as he destroyed the Second Bank of the United States. The Bank's end led to the Panic of 1837 and the downfall of the Van Buren administration. Jackson's other main legacy was forcefully removing 60,000 Indians from the Southeastern US, an ethnic cleansing known to history as the Trail of Tears.

Calhoun allied with Jackson while serving as Adams' Vice President. He became Jackson's Vice President during his first term but they opposed each other during the Nullification Crisis, with Jackson threatening to hang Calhoun and his fellow South Carolinians if they seceded. Calhoun became increasingly extreme, setting the ideological groundwork for the Confederacy and the Civil War. Ironically, his efforts as Monroe's Secretary of War provided President Lincoln with the bureaucratic infrastructure to save the Union.

The Whig Party kept Adams' vision alive and it was largely implemented by President Lincoln as the South was not present in Congress to oppose him. These policies, such as the Homestead Act and Transcontinental Railroad, contributed to America becoming the world's largest economy in 1871.

Historians classify him as an average President for proposing such a bold vision for the country but proving unable to enact it. In 2021, C-Span ranked him number 17 out of the 44 men who had served up to that time.

George Washington Adams' mental health continued to deteriorate. He fathered a child out of wedlock and was terrified when his father told him to come to Washington to help him vacate the Executive Mansion in 1829. George fell off his steamship and is believed to have committed suicide. Adams read the news and told Louisa. They were devastated and Adams blamed himself.

He rebuilt himself after his defeat and George's demise, representing Massachusetts' Plymouth District and becoming America's moral center and greatest critic of slavery. No longer representing the entire Union, he did not have to restrain his opposition to human bondage. He brought so many citizen petitions requesting for slavery to be abolished within the District of Columbia that Southern congressmen imposed a gag rule, tabling any discussions on slavery within the House. Adams persisted, insisting the rule violated the First Amendment right to petition. It was repealed in 1844, after seven years.

In a late-career climax, he represented African slaves smuggled into the US aboard *La Amistad* and argued their case at the Supreme Court for four hours. He won and the Africans returned home.

Adams suffered a fatal stroke while denouncing President Polk's war against Mexico, which was intended to expand slavery westward, in 1848. His last words were, "This is the last of Earth. I am content." Abraham Lincoln, congressman from Illinois and an Adams protégé, was present.

Adams' personality softened during his post-presidency since he was less ambitious and afraid of failure. He and Louisa grew closer after George died and their marriage entered its most successful period. She passed away in 1852.

John Adams II married Mary at the Executive Mansion in 1828, near the end of his father's administration, but he failed as a lawyer and became an alcoholic after George's suicide. He died in 1834.

Charles proved the only successful child, serving as Lincoln's minister to the Court of St. James in London and keeping Europe from recognizing the Confederacy. He later became a historian of his family and of the country. Most importantly, he broke the parenting cycle of his father and grandfather, raising seven children who lived to adulthood.

In 2021, my wife and I visited her grandfather in Virginia, and it was at that time I first considered writing a sister novel to *The Eisenhower Chronicles*. That book utilizes an episodic structure to tell the story of Ike's involvement in World War II, the Cold War, and the Civil Rights Movement. I wanted a subject with a long career that intersected multiple international conflicts. My initial choice was Marquis de La Fayette, so I could write about his time in the American and French Revolutions and during Napoleon's reign. But my online discussions with the Council on JQA (see *Acknowledgements*) turned my attention to John Quincy Adams.

Adams intrigued me since he was a bridge between Washington and Lincoln, correctly prophesied how a future President would end slavery, and, like Ike, was a foreign policy genius. At first I decided upon writing a novel consisting of ten episodes that would start with Adams escorting his father to France as a child and which followed his rise, fall, and return as an elder statesman. I quickly decided I wanted to write a more cohesive narrative and upon learning about how his showdown with the Holy Alliance led to the Monroe Doctrine, I knew I had my tale. The story could be framed as a diplomatic chess match between Adams and Metternich and a conflict between America's greatest Secretary of State and Europe's most cunning diplomat was an ideal premise to craft a political thriller.

Historical fiction, especially when focusing on real people and events (known as biographical fiction), contains a constant tension between the two words forming the term. My philosophy of the genre is that historical fiction must be well researched in order to do justice to its subject but is, ultimately, a work of art and not an exact duplication of fact. That is how I approached *The Middle Generation*—I accumulated over 400 pages of research notes that I referred to at every paragraph, but this is still a novel dramatizing John Quincy Adams and not a perfect recreation of his experiences. Those interested in precise accounts can find them in various nonfiction works, many of which are listed in *Acknowledgements*.

The Middle Generation's artistic dimensions and narrative cohesion required various simplifications or interpretations of historical details. The largest liberties taken were the following:

Numerous secondary sources that I read gave conflicting accounts of whether President Monroe's direction to General Jackson was intended to encourage his conquest of Florida. I chose to imply this but leave it unclear to Adams to maximize the revelation's dramatic impact in Chapter XV.

Although Emperor Alexander's edict was real, most of the story in Part Seven was fictional. The idea of Adams playing Russia and Britain off each other was inspired by President Nixon's triangular diplomacy with China and the Soviet Union. The Anacostia River episode in Chapter XLIX was fictional.

While the story of Adams helping Dorcas Allen in Chapter LVI was real, it occurred in 1837, when Adams was a congressman, not when he was Secretary of State.

Adams' visit to Braintree in Chapter LXV was fictional.

I decided to portray the Baron de Tuyll in a darker light than his real life counterpart to give Adams a more compelling antagonist.

Some purists may take issue, in good faith, with my choices. To them I apologize. Every historical fiction writer must make such decisions with his or her own judgment. I made mine hoping to produce an account of John Quincy Adams and the generation that came of age between the Revolution and the Civil War that was both compelling and true in substance if not always in exactness. I hope that I have honored their memory, for that is historical fiction's raison d'etre.

Acknowledgements

Thank you to Amanda Makhoul Zucker, my wife, for supporting the idea of writing a novel about John Quincy Adams. I explained my reasoning while editing *The Eisenhower Chronicles* and she instantly endorsed following my book about a giant of twentieth century America with one of the nineteenth. She encouraged me throughout the laborious process of writing this novel and proofread it more than once.

Thank you to my Council on JQA, a group of Twitter friends who both inspired me to write this novel and who discussed specific plot points and facts while writing the first draft. The Council is formed of Dr. Jeffery Tyler Syck, Mr. Sebastian Stock, and Mr. Daniel Vargas. An additional thanks to Dr. Syck for fact-checking the novel and providing his foreword.

Thank you to Dustin Prisley for editing the novel.

Thank you to White Rabbit Arts for designing the cover.

The following sources were invaluable to my research. I recommend all of them to readers interested in nonfiction accounts about Adams and his world.

The Massachusetts Historical Society digitized Adams' 51 volume diary, which was the most important source. I cannot thank them enough for doing so and for adding a search function, without which this project may have proved impossible. The diary influenced every scene of this work.

The three most important secondary sources were:

John Quincy Adams: Militant Spirit by James Taub
What Hath God Wrought: The Transformation of America, 1815-1848 by Dr. Daniel Walker Howe

Nation Builder: John Quincy Adams and the Grand Strategy of the Republic by Dr. Charles Edel

Other sources include:

From Colony to Superpower: U.S. Foreign Relations since 1776 by George Herring

Henry Clay: The Essential American by David Stephen Heidler

Calhoun: American Heretic by Robert Elder

James Monroe by Gary Hart

Metternich: Strategist and Visionary by Wolfram Siemann

Thomas Jefferson: The Art of Power by Jon Meacham

Andrew Jackson: An American Populist by Jon Meacham

The Adams Women: Abigail and Louisa Adams, Their Sisters and Daughters by Dr. Paul Nagel

Imagining the Bounds of History, Shannon Selin's website, particularly the pages "The Inauguration of John Quincy Adams" and "A Skeleton City: Washington DC in the 1820s"

"Missouri Compromise" at the Lehrman Institute

"The Missouri Compromise" by *UShistory.org*

"Cicero and America" by Timothy Casper at Hillsdale College

"Cicero on Justice, Empire, and the Exceptional Republic" by Michael C. Hawley at *Classics of Strategy and Diplomacy*

"An interview with historian Gordon Wood on the New York Times' 1619 Project" by Tom Mackaman at *World Socialist Website*

"Slavery at Monticello" on *The Jefferson Monticello* site

"Master John Marshall and the Problem of Slavery" by Paul Finkelman at *The University of Chicago Law Review*

"The Enslaved Household of President John Quincy Adams" by Dr. Lindsay Chervinsky and Ms. Callie Hopkins at *The White House Historical Association*

"Northeast Executive Building: August, September 1819-November 1866" by *The Office of the Historian* on the Department of State's Website

"Maria Hester Monroe: The First Daughter Wedding" by Feather Foster at the *Presidential History Blog*

"Louisa Adams and the Jackson Ball" by Feather Foster at the *Presidential History Blog*

"Anne Royall and the President's Clothes" by Katherine Brodt at PBS

"Rebelling and Expelling: The Class of 1823 goes rogue and gets booted" by Jacob Sweet at *Harvard Magazine*

"Great Britain and the Russian Ukase of September 16, 1821" by Richard Allen Ward and part of the UNT Theses and Dissertations collection

"The Later American Policy of George Canning" by H. W. V. Temperley of *The American Historical Review* and the *Oxford Press*

"British Foreign Policy Under Canning" by Andrew Montgomery Endorf at The University of Montana's *Graduate Student Theses, Dissertations,& Professional Papers*

"Metternich and the Greek Question 1821-29" by Stavros Stavridis at *The National Herald*

Finally, I give the opposite of an acknowledgement to Maggie, my beagle, who did everything in her power to distract me from writing this book.

About the Author

M. B. Zucker has been interested in storytelling for as long as he can remember. He devoted himself to historical fiction at fifteen and earned his B.A. at Occidental College and his J.D. at Case Western Reserve University School of Law. He lives in Virginia with his family. He is the author of three other novels. Among his honors is the Best Fictional Biography Award at the 2023 BookFest.

The Middle Generation: A Novel of John Quincy Adams and the Monroe Doctrine is M. B. Zucker's fourth novel.

www.historiumpress.com

A subsidiary of
The Historical Fiction Company

New York, NY U.S.A.
Macon, GA U.S.A.

Printed in the USA
CPSIA information can be obtained
at www.ICGtesting.com
LVHW071928121023
760965LV00016B/27/J